SUNLIGHT ON VENUS

First edition
June 2021

Sunlight on Venus

John C. Sable

Chapter 1

The Earth has turned against us.
There are few humans left.

Aldai stared out of the thick plastiglass window of the Special Ops locker room. Below, he could see the vast expanse of boiling cloud, spreading as far as the horizon and then bending to show the curvature of the Earth. The cloud was an angry mix of slowly moving colours: dark patches of thicker gas folding against lighter browns and reds.

The storm swirled and flowed with a lazy volatility. Beneath the StratoPort, the maelstrom spread out in all directions, homogenous and tortuous. All around the circular sky city, the cloud rolled over itself like colossal leviathans, heaving themselves through the air as they fought over a planet-sized carcass.

But the view above was clear and blue. In the canopy of Earth, the sky was thin and vast, and lorded over the

1

miasma of cloud beneath. It was azure at the edges, leading to a deep blue directly above that gave tantalising glimpses of stars, as it almost became transparent to the darkness of space beyond.

The upper atmosphere was the sun's domain, wide and featureless. Floating in the heavens, the StratoPort provided its population with a never-changing sequence of light. At fifty thousand feet there was nothing to obstruct the afternoon brightness apart from the steel structure and the smart-dimming of the windows. Whirring systems kept the internal conditions habitable, but the unimpeded solar rays always beat down on a faded exterior. The only relief was when the sun dipped below the horizon, turning the vista red, before revealing a night sky of clear constellations.

Aldai turned to resume his preparations.

Team-6 had been called in unexpectedly. It was meant to have been an afternoon off, after several busy weeks of extended overtime. He had just settled down in his cabin and had dimmed the wall screen to a dusky half-light, as low as the interface would allow. It had got stuck on a view of Old Wisconsin, showing an image of gently rolling hills of green and olive from a time long before. The wall screens were Government mandated and controlled; however much you wanted to, you couldn't turn them off or change the vista. They were supposed to nourish a part of human nature that you couldn't scratch in a metal station in the stratosphere. They were welcoming and infuriating in equal measure. *Old Wisconsin looked nice. Shame it would only ever be just a memory.*

Aldai had switched on the holovision to watch endless news and reruns. Leaning back on his bed, he soothed his tired muscles and aching metal calf-splint. He needed the respite, despite his near-youthful twenty-nine years.

But to his annoyance, the settling calm was disturbed. Sergeant Halderford had called in on the only frequency that Aldai couldn't block. Ten minutes later, Team-6 was assembling in the Military Quarter.

Out of his locker he took his flak jacket and forearm protectors, fitting them over his handsome six-foot frame. He inspected his helmet and vis-goggles and pulled them snugly over his short, dark hair. He lifted out his hefty carbine, checking it over with military precision. The recharge lever provided a reassuring amount of resistance as he engaged it, and it rebounded back with a satisfying click of metal upon metal. Running his finger down the slot in the ammo cartridge, he registered a full slug of shard needles.

He sat against his bruised and dented locker as the clatter of the six team members slowly died down. They took seats on the benches and waited patiently for Sergeant Halderford to tell them what the hell this was all about.

Rongal was opposite him, fiddling with a cross around his neck. He was the shortest of the group, though still five-eight, and slightly overweight from an unhealthy addiction to synth-chips.

"You know the gods left a long time ago," said Jones, sitting next to Aldai.

"They're still here," replied Rongal in a low, measured tone.

"Maybe you can ask them to sort out the surface," Jones continued, deliberately stoking the fire. "And make it a little less cloudy."

Rongal scowled at him. "If you don't believe, then there's more attention for me."

Jones shook his head with the arrogance of youth, as if he didn't need looking after. He'd only just passed the cusp of adulthood, and the locks and bolts of life were yet to slide into place and solidify his outlook.

But Aldai couldn't help but agree with him. The surface was scoured and uninhabitable, trapped under a thick blanket of angry storms. In the twenty-sixth century there was no way that the gods still presided. They had slowly dwindled, either diminishing into vacuum or leaving to travel to distant stars in search of more worthy reverence. And regardless, they needed large numbers of people to look to them, and there were few people left here to provide worship.

By all accounts, the gods had long abandoned the whispered prayers. If they were still here, then they weren't listening, they were simply applying their vengeance, fury and retribution on the planet, releasing karma and payback on its arrogant population.

There was only one god that had stayed: the sun. But it had no personality anymore. It was no longer Ra, with the head of a proud hawk, riding majestically across the sky on a flaming chariot. It was no longer Xihe, the mother of ten three-legged crows, who took it in turns to fly around the Earth. It was no longer Shamash, Sol, Apollo or Hors. It was simply a lifeless ball of flame, slowly and methodically turning hydrogen into helium.

The only altars to it were the four fusion reactors in the Heart of the StratoPort, constantly chanting and wailing in a pale imitation of the solar process and pouring out energy to drive the gravity cascade of the giant Levitation Engines. It made for little adulation, but the sun didn't care; it didn't need glory. That was probably the reason it was the only god left. It had the power to create life, sustain it and watch it grow, live and die. But that was all irrelevant to this deity. It didn't care what happened to its power. It was too engrossed in its own purpose, looking inwards and caring little for the planets, comets or debris that got caught in its gravity well.

It didn't matter to the sun that the only living beings that even noticed it were the fifty thousand inhabitants of the StratoPort, who merely acknowledged its lazy rise every morning with dispassion.

The gods had left and been replaced by the fleeting and fragile purposes that you could find on the Port. You found something to consume your mind and fill your days, and that's what became your church service.

Aldai felt the winged eagle of his Special Ops insignia. That was all he needed. That was all he had. It was his god, lectern and prayer book. You didn't look up anymore. Other than Rongal and a few people still holding on to vanishing threads of godly coat-tails, you didn't look to the heavens. You looked down, at your feet, to the metal below, or to the fifty thousand feet of nothingness below that. You looked at your feet, and kept your eyes down, and simply took one step in front of the other. You kept your focus on a point, an idea: fragile and ephemeral.

Aldai's goal was the mission. One day to the next, one mission after another. That was his focus. That kept his mind from wandering. Wandering to Deradin, to freefall and to claustrophobia, or to thin walls keeping life alive on the most fleeting of margins.

Aldai was a mutt. That's what they called them anyway, in hushed voices, when people thought they were out of hearing, and in the recreation halls of the four quarter-schools. Children make a habit of the tritest aspects of subculture. The two-for-twos would bring it up in the schoolyards, scoring cheap points, trying to create rough, primal hierarchies among the innocence of childhood.

Fifty thousand people, no more, no less. When the population fell, it would be raised. When it went above, it would be lowered. The natural cycle of life was reduced to permits, applications and statistics. When hope wore thin and love and passion receded, children were brought into the world through projects, drives and rewards.

They were called mutts. Aldai was born during such a time. He was born to fill the population, to keep humanity going.

And now he was military. Now he was part of the sharp end of keeping the sky-city defended.

He was in the armed forces, tasked with the dirty work of regulating the more insidious aspects of the population. And there was work for Special Ops aplenty. Humans would always find ways to be dissident and resist governance, more so in more desperate times. In the dark corners of the Uppercone or the vast Undercity that hung underneath, there were hoarders, dealers and the drug-addled. There were those who had lost hope or sought escalated vengeance for petty squabbles.

There would always be crime and misdemeanour. There would always be those at the fringes of society, angry at the way things are. But until recently, they had at least shared the common purpose of staying afloat, keeping the StratoPort in the air.

Recently that had changed.

A few years ago, a bomb had gone off. It was deep in the Undercity, not even near one of the giant Levitation Engines or the Fusion Heart, and it didn't even make the news. But it was unmistakably a marker, and it was followed by more, until a few weeks ago one had gone off that had shaken the entire structure. It had ripped through a generator and disintegrated two workmen. The whole Port had shuddered, to the general panic of its population. It was like an earthquake that could be followed by the floor dropping away from you. And it was a directed plasma charge, not a home-made bomb like most of the recent incidents had been. As far as anyone was aware, that kind of plasma weaponry was only available in the tightly regulated science labs up on Five-deck.

As people picked up smashed glass and fallen picture frames and shops restocked ruffled shelves, the two news channels started reporting that it was a bomb. Red lights beamed out across the ceilings of habitation spaces as the Port went into lockdown, and concern and panic had spread. For those still brave or desperate enough not to scurry down to the cabin decks after work, a curfew rang out every night as the sun went down. Weary and inebriated revellers were urged out of the main Concourse, so that the area could be patrolled by the Scout Police in the dimly lit darkness of the night.

"We've got a briefing from General Gumpert," said Sergeant Halderford, as the six military personnel that made up Team-6 sat against the lockers.

Gumpert...! What does he want with Team-6? Aldai felt a twist in his stomach. He'd only ever seen Gumpert once, at his passing-out ceremony nine years ago. Other than that, the General was rarely seen in public apart from a few occasions, standing next to the President when public briefings required it.

Team-6 exchanged glances that only Halderford refused to take part in. Halderford held his sergeant's professionalism and kept his eyes on the door intently and expectantly.

"I heard that Gumpert keeps a stuffed gazelle in his office," said Bekka. "As some sort of memento of a time long forgotten."

"I heard it's a horse, and he's obsessed with old Westerns," replied Jones.

Aldai smiled and shook his head, preferring not to join in the idle speculation. Rongal eyed Jones with a level of revengeful contempt, and only Tiernan and Halderford managed to ignore it completely. Tiernan was old, long past retirement. He was a lifer. Like many on the StratoPort, you just kept working, because otherwise you'd just be rattling around. He wasn't any less athletic however. Tiernan kept up with the others with quiet energy.

"I heard he's descended from Habersmith and he still has the family bonsai tree. The one Habersmith kept in his office before the StratoPort being raised into the air," replied Bekka, spurred on by Jones' competitiveness.

"That would make it like over two hundred," Jones shot back.

"That's enough," chimed in Sergeant Halderford, sensing an escalation of argument.

Halderford kept a tight ship. He was a tall, reserved man. His face was impassive and stern, and his thin lips rarely broke into a smile. He was a product of a military upbringing, and had searching eyes that tried to hide what they'd seen in the past. There were rumours that in his youth he'd run Special Ops on the now-scoured surface of Earth, before it was deemed too hazardous, and any travel to the surface was blacklisted.

They sat in silence, Bekka and Jones looking like they were holding back from more competitive gossip, but managing to contain it. Rongal was mouthing the words of a prayer, and Tiernan's hand fumbled with his shoulder strap.

After a short while, the door banged open, and in came three large military men, covered in medals and stern confidence. General Gumpert strode in first, with grizzled face and piercing eyes under unkempt eyebrows.

Following him was a man wearing a dark blue flight uniform. He looked thin compared to the other two, but was still tall and broad shouldered. Aldai recognised him from the Special Ops flight training and aerial manoeuvres, back in the Academy, and distinctly remembered him giving a tongue lashing to some of the weaker recruits whose stomachs had revolted from high-G turns.

The other man Aldai had never seen before. His black uniform signified an Intelligence Officer. It wasn't a uniform that you saw very often, and if you did then it generally meant you were about to get familiar with the inside of a SeaPort cell block. The Intelligence Department, positioned high up in the upper habitation cone of the StratoPort, was a place few saw the inside of. *Whatever they know is their business, and things are better if they stay that way.*

"Ops Team-6," started General Gumpert, without any introduction or pleasantries. "This mission is to be classified as Code Gamma. Certain circumstances that I am unable to disclose have pulled you into this task. I have no doubt you are acutely familiar with the subsequent responsibilities, but nevertheless I remind you that anything that happens on this mission must never be spoken, disseminated or even whispered, other than to official state channels, through Orcanciz here," Gumpert said, motioning to the man in the black Intelligence uniform. "At the end of the mission, you will not talk about it to anyone other than Orcanciz, including amongst yourselves. Do I make myself clear?"

"Yes, sir!" they all said in unison. Aldai glanced at Sergeant Halderford, confused as to what could be requiring such high-level security. He had heard of Code Gamma in training, but never in practice. It was usually Ops Team-1 and Team-2 that would deal with Intelligence missions. Halderford was impassive as ever, his attention unwavering towards General Gumpert.

"Very well, proceed," said Gumpert, and the three high ranking officers left the room without any parting formalities. The team sat in silence for a moment. Aldai half-expected Jones or Bekka to make light of the situation, but neither spoke.

"We've got a mark down in the ARC district of the Undercity," said Halderford. "You heard the general; this is Code Gamma. You know your responsibilities. God help you if you step over the line; this one goes way above my head." He got up to lead them out of the locker room, "Let's go, side exit."

Their military focus switched on. Whatever it was, it was orders, a target and a job.

They exited the Special Ops centre through the back entrance, which led onto a large circular service corridor that ran around the circumference of the StratoPort. The corridor was long and gently curved. There were many like it in the Uppercone, the habitable area where the population lived. Splintered around the outside of the circular Port, these corridors covered nearly every deck. If you wanted to move, to run as if you weren't trapped in a giant tin can, then they were your only option.

This one was bare and functional, empty and lifeless. Its only features were slit windows, just too high to see through, that had created a striped pattern on the opposing wall where their light had bleached the white paint yellow. A gentle breeze caught the team as a fresh-air purge gently coursed around, whipping up dust off the floor to hang briefly in the air around them.

These corridors gave Aldai the jitters. Their constant curvature always obscured their full extent from view, just around the bend. However much you chased the hidden distance, however fast you ran, you'd never see it. They gave Aldai a recurring nightmare where he was in one of these curved passages, walking around it until something would appear silently in front of him, revealing itself from around the bend as the repetitive, featureless walls slowly rolled past.

They followed the service corridor for fifty metres before arriving at a solid door with the appearance of an air lock. It had a heavy block handle linked to a robust mechanism, and it bulged outwards as if ready to brace against an oncoming pressure gradient. It was surrounded by a red dotted line just inside of its circumference that looked as if it had been painted two hundred years ago when the StratoPort first lifted off the ground.

"Leaving the upper containment area," Halderford spoke into his voice channel on his wrist link. He heaved the lever down and the door clunked open, releasing a smell of stale air and causing an adjustment in their ears as the pressure around them momentarily fluctuated.

You got used to it after a while. The StratoPort was old, and its seals and joins were past their working lifetimes. There were the occasional gaps and slits that opened up to release pressure fluctuations as the structure groaned and stressed under its own weight. Bug-drones occasionally zipped through the air, following air currents to seek out the crevices and nest in them with expanding plastifoam. They nestled in the gaps as if they were forming some sort of life-ending chrysalis, but there were always new holes to find. They kept the habitation zone at fairly constant pressure, but as soon as you went below, into the Undercity, then each new section carried pressure fluctuations that caused popping of ears as the body registered the differences. This ladder-duct hadn't been used for a while, and it had leaked pressure and smelt like dull metal.

"Down to Z2 deck," said Halderford.

"One hundred metres of climbing. Just what I wanted today," said Jones.

"I can think of a faster way you could get there," said Bekka with a certain self-satisfaction. "If you didn't want to climb."

Jones scoffed from inside the tube.

"As quiet as possible, Team-6. Holster and secure weapons," came Halderford's stern response.

Aldai slung his carbine over his shoulder and pulled on the rubber covering to prevent it clanging against the metal casing of the vertical pipe.

He stepped into the ladder-duct, twisting to let his feet find a hold, and started his descent. It led down, deep into the structure, its end further than the eye could see, and it sloped gently, pointing towards the low-peak of the Port far below.

The StratoPort was made of two cones. The Uppercone pointed towards the heavens and was squat, with forty-five-degree sides that sloped down towards the planet below. It was where the majority of people lived and worked. On the other hand, the Undercity was an inverted cone, aiming down towards the planet. It was twice as long as it was wide, giving the entire StratoPort the appearance of a pointed shield or a stretched diamond in the air.

Unlike the bustling Uppercone, the Undercity was more sparsely populated. It housed the Heart, where the four Fusion Reactors provided the station with power, and it housed the eight sky-scraper-sized Levitation Engines that kept the StratoPort in the air. Otherwise, it was an industrial sprawl with only a few small hubs of human activity. In those hubs, workers, engineers and technicians tended to the vital task of keeping the station afloat, but that left large swathes of uninhabited nooks and crannies, a tangled maze of steel panels and girders that made up the majority of the under structure. It was an area ripe for hiding nefarious deeds, and it was Team-6's main hunting ground.

They knew it well from years of surveillance. They avoided the Undercity express elevators that zipped around its cavernous extent like a nervous system, preferring instead to use the rarely trodden hand-rail routes and service tubes. That way they could deploy themselves throughout the unkempt mass of the various technical districts while remaining out of sight, before descending upon unsuspecting crumps.

But even they didn't know the full layout of the Undercity. The Sergeants carried the rare wrist-link interfaces that housed the augmented holomaps, built up over decades of exploration, but the holomaps only went so far, and there were uncharted parts. The Undercity was full of unexpected bulkheads and dead ends as if the whole industrial structure was an afterthought, or so hastily assembled that building plans went out the window. There were channels and caverns where there shouldn't be, and unless you had experience, you'd be lost before you even realised that you'd left the habitable space of the Uppercone.

They exited the vertical shaft through a second heavy airlock door into another circular corridor. This was smaller, with tighter curvature than the one above, and instead of white-painted walls it was bare metal with rivet joints. Their boots cushioned their steps over the floor grating, and without orders they readied their weapons. They followed the corridor around until a flat bulkhead end wall appeared around the curve.

"Partial pressure on the other side," said Halderford. "Masks on." They all pulled on breathing masks instinctively, and Halderford opened a hatch. Aldai was pulled forwards by the release of air.

Even partial pressure was uncomfortable. It meant you were no longer washed over by the recycled and pressurised air of the Port, and instead you felt the effects of the external environment. At fifty thousand feet that meant a chill that struck your exposed skin like needles. Your body felt bloated, stretched and strained. You could survive it for a few minutes, even if you found yourself fully outside without oxygen, but it wasn't a statistic that you'd ever want to test.

They made their way quickly through the depressurised section until they came to a second pressure hatch. Hurrying through, Halderford pushed it shut, aided by the pressure gradient that seemed to want to help close the hatch as quickly as possible. He fought its last few degrees, just about managing to close it softly, and prevented it clanging out through the surrounding area. They waited for conditions to stabilise before taking off their masks.

"Never gets any easier," said Bekka, and they all took a moment to readjust to pressurised air, rubbing sore faces and waiting for ears to pop and eyes to refocus.

Aldai had never been to this part of the Port, it made him uneasy. *Code Gamma. What is General Gumpert sending us towards?* He sorely wanted to ask Halderford for more information, but knew this was one chase he'd have to go in blind.

They entered a cathedral-like area, with regular giant square columns ascending from the floor, spaced evenly like a city grid, with gaps in between where roadways could criss-cross. The columns were each painted with twenty-foot numbers designating their identification, and they were clad in occasional pipework that hissed and released steam intermittently. Each column could have

16

been an office block housing countless workers and countless computers, rising up through the ceiling, many decks above. The reality was that they were probably storage or disused and empty, long forgotten and devoid of purpose.

The whole area felt abandoned, and the base of each column was littered with discarded rubbish. Cups, papers and magazines had started their decomposition process, and were worn and brown. Some looked as if they were old enough to have been left by the people that built the station. The place felt old, as if from a different time. It was one of the many deserted and dilapidated sections strung through the Undercity.

The team made like ghosts along the central causeway, passing perpendicular routes that they examined with the point of a rifle. But it was quiet and empty, and the only movement they saw was a bot that scuttled towards them erratically down a roadway-sized side alley. It was dusty and sagging on one side, its front axle scraping along the floor.

"Looks like a cleaning workbot," said Bekka. "Must be lost down here."

"It could have been down here for decades," Jones replied, stepping towards it cautiously. But before he had a chance to investigate it, Rongal strode towards it more confidently.

"I'm not taking any chances," he said, firing a silenced carbine needle through its outer shell. Its movements stuttered and its lights extinguished. Jones shook his head, but no one batted an eyelid. Workbots had it hard on the StratoPort. They often took frustrated kicks from disgruntled inhabitants. "Can never be too sure," Rongal continued, re-joining the group as they stepped quietly along.

The rest of the area was empty, and they made their way to the back of the vault, where a set of wide stairs with two flat ramps for vehicles tyres took them up into a football-pitch-sized area that appeared to be an abandoned workshop.

The room was dusty and untended, as if it had been shoe-horned into the Undercity as a relic of the surface world. Machines piled up around the edges where they once would have stood in neat rows. Perhaps, in the past, they would have been used to train fresh apprentices in the art of tending to elevators, pumps, fusion reactors or the eight Levitation Engines, but now they were just undocumented storage. There were crates and containers strewn across the floorspace. A musty smell and only the faintest amount of light wound its way through the urban sprawl of the Undercity in order to illuminate the scene in front of them.

Halderford motioned to the team to split up, cocking two fingers left and three fingers right. They obediently spread out around the outside cover, each member adopting readied poses, coiled like springs as they silently approached.

They could hear quiet voices up ahead. It sounded like a small group having a muted but intense argument. In the centre of the room were three shapes, one short and round and one that seemed fainter than the others.

Aldai activated the thermal mode on his goggles as Jones and Bekka positioned themselves out left and Tiernan and Rongal out right. He listened intently for the rustling of hands in pockets, the movement of feet indicating body language, the dynamic of the voices and the vibrations through the floor, his keen military senses on high alert.

Motioning with three fingers on his forearm, Halderford nodded back in agreement.

"We need more plasma cores," said one voice, hoarse and wispy.

"I can only get so many before people start noticing them disappearing," came a second.

"Do you think I care about that? We need them, what else matters, Dart?" said the hoarse voice, before coughing meekly.

"If we get caught, we'll lose this supply route completely," said the third voice. "Do not pressure them, we need those cores but we must be patient."

"Patient? What for? You know as well as I do how little time we all have left."

Aldai was watching Halderford intently for any sign of command. They were all ready at any moment, like tigers waiting in the tall grass. Halderford stared back, allowing the conversation to go on as long as possible. He wanted the trio to splurge their inner intentions, unaware they were being listened in on and surrounded by Special Forces.

"I'm having second thoughts," came the voice that was referred to as Dart. "What if Venus is successful?"

"What hope is there on Venus?" replied the rasping voice, coughing compulsively. "The StratoPort is a bloated charade on a dying world. It's arrogant and offensive, doomed and futile," he spat. "We strike one of the main engines next and bring this abomination to the ground."

That was all Halderford needed. He rotated the dial on his wrist-link to signal the others and motioned a deft hand gesture to Aldai, and the team pounced gracefully into readiness. Bekka and Jones had inched around to the left and were the first to break cover, aiming rifles at the three.

"Stay where you are. You are under arrest on charges of terrorism," came Bekka's voice.

Aldai and Halderford moved out from their position slowly, initially unnoticed by the startled trio. The small man who they referred to as Dart was backing away. He was short and heavyset and had a full, unkempt beard that spilled over his technician's overalls, green for habitation. One of the others, a man with shoulder-length hair, appeared calm, with hands up. He was also wearing overalls, but they looked as if they were covering more formal clothes underneath.

The third was different altogether. He had his back to Aldai, and was wearing a long, worn cape, full of notches and scars. Aldai couldn't make out his face behind a hood that was pulled down over his features.

"Sun's wrath," exclaimed the short man as he noticed Aldai and Halderford and realised that they were now surrounded by six Special Ops.

The caped man turned to look, exchanging glances with Aldai. His face was pale and skeletal, barely human. His features were withdrawn, and his eyes were white with dull pupils. It stopped Aldai in his tracks. It looked like a Gaunt or a Blood-feeder from old comic books. *What the hell is that?*

The Gaunt-like figure reached into its cape. Aldai pulled up his rifle ready to shoot, but before he got a chance there was a blinding light from a flash bomb. It dulled sight and sound, disorienting Aldai until his vis-goggles compensated. The room filled with smoke cascading out of a canister on the floor, and Aldai caught a glimpse of the caped man diving into a gap in the piled machinery at the far end, moving ungainly but fast. He instinctively made pursuit.

Aldai slid between the contorted metal of piled-up machines, finding a door hidden behind the uncoordinated dumping ground that the workshop had become. He wrenched it open and saw the Gaunt-man disappear around a corner. He sprinted as fast as he could, finding a staircase heading down to the deck below that he took in two bounding steps, landing heavily on a gantry.

"Need alive," came a garbled message in his right ear, but Aldai was too focussed to respond. He ducked under overhead pipework as the gantry swung around to the right, revealing a long section with a low roof, and the Gaunt-man up ahead. He hunched over and ran, seeing the Gaunt-man's cape whip around as he disappeared to the left. Aldai followed, finding a weaving corridor painted grey with multicoloured cables running along the ceiling.

Just as he turned a corner, he was almost floored by the suction of air from in front of him. The Gaunt-man had opened a hatch, blowing an airlock without depressurisation.

Aldai's senses swam, his ears ringing, his forehead burning. The air squeezed out of his lungs, and his chest pulled in, as every other part of his body tried to push outwards. He positioned his oxygen mask and steadied himself, his breath rasping as his lungs regained composure. As his visor adjusted, he headed into the brightness of the outside section beyond. It was a hanging gantry perched against the side of the Undercity, exposed to the wind, high altitude and vast fall below. But the Gaunt-man was nowhere to be seen. All Aldai saw was a clip releasing from a metal handrail, pulled down by a cable below.

The Gaunt had jumped.

Aldai braced himself over the handrail, peering down and trying to make out where the Gaunt-man had swung to, but it was no good. As the inverted cone shape of the Undercity fell away below and behind him, he couldn't make out any movement against the jutting industrial sprawl.

"Crak!" he cried.

The high-altitude currents bluffed past him, and he steadied himself on the ice-cold rail, peering one last time for a potential hatch or ledge that the Gaunt could have landed on. But it was no good. The section below him was unmoving with the sterility of metal. The Gaunt-man was long gone, and could be scurrying through a distant lower section unknown even to the holomaps.

Aldai heaved air through his oxygen mask. He rarely let a target escape, but he hadn't even got close to this one. Reluctant to head back with bad news, he withstood the discomfort of the altitude and took in the surroundings.

Below him was the Rift. The storm swirled around this vast black void, objects whipping round and gleaming in the sunlight before being lost in the blackness of the depths. It was a chasm in the endless clouds, a needle of calm like the inside of a tornado, maintained constantly against the swirling planet-storm beyond.

The StratoPort was perched above it, as if holding on with one last umbilical cord to the surface below. It was like a ship stuck over a deep whirlpool in a raging sea, waiting to be sucked down to the depths.

The Rift spoke to Aldai. His eyes were lost in it, and he stared intently, wanting to make out shapes, or see something to focus on. But there was nothing, just darkness surrounded by slowly circling clouds. It was hypnotic, like it was calling to humanity. It was the last breach in the planetary storms, patiently waiting for the StratoPort to slowly give up resistance and fall into it. However much energy the Fusion Reactors burned, and however much force propelled the StratoPort upwards to maintain its delicate hover, the Rift simply waited below.

This is why people only live in the Uppercone. In the Uppercone, the Rift was shielded from view, and you could ignore its existence, focussing only on distant clouds below that moved slowly, too far away to reveal their destructive nature. It was only if you went down to the Undercity that you were reminded of its presence.

And yet something lived down there. Far below him was the StratoPort's sister construction, the Seaport. Beneath the dark void of the Rift, down many miles of storms and below a raging sea, was the other last vestige of humanity. Their symbiotic relationship, using the Rift as a last transport route, was all that kept humanity still surviving. Dropships were sent down with supplies for the SeaPort, and they returned laden with goods in kind.

Two Ports. That was all that was left. Aldai had always thought it was a sick joke that the two structures were called ports. A port is something looking outwards, the start of journeys and the link to lands distant and unknown. The StratoPort and SeaPort were only connected to each other, a closed feedback loop of exploration that belied their desperate nature.

He shuddered and counted his blessings that he was living high above the clouds.

Finally wrenching himself away from the view, he made his way back up to the others. He found them with Dart in handcuffs and white blow-out marks on the floor where the smoke bomb had gone off. Sergeant Halderford looked at Aldai expectantly, but quickly realised he was alone.

"The caped man got away sir, blew a hatch and abseiled below before I could get anywhere close to him."

"Roger that, Aldai. They were expecting us, or at least had planned escape routes. Dart is all we have. Better than nothing."

Aldai looked at Dart, who briefly met his stare before looking away.

"Let's head back up to civilisation," said Halderford.

Chapter 2

They made their way up several decks, by stairs and rickety slide-door elevators. Tiernan gripped Dart tightly, and Team-6 were on high alert in case of assailants from the dingy corners of the Undercity. They had just grappled with an unknown entity, a Gaunt-man, something they'd never seen or heard of before, and its inhuman nature put them on edge.

They passed between two large bulkheads and found themselves in a windowed gallery overlooking a hangar, open to the elements and bathed in blazing sunshine. Halderford called in a flight, and after a few minutes a black-clad Intelligence transport swung in and landed softly on the wide expanse of metal floor plating. It connected to an atmospheric pressure tube, and Team-6 made their way into the craft.

The pilot wore dark glasses and said nothing, and the team sat in an uncomfortable silence as the heavily laden shuttle lifted off and slid sideways, pointing its nose away from the Undercity and across the expanse of cloud in front of them. The ship left the confines of the hangar and was greeted by the buffeting of high-altitude air currents that whipped around the StratoPort, creating dangerous and invisible turbulence patterns for skilled pilots to navigate. The shuttle wobbled before stabilising, causing Team-6 to shift uncomfortably in their seats. Dart appeared not to even notice, as if falling out of the sky wouldn't be an unwelcome turn of events.

The transport rose, slowly winding itself around the lower inverted cone of the Undercity, providing rare views of the outside of the sky-station. The craft shadowed it, keeping its vast structures about a hundred metres to the port side, climbing around the Levitation Engines and unclad structures. As it reached the apex between the Undercity and the Uppercone, the widest part of the StratoPort, the sun appeared around the side of the structure, dimming the autoshades.

Aldai sat opposite Dart in the transport, watching him intently.

Normally they would have started the process of interrogating a suspect by now, or at least laying some foundations. Halderford and Aldai had honed a double act over years working together, and could normally get a charge to talk. You started with idle questions, each building on the last, guiding suspects towards answers before they realised where they were heading. Sometimes you pushed anger, sometimes fear, sometimes guilt.

However, Dart was unusual. He was difficult to read. He didn't look like he was part of a crime syndicate. He didn't look purposeful or angst ridden. He didn't fidget with nervous anticipation at what might happen to him. There was nothing to go on yet, which made it all the more tantalising to start the line of questions. He appeared to be just an average under-tech, caught up with a plot that could bring down the entire StratoPort, himself too.

Who, or what, was the Gaunt-man?

That was the question Aldai wanted to ask most of all. He'd never seen or heard of such a creature. It looked just about human, but warped and twisted, a shallow reflection of those around him. Its face haunted Aldai. It looked like a ghost, and there was something about its rasping voice, its ungainly athleticism and its frightened yet piercing face that unnerved and revolted Aldai. It was a question that was slowly boring into Aldai's mind, resisted only by military doctrine and the need to keep your mind trained on an idea that holds steady.

Mutt. Damn seed.

The fringes of Aldai's mind clamoured quietly, places he didn't want to go to. Providing he held the straining bow line and kept the boat flat against buffeting winds, then he could sail true. The Gaunt-man was both a thunderstorm and a rock-strewn coastline. Focus on the job. Put it out of your mind. One day on the StratoPort at a time.

It didn't matter anyway. Halderford was a stickler for rules and authority, and while the team was more than just work, Halderford would reluctantly report any one of them without a second of hesitation. Maybe that was why he was Sergeant; he was able to put his emotions aside, bury them and carry out orders without question. It was uncaring and impassive, but predictable and professional. Sergeant Halderford ran a tight ship, and Aldai was pleased for his dogmatic inevitability.

Dart never met his glare, but simply stared down at the floor. He had resigned himself to fate. Maybe that was where Aldai would have started his questions. Perhaps there was a glimmer of relief at being caught. That could provide results; it had worked in the past. People would often work themselves into trouble that they neither wanted nor could escape from, and it was often a button that could be pressed in order to extract information. Yet something about Dart's demeanour suggested he would take his knowledge with him to whatever depths of the SeaPort holding cells he might end up in.

Aldai glanced at Sergeant Halderford, who ignored him. But even his normal unwavering exterior had the slimmest of cracks that said he was trying to resist a certain temptation himself. Still, General Gumpert's words of warning and Code Gamma's doctrine were resonating in all of their minds, and no one dared verbalise their thoughts.

Venus. The saviour. Dart had mentioned it with some optimism. What did he know? What were people saying in the depths of the Undercity? What news was there beyond the excuses and distractions perpetrated by politicians?

But it was no use, he would be court-martialled simply for opening his mouth. He looked around the team and saw a mix of faces that seemed to be turning over similar quandaries.

The transport flew past the main hangar system and zoned in on a higher, smaller hangar that Aldai had never been to before, near the spire at the top of the Uppercone. The craft slowly transitioned from the jet stream to the bluff turbulence of the StratoPort, rocking from invisible, swirling air currents, the serene views out the front view-screen belying the perilous hidden flying conditions.

Landing in the Intelligence hangar, Team-6 exited the craft down another pressure tube to where Orcanciz and two black-clad Intelligence Officials were waiting in the hangar maintenance foyer.

"I must remind you of your vows of secrecy, Team-6," Orcanciz said over the noise of the auxiliary equipment around them. "You will say nothing of this to anyone, and if there are any developments you come straight to me." He walked off abruptly, and Dart was led away with an unnecessary level of restraint.

One officer remained and led Team-6 to darkened rooms in the Intelligence Department. They were separated and individually debriefed, and it felt like an interrogation. The Interviewers sat opposite them without any hint of small-talk and asked relentless questions for an exhausting amount of time.

But what struck Aldai most about the process was the way they were seemingly unmoved by the appearance of the Gaunt-man and refused to answer any questions in response.

"Why do I get the feeling we'll never see Dart again," said Jones, when they were back in the Team-6 locker room, but no one dared reply. They quietly stored away their gear, all thinking silent questions that they had to simply push aside and follow orders.

"I'm heading to the Crescent for a send-off for Sam," said Aldai. "Anyone want to join me? They won't be there until clocking off, so I got some time to kill."

"Sure, I'll come along," Bekka replied as she holstered her carbine in its weapon case.

The other members of Team-6 went their separate ways, ready to resume whatever activity they had planned for their afternoon off before it was unceremoniously interrupted.

* * *

The Concourse was the largest open space in the StratoPort, and effectively acted as the city centre. It was cavernous, covered in criss-crossed walkways and pressed up against one side near the top of the Uppercone, wedged in between offices of the business districts. High above, the Government offices assumed the peak of the station, and below them were the accommodation levels.

It had vast windows that offered panoramic views of the clouds below and sky beyond, and it always let in sun, as the StratoPort slowly rotated in the sky. Several columns ascended from the floor, breaking up the space and creating countless nooks, walkways, alleyways and vistas where small bars, shops and restaurants hid out of view, available only to those brave enough to explore the full extent of the Concourse and find every hidden gem.

The Crescent occupied such a position. It was shaped like its namesake, a small bar with an entrance at each end. It commanded some of the best views over the Concourse and across to the sky-windows, yet was often quiet, just the way Aldai liked it.

He moved his glass in circles on the carbon bench, looking out to the mass of shops, restaurants and bars beyond.

"So, I guess we can't even talk about the fact we can't talk about stuff," said Bekka.

He smiled. She looked different in civilian clothes. Most of his colleagues he rarely met outside of work, so he only ever saw them in flak jackets and uniform. She had let her auburn hair down to her shoulders and there was a freshness about her appearance.

"I'm afraid I'm going to have to report you for merely mentioning the thing we're not allowed to talk about," Aldai replied, looking around and half expecting Orcanciz to be standing behind them.

"I think you'll have to report yourself for acknowledging me," she quipped, and they both laughed.

It was a lazy afternoon across the centre, only servicing the mid-afternoon people-traffic, and bracing itself for the bell-toll of clocking off. Then, the evening revelry would take over, and the noise and bustle would rise, until it was cut short by curfew.

A sparrow landed near them, taking advantage of the rare post-meridian guests, cocking its head, either out of inquisitiveness or more likely in expectation of being fed. The Concourse was like a giant aviary for birds and humans alike. Aldai shooed the sparrow away. It was carrying too much bulk as it was.

"You know, I'm glad I don't have a nine-to-five," he said. "I don't think I could imagine trudging to offices to push numbers around. It's not much, but at least we get to move around the Port."

"I know what you mean," Bekka replied. "My parents wanted me to follow them into healthcare. I resisted, of course. The look on my dad's face when I'd told him I'd signed up for Special Ops was priceless."

Aldai picked up a kernel from a small bowl on the table, a tightly compressed ball of powdered run-off nutrients shaped like a nut. It disintegrated in his mouth, only palatable because of the high levels of salt in it, that cut through the bitterness of the synth-alcohol.

"What would you do if you weren't Special Forces?" she asked

"Drug cartel," Aldai said, after thinking about it.

"That I can see," laughed Bekka, with mock approval "You'd be good at it, I bet."

"Yeah, I'd find a small corner of the Undercity and create my empire. It's probably be just me, and maybe a few sparrows that I'd train to run errands."

"You're treading a fine line, Aldai," she replied with sarcastic sincerity. "I may have to report you to Intelligence for merely suggesting such vagabond activities. We report to higher powers now."

"True," Aldai laughed. "But I trust you'll keep my nefarious plans in confidence." He paused, trying to make sense of their mission earlier, and the intervention of Orcanciz. "I feel like they were desperately short of manpower and we just happened to be available. A one-time thing. It'll be back to normal now, no questions asked. It was a peek behind the curtain before it is emphatically closed again."

"And we have to put it out of our minds and pretend it never happened," she said quietly.

Aldai silently agreed.

His attention was caught by the screen above, showing the daily news. It was displayed round the clock, and so tightly linked to the Government that it was effectively state controlled. He half expected to see a story about their arrest in the Undercity. He was expecting to see the Gaunt-man's face, now etched into his conscience against his wishes, with the hope of some explanation by an overly professional news reader. But he wasn't surprised to see them still covering the bomb that went off last week. News was slow at the edge of time, and they were currently interviewing an old man who was describing the tremor he felt, and desperately trying to cut him off before he got lost in who he blamed for the incident.

Then Aldai saw her. The woman he'd caught glimpses of over the last few weeks. She was walking across the Concourse below. Tall, dark haired, with a fair complexion.

His stomach twisted. She must have transferred here from south quarter. She was serenely beautiful, as if she floated as she walked. He had seen her the week before through a side window of the market, but once he'd high-tailed for the exit, willing the check-out assistant to scan his surplus rations with more than the usual disinterest, she'd gone.

"What are your plans for summer break?" interrupted Bekka, pulling Aldai out of his daydream.

"The usual, I imagine," he replied. "Though I want to take out a transport and drop a mag-line. I haven't done it in years: not since I was a teenager. Most of the time you don't get anything, it's not really about what you find, it's more about the peace and quiet, a sense of freedom. I don't know, its relaxing anyway."

"I've never done that before," replied Bekka.

"You should try it. There's something about it, being able to just fly into the distance. You feel as if you're moving, or going somewhere. The view doesn't change; you still just see an endless expanse of cloud, but you at least feel a little more free."

"I'd like that," said Bekka, pondering Aldai's words. "I want to go to the surface," she said after a short pause.

"The surface? You're crazy," Aldai smiled. "Even if it wasn't blacklisted, is it even possible?"

"I think so . . . well, technically it's possible, I mean if people can walk around on Venus these days then you can walk around on the surface of Earth, right?"

"I suppose so."

"Don't you think that would be amazing? To walk through ancient cities, dig amongst piles of rubble and find treasures and keepsakes of people long gone?"

"I suppose it would, if you could put up with the three-hundred miles-per-hour winds, heat, lack of visibility and flying debris that could floor you at any moment. Not to mention you'd have to wear a full survival suit the whole time."

"True," laughed Bekka. "I still want to do it. If it wasn't outlawed, I'd sign up tomorrow."

"I think you just want to break the rules," joked Aldai.

"You're probably right. But what's life without a little rule-breaking right?" she said, catching Aldai with a mischievous look. "You've got to let off steam somehow, and anyway it's my planet. I'm not going to run scared of a few storms. We've got to show it we're not scared, right?"

"Your planet?" Aldai replied. "I didn't realise, your majesty. I'll keep in your good books for when we reshape Earth."

"You know what I mean. It's *our* planet, all of ours. It doesn't feel right being kept from something you feel is yours."

Aldai nodded. It was a thought they all had. Something had been taken away from them without fair discourse. They'd been ejected from territory that was theirs. So perhaps she was right; perhaps he did want to see the surface. Part of him did anyway. Maybe it was to counteract the feeling of being denied access to the man-made cities, towns and empty roads. Long ago, humans had made their mark with civilisations and monuments, before they were pushed out unscrupulously by overwhelming natural force.

But another part of him rejected the idea. The past was gone, unreachable. To see the surface as it was now would be like excavating your own house or digging amongst your neighbour's rubble. It would be like uncovering your own grave. One minute you're discovering a lost civilisation, and the next minute you're lost with it.

High above, the bell started tolling five o'clock. Despite all the technology around them, the designers of the StratoPort had decided to take a more rustic approach to the daily clock, as if they were still in some medieval village or market town. To some extent it worked, giving a more homely feel to the Concourse. The bell reverberated and echoed in a way that a digital sound never could. It's deep clanging, from heavy copper on copper, resonated across its old, imperfect surface, and around its convex interior, before ringing out across the space-age living area.

It was said that it was taken from a clock tower of a small town in Belgium, where Habersmith, the great designer, grew up. As it rang, it conjured up images of traders and merchants walking cobbled streets or emptying onto a town square after Christmas carols. Its sonorous clangs hinted of children growing up under its gentle tolling, feeling a cool summer breeze at a lazy afternoon garden party. It gave a tantalising glimpse of a human bond to the Earth. But, just like the last humans, the bell had been relocated to the sky, and could never return. Well, unless they found some success on Venus. They *would* return. *Venus would succeed.* It had to.

As the bell struck five, and the first groups of people started to mingle into the Concourse from the offices, Bekka gathered her bag and gossamer-thin pullover.

"That's my cue to leave. Have fun with the send-off," she said with a smile, fully aware of the reputation that Aldai, Sam and Wes had when they had any excuse to celebrate.

"Thanks," replied Aldai, watching her go, a slight furrow on his brow. He suddenly saw her in a different light, and a question brewed deep in his brain that had never appeared there before.

A few minutes later, Wes and Sam arrived, Wes slapping Aldai on his back, but so expectedly that Aldai barely flinched a millimetre.

"Who'd ya arrest today then, robo-cop?" said Wes, referring to his metal leg splint, from when a Sayen cartel member had fractured his tibia when they took down a ration-hoard. Wes had already taken off his tie, and it hung loosely out of his pocket, no doubt destined to end up lost in some dark corner of a bar, only to be found by a cleaner the following morning. "Let's get some drinks in," he said to no one in particular, heading over to the bar without even asking what the orders were.

Sam seemed a little more reserved.

"You looking forward to it?" asked Aldai.

"Does anyone ever look forward to the Seaport secondment?" he replied, with a reluctant smile.

Aldai let the question hang and avoided answering it. It was true; everyone had to do two years in the Seaport. At some point in your life, your conscription came up, and down you went. If you were unlucky, you had to go down twice. It was the only way people would work down there, compared to the sun-bathed StratoPort. Or at least the only fair way. Aldai had got his stint out the way in his early twenties, a time when he should have been spending each night in the Gallery night club pretending like the world wasn't about to end.

He thought about the view he got earlier, leaning over the rail and looking directly into the blackness of the Storm's Rift. It gave him chills that he tried to hide. It reminded him of the view from the drop-ship at the start of his two-year service, as it fell out of the sky, taking him down to month after month of the damp corridors and artificial light of the SeaPort.

"It's not easy, buddy," said Aldai. "But it goes quickly, and you'll be back up here in no time. And then you get to enjoy watching Wes have his turn next."

Sam raised his eyebrows and nodded in approval, just as Wes returned with three glasses full of thin brown liquid and perfect cubes of ice, expertly balanced between his hands, a task he could do with his eyes closed or blind drunk.

"True," replied Sam. "If there's anything to return to."

"I'll not hear that kinda talk today," said Wes, unreasonably optimistic. "What about the Facility on Venus? You saw the program the other day. The Second Expedition are on their way to help the First figure out the power source. It's a climate changing device. Maybe they're even on their way back with it right now. Pretty soon we'll be back on Bondi Beach, and even better, we'll have it all to ourselves."

Sam smiled, at least for Wes' optimism. As much as he found it irritating, it was exactly what he needed right now.

"You do realise that's just propaganda?" said Sam, unable to allow the optimism to settle. "Don't you think it's strange that we find an unused, abandoned alien device, just when it's almost too late for us to use it?"

"What I find strange is that you don't see the optimism. And we don't exactly have many other options. Whatever it is, it means there's something out there with the power to help us reverse the climate. I, for one, believe in it, and I, for one, am excited."

Sam smiled. Hard to argue with that. For all he knew it was true: the Venusian device really could offer salvation. And whether Wes really believed it or not, they all knew that after a while you had no choice, and you *did* believe it regardless. Sam had to believe it now more than ever. He had to believe that when his armoured dropship broke out of the Rift, rising into the glare of the sun, his eyes squinting at its brightness for the first time in two years, then it wasn't just the StratoPort's steel-cage exterior that he was returning to. He had to believe that, instead, there would be some concrete hope that they could live on the surface once more, and wouldn't be forever outlawed to the stratosphere.

"If you say so," he said reluctantly, despite being grateful to have someone like Wes around to make him believe it, even if only for a moment.

"Well, if you don't believe it now," said Aldai. "Then perhaps you'll believe it after a few more slammers," which finally broke Sam's sombre complexion into a laugh.

Chapter 3

If hell existed, this was it.

Colonel Seerman was the first to leave the Venus Lander, taking in the surroundings as his heavy environmental suit groaned and creaked against the immense temperature and pressure gradient for the first time. It was a moment he'd dreaded ever since he'd been selected to lead the Second Venus Expedition. You could push it out of your mind when you were training or travelling, but when you were faced with the eerily quiet furnace of a planet, you had to steel your mind against an atmosphere that would crush, burn, boil and disintegrate you in a fraction of a second. It was like walking on a highwire. But there was a mission to do: recon the alien power source in the Facility. That's what you had to focus on. That's what you had to fill your thoughts with.

The lander had disengaged from the *Molniya-V* interplanetary craft a few hours before, leaving it to float around in orbit like an arrow without an arrowhead. It hadn't exactly been spacious, but the interplanetary craft at least had room to move around in and places you could go to get some peace and quiet.

The Lander, on the other hand, was more cramped, bristling with oversized pressure pumps and coolant circuits inside a thick metal skin. The main habitation space and bunk rooms were squeezed towards the front, behind the cockpit, and the rear of the craft was taken up with a large five-man airlock and decontamination area, where the environmental suits were stored. It was functional and tight, but it was only for seven days. Seven days in this tank was all they needed to withstand.

They'd descended through the thick clouds of sulphuric gas, the ship walls making unnatural sounds as the pressure increased and increased, and the temperature gauge slowly turned further and further towards four hundred and fifty degrees. The ship was buffeted one way and then another by swirling air currents, and the cockpit viewscreen was splattered with sulphuric rain, occasionally calm and pattering, occasionally lashing and juddering the entire ship, as if some planet-sized entity was fighting their approach and warning them away.

Yet their landing was calm. Despite the turbulence, the thick atmosphere slowed the craft naturally, allowing an easy final descent. Closer to the surface, the clouds broke, and the ship entered a serene and ghostly new world. Forever blocked from the sun, it felt like an underground cavern, with the clouds above appearing as an impenetrable rock canopy, and the ground below dimly lit by an even light that resisted the formation of shadows.

They had descended into the furnace of Venus. Beneath the sulphuric clouds, the intense heat and pressure created a void of tranquillity next to the surface. Even the storms of Venus' upper atmosphere didn't want to go anywhere near the ground below.

Now, as he stepped down the exit ramp, Seerman was met with an other-worldly view that sent a wave of resistance to every sinew in his body. Your first step onto a new planet was supposed to feel like an endeavour, an exploratory achievement. Seerman had felt that when he first felt Martian soil under his boots, but he felt none of that from Earth's other neighbouring planet.

And the view that greeted him wasn't a comfortable one. Soon after they landed, touching down in a large U-shaped valley just north of the vast plateau of Ishtar Terra, a dust storm passed over, kicking up a thick soup of particles that hung in the air even after it had gone. It obscured the distance from view, and as Seerman's environmental suit landed its first foot on the Venusian ground, he was greeted by a wall of mustard-gas haze.

Their suits were cumbersome and heavy. The main body was a coffin-like pressure vessel that housed their rigid upright bodies and the habitation systems. Outside there were four legs, the rear two facing backwards so that as they walked it gave the appearance of a scuttling crab. Two mechanical arms extended from the suit hull, controlled through a brain interface and hand contacts by their waists, and they were mercifully allowed to see outwards through a large transparent visor.

The suits resisted the oppressive external environment. Pressure systems were mounted on their backs, with coolant systems inside, that together fought the ingress of four-hundred-degree heat and ninety atmospheres of pressure. They were a technological marvel of the twenty-sixth century, and a safety line on the precipice of a last hope.

But they certainly weren't comfortable. The various systems left little room for moving around inside. The astronauts' bodies were cocooned by humming and gurgling survival units, which meant you could just about shift your body weight before it was met by thin resistance pads. Movement felt lurchy and ungainly and took a while to get used to. You were effectively a passenger no longer in control of your balance or sensory feedback, and you had to rely on the suit to keep you upright, and learn to trust its movements and resistance.

First Officer Sandra Caellyn followed Colonel Seerman. *First Officer.* It was a title she still hadn't got used to. She wasn't military: far from it. She was a xeno-archaeologist, with full intentions of developing a career studying Venusian civilisation from a comfortable office on the StratoPort. It was a surprise when she got the invitation from Space Division, after which she found herself tumbling down a hillside of pressure and coercion. It was only late in her training that she learnt the uncomfortable truth that they'd lost contact with the First

Expedition shortly after it landed, and the Second Expedition was supposed to pick up the scattered pieces. Once she learnt that, her superiors made it perfectly clear to her that there was no turning back. Any retreat from the mission was blocked off; she was going to Venus, willing or otherwise.

I am Sandra Caellyn.

I will get through this.

Seven days in these suits. Goddamn they better hold.

Following her was the large frame of Kowalski, managing to walk with broad military bluffness even inside the suit, and behind him was Yakun, the engineer, and Arundel, the pilot.

"Acclimatisation," came Seerman's voice through the comms. "Get used to your suit, the way it moves. It'll be your home away from home for the next seven days."

More like test them to see if they actually work.

"We're two hundred metres from the First Expedition Lander. Let's go and see what we can find."

Caellyn wasn't sure how she'd feel when she took her first steps on Venus. As they travelled through space towards it, her mind had gone through fear, unease, wonder and excitement.

On one hand, she would get to walk on a different planet and discover a remnant from an alien civilisation. She would get to see the Facility first-hand, rather than just studying it from hazy vid-clips and digital images. Maybe she would even get to see the Star-Sphere itself, the name they had given to the power source hidden deep within the underground building.

She had felt a brief buzz of excitement. You had to search for it. You had to push down the fear, dread and discomfort, but once you did, the enthusiasm was there. Or perhaps it was nerves, as her brain misinterpreted rapidly firing neurons. Maybe it was her brain's diversionary tactics in the face of imminent danger.

On the other hand, they were so far from home. Eighty-one days: that's how long it had taken to get here. That's how far from home they were. Eighty-one days since they had left the confines of the StratoPort and headed out into space in the *Molniya-V* craft.

Now she was on the surface, Caellyn's thoughts couldn't help but encourage retreat. They briefly turned to her comfortable and well-furnished cabin in the StratoPort's Palmas district, but she pushed them away. It was too distant. She and her shipmates were explorers, charged with the highest of responsibilities. That framed their current circumstances. But her mind still wanted an escape route. *The Molniya-V.* It wasn't too far away, up there in orbit. That would suffice for now. Right then, the *Molniya-V* was the only security in this portion of the expansive galaxy.

The *Molniya-V* at least felt safe. As they travelled, she had wished their interplanetary journey didn't have to end. It was enjoyable, destination aside, and spirits had been high as they took in the freedom of the stars. Perhaps it was the feeling of going somewhere, wherever it was. With an eighty-one-day journey, you can forget the destination and just focus on the travel.

And the views had been spectacular. Their *Molniya-V* craft floated through space on a quiet trajectory, surrounded by constellations that you almost felt you could reach out and touch. And they didn't change, like they did on the StratoPort as the Earth slowly rotated. As you headed out through the solar system on an unchanging path, the constellations stayed in place, and you were constantly watched by Orion, Aires, Gemini, Taurus and Leo.

It was a freedom rarely felt on Earth, and it filtered a sense of optimism and adventure into the crew. They drank spirits and played card games, betting small hands of ration-bags, which Kowalski always seemed to win. They told stories and dreamed of better times.

You could almost forget where you were coming from, and where you were going.

Yakun, the ship's engineer, was always busying himself in the depths of the ship, normally disappearing for a day, and returning covered in oil and claiming that he'd increased the efficiency of some system or other by a fraction of a percent, and chastising the ship builders as if they should have let him build the whole things himself. He would even head out for unscheduled space walks, claiming the solar sail was damaged, and Caellyn suspected that it was an excuse to spend more time with machinery than human beings. Still, he was amenable enough. One time he'd taken her out for a spacewalk, but they'd only got as far as the third support strut before he'd noticed a dull cell and become so engrossed in it that she floated herself back in.

Caellyn's hideaway was about half way down the *Molniya-V*, where she'd cleared out a side capsule that was meant for storing spare guidance systems. According to Yakun they were completely unnecessary, so he'd helped her relocate them to a more cramped cupboard near the air filters. She'd turned it into a small library, fashioning a bookshelf out of back-pack supports, and filled it with the small number of novels she'd smuggled on board. The *Molniya-V* was designed for a larger crew than five, so no one had complained when each crew member carried on more than the designated luggage limit.

Before they left, Caellyn had been down to the StratoPort library. It was hidden beneath the Offices District, where it sat full of old dusty books and a librarian who looked as if he was protecting a dragon-hoard of gold. He'd protested vehemently against Caellyn taking so many, as if he was worried that he'd never see them again, but without saying it out loud. He didn't even know they were going to Venus. He only relented when Caellyn told him she knew General Gumpert personally, and would bring him down to see their extraction under military duress. The Librarian conceded at this point and resigned himself to accepting that military needs outranked the Consolidated Rules on Ancient Books.

She'd hastily grabbed as many as she could carry before the librarian could come back with statutes that refuted her brief victory. And she was pleased to have them. The books had passed the time on the journey well, and she'd been lost in romance stories set on the Biarritz coast,

49

thrillers in Moscow, and several books about Venus. One was an early twentieth century novel about a civilisation of Amazonian women living under Venus' thick clouds, written before humanity had developed the technology to look through them and realise that the surface was inhospitable and barren. Another detailed Venus' history. Seven hundred million years ago, its climate wasn't dissimilar to Earth, before it went through a runaway greenhouse effect that rendered its atmosphere the inhospitable oven it is today. She'd spent many hours in her den, only occasionally disturbed by Kowalski, who brought her rehydrated meals when she didn't turn up to mess time.

Arundel was busy in her own books, the ship's manuals. As the pilot, she felt a certain responsibility to know exactly how everything worked, which only infuriated Yakun, who saw the manuals as blasphemous to the art of tinkering. Luckily, she was professional enough to ignore him, and he finally relented his disapproval when she fixed a broken water disinfector that cleaned the recycled runoff water.

Arundel was the only crew member to take a genuine interest in Caellyn's line of work: the search for the Venusian civilisation. Or to at least feign an interest. It had been Caellyn's job for the last few years, leading a team in the Government's Venusian Archaeology department. They had been charged with finding other evidence that could explain the existence of the Facility. The Government was desperate for information that might prove its origins.

Caellyn showed Arundel the topological maps and research data they had from probe sensing across the surface, as well as the potential dig sites they had identified, where ground scouring or dark patches gave motivation to investigate further. There was hope that there might be other structures hidden under the topsoil, or, perhaps, as the media channels were frenzied to believe, evidence of an entire space-faring alien civilisation. But Arundel's interest waned when she realised that the evidence was almost non-existent, based on possibilities and, more likely, Governmental propaganda.

"So you're telling me we have nothing to explain the Facility?" Arundel said.

Caellyn didn't know how to respond. *I thought they knew.* They had all been kept in the dark, fed just enough information to keep them barely prepared on an unwilling path.

Arundel looked horrified before leaving to compose herself in the cockpit.

And at that moment, Caellyn didn't blame her. She remembered her own feelings when she was told they were going to enter the unknown Facility. It was just an unexplained door in the side of the valley, leading into a long shallow incline, through several well-spaced rooms, like a burial shaft in a pyramid.

"My Lidar's not working," she reported as she stepped onto the soft, crust-like soil of Venus. She cursed into her visor, suddenly feeling vulnerable and senseless. The human-shaped figure on her heads-up display showed a

51

malfunction, with a red flashing block above its cartoonised head. A readout scrolled across the top of her vision, telling her a malfunction code that was just a string of numbers and letters, clearly designed by someone who never had field experience. Afraid to look up at an endlessly obscured view, she hammered her interface keypad, willing the circuitry to connect and align. But the readout kept scrolling, and the red block turned solid. "I'm on vis only," she said.

"Copy that, stay close," replied Seerman. "Team report malfunctions, I want constant updates on how the equipment is holding up."

Seven days. That's all they needed to last. In fact, that's all they were guaranteed for in this heat and pressure. Taking into account safety factors and margins, that would push them to their limits.

That was all strictly confidential information of course. As far as the general population knew, you could walk around for a whole year down here. The Government-controlled StratoPort news channels had reported that the First Expedition had been there for two months, before they'd returned to Earth, and then headed back to Venus. It was a lie that they'd hope to keep stringing along until they had worked out how to operate the planet-shaping alien power source, and the means to the end became irrelevant.

Without the Lidar laser visual system, Caellyn took in her surroundings unaided. Flat, crumpled earth spread out in a circle around her. It was red and angry, a rusty colour that refused to support even the most basic forms of life. It stretched out for about ten metres in each direction before being obscured behind a camo dust-cloud.

As she moved forwards the circle followed her. She got the feeling of being trapped in an up-turned glass that was mercifully being slid across the surface, at least allowing her some freedom in captivity. *Breath.* She focussed on breathing, slowing it down as the monotony of inhales and exhales filled the quiet around them, save for the soft thud of her solid footpads on Venusian soil, and the occasional clanging from inside her suit.

They trudged on through the foggy conditions, a line of five beings in an otherwise empty world. An eerie silence oozed from the environment, the silence you'd only get when there was no other life on the planet. They could carry on walking for forty thousand kilometres, around the entire circumference, almost the same size as Earth, and see nothing but rocks, flat soil and dormant volcanoes.

But right now, all Caellyn could see was the back of Seerman's suit before everything else was lost behind dust. With her Lidar broken, she was blind to her surroundings.

She couldn't see a laser-rebound image of the cliff wall to the right, extending into the distance along a straight line in either direction, that housed the Facility doorway near their landing site. She couldn't see to her left, where the flat valley floor spread out beyond Lidar range. And without Lidar, right then she couldn't see the ship of the First Expedition ahead of them. She kept her head down, following Seerman's footsteps and trying not to acknowledge the circular cloud-wall around her.

"It's a toxic wasteland," came the crackled voice of Arundel through the comm system. "We're supposed to believe that there might be something of the First Expedition still worth finding?"

"That's our first task, private," came Seerman's response, stern, but with an air of uncertainty.

"There could be habitable areas inside the Facility," said Yakun hopefully, but no one dared reply.

"Our mission is to head into the Facility and recon the Star-Sphere," came Seerman's voice after a pause. "That is our focus. Secondary objective is to work out what went wrong on the First Mission. We investigate the First Expedition's Lander, then we forget about them and get on with the job."

Twelve years ago, a robotic survey had stumbled across the Facility door. Hidden in the rockface, up a short incline from the valley floor, the door was almost indistinguishable from the rock around it. It looked human sized, and if it hadn't been slightly ajar it probably would have gone unnoticed. The drone had managed to push the door open before its signal was lost. A second autonomous mission was planned, and several more drones were lost before it was established that the entrance was damping any kind of signal getting in or out. The engineers on Earth changed tactics, and drones were programmed to go in, fly off radar against whatever structure was inside, and then retrace their route back out again.

After several attempts, one went in, and after fifteen minutes of radio silence, came out, and the first internal pictures were beamed back to the StratoPort. It was just a regular rectangular room, empty apart from a shaft at the far end that headed downwards at a five-degree angle, but it was enough to be met with rapturous applause in the Earth control centre, and a renewed sense of hope. It was like digging for treasure and finding your spade clang as it hit something hard.

News of the discovery had spread like wildfire around the StratoPort and SeaPort, and everyone was abuzz with hope. It was a strange optimism with nothing immediate to hang it on, but it left a tantalising desire that there was *something* that could provide some salvation. It at least provided an avenue, when before the discovery none other existed. It answered questions and posed many more. It was positive news, when other avenues were being closed off.

A third probe mission was sent, this time better prepared, with probes intended to reach further inside the structure before making their way out again. Most didn't make it, and were seen in final resting places by later entrants, who gently hovered past them, the victor in some mechanical survival challenge. The number of probes slowly dwindled, as hope faded that they'd find something of interest, until one of the early drones, that they thought they'd lost, suddenly emerged. It had penetrated far into the structure, past several rooms where the shaft opened out, until it had found a control room overlooking a huge, circular reactor hall, dimly lit.

There, in the middle, it had glimpsed the Star-Sphere. Sixteen beach-ball-sized orbs, black and lifeless, hovering in a formation as if they were perched on the surface of a large invisible globe, all equidistant from each other.

It had taken everyone aback, and the team on Earth were in disbelief. They had found technology that appeared to still be operational.

A later probe returned with a blurred video of a mural carved into a wall, from further up in the Facility. The mural seemed to indicate the orbs could reshape the surface of a planet. It showed the Star-Sphere amongst pictograms of planets with atmospheres in a state of alteration. It was slim information, but it was enough for Venus fever to grip the Ports.

It was salvation. *It had to be.* The celebrations that rang out back on Earth lasted a full week, with people talking about staking out plots of land on the surface, as if they could recolonise the surface of Earth the next day. It was like the Nineteenth Century gold rush, with everyone eager to face the Rocky Mountains for a slice of what was beyond. But soon the optimism dwindled, and the serious task of understanding and recovering the Star-Sphere began.

A manned mission was planned to investigate the depths of the Facility. It was clear that this Facility was built for organic life. No signals could get in or out, not even down a wire, and the guidance systems of the probes were struggling against unknown drifting and malfunctioning. People would have to go to Venus and walk on its surface. It was a decision that reflected their desperation. The public needed hope and answers, and the surface temperature on Earth was slowly creeping upwards.

The First Expedition had landed just over a year ago. They had reported back that they were entering the Facility, and then all communication went quiet. The mission's failure was covered up, and the population was kept in the dark, with the Government in fear of rioting and the descent of all hope. They covered it up, and as far as anyone knew, the First Expedition were very much alive and making slow progress, while a second team was hastily assembled.

"Almost there, Caellyn," came Seerman's voice through comms, aware that all Caellyn could see was the back of his suit slowly moving forwards.

"Roger," she replied breathlessly. "Can you see any damage, Colonel?"

"Negative, looks OK from laser-rebound. Need visual," came the reply.

The nose of the Lander peeked through the fog first, startling Caellyn. As she walked forwards, the ship emerged from the dust-mist, its nose pointing proudly despite being isolated here for almost a year. She reached up an autonomous arm and touched its armoured metal surface, half expecting it to crumble away, but reassured to find it still solid, but mottled like acid rain on limestone. She ran her disconnected metal hand along its angular shape. It was identical to theirs and had an uncomfortable level of familiarity. It gave her an unnerving feeling that they had walked in circles and had simply settled upon their own Lander. But then markings appeared on the side designating its ship reference, and a picture emerged of a sun supported on the back of an eagle. It was the First Expedition's insignia, emblazoned on the Lander's skin like a tattoo.

She moved around the front-left rocket drive, a twelve-foot-high column, that, with its three siblings at the other corners of the ship, could provide multi-axis thrust to manoeuvre the Lander. Beneath it was blasted earth from the force of the landing, and just inside that was one of the large landing pads that had crumpled the ground beneath it. It had sunk through a few centimetres of the Venusian crust before finding enough purchase to support the tank-like weight of the craft. The ground looked perfectly preserved, as if the landing had happened yesterday, rather than a year ago.

"Oh my god," said Seerman, from further around the ship.

"What is it?" came a worried reply from Kowalski, still a few metres behind them. Seerman didn't respond.

Caellyn rounded the ship, pushing the suit as fast as its assisted bionics would allow, until she was standing next to him.

She meant to say something, but couldn't form words. The ship had been sliced neatly down its fuselage, like a razor-sharp sword had plunged through it. The slice had separated the engines from the main ship down most of its height, so that they were weakly supported by only a small section of the undercarriage.

The rest of the team joined them.

"Holy shit," murmured Yakun, looking around nervously. "What the..."

"Kowalski, Caellyn, check inside for information, Kowalski take point," Seerman barked, regaining composure and cutting off Yakun's concern.

"Sir?" said Kowalski, unbecoming of his military experience.

"We should never have left our ship," said Yakun. "We need to go back."

"Negative Yakun," shouted Seerman. Arundel was murmuring to herself, unaware it was being broadcast through the comms. "Kowalski check that airlock now," he said.

"Yes, sir," came the response, the second order snapping him into focus. He slowly stepped up the deployed ramp to the airlock aft of mid-section and keyed in the opening code. The door slid across, but jammed before being fully open. He leant the full weight of his environmental suit against it and it relented, allowing them past. He stepped inside, and Caellyn followed.

"Inside airlock blown out," said Kowalski, his regimented training now guiding his actions. Caellyn followed him through the depressurisation airlock and through into the decontamination room. Normally you would sit in each area for half an hour or so, and it felt wrong to be walking through without stopping. But it felt doubly wrong to see a Lander in this shape. It was decimated, with a mess of equipment strewn over the floor.

They moved down the starboard side and into the habitation room just behind the cockpit. "Nothing inside main digs," came Kowalski's voice.

The main room was as lifeless as the surface, covered in a thick layer of dust. It was the same layout as its Second Expedition sister ship, with a large round table against the starboard wall, the cockpit ahead, storage space on the port side and the space in the centre for exercise. But the planet had begun its slow process of consuming it, and it resembled an archaeological find, or a prophetic vision.

Caellyn flicked on her helmet lights, and three beams sniped out in front of her, illuminating the heavy atmosphere inside the ship. She turned to be met by a large round face a metre away, sharply drawing breath and letting out a wailed gasp.

"Just a space-walk suit," said Kowalski, turning quickly. "Nothing to worry about. You OK?"

"Fine," said Caellyn, steadying herself on uneasy legs. "Let's check the quarters," she said in mock confidence.

Kowalski moved his bulk down the port-side corridor to the aft section, squeezing through gaps not designed for full atmospheric rig, with Caellyn holding back, scouring the main living area and half expecting to see more than just the empty remains of a chewed-out husk of a ship. She felt movement up her spine and closed her eyes, convincing herself it was muscle spasm caused by her heightened senses going into overdrive in an unfamiliar environment. The heavy metal pressure suits allowed little room for scratching an itch, and she forced her thoughts away, spreading her search lights across the pilot cabin.

"You think that was natural?" came Arundel's voice from outside, startling Caellyn for a split second.

"Keep it to yourself private," crackled Seerman's short reply. "One step at a time."

"Sir, bunk 5 door jammed shut," came Kowalski's report over the banging of his progress into the sleep-cabin and shower-room corridor. "I'm going to try and force it open." He braced against the bulkhead and heaved the heavy door. The noises pinged and echoed unnaturally in the highly pressurised atmosphere, like the zip of creaking metal underwater. Caellyn watched from the main living quarters, her ears filled with the metal jamming against metal, and her other senses on high alert. There was a crack as Kowalski lurched and steadied himself.

"Kowalski, report," Seerman's voice came urgently.

"Door open, nothing inside."

There was silence in reply. It meant the First Expedition members were nowhere on the ship.

A morbid part of Caellyn had wanted to find bodies and a rational explanation. Now the reality looked to be that they had vanished in the Facility itself. Caellyn couldn't help but feel Seerman had turned off his comms and was swearing profusely into his visor, but it was a scenario she'd never get to witness.

"Return to the ship. We need to communicate this to the StratoPort," Seerman said through the comms.

Caellyn and Kowalski made their way out, to be greeted by concerned faces from the others. They regrouped and slowly made their way back to the Second Lander, leaving behind the first to be abandoned again, as the dust-fog slowly enveloped it.

Seerman and Caellyn took the front, and the team followed closely, a tight line of five retracing their footsteps.

"We never should have come here," said Yakun.

Seerman rounded on him, taking a few steps forward until their visors butted together.

"You listen to me, Private. This is a military mission. I don't care how you feel, we've got one job: recon the Star-Sphere and get off this god-forsaken planet. Do you understand me?"

"Yes sir," came the shell-shocked reply.

"Good, back to the ship, our ship, that's the orders," continued Seerman. He pressed a few buttons on his wrist interface and Caellyn heard his voice again in her helmet.

"This is a private channel, First Officer. Speculate on what we just saw."

"Captain, I..." came Caellyn's response, trailing off. She was taken aback. It was the first time Seerman had approached her for counsel and advice. On the *Molniya-V* they had operated a loose and casual hierarchy.

"Officer, I need the best assessment we have, and I need it quickly, speculate on what we just saw."

"Well... it's possible it was debris during a storm, something large and thin that just sliced through the ship."

"These ships are designed to take a nuclear blast and carry on flying," came Seerman's response.

"I know that," said Caellyn. She paused, unsure how to say the next few words. "I've heard of dropship being taken out by stray debris. I remember it on the news. The wall of the Rift collapsed momentarily and something hit it. Apparently, it disintegrated as it was slammed into the Rift-wall. Perhaps this could have been from a storm, and a thin plate of rock was whipped through the air and sliced the ship like that," she said, as if not believing her own words. "But these ships are tanks sir, I can't imagine anything that could do that. It looked..."

"Speculate," he said again, more urgently, as if forcing Caellyn to say the words he already knew she was going to say. Caellyn fought a rising unease and swallowed awkwardly.

"I think it was intentional sir, intended to disable the ship without being visible to planetary sensors."

"Agreed," came Seerman's sombre reply.

They marched on in silence, Caellyn's view only interrupted by a warning sign that registered a brief temperature spike before the internal systems compensated.

"Did you see that?" came Yakun's voice, from a few paces behind her.

"See what?" Arundel replied.

"I saw something move, in the fog."

"You're jumping at shadows," interjected Kowalski. "I'm on Lidar, and I see nothing but empty ground."

"I saw something," replied Yakun. He changed path, starting to walk towards the dust-cloud on their right.

"Yakun, get back in line," said Kowalski, moving to grab Yakun until he relented and re-joined the single file.

"I definitely saw something," Yakun said insistently. "It was there on the edge of the fog, then it was gone."

"You're jumping at shadows, Yakun," Colonel Seerman interrupted "We head back to the ship; keep your eyes down if you need to."

They moved in silence from that point onwards, Caellyn keeping her attention heightened, as they crossed the valley floor back to their Lander. It was only disturbed by her Lidar, which briefly resurged into life, providing a hazy mass of pixels overlying the featureless terrain in front of her before disappearing just as quickly.

Their footsteps padded on, and as they approached the Second Lander, she got an unsettling feeling that they'd find it slashed as well, or somehow in a similar state of decay, despite only a few hours passing since they landed. She looked at the barren ground around her, imagining it as her tomb. *Where the hell are the First Expedition?* Five souls marooned on a hostile planet.

But their Lander was still in one piece, standing proud and undamaged. *What could treat this like tinfoil? I mean, it's a tank.* It was squat and loaded with armour like an overfed pet. It looked solid and unbreakable, with its four rocket drives pointed uniformly and diligently up to the sky. They were like holstered lances, ready to defend against any attack.

The five astronauts stood in the decompression chamber for what felt like an age, struggling to meet each other's gazes. As they waited for the pressure to drop, with the evacuation pumps running double time, Caellyn couldn't escape visualising the images of the First Lander's equivalent room, exposed to the atmosphere and full of rotting equipment. It took willpower not to imagine the walls around her splitting open and their Lander sharing a similar fate.

"I think we should arm ourselves from this point forwards," said Kowalski.

"Agreed," came Colonel Seerman's reply, after a short, weary pause as if he felt the entire weight of Venus' oppressive atmosphere on his shoulders.

The inner door shone a green light around its circumference, and they moved into the second chamber to spray their suits. The air jets removed the toxic coating that a short stint outside produced, allowing them to finally open their pressure vessels and step out before heading further into the living quarters.

"I'm going to report back to Earth," said Seerman, "Kowalski, make contact with the *Molniya-V* AI and see if you can get some readout on this dust-fog." He headed into the communications room and closed the door so that the crew couldn't hear his report to the base on the StratoPort.

Caellyn may have been First Officer, but right now Seerman was clearly relying on Kowalski's military background to stand firm against uncertainty. She wanted to resist, to prove to Seerman she deserved the title, but her wits deserted her. She wasn't a leader. She'd only been given the rank of First Officer because whoever organised the mission didn't want to accept that it was entirely military. What would she even say right now, if she assumed command? Reassurance? Hope?

Arundel had disappeared into the cockpit to divert herself in more manuals, probably trying to work out how fast she could pilot the craft off the surface in an emergency, and how hard she could push the engines. Yakun had silently followed Kowalski to the systems interface opposite the round table, without even making his usual moan at being ordered around by a "meathead."

Caellyn sat at the table and allowed herself to stare out the window into the cloud of dust, as the ever-present hum and faint whine of habitation systems coursed through the Lander. *Seven days. That's all it is. Seven days, and we'll be back in the Molniya-V, with or without the Star-Sphere, but at least on our way home. But I hope to God we find something. They wont like it if we come back empty handed.*

Chapter 4

In the days that passed since Aldai's encounter with the Gaunt, he found his thoughts return more and more to the haunting face. It was still in the Port somewhere, hidden away in a dark crevice of the Undercity. They should be down there, finding it and finding answers. The Gaunt should be behind bars in a SeaPort cell. He felt revulsion and unease at the barely human features, the rasping voice and the rattle of the Gaunt's breathing.

But the knowledge had just been sequestered in the Intelligence Department. Team-6 had opened the box, and then the lid had been shut, without a chance for protest. The answers were inside the box, but the box had been locked, closed and taken away for processing. It was infuriating for Aldai, with the Government in control of his actions and blindsiding his conscience.

When their transport had landed in the Intelligence hangar, Team-6 had been split up and questioned. Each had been taken to a different room, small, plain and with dark walls, and empty apart from only a table and two chairs. They'd each been interviewed by a bureaucrat, someone only interested in facts, and not what they meant.

The woman interviewing Aldai had long blond hair that was thin and straight, thick glasses and a neatly pressed suit. She had no interest in small talk. Aldai still couldn't get over the fact that when he mentioned the Gaunt, she didn't even raised an eyebrow. I mean, seriously? How could she remain deadpan? There was *something* in the structure below them, a twisted Gaunt, or, well, alien? It was unnatural. It was right here on Earth and no one knew about it. Yet the Intelligence Officer had barely flinched, as if she was so accustomed to the idea that it was irrelevant.

Aldai was prepared for a gasp. He was expecting shock as the news sunk into another human being. He thought he would watch her pen hover as her brain processed the ideas. But the pen simply carried on looping and sliding, noting down words as if they were irrelevant, a chore. They would be filed at the back of an old steel cabinet and forgotten about, while the Intelligence Department focussed on more pressing issues, like how to convince everyone Venus was going to be a success.

The lid of the box had been well and truly shut. It was exactly what Aldai didn't need. On the StratoPort you needed monotony, you needed things to be regular and unchanging. Life was as solid as the floor below you, tenuously balanced above fifty thousand feet. If you pulled at loose threads you could unravel the whole garment. But his actions and conscience were no longer in his hands. He tried to push the thoughts away and put the Gaunt out of his mind. Let someone else worry about that. Do your job. Let the sun rise and set. Keep the machine turning.

* * *

Sam had had a more formal leaving party before he took the dropship down to the SeaPort. It was a solemn affair, with the only brightness coming from the coloured surplus-ration cakes. But even they were just for show, and their substance was dry, so that not all of them were eaten. Still, Wes was on good form, and it was a welcome distraction for Aldai. Sam's parents had given a speech, which sounded like a Government advert, reminding Sam of his duty and that the secondment was something everyone had to do, but what else do you say? Everyone gave him advice about how to pass time down there, but absolutely no one said "We'll come and visit." You couldn't even if you wanted to; the dropships were so full of cargo that seats were reserved only for official purposes. They'd all got drunk and danced in Sam's cabin while the window-screen showed a view of the Old Himalayas, until someone smashed a glass against it and they covered it with a sheet. Sam's mum had too much to drink and was taken home by his dad, and the numbers slowly dwindled until Aldai made an excuse and somehow found his way back to his cabin.

Life went on.

Aldai sat in the Crescent one evening, this time alone. He didn't feel like he wanted to see Wes at that moment, not without Sam around to offset his relentless chatter. He watched the sun go down, lost in thoughtfulness. It was the same as it was every day, a stellar lightshow of the lightest orange, the sun rays battling through the low angle from the horizon and becoming redder and angrier as particles blocked their path, shedding energy and becoming lethargic as their wavelengths stretched.

Then the sun disappeared to the dark side of Earth. Or that's what they called it these days. The StratoPort could only see so far, and when the sun went over the horizon, no human saw it until it reappeared the next day. *The dark side of Earth might as well be the underworld. The Earth could be flat, and underneath was Ma'at or Hades. When the sun goes down, maybe it really does fight the giant snake Apophis, who is intent on the destruction of the world.* He filtered these thoughts through his mind until he was ushered out by the Scout Police who were emptying the concourse for curfew.

Tuesday came around, the evening he spent with his mother. It was normally an uncomfortable affair. They'd go to the Concourse and look for a restaurant, but in reality they were just wandering around until they zoned in on the same Thai joint they went to every time. It had neatly laid tables and an air of sophistication, hidden by the side of the Concourse away from the crowds. His mother would normally stare out the door and could barely make eye contact with Aldai, and it was a chore for

70

both of them until they'd finished their beige and grey food and made their separate ways.

The food was good at least, relatively speaking. The chef, unnaturally positive, would somehow manage to get the best out of the standard nutrition paste from the artificial farms, reformed into different constitutions for variety. It was the same thing you got in every restaurant, with each chef simply forming it with a different arrangement of synth-spices and salt level, and occasionally a vegetable or fresh egg, depending on what the chefs had managed to get their hands on. Somehow the Thai joint managed to get something more out of it, their thin menu offering some of the more palatable dishes on the Port.

Aldai was preparing for the Tuesday ritual, and made his way through the habitation warren to his mother's quarters in the top cabins. But with his thoughts awry, he almost got lost in the mess of corridors that all looked the same. It was easy to do; there were hundreds of similar corridors, all with the same worn carpet and regular grey-gloss plastisteel doors, inlaid to make them look like wood. It was a labyrinth, and you could only tell where you were by the arrows in the floor every ten or so metres that always pointed towards the centre of the Port. If you got lost, you simply followed them in, and then headed back into the warren for a second try.

He entered her cabin to find his mother unusually glammed up.

"Sorry darling," she said, without turning from the mirror "I've got a date tonight, I meant to tell you but it slipped my mind."

"Anyone I know?" said Aldai, with both relief and rejection, at having their weekly meal cancelled.

"I wouldn't think so; he runs the legal firm by the 6-strut."

Great, another desk jockey. He'd probably look down on military just as much as Aldai would reciprocate. Still, none of them were allowed to hang around long; his mother drew them in and then spat them out. *At least she isn't a Loper. At least she hasn't lost hope.* He headed to the casino to blow his surplus rations on blackjack and synthetic alcohol.

The following day they were posted to the Undercity again. Team-6 waited expectantly in the locker room as if Halderford would announce another appearance from General Gumpert, or Orcanciz even, but it never came. This was regular patrol and reconnaissance, back to the mundane. They all had to bury their questions and ride the anti-climax. The chain of command closed above them, and again they were grunts following orders, demeaning and comforting in equal measure.

They'd been assigned to the Mendocino district around Levitation Engine 7, one of the eight giant engines that kept the StratoPort in the air. It was mostly workshops and build yards, one of the busier areas of the Undercity, and it was a welcome outing after a few days of training and perch-watching.

With the whole Port on lockdown and high alert, the Special Ops had become more of a visible presence. Under normal circumstances they wouldn't be asked to bother with simple reconnaissance, but right now they were needed as a public relations exercise. Seeing armoured troops walking around in industrial camo and carrying carbines was a reminder to everyone to be on their guard. It was intended to make people feel reassured and protected, but also to make it harder to forget the crack of the whip.

"Never understood how these things work," said Jones, motioning to the huge Levitation Engine, as they slowly made their way around its gargantuan bulk. It was the size of a small mountain, shaped like an upturned egg but ferocious in its power. From the inner deckways all they could see was a gently curved metal surface arcing away from them into the distance, until the view was blocked by metal grating that butted up against it.

"I've never understood how your brain could work, given half of it was replaced with smushed banana," came Bekka's response.

"You explain it to me then," Jones challenged. Bekka went quiet for a moment, as if unsure whether to formulate a serious answer or an even better put down.

"I suppose the smushed banana is an equal match to your remaining brain, so the two halves work together," she replied, choosing the latter.

"I meant the engine, cloud-head."

"All I remember," interrupted Rongal, as if trying to diffuse an argument destined to escalate. "Is my teacher saying 'everything has an opposite'. Gravity pulls, but something must resist. It's just that in a universe full of gravity, it took a long time to find it."

"From a different dimension," chimed in Jones, as if unwilling to allow the conversation to become serious.

"What would you know, Jones?" said Bekka. "All I remember from our Levitation Physics class was watching you trying to chase Sarah Randfen, and her trying to ignore you."

"Sounds like jealousy to me," he replied.

"Hardly," Bekka scoffed.

"Entering Mendocino district," interrupted Sergeant Halderford's voice from the front of the group. "Eyes up."

It had the desired effect, and the team walked on in silence, peering into the corridors and recesses as the main floor curved around the Engine. They split off and changed direction towards the Port central axis and entered a large open area with a ceiling several floors above. It had the appearance of an atrium of a multinational corporation, but was empty, save for two giant figures embossed into the far wall. One was reaching out to a ball of energy, another holding a spanner in one hand and a miniature StratoPort in the other.

Between the two figures was a receptionist, sitting alone in the huge space, her desk looking like a goalpost in an empty Slamball pitch. As Team-6 walked past, she barely even looked up from her computer screen.

"Ma'am," said Halderford.

"Sirs," she replied nonchalantly. The Undercity folk kept themselves to themselves. It wasn't about social hierarchy, because in the twenty-sixth century there wasn't an economy to base it on. It wasn't even about people looking down on the Undercity. The engineers and technicians were held in high regard. They kept everyone afloat somehow, so they were quietly appreciated.

Having spent a long time in the Undercity's twisting, endless sprawling mass of metal, Aldai got the feeling that the environment down here just changed a person's outlook. The Undercity was sparse, unkempt and industrial, compared to the bustle of the relatively clean habitation spaces in the Uppercone. It was a different perspective. In the Uppercone, it was as if people were trying to forget the circumstances and live lives of work and recreation, while in the Undercity there was the grim reality of keeping the lifeboat afloat. Down here there were endless work shifts that cared little for rising and setting of the sun, whereas in the Uppercone you could almost pretend like you were still on the surface.

Plus, there was the Rift. From the external reaches of the Undercity, you couldn't avoid seeing it and looking down into its black, empty pupil. Perhaps that changed people's views.

The team walked into a large, straight hallway with a plasticrete floor. Left and right, through gaps in half-closed doors, they could see people at work in small rooms full of wires and hardware. The air was full of the buzz of mini saws, the crackle of welding torches and the dull roar of extraction systems.

They walked on until they reached a large vertical shaft like a ten-metre diameter water main that ran down into the depths of the Port. It was full of large pipes that ran from the ceiling a few floors above, and opposite a workman was welding on the far wall, hanging by straps from the walkway above. They took a set of spiral stairs down a few floors, passing a woman who walked on by without acknowledgement, her hardhat covered in soot and her overalls decorated with grease marks.

Near the bottom they entered the Mendocino lower reaches. There, the scene became more expansive, with a low ceiling framing open metal flooring spreading in all directions, revealing a wide deck area dotted with machinery and ducting. A portion of the egg-shaped Levitation Engine obscured the view to the right, and up ahead there was the faintest glimpse of natural light.

"Split up. Tiernan, Jones walk around right, Aldai and Bekka you head over there," said Halderford. "Eyes up, you know the drill, everything under order," he said, as if reminding the team that, despite their curiosity fuelled by the fracas with the Gaunt a few days before, they were to act as if that had never happened. To their frustration, they had to pretend they'd never even been on the Code Gamma mission. Halderford had discreetly reminded them of this several times, perhaps knowing it was a thought brewing in their minds. Maybe it was brewing in his mind too. *Who knows with Halderford; he plays his cards close to his chest. Crak, he's annoying sometimes.*

Aldai and Bekka walked in silence, their attention on the noise and bustle of clanking metal around them, as they passed the occasional workmen who only shot them glances before resuming their errands. The two crossed the platform, heading towards the glint of sunlight in the distant reaches of the deck. They made a left turn, and the ceiling gave way to an area of double height, housing a gently purring generator that chugged like a diesel engine. A man was viewing an interface panel and occasionally touching buttons that caused minor changes in frequency of the whirring machine. He looked up at them, his features soft and fresh, as if he was barely out of college.

"Upconers!" he said with an element of surprise, holding his hands up in sarcastic repost. "Don't shoot."

"At ease, private," quipped Bekka, as Aldai split off to walk around the house-sized generator, taking in its complex array of wires, exposed circuit boards, and pipes that coursed rigid with through-flow. "Just keeping the peace," said Bekka.

"Well, keep your guns pointed away from Brenda here, she's running smooth but doesn't appreciate the end of a rifle," said the workman.

"Of course," replied Bekka, relaxing her gun and pointing it down. "With the high alert we've been drafted to have a look around . . ." her glance invited response.

The workman looked away, keying codes into the device before sliding an interface column upwards on his display.

"Nasty business," the workman said. "Took out one of these a few weeks ago. I didn't get a chance to look at it but Holedy over in Leeuwin District said it was reduced to a mangled mess. You can't imagine it can you, something like this reduced to cinders, but that's what directed plasma charge can do."

"Directed plasma charge?" Bekka replied.

"Oh, well, you know, that's what they said it was. Can't think of anything else that powerful, but it was only a small charge."

"What's the feeling like down here after that?" asked Bekka.

"Just gotta get on with it, haven't you," replied the Workman, resting his hands on either side of the panel, his attention finally drawn away from his testing schedule. "They'd have to do a lot more than that to have any impact on the station, I mean you've seen the size of the Levitation Engines, plus there's eight of them right? And we only need five working," he said, before suddenly realising he shouldn't have said that to people he'd never met. Bekka's mild perfume must have briefly released him from his professionalism. "Well, four or five, three even," he said, before moving around to the side of the machine, slipping past Aldai, who'd completed his circuit of Bertha. Aldai exchanged amused glances with his teammate as she followed the workman.

"Have you seen anything suspicious going on?" enquired Bekka.

"Me? No. Lev-7 has been pretty quiet. I don't think we've been targeted once in the last few years," he said, now engrossed in installing some sort of sensor. "You know, I was always in favour of taking the StratoPort into space. With a bit of extra work on the hull you could withstand the pressure" he said, keen to get the topic back on to engineering. "But then it'd be harder to transport stuff from the SeaPort, but not that much harder. No oxygen though. Atmosphere would all have to be artificial. Less radiation protection though, but I mean, it's space, right? You want to hear a joke?"

"Sure," said Bekka reluctantly.

"What are three things a foetus needs?" he said.

"I don't know," said Bekka uncomfortably, shooting Aldai a questioning glare.

Aldai smiled, pleased he wasn't talking directly with the workman.

"Gravity, radiation protection and insemination," he said, clearly pleased with himself, and unaware no one was laughing. "I'm serious though, that's why we gave up on Mars. Gravity's all wrong to raise children. Well, that and we had to focus our attention on surviving on Earth, I suppose."

Bekka sighed, unsure if the workman even knew what insemination was, but kept her eyes away in embarrassment.

"And was good luck that we'd got the levitation technology, you know, otherwise we'd be swamped by those clouds. We'd all be in the SeaPort without it. Think I'd rather be a jumper," he said jovially.

"You think jumpers are funny?" Aldai interjected, cutting through the workman's cheery tone.

"I...no, no of course not," he replied, taken aback "I meant no offence. Did you know Mars colony is all but abandoned?" he said, changing the subject quickly. "Had to commandeer the ships for Venus. That's where I wanted to work: interplanetary ship-building. Never meant to be down here in power systems. Qualified top of my class in solar sail design. But you go where you're told, right? Sounds like ship-building might be expanding again though. Maybe I'll get a chance."

Aldai eyed him with bubbling contempt before shaking his head and inspecting a schedule board on the side of the room. It was covered in electronic-marker-pen maths instead of task priorities.

"Well, you know where we are if you see anything," Bekka said, motioning to Aldai for them to make a quick exit before the workman strayed into a new topic.

"No... problem," said the workman. "You want to see..." he said, before cutting himself off as he realised they were leaving.

Aldai turned to see him already back at the interface panel and resuming his tests. The generator increased in velocity so that it sounded more strained and powerful, sending minor vibrations through the metal-panelled floor.

"Maybe that's why they're so weird down here," Bekka joked to Aldai, when there were a few bulkheads between them and the workman. "They have to talk to people like that." But Aldai remained silent.

They passed along banks of humming cabinets before taking stairs further down, finding themselves back next to the giant Lev-engine, this time lower, with the curvature of the engine falling away from them as it slid towards the egg-point tip far below.

They walked around a giant support strut, so large that you could fit the Statue of Liberty inside it. It extended up through floor after floor of the structure, bearing the immense loads of the Port, like a thick bone of an inner structural skeleton. It pushed through deck after deck, claiming priority over any attempts to create ordered square workspaces next to it. High above them, it would split into tributaries like a river delta, to support the Uppercone far above.

They moved underneath it, through an area lit by a faded yellow translucent ceiling that must have been fed by a light well, giving everything a soft orange glow. It was a quieter area, with the hum of the Mendocino main deck some distance away, and it was full of rectangular metal canisters that looked like large oil containers.

As they made their way through a man poked his head up in front of them before ducking down and hastily making for a door.

Aldai nodded at Bekka and they followed his path. They approached the door with caution, maintaining routine professionalism but with rifles poised. Through the door was a dark corridor that headed down a short distance before dog-legging left.

There was a dimly lit workshop to one side, with windows onto the corridor, and a light was on in the corner, behind a door that was slightly ajar. Aldai flicked on his torch light and made his way into the workshop towards it, cautiously surveying the array of lathes and pillar-drills that filled the space. Approaching the lit side-room, he pushed the door with his rifle to inch it open quietly.

"Can't a man get some peace around here?" came the response from the cupboard. Aldai could see a cork-topped bench running along one side, covered in electronics and solder-iron burn marks.

"Just doing the rounds," came Aldai's calm response, remaining motionless, the door half open and blocking his view of the person within. He paused before taking a few steps back, with Bekka joining him. "We have a few questions," he said.

The technician sighed in frustration. He slowly opened the door, revealing a medium-sized man with disgruntled, rounded features, who eyed them beadily through upturned spectacles.

"What sort of questions?" he said, noticing their weaponry, but resigned to having been cornered. "You don't look like you're interested in flux capacitors."

"Port's in alert," said Aldai. "We're just patrolling. Have you seen anything suspicious? I'm sure it didn't escape your attention that there was a bomb a few weeks ago."

"You think I'm a terrorist? Far from it, they can all..." but he trailed off before finishing the sentence.

"Have you seen anything?" asked Bekka, interrupting Aldai with a lighter tone of voice. "Anyone you don't recognise, any shipments or strange behaviour?"

The technician studied Bekka, appearing to at least acknowledge her more than Aldai.

"Not my place to say," he replied. "I just keep my head down, got myself a nice quiet workshop out of the way and I intend to keep it that way."

Aldai eyed him up, he looked fidgety, and not just because they'd cornered him. He looked afraid. Aldai had initially taken his startled response as guilt, but now it looked more like fear.

"You've seen something haven't you?" he said more directly.

"Aldai," Bekka interrupted. "Be careful what you say." But Aldai held his focus on the technician, who shuffled and retreated a step towards the alcove they found him in.

"I... haven't seen anything. Lev-7 hasn't had anything unusual in several years. Now if you must, I've got a lot of work to get through, or I'll be on night shift."

Aldai turned looking towards the door of the main workshop, half expecting to see someone watching them, but there was no one there, just the sound of distant machinery turning and thumping. He looked back at the man, who'd taken a step further towards the alcove, his hand resting on the door frame. Aldai's rifle twitched, aware that the workman's hand could disappear and grab something from behind the door at any moment.

"Have you seen a Gaunt-man, like a skeleton, rasping voice, trouble breathing?" said Aldai emotionless.

"Aldai!" exclaimed Bekka, with brief alarm that quickly faded to let the man answer. As much as that kind of question could land them in a lot of trouble, she too was wanting to hear what the man said.

The man froze, staring at the windows. He heaved air, composed himself, then reached inside the door. Aldai raised his gun, but the man barely flinched at the prospect of staring down the barrel.

But then he must have flicked a switch, because the room suddenly spun into life, lights on, extractor fans whirring, and the wailing of safety systems engaging in the various workshop machinery. Bekka wheeled at the scene around them, but found nothing to aim her gun at. Aldai remained resolutely trained on the man, who now held his hands up in defence.

His hands empty, he motioned to Aldai to come closer. Aldai slowly followed his command behind the protection of his rifle.

"You just had to keep asking questions, didn't you? You could get me in a lot of trouble, you know."

"Tell me about the Gaunt, who is he?" he said over the cacophony around them.

The technician stepped in closer. "He? You have no idea, do you? Take the corridor round to the left, remove the third bulkhead, see what you find," he said through gritted teeth. "I just want it out of this section and away from my workshop. But you didn't hear this from me, right? If this ever comes back to me, I'm a dead man."

"We'll protect you," said Aldai, but the technician laughed.

"The long arm of the Uppercone has little influence down here, Upsider," he said, staring Aldai down. He held Aldai's gaze as he backed off, slowly reaching inside the door and flicking a switch so that the room quietened.

"Get out!" he shouted. "You only went and tripped the safety switch. How much more damage will you Upsiders do!" he said in mock anger, shaking his head disparagingly before disappearing back into the cupboard room.

"Let's go, Bekka," Aldai responded aloud. "Nothing more to be gleaned from this one."

They made out of the workshop, its safety systems still spinning down, and Aldai motioned for Bekka to follow him around the corridor towards the loose bulkhead, signalling to stay quiet and remain alert. Sure enough, they found that the third panel in the wall had a broken corner that looked like you could hook a finger around it. Bekka shot Aldai a questioning glare that hid a level of concern, but resigned herself to keeping watch, as Aldai focussed on the panel with tentative anticipation.

He rested his ear gently against it, listening intently for anything inside, but heard nothing, not even breathing.

"Aldai what is this? We should call back-up," Bekka said quietly.

"Negative," Aldai replied.

If they called for back-up now, it would be taken out of their hands. This was a box with a lid that they could open. It was a loose thread begging to be pulled. This was a chance at answers, and it wasn't a chance that Aldai had any intention of giving up.

Reaching down, he pulled the broken corner, and the plating came away. Steadying himself, he braced it between his arms, as Bekka instinctively provided cover against whatever was revealed inside. Aldai placed the plating to one side, looking at Bekka, who gave him a reluctant all-clear signal, and he stepped inside the gap.

It looked like a server room, with wires running down the walls. In the middle of the floor was a sleeping bag, half open and dirty. A chair and small makeshift desk stood in the corner, and a loose cape hung over the chair. It had markings down it, exactly like the Gaunt's clothing from before.

"We should move," said Bekka nervously, keeping watch just outside the hatch.

Aldai moved up to the desk, almost tripping over a pair of shoes that were camouflaged in the darkness. He looked down, seeing them covered in a mud he didn't recognise. It was heavy and clumpy, nothing like the fine soil up in the hydroponics floors.

"Aldai," hissed Bekka. "We should move."

Aldai reached the desk and drew in his breath. There were blueprints of the entire StratoPort. But they were old, as if they were originals. They were faded and worn at the edges, as if they had seen wind and rain., and were splotched with acid dots. Marked across them were notes and arrows, as if plotting routes and objectives. Against Levitation Engine 7 was a large cross.

"Aldai, I think someone's coming," said Bekka urgently.

"Roger," he said, moving swiftly out of the room, and carefully replacing the plating. He managed to reposition it softly, before re-slinging his rifle, and they retraced their steps along the corridor towards the dogleg. There were footsteps ahead, and they turned the corner to see a maintenance staff in red overalls coming towards them, carrying a heavy toolbox under one arm and a metal sheet under the other. Bekka waved at him awkwardly, only to be met with an impassive stare as the workman went about his daily tasks.

"What did you see?" said Bekka, as they made their way up to the others.

"It was a map, I think they'd marked points, like transport routes and... Lev-7 had a cross on it."

"Krak," she replied flustered. "What do we do, shall we tell Halderford?"

"I don't know..." said Aldai, lost in thought.

"We've got to tell Orcanciz, Aldai," she replied. "This is bigger than us."

"You're right," he said reluctantly.

What had he expected? He half thought he was going to save the StratoPort single-handedly, foiling the Gauntman's plot to the reward of his heroism.

Or maybe he didn't care, maybe he just needed to know answers, to resist being kept in the dark, and to follow the human instinct of resistance to bluff and controlling authority. But it dawned on him that they had walked into a hornet's nest without the proper equipment, or they had chased down a rabbit like a hound, only to find it turn and bare its teeth. "You're right," he repeated. "Let's go to Intelligence after debrief. I think we should keep it from the others".

Chapter 5

Caellyn awoke from the night cycle to see the dust-fog partially lifted, but the same ghost-light illuminating the surroundings. The sun had barely moved at all. A Venusian day lasts one-hundred and sixteen Earth days, so the sun wasn't due to set for another month. Venus would hold them facing the sun as it slowly rotated, making only one-and-a-half revolutions as it circumnavigated the galaxy.

Their night cycles were simply times set aside for sleep. But without the darkness of night, it felt like the body was fighting itself. Part of it wanted to carry on without rest, and another part dog-tired but unsure what to do with itself without the proper cues and indicators. You had to force yourself to sleep. You had to convince yourself you were on Earth, and to imagine your cabin-bed and soft linen sheets, and the whole StratoPort getting drowsy as the bustle of the day died down.

Yakun looked like he hadn't slept at all. Colonel Seerman had ordered him to fix what he could of the environmental suits before he, Caellyn and Kowalski headed into the Facility, and he was still grumbling about corrosive heat as he brough Caellyn the morning coffee.

"Fixed your Lidar," he said, waiting for praise, but Caellyn was too tired to answer first thing in the morning. Yakun simply moved on, heading back to the decontamination room to grumble to mechanical parts instead.

At least he'd brought her coffee. For most of the journey from Earth he'd only make himself coffee before disappearing down to the engines, so perhaps being trapped in a small pocket of Earth's atmosphere in the pressure cooker of Venus was bringing out his sociable side. Caellyn drank the dark liquid spiked with artificial caffeine and went to review the readouts from *Molniya-V.*

Arundel was up and checking engine diagnostics, her hand over her forehead in thoughtful exasperation.

"Morning," she said. "You know I'm not sure what's worse, heading into an alien Facility, staying on the lander when there's something out there that can slice through it like butter, or being left alone with Yakun."

"He'll keep himself to himself," Caellyn said, managing a sombre laugh at Arundel's attempt to make light of the impending tasks.

They spent an hour getting back into their environmental suits.

It seemed to take longer this time, as if even the cold metal and vacuum layers had some hesitancy about where they were going. The seals hissed and the mechanical clamps struck into place, while the power and environmental systems whirred and gurgled into life.

Caellyn, Seerman and Kowalski sat in the air-lock as the temperature and pressure slowly rose and the Venusian atmosphere was let in.

It gave you a lot of time to think, and there wasn't a lot to distract you from your circumstances. Caellyn's thoughts turned to the old fable of the frog in a pan of water, the temperature increasing incrementally so that the frog didn't notice until it was too late. She pushed that away. Seerman and Kowalski looked impassive through their visors, as if their regimented lifestyle made this easy. At one point, Kowalski told a joke about his Aunt's cooking, which at least gave a momentary relief.

When things got difficult on the StratoPort, Caellyn would go to the abandoned hydroponics deck. It was only two floors high, but spread out a large distance across the Port, just below the border between the Uppercone and the Undercity. It was full of thick trees, palms and vines, cramped into a thin disk. The plants leaned and craned towards the light boxes that dotted across the ceiling, and the trees bent over as if they were supporting the weight of the Uppercone by themselves. The area was supposed to be used for recreation and oxygen generation, the Central Park of its day, but it had long ago turned into an unkempt and overgrown tangle of nature that was only tended to in order to prevent it spreading further across the Port and escaping its cage. Most people avoided it, as it was full of soil and bugs that revolted you when you'd grown up inside the clean metal walls of the Port.

Caellyn liked it, however. You could get some real peace and quiet down there. You could battle through foliage like an early explorer and find a curved nook of a tree where you could read a book undisturbed. You could even cut away bush and try and cultivate things yourself in the thin soil. She'd once managed to get carrots to grow there, after stealing some seeds from the small plant archive centre up on 7VX deck, just above the large artificial farms that mass produced algae and insects for the nutrition paste. She'd managed to get one good crop before they lost the struggle to grow in the thread-bare soil, but the crack of their freshness as she bit into them was a memory she could savour for a long time.

It was there that she had first met Colonel Seerman.

She'd been leading the Venusian Civilisation research team at the time, when an unexpected invitation had come from Space Division. Curious, she found herself being interviewed for a mission to Venus. It was only for a back-up team, they'd said. They were there to assist the First Expedition if they needed more hands-on expertise or support. She declined, of course, since no one in their right mind wanted to go to Venus. It was a furnace.

Still, they hadn't taken it well. There was quiet pressure to say yes, and she'd been taken aside for a casual chat with several high-ranking officials about the consequences of the refusal on her career. It was duty, or bravery, or honour, depending on who was trying to convince her.

They would remind her that when the Expeditions returned, they'd have people who'd had first-hand experience of the civilisation, which was apparently now an invaluable trait for the next Head of Research. And most of all, they remind her that all this was the highest level of secrecy, and that if she spoke of her involvement in the Venus project to anyone then there would be the direst of consequences.

She'd been clearing brush amongst the foliage, partly to attempt another allotment and partly to simply vent emotions at the situation, when down one of the machete-hacked paths came a stocky man in civilian clothes, looking in his early fifties, with a rocking gait at odds with his unmoving stare. It startled her somewhat; she rarely bumped into another human being down here.

"Caellyn, Colonel Seerman." He held out his hand. "I'm sorry to bother you. They said you were down here, and I used to spend a lot of time on this deck myself. I couldn't pass up an excuse to do some exploring again." He paced to the side, taking in the surroundings like an old friend. "You know, when I was your age, in my mid-twenties, they actually banned me from coming down here when I tried to help a tree break through into a bathroom on the floor above."

At least he didn't seem like an impassive career jerk, who thought humans were just numbers, to be simply coerced using soft-skills from a management book.

He sat by a tree and told her about how he used to bring his children down here until they'd hit their teenage years and become more interested in Slamball. He at least managed to divert Caellyn's frustrations, despite the impending turn of conversation. But sure enough it came, and another sales pitch emerged about the expedition to Venus. However, this time it didn't carry the normal lecture. Seerman was going to lead the mission. He was actually going there himself, and it gave his speech a different tone.

He said the usual, about how Caellyn was the best for the job, which he managed to deliver with a candour that flattered her. She gave the usual response, which was that if she was the best, she would have been in the First Expedition, to which he laughed and said how the first team was less focussed on the wider potential of a Venusian Civilisation. He talked about his own reservations and sacrifices, about how he was going to have to lie to his children and tell them he was going to the SeaPort, and it left Caellyn defenceless to her own lack of fortitude. All she'd leave behind was a comfortable life, and an irritating younger brother who'd probably just be pleased to get his hands on her collection of ancient bottlecaps, that she mostly just kept because he wanted them.

He outlined the same spiel about how time was running out for humanity, and soon they would all have to make brave choices and push themselves beyond what a human should do. But when it came from him, someone who was actually putting his money where his mouth was, it carried a weight that was difficult to ignore. She'd felt the possibility of maintaining resistance slip away as he talked, and she'd eventually agreed.

She wasn't sure why, but as he left, she'd actually felt a certain excitement. Seerman had a reassuring confidence that gave the impression he'd protect his team from the hostile planet regardless of what they encountered, and it left her to dream of the possibility of actually seeing the inside of a building from a different civilisation.

But after that point, there was no going back, and she was in a lifeboat floating down rapids.

Now, many months later, she was standing at the base of the incline that led to the entrance to the Venusian Facility.

They slowly made their way up the slope to the door, their heavy suits gripping the hard soil and rock with mechanical assistance, until they found themselves face to face with the entrance. It was ten feet high, large enough for their suits to pass through, and was about three-quarters open. Where it swung across the ground it left scrape marks in a sweeping arc along the flat soil.

"First Expedition must've opened the door like this," said Caellyn. "The drones before them only opened it part way."

"Roger that, Officer," came Seerman's response. He carried no less reassurance, but the warmth he had conveyed a few years before in the abandoned hydroponics deck had been replaced with sternness now that they had landed on Venus.

They walked through the door and into a short corridor that dog-legged left and right to obscure the view inside and out. They switched on headlamps and unholstered their bolt pistols to use as torches, but the darkness was oppressive and seemed to resist light.

Caellyn gripped her gun. *A gun.* Even through the brain-interface it felt heavy. Her actual hands were down by her side in the pressure vessel, but even so there was feedback from the robotic external arms that made the gun feel weighty. She turned the gun over in her hands. It was heavy, reminding her of its potential. She had never fired a weapon before, at least beyond the brief firearms training she received in the weeks leading up to the mission, and she dreaded having to actually use it. Or perhaps it was a dread about what she would have to use it against.

They made their way through the passage and into the first room, which opened up as their torches roamed around it like search lights.

"Comm check," said Seerman as he placed a lamp on the floor, illuminating the area.

"Roger," said Kowalski, followed by Caellyn.

"Must just be that entrance that blocks signals. Kowalski head out and see if you can hear us."

Kowalski turned and retraced his steps. Seerman whistled Vivaldi's Spring in order to give the comms channel a constant noise. Caellyn only recognised the tune from hearing Seerman play a selection of classical music on the *Molniya-V* journey over.

Kowalski disappeared into the corridor before reappearing a few moments later. "Cut out halfway through the corridor. On the outside, I wasn't fortunate enough to hear your whistling."

"Roger," said Seerman with impassive tension.

The entrance room was rectangular and simple, with the only exit being the square shaft that led down a mile or so at a shallow angle. Caellyn's team, back on Earth, had hypothesized that it could have once been an elevator shaft, as there were two grooves that ran down its length that could have guided a capsule that was no longer there.

The first room was strewn with old drones: four near the entrance from the first missions, that fell from their hover as soon as the entrance cut their guidance comms to Earth. Further in, about a dozen or so were lying in a decrepit state. They were the updated design from one of the later missions that were supposed to fly intelligently before their navigational systems went haywire and they never made it back out of the Facility.

"You think Yakun could fix one of these drones?" said Caellyn, checking each one. Their spherical white outer casing looked like it had rotted through and the mechanical arms that extended from each side were twisted and crumpled like melted chocolate.

"I think it might keep him quiet for a bit either way," replied Kowalski. "Footprints from the First Expedition. They made it in this far at least. Hell, where are they?"

"I'm trying to make out numbers; difficult to see," said Seerman. The prints followed a trail in the light dusting of soil that covered the floor of the room, near the entrance.

"Same size footpads as ours," Caellyn said. "Looks like they moved around a bit before heading towards the elevator shaft and back again, there's no dust over there so difficult to say."

"This place gives me the creeps," said Kowalski.

Caellyn couldn't help but agree. She'd half expected to walk in and see five husks of the First Expedition lying there like coffins.

But everything about it was unsettling. The entrance passageway, the discarded drones, and the fact that they were going to have to head further into it. Even the walls looked strange. She walked up to one to get a closer look. Despite being black and smooth like obsidian, the surface gave the impression it was moving, like there was something lightly flowing over it that obscured the eye. Or at least it did until you focussed on a particular point, when it then looked still, dry and solid. She reached out a bionic arm to touch it, the heavy suit arm lifting towards the wall, and lightly tapped a finger on it.

A crackle of feedback shot through her suit, causing her to recoil. An energy coursed through her body, with something electrostatic running through her bones and over her teeth. Her heads-up display blurred and skewed, flashing colours across her visor before resetting as she caught her breath.

"Shit!" Her mouth tasted like aluminium. She ran a diagnostic of suit systems, waiting with morbid anticipation as the diagnostic bar on her display rose to one-hundred percent before flashing green.

"Everything all right?" asked Seerman concerned.

"I think so," Caellyn gasped. "Not registering any damage. Damn, that made me jump. Don't touch the walls. I think they have similar damping to the entrance passage."

"Roger," Seerman replied. "Keep alert, no unnecessary risks. Let's head down the elevator shaft. We've got a fair walk to the second room."

They each knew the layout of the Facility well, having spent many hours studying the drone footage from the ones that made it out. They'd watch the camera slide awkwardly down these corridors, catching fleeting and blurred images of the extent of the Facility. When she'd been selected for the mission, Caellyn had watched them even more intently, looking for any anomaly in the darkness, turning from the analysis of a professional excavator to the morbid curiosity of someone entering a tomb on a distant planet. Now she was here, it felt surreal as it was framed by the heads-up display in her visor.

They slowly made their way down the passage, taking in the walls with a freedom the drones never had, but finding nothing but the bare extent of the obsidian black material. There were no markings and no scrapes. There were no messages hewn into the solid material from its age-old inhabitants, or imprints of lettering designating even the most trivial of features. It was just flat surface, functional and lifeless.

The corridor was wide enough for two people in atmospheric suits, but they walked in single file, with Seerman at the front and Kowalski at the rear. Their suits clanked repeatedly on the black rock floor as they slowly made their way down the incline.

Arriving at the second room, the floor levelled back to horizontal, and they were met by a space similar to the entrance that looked like some sort of checkpoint. It was flanked by two buttresses that created only a narrow walkway between them.

The buttresses were far more imposing when you stood in front of them in person, compared to viewing them through recorded video feed. They were angled slightly backwards and away from the walkway between them as they rose above head height. Behind them was a platform for someone to stand on and look over whoever dared approach, like an archer over a parapet. The shape of the buttresses almost invited a person to walk through, while their overstated bulk reinforced the power of whoever was watching them from the other side.

"Didn't even check our papers," Kowalski said as they passed through the gap and stood on the other side behind the buttresses.

"Take a moment to catch your breath," replied Seerman. "We head on in five."

"Sir, I need to check the top of these buttresses," said Caellyn. "There looks to be something on them, but the drones never got a clear shot."

"Okay, do what you must, but be careful," Seerman responded.

Caellyn climbed the few steps, one at a time, and found herself at the top of the buttress looking down at the second room entrance, like a guard might have done once before.

In front of her was a keypad.

"Oh my God," she said. "Sir, I think it's a keypad. It's made of similar materials to the walls, but it's unmistakable, there's eight square keys here."

She moved her visor closer, trying to discern markings on the individual keys, but each key looked smooth and bare. If there had been any labels on them, they had disappeared many years ago.

"This is incredible," she said. "It's almost perfectly preserved. The drones never got a good image, I tried to get them to pre-program one to head inside and capture this point, but none of them came out. They're probably the ones up by the entrance."

"Caellyn, remember the mission, I'm not taking any risks," came Seerman's response.

"Sure, sure," said Caellyn, lost in childhood wonder for a moment. "I mean it just invites you to press it, right?"

"I don't think that's a good idea," chimed in Kowalski.

"No, of course," said Caellyn, unable to take her eyes off it. "Probably doesn't work anyway. It seems the obsidian material is the only thing preserved; everything else is gone. The size of the keys looks almost as if it was made for human fingers."

"So, they're human now, whoever lived here?" said Kowalski.

"Maybe, yes, I mean it's difficult to say," she said. "I think... *we* think, well... before this, all we had to go on was the size of doors." she said.

"That's all we had to go on? I thought there were other excavations?" he replied.

"Well...we haven't exactly found much else, maybe some areas that could be foundations."

"But the Government said we found a civilisation?" he said with some frustration.

"There must have been a civilisation for this to exist. The Mural gives some indication they were trying to change their climate."

"Goddamit," he said, surprising Caellyn. "We know so little about this."

"That's enough, private," said Seerman. "We're all doing the best we can."

"So were the First Expedition," Kowalski muttered.

"Sir, if we could press one of these buttons," said Caellyn, trying to put Kowalski's frustration behind her. "We might be able to get a better understanding."

"Negative, officer, we're not here for archaeology or to take risks. We're here to recon the Star-Sphere, understand it as best as we can, and then get out. Today we recon the labs, tomorrow the sphere, and we only take steps we understand."

"Amen to that," Kowalski responded. "Let's get this done and get out of here."

They headed further into the structure, down another passage on a shallow incline that looked like another elevator shaft similar to the first, moving another kilometre or so deeper underground. As they passed about halfway down, they registered a faint breeze in their suit heads-up displays, coming from the depths below. It would have been imperceivable through their heavy bionics had it not flashed up as a minor wind speed and temperature dip. They didn't even mention it to each other. It was on all their minds that the First Expedition was likely missing in these tunnels, and they'd resigned themselves to walking through uncertainty. Caellyn saw Seerman ready his gun up ahead, and she did the same.

She pushed her thoughts back to the hydroponics deck. There you'd get a light breeze every now and again when the air-purge initiated, and the plants went from still and rigid to waving and swaying leaves. She forced her thoughts to stay there, as if willing her consciousness to travel across the galaxy.

After another half hour of walking, they reached the complex of labs, with eight rooms arranged neatly and symmetrically, four on each side, off a wide central chamber with two round support struts in the middle.

"The Murals are up on the right, third room," said Caellyn.

"Roger, do what you need to," said Seerman. "Kowalski, let's check the other rooms, see if we can find anything else. We need all the information we can get, and these labs seem like the best place to get it."

"Copy that."

Caellyn entered the lab-room. It looked like a classroom with rows of black rock benches, but there were no stools or books or students. The only other feature was the Mural on the far wall.

Caellyn gasped as she saw it up close. It covered the entire wall, inlaid with graphics all over, beautifully sculpted as if by a master craftsman, but imperfect with chip and gouge marks. In the centre was the image that everyone on Earth knew so well. There was the half-dome, signifying a planet, with a thin circumferential band that looked like a raging atmosphere. At the top of the half-dome was a collection of small discs, arranged in a ball shape, and stretching upwards was a line that led beyond the atmosphere and up into space, before bursting into an array of arcs that slowly bent through space, landing back on the surface. To the left of the main image were scenes of a raging sky, and to the right were scenes of a sun unimpeded over a mountain. Caellyn reached out, as close as she dared take her hand before her suit's feedback systems registered a tingle of electrostatic damping.

"What went wrong?" she whispered.

"Repeat," came Seerman's voice, from a neighbouring room.

It made Caellyn jump. "Nothing... sorry. I was... I was just talking to myself," she replied. She refocussed her mind and spent a while examining the remaining inlaid images. There were scenes of the solar system, constellations, strands of DNA and cellular mitosis. It was inlaid with swirls and lines that looked like artistic flair, but would consume countless careers deciphering their meaning. There were images of tools crafting the orbs and arranging them in the larger layout of the Star-Sphere shape. In the far right-hand corner she looked down, trying to focus on a small patch of swirling ridges that appeared to be an extension of the cloud, but she couldn't help but see a human face staring back at her.

But there was nothing concrete to help them understand the Star-Sphere further. She shook her head, feeling Kowalski's exasperation. *He's right. We know so little about this. Where the hell are we supposed to go from here? We need to bring back answers. Everything rests on this.* She stood back and took detailed pictures of the wall, before checking the rest of the room but finding nothing on its featureless extent.

"Anything useful?" came Seerman's voice, the line crackling a little from the distance between them and the damping from the walls.

"I've got better images of the Mural than the probes at least," she replied. "But nothing ground-breaking here. Sorry, sir. We'll see what they think on Earth when we get out and transmit them back," she said. "I'm going to check the next room."

"Roger," came the slightly garbled reply.

Caellyn left the third room, and could just make out Seerman in one of the far labs, before entering the next one. This room was different, being partitioned into bays, each with a shelf that looked like it could have once been used as a desk.

"Hell, found a gun," came Kowalski's voice from somewhere across the complex of labs.

"Report condition," Seerman responded.

"It's corroded pretty bad, you can only just make out the outline," Kowalski replied.

"Noted," came Seerman's response after a short pause. It was as if he wanted to say something more, but couldn't think of anything helpful to say. They all thought it.

Where was the First Expedition, and why was a gun discarded in the corner of an empty room?

Caellyn heard a rustle coming from one of the far bays.

She stopped, trying to remain as still as possible, craning her hearing over the humming and bubbling of her suit systems. She stepped closer, despite her body urging her not to.

"I think I heard something here," she whispered.

"Roger, where are you?"

"I...the...fourth lab on the right," she said, momentarily losing her bearings.

The rustling turned into a scraping, louder and more distinct. It started to sound like a heavy sword being drawn across a stone floor. Suddenly a mangled metal object burst from the far bay, rising straight towards Caellyn's head, a tangle of metallic arms, floating in ungainly swoops like a bird with a damaged wing. She raised her gun, firing in panic as the machine fell awkwardly to the side and into another bay.

"Caellyn!" shouted Seerman, as she backed away, hearing Seerman's heavy footsteps come from across the central chamber. "What was it?" he said, arriving by her side. His gun was raised with military alertness.

"It's ok," she breathed, catching her breath. "I think it's just an old drone."

"Take no chances officer, weapon up," came his response.

He inched forward, one careful step after another, slowly rounding the bay side until he was staring down at it. He fired three shots, making Caellyn jump as the sound rang out through the Facility. She cautiously approached and stared down at the corroded, twisted metal.

"I didn't think they would last this long," she said, now seeing the clear "V" of Venus mission on a patch of uncorroded metal. It looked helpless. It had been stuck in this boiling inferno for years, its power slowly dwindling. She almost felt pity for it and imagined it had tried to fly at her as a cry for help.

"Neither did mission control," said Seerman.

They turned to find Kowalski at the door entrance, a pained expression on his face. He appeared to be mouthing words, but nothing was coming through the comms. He raised his arm and gave a "cut-out" signal near his neck.

"Heck," said Seerman. "I think his comms are down. Kowalski do you read?" he said, but nothing came back despite Kowalski's efforts.

"You still reading me Caellyn?" he said, as if half expecting to find her gone too.

"I'm still here," she replied.

Kowalski motioned to his arm pad readout.

"Heaven above, he's leaking power too, he's a few percent below nominal," Seerman said. "We need to head back. These labs are goddamn empty anyway."

"Copy that," Caellyn said, briefly meeting Kowalski's resolute gaze before looking away. They were all aware of what would happen if a suit ran out of power. The containment system would fail, and pressurisation would fall off. A human being would be exposed to the temperature and pressure of the Venusian atmosphere, and would burn, boil and disintegrate at the same time. The only reprieve would be that it would be a quick death.

They moved the now silent Kowalski back up towards the entrance. It felt faster on the way back, but still took nearly two hours. The bionics creaked as they urged them as fast as the suits would allow up the shallow inclines, stopping every few minutes to check Kowalski's power readout. Seerman communicated with him through sign-language that they'd all practiced for such an occasion, but Caellyn found it difficult to look.

"Sir, I'll send the images of the Mural to the Port, but there's a lot of detail. It could take a while for them to make sense of it all, if we ever could," she said to Seerman as they approached the room with the buttresses.

"Copy that, Caellyn. Let's hope they find something in it. Either way we've got a tight schedule. Tomorrow we survey the orbs and then we only have four days."

"Right, yes sir," she said.

As they passed between the check-point buttresses, Caellyn barely thought about the keypad, her earlier wonder now flattened by the reality of surviving in this hellhole. As they left the room she turned around, peering into the darkness, imagining the room in operational state long ago. The buttresses stood immobile and imposing. It felt like they were watching her, or someone was watching her. She shuddered and re-joined the slow march up to the first room.

As they arrived at the entrance, passing the mangled and burnt-out drones, they heard a raging and scraping coming from the front door.

"What is that?" said Caellyn.

"Sounds like a storm," came Seerman's response. He disappeared through the dog-leg entrance corridor, leaving Caellyn and Kowalski alone in the room.

He returned a few moments later. "There's just a shower of volcanic debris, nearly floored me; sin, it's strong. I tried to call the Lander but no response. I doubt we could make much progress through that anyway," he said. "How much power does Kowalski have?"

"Seventy-two percent sir," Caellyn said, checking Kowalski's arm.

"Heck. Shit. Enough to last the night cycle at least. We're going to have to wait it out here. Get some food and rest, hopefully it'll pass soon and we can get out of these suits," he said, his voice rising in frustration.

"Yes sir," she said.

"*Goddamn this hell-hole planet!*" he shouted, making Caellyn jump. "Sorry," he said. "We just need to stick to the schedule. Shit, the ship can withstand that, right? I mean they're build to withstand a nuclear blast. It had better survive that."

"I hope so," Caellyn said, trying to maintain composure.

Seerman went over to Kowalski and signed the plan. The soldier nodded as if trying to convey confidence.

Caellyn breathed deeply, trying to find some confidence against a barrage of Venus.

Chapter 6

VENUS CELEBRATION – SECOND EXPEDITION LANDED!

Aldai looked at the poster a man was hastily putting up. It showed large block lettering and the Mural below; the symbol of the Star-Sphere; a half dome with lines arcing through space and back into the atmosphere of the pictogram planet. He raised his eyebrows; he'd seen these before. He couldn't help but feel it was just more propaganda.

No one had actually explained why a Second Expedition was even needed. The President was on television a while ago explaining that the First Expedition had initiated the Star-Sphere but needed more manpower and expertise, and that a Second Expedition was being sent to assist. He'd said it with all the bluster of a politician trying to sound convincing, and he batted away questions with repetition and recurring points. Everyone watching felt some lack of transparency, but nevertheless it seemed to work. No one complained or resisted, and everyone was pleased to hear good news for a change.

It gave people hope that was desperately needed. Venus provided optimism. Before the Facility was found, faith in the continued future of humanity had been slowly dwindling.

Ten years ago, the situation was at its bleakest. Options were running thin, and when the surface was blacklisted it felt like the final nail in the coffin. Aldai had just returned from his assignment in the SeaPort, looking forward to spending days basking in the sun that he'd missed for two whole years, to find that things had changed. Travel to the surface of Earth was prohibited, and the last humans were restricted to the StratoPort and the SeaPort and nowhere else.

In some ways, it wasn't a major difference; hardly anyone got to feel the solid ground of Earth beneath their boots. Only a few people would be sent down in specialist teams, risking the storm winds to gather remnants of machinery and rare metal stores. But over time the losses mounted. The Government decided to pull the plug to avoid another set of bodyless funerals.

Despite the fact that few people would even dream of going to the surface, its blacklisting represented something far bigger. It was an element of finality, a reminder that the point of no return had passed. Perhaps that point had been passed centuries before, but it mattered little. To be denied any chance of going to the surface felt like the final abandonment of Earth.

After that, and on seeing the fallout in the population, the Government had gone into overdrive with campaigns to change the outlook. There were flavours of the day, depending on what ideas the marketing department could drum up.

At one point it was Mars, with a scientist vehemently reviving the solution to pregnancy and adolescence by keeping pregnant mothers, and children under the age of eighteen in a one-G centrifugal space station. It would allow the foetus to develop normally, and the child's organs and bones to grow under the conditions the DNA expected. After all, everyone remembered the unplanned Martian pregnancy from decades ago that birthed something that was barely recognisable as human. And there was the youngster who spent a year at the Mars colony, when the low gravity caused growth acceleration that resulted in an untimely and painful death. But even if a one-G centrifugal station could work, it just didn't gain any traction in the people of the StratoPort. It was like swapping the StratoPort for something less comfortable, and without even the illusion that you were still connected to the planet we evolved on.

Then there was the Alpha Centauri project. Well, that was even more desperate. It would only entail humans spending several decades in a deep space travel pod, where they would then find themselves four-point-two light-years away in the vain hope that Proxima-B might not be a sterile, atmosphere-less Earth substitute. It was the smallest, slimmest nugget of hope. The reality was, even if you made it to our neighbouring galaxy there wouldn't be any habitable planets. A habitable planet was like a grain of sand flowing past you in a river a mile wide. Even if you found one the right size and the right distance from the sun, it still needed a magnetosphere and an atmosphere at the right stage of development. Even Earth was uninhabitable to humans if you wound back the clock on geological timescales. For example, seven hundred million years ago, when Venus was undergoing a runaway climate change, Earth was just a ball of ice with barely any oxygen.

The Alpha Centauri project was a short-lived distraction. It got a following in the young people, who boldly claimed they would jump into a capsule and colonise a new galaxy like some ancient explorers. But it was only ever propaganda. There wasn't even the technology to back it up. Not even close. The deep-space engines wouldn't even make it there in a lifetime with human cargo. It kept the news channels babbling for a few weeks, but then it went quiet.

There were other projects, but none that were palatable. It seemed that whatever options the Government could dream up, each one involved living in a tin can, and none of them were more appealing than the StratoPort. At least on the StratoPort you could imagine you still had some connection to Earth.

When they found the Facility on Venus, with a tantalising glimpse that they could change a climate, it became the gold dust they were searching for. It didn't matter that Venus had some of the most inhospitable conditions in the galaxy. It didn't matter that they knew little about the Star-Sphere, and even less about how they might get it to work. The public lapped it up despite the difficulty. It provided the slightest possibility of redemption, that was all you needed to hang a hope on.

And here they were, another Venus Celebration. Another weekend of festivities, despite no visible results. Aldai cursed himself, knowing it was foolish hope, but even he couldn't resist it.

His mind wandered to Spain. That was where he'd go. When the clouds left, he would return to Andalucía. His uncle had told him that his family used to have a vineyard there, many generations before. There were rows upon rows of loose-tied brackets supporting huge ripe grapes that looked like they were going to burst. The vineyard was on the side of a hill, surrounded by lush, green, rolling landscape, the dusty ground rich in nutrients and bees and swallows darting lazily through the air. His uncle had kept a bottle from it, old and scuffed. The label was worn, but you could just make out "Sarenca Vineyard" on it, as well as a sketch of the vineyard itself. Their wine was drunk all over the world, as far away as Beijing, Mumbai, Adelaide and Montevideo.

Now that bottle was in Aldai's cabin, hidden at the back of a cupboard.

Team-6 had spent the last few days running heavy suit training in the water column. When he'd asked what it was for, Sergeant Halderford had simply said it was to give them a more rounded training, to be able to deal with a wider range of threats. It brought back memories of watching deep sea mining drones from the SeaPort, where all you could see was a restricted, claustrophobic view through dark sea. And it was even worse when you were underwater yourself, in a cramped, hot suit. Apparently, they were one size fits all, but that meant they fitted no one particularly well. The leg plates chafed against his calves and left them bruised and battered. He was pleased when he could take off the marine gear and get back onto dry floors.

With the training behind him, he needed to move his sore limbs with some freedom, so he headed up to the recreation deck. It was a bright morning, and flowers had been placed around the area. They were releasing their pollen dust and pheromones, bestowing a freshness to the air, unaware that their stems and petals were trapped in a steel box in the stratosphere.

Aldai stretched his muscles near the deck entrance, readying himself for exertion, as he checked the temperature readouts on the interactive World Map next to the Venus Celebration poster. It showed the land masses as if they still mattered. A recent update overlaid the wind patterns of the storm, and above that the jet streams. Right in the centre, just off the coast of Brazil on the equator, was the Rift, maintained by the counterflow of winds between the northern and southern hemispheres, near where the Amazon emptied into the sea. Aldai couldn't help but wonder what the Amazon River looked like now. *It was probably swollen and raging, dark and full of mud and ash.*

Above the Rift was a little dot that signified the StratoPort. It had the freedom of the entire globe, but there was no place for it anywhere else. Next to it on the map were its vital signs of altitude and positional variance, and to the corner was the global surface temperature, that had held just about steady over the last few decades. Occasionally it would slowly creep upwards. It never went down.

He shook his head like a child looking at a shop window display of toys he'd never afford, and went for a run.

The gym section of the recreation deck was quiet for a Friday morning. He ran past alcoves on his left housing coffee shops, weights areas and yoga floors, and a curved seating area on the right, beneath the large angled window that ran along the edge of the deck.

He had expected more people to be there, but there were only the regulars. He ran past an old man in his seventies, an unusual age for the time, wearing a gym kit that looked like it had been given to him in his twenties. He was in here every day, and it kept him surprisingly spritely. He ran the other way, a look of quiet determination on his face. There was a cycle class happening on the left, and a toddler class with a gym leader trying to herd young children onto exercise mats, in order to pay attention for just a moment.

The gym section was one of the more buoyant areas of the StratoPort, as if exercise freed the spirit. The Concourse had its bustle, but it also carried the frustrations of those who'd finished a day's work, and those drowning their surplus rations in synthetic alcohol. On the recreation deck, you could feel like you were moving forwards, even if you were literally running in circles.

And then there she was.

Sitting at a small drinks stand near the windows, there was the woman with dark hair. Aldai immediately flushed with anxiety, but it was the good type of panic when you want something badly and it is only your head versus your body that is stopping you doing it. He slowed to a jog, his brain now in overdrive and double thinking itself.

She was sitting reading a book. Her hair was up in a ponytail, and she wore a gym kit that showed off her slim body and long legs. She carried a poise of gentle confidence, her exposed neck standing straight as her fingers slowly leafed one page over the next.

Go and talk to her said Aldai's brain, before thinking of every excuse on Earth not to.

He stopped running, casually staring into the distance at nothing in particular. It was a first step at least. It gave his brain time to think over the quandary, and it left the possibility of simply restarting his run, as if nothing unusual had happened. But what if she'd seen him? It was too late; he'd gone past the point of no return.

The drinks stand.

He headed over to it. He was close enough to catch a faint scent of her perfume, but became immediately aware that he was wearing his second-best gym kit and was sweating from his brief exertion at the start of his run.

"Sir, how can I help?" said the man at the stand. It took Aldai by surprise, despite being exactly what a kiosk person should say. He quickly searched around their menu, trying to find something to buy.

"Orange juice please."

"I'm afraid all we have is powdered today, will that suffice?" came the polite reply, testing Aldai's patience.

"Sure," he said, imagining the attendant saying this to everyone, all the time, as if he had to at least pretend there was the remotest possibility that one time they might have actual oranges.

The water pump whirred into action as the attendant scooped a spoonful of orange powder into a plastic cup and filled it, giving the illusion of freshly squeezed juice. Aldai was almost sure he could feel the woman's eyes on him now, sitting a few paces away, but dared not look. *This had to appear natural,* he thought. After what seemed like an age, the cup filled, and Aldai paid with a thumbprint. He sipped the juice, which actually didn't taste as bad as he thought it would, before counting to three and diving off the high board.

"Is this seat taken?" he grinned and motioned to the clearly empty seat next to the lady.

"Er, no," she replied, smiling briefly before shifting slightly away and continuing to read her book. *That was ok, that was ok. It was unlikely she'd make it easy for me.* She was stunning after all, and probably got approached like this all the time.

"I see you're reading twenty-second century history," he said, thankful that she was reading a book with a title highly visible. "Guess we've got them to thank for all of this," he said, trying to make light of climate catastrophe, and wincing slightly at his hastily-thought-out joke. At least it got her attention, and she half closed the book and looked at him, her eyes deep and brown.

"They inherited a world already slowly crumbling, so I'm not sure we can blame them," she said matter-of-factly, neither putting Aldai down nor giving him encouragement. "The hardships they endured, and the atrocities that happened as people scrambled away from disaster, made it a very difficult time to be alive."

"That's true," he said. "Everyone inherits a world of the generation before." He wracked his brains quickly, checking he hadn't stolen that line from a recent Government advert, and was pleased to find that he couldn't pin it down to anything. It had sounded good, and it may even have been original.

She nodded, at least.

"I suppose all we can do is rebuild the world better once it's habitable again, as a legacy to their struggle," he said, trying to divert the conversation from historical facts - on which his knowledge of was fairly threadbare - at least compared to someone intelligent and well read.

"It's true," she agreed. "I mean, I'm not sure we can ever do them justice. We'd have to build monuments in every city and country to remember them."

This is good. At least she's not blowing me off completely.

"Where do you think you'll settle?" Aldai asked.

"I'm not sure, my family comes from all over; my dad's side comes from Russia and China, while my mother's South American. I'm a bit of a mixed breed," she laughed, rubbing her temple and averting her eyes briefly. "But I think I'll just travel and find monuments and ancient cities, as if I was one of the first explorers, and rediscover ancient buildings for the second time."

"That sounds good, I'm not sure if they'd still be there but I'd enjoy hacking through jungles and camping under the stars looking for ancient treasures," replied Aldai.

"Oh...I'd probably fly," she replied. "I don't think I'd like the mud. I'd be a first-class explorer, you know. But it'd be great to be in remote places, without another human being around for miles. Did you know there was a city in Canada that built a dome over itself? Saskatoon I think it was called. I'd like to see that, or what's left of it. Although maybe you'd see bones, that'd be gross wouldn't it? Maybe I'd just stay up here!"

"I know what you mean," replied Aldai. "It's just the open space that would be great, and to be in nature again, amongst vast expanses of clear landscape."

She nodded as she shifted in her seat, briefly pushing out her chest, rendering Aldai's thought processes null and void for a moment.

"I'm Aldai, by the way."

"Irina," she replied with a smile.

"I haven't seen you around," he said. "What do you do up here?"

"I work in accounts," she replied. "We run inventory, logistics, all that kind of stuff. How about yourself?"

"I'm military operations," he replied

"Oh right," she replied. "Who are the bad guys these days?"

The question struck Aldai. It was meant innocently, but he couldn't help but think of the Gaunt. Lost in Irina's intoxicating presence, he'd been pulled away from his daily life for a moment. He couldn't say it though. He couldn't talk to anyone about it. There were inhuman beings trying to take down the StratoPort, and it was a secret trapped in Aldai's conscience, while people went about their daily lives unaware of the danger lurking below. Whatever sacrifices people had made in the past could be wiped out in an instance.

"Just the usual," he said, trying to divert both his thoughts and the conversation. After a short pause, he said, "There's another Venus Celebration, are you going?"

"When is it, next Tuesday right? I don't think I am, there's a SeaPort shipment coming in and I'm running shift, unfortunately. Maybe I'll be able to get out of it."

"Well, er, can I take you for a drink some other time? You can't get away without celebrating Venus completely, you know," he said, surprised by his own quick thinking.

"Okay," Irina smiled.

Wow, play it cool, he thought, as his body swam with endorphins.

"Can I get your number?" Aldai said hopefully.

"Sure," she replied, offering the thumb that contained her info chip. Aldai lent across and offered his, and she gracefully pressed them together, exchanging electromagnetic currents.

"Great," Aldai said, trying to hide a smile from breaking out across his entire face. "I'll give you a call."

He got up, and made to head off. "Great to meet you, I'll see you around," he said, as she met his gaze with a faint smile and gave him a light wave. Aldai headed off around the running track, picking up an unusual amount of speed, as if gravity had suddenly lightened.

Orange juice he suddenly thought. He'd completely forgotten about it, leaving a full cup next to her. Feeling sheepish, he resolved that at least he could make a joke out of it next time they met.

* * *

"You old dog!" Wes said, slapping him on the back, Aldai barely flinching as per normal. "Accounts, right? Not sure I know her. Good on you."

They'd met up that evening after Wes came out of work, his tie loosened but still around his neck, giving it at least some chance of making it back to his cabin.

"You heard from Sam at all?" Aldai asked hastily.

"The wife got a message. It sounds like he's settling in all right, but you'd say that either way, right? Can't exactly come back early."

"Even if you wanted to. I'll send him a message once he's got into the routine of it."

"It's just, you know, what do you say? How's the fish? How's the lack of natural sunlight and constant dripping of water? And it's not like there's much news up here. Apart from the Slamball game between the Powerhouse and Glaciers on Saturday. Did you see that? Part of the

Venus Celebration, bringing some of the legends back! We're definitely going."

"You serious? That's incredible. I grew up on those guys," Aldai said.

"Though what about what's-her-name? You meeting up with her?"

"Irina? I haven't organised anything yet...don't want to seem too keen. But Saturday is definitely off the cards now. She'll have to wait."

"Yeah, right," Wes said, swirling his water in his glass, as a group of young office types congregated near them. They'd met up at a café down near the windows, so that you got a panoramic view of the outside clouds that looked darker and blacker than normal, as if they'd kicked up a soot deposit off the surface. It was just starting to get busy, and there were already a few groups getting rounds of drinks in, and a few old drunks by the bar with their faces scuffed and sombre. "Well, I'll send Sam a message once you've met up with Irina, let him know someone's taking his buddy away."

Aldai smiled reflectively. He thought of what Sam would be going through right then. It was easy to make light of it when you were up in the StratoPort, but harder when you were under the sea and facing the reality first hand. You spent the first week or so acclimatising to the SeaPort, so Sam would be sitting through presentations on what to do if a section flooded, and how to resuscitate someone if their lungs were full of water. Then they'd teach you about the various systems down there: fishing, deuterium mining, deep sea mining, salt production, all the exciting parts. Then they'd assign you your job, and you spent the next two years looking after yourself.

"How's the family?" Aldai asked. Despite seeing Wes often, it wasn't a topic they regularly discussed. Normally, when he, Sam and Wes met up, it was about finding a distraction from the daily bustle of life.

"Good thanks," Wes said. "Tyler's almost five now, about to start school. Jane doesn't like the south quarter primary though, so she wants to get him into the one over by the zoo, museum, whatever it's called, you know, where they keep the small number of animals. Apparently, the teachers are more engaging and it's got a bigger rec hall. His sister wants to go with him. She thinks she should be doing the same, so we have to remind her she's not old enough yet."

"Sounds fun," Aldai said.

"They keep us on our toes at least. You should come over sometime. Tyler asks after his Uncle Aldai, you know."

"Sure, we'll have to arrange something."

They talked until the sun was low, the groups around them got too loud and the conversation ran dry, so they both made excuses and headed back to their cabins. The ever-present cabin wall screen was showing a vista of the Savannah, but Aldai wasn't in the mood. He put a sheet over it and switched on the holovision. The news channel was interviewing Landarus, the high-forward for the Powerhouse's winning season eight years ago. *Now this is something to look forward to.*

Chapter 7

The StratoPort had a habit of not giving people what they wanted. Whether it was the cage-like metal exterior that kept you running in circles, or the temptation of the surface, who's ancient vistas were force fed on cabin wallscreens, nothing quite scratched the human itch. Oh, and not to forget the Government itself, that kept secrets holed up in the Intelligence Department, like the fact there were Gaunt-men running around the Undercity trying to blow the whole station up.

You just had to keep your head down and try and eke out a life. If you let your thoughts wander, they'd stray into unwelcome places. You were a lion in a cramped safari park, trying not to dream of the Savannah, trying not to dream of lying in the sun under a Baobab tree with your pride, and the thrill of the hunt, and sinking your teeth into the warm flesh of exhausted muscle. You were a lion in a cage, being fed nutrition paste and trying to pretend none of it was true.

Slamball, a cross between American football, lacrosse and handball, was an outlet. Two teams would line up against each other, taking positions across an arena like a basketball court, with the quarterback at the far end, eyeing the field as they held a tennis-ball-sized gyrosphere that you could spin up and curve around players. Then the quarterback's grunt-call went out and all hell broke loose until the gyro-ball hit the back of the goal board.

The game had risen to prominence due to its brutality, with players wearing heavy protection that was weaponised as much as it was successful at preventing injuries. Order was kept from a distance, and maintained only due to dog tag shock collars that prevented the players descending into all-out fighting. It generally kept the play above board, and even provided some light relief when an enraged forward was shocked to the ground to prevent them swinging a punch. The crowd bathed in the melee, a momentary release from their daily lives, a place where you could shout at the top of your lungs with unchecked vigour. You could feel the ecstasy of victory and bitterness of defeat, both of which nourished a part of the human soul in a way that felt primal and necessary. It was tolerated by the Government only because of its popularity, and they had given up trying to wean people off it when their efforts to water down the rules and the physical contact were met with minor rioting.

But the StratoPort never quite gave you what you wanted, and Team-6 had been called in to guard the passages beneath the Stadium. The powers that be cared little for Aldai's desire to scream from the stands. Their only interest was the high alert from the station, and making sure people woke up tomorrow, forgot about the match and went back to their daily drudgery. Team-6 were to miss the game in order to make sure that some malicious force, unidentified in the briefing, wasn't able to set off another bomb around the tightly packed arena.

"Did I mention I was a Powerhouse fan?" said Aldai to Halderford, as they walked through a darkened storeroom a few floors below the stadium. It was full of rows of floor-to-ceiling struts like an apple orchard, and littered with boxes. He scanned his night vision around, barely interested in whether they found anything or not, focussing instead on the faint sounds of the match above. The noise of the crowd and the squeak of feet on polished wood from the players warming up filtered through the structure to where Aldai, Halderford and Bekka were positioned. At least they had that; Jones, Tiernan and Rongal were patrolling the Concourse, missing the atmosphere of the game completely.

"I'm sorry, you know we don't have a choice in the matter," Halderford replied impassively, but with the tone of someone who doesn't understand the importance of Slamball.

"I mean, it's the game of the century," muttered Aldai.

"Someone's got to guard the under passages," came Halderford's reply. "You know the state of alert we're in," he said, with a hint of a reminder of the Gaunt-man that they could never actually talk about directly. "At least you're close to the action," he said.

A joke? Halderford was in an unusually good mood. Aldai let it go; if he responded how he wanted to he'd be court martialled. *Some people just don't understand how much Slamball could mean to someone.*

It hadn't exactly been the best day so far. He'd had his tri-monthly medical, which was a painful affair for even the healthiest of people. He'd been up in a med bay with a long-faced doctor sick of giving bad news, who at least found some relief in only having to remove two melanomas with his gouge-gun that saw far too much use.

At this altitude, you couldn't avoid medical problems. They may have been on the equator where the magnetic field was strongest, providing a protective barrier to cosmic radiation, and just beneath the ozone layer that provided a defence against harmful ultraviolet light, and encased in the radiation protection of the StratoPort outer hull, but you just couldn't fight it all. The StratoPort was holding people at an unnatural height that meant the higher radiation-produced cancers and degenerative diseases with greater frequency. Life expectancy was in the late fifties on average.

Aldai was given a clean bill, with only minor cataract formation that wasn't affecting his sight but might need to be removed in a year or two.

So Halderford's joke was poorly timed, but he wasn't to know. And anyway, most of the time he was a pretty good sergeant.

The starting horn went off above them, and the sound of the crowd rose to the muffled scuffing of boots, armpads and helmets on polished wood. Aldai leaned against a strut, craning his hearing and trying to visualise the play above them from the noises.

It was Pacific Powerhouse against the Glacial Wanderers, the two biggest teams, an exhibition match full of retired players, some of the greats of the game, to honour the supposed progress on Venus. It was a rare extra game in a fairly thin season that only stretched to five weekends most years. Five weekends, that was all they'd get normally, to sate the population's bloodlust. The five teams, all full of amateur players, would play round robin before the title-decider weekend.

Long before Aldai was born, the season used to be bigger. You would see it on the highlights reels on the holovision, covering matches going back two hundred years, and even some archival footage of before that when it was played on the surface. In fact, the whole following used to be larger and more fanatical. In the early days of the StratoPort the station was arbitrarily split into four quarters, with each quarter having a Slamball team. The problem was that there were cultural divisions between the quarters that were deepened by Slamball rivalries. After the North quarter lost the '22 final to the South quarter, the after-game score settling turned into riots that set fire to a portion of the station. The Government seized on a rare opportunity to pare back the sport from the public conscience, and from that point onwards it existed in its current form. Teams were renamed and the station quarter system officially abolished.

Aldai had been a lifelong Powerhouse fan. This season they were 3-0 in the league, joint top with the Wanderers, whom they were due to meet in a few weeks' time. To see an extra game would have made Aldai's year. He'd grown up seeing "long arm" Landarus spinning balls down the left field, and Howey Huffman slamming the ball so hard you thought it would break the backboard. They may not be at the top of their game these days, but he bet they could still sling passes like some of the half-baked modern stars.

"You know I played for Powerhouse once," said Aldai.

"Shut up," said Bekka encouragingly. "You? You kept that one quiet. What happened?"

"In the game? I scored one point, but we lost 5-3."

"No, I meant with your life. How come you're not up there right now playing in the game, and not down here listening to their feet squeaking."

"Get out of here," Aldai laughed. "I wasn't the best, you know. I mean I thought I was. I was going to be the greatest, but I didn't have the time to dedicate to it like some of the other guys."

"Sure, so it was just time," Bekka replied.

Aldai pushed her lightly. "And breaking my tibia didn't help. I was pretty good, though. Threw a ball curved between two forwards, even made it to the highlights reel. You must remember that right?" he said to Bekka.

"I'm afraid I don't," she said, as they left the storeroom and its field of struts, and headed into a corridor so full of air conditioning ducts that it barely left enough space to walk through. "I was an Atlantic fan anyway. I was infatuated with Strulight growing up. She was incredible."

"Okay, this just got worse," said Aldai, with an air of amusement and false frustration. "You kept that quiet. I think I'd just imagined you'd be a Powerhouse fan, given, you know they're the best. I mean, because Team-6 are the best. Halder, can we switch places? I'd like some distance between myself and an Atlantic fan."

"Hey!" Bekka replied, trying to work out if Aldai had just paid her an accidental compliment.

The air conditioning passageway reached an end, and a set of stairs that took them down a level and back in the direction they came. "How about you Halderford, who do you support?"

"Powerhouse, I suppose," he said after a brief pause.

"There we go," said Aldai. "See, that's more befitting of Team-6."

"Can't say it was my thing though," Halderford replied dryly. "Just unnecessarily violent."

That made sense at least, thought Aldai. You wouldn't want to face Halderford in a fight, but he wasn't exactly the outwardly boisterous type. Though maybe he'd been different in the past. Aldai got visions of a younger Halderford, fresh into the military, putting down violent uprisings and criminals with cool intensity of force, before it gave the man his overfill of primalism and turned him into the impassive, quiet sergeant he was today. It probably wasn't true, but either way, if he'd been a Slamball fan at all, then he'd have moved heaven and earth not to take this shift.

They reached another storeroom, directly under the previous one, and scanned it with night vision before taking seats on a few boxes in the corner. Halderford played with his wrist-link, reporting back to command and manipulating augmented displays that only he could see through his visor.

For a while they sat in silence, only punctuated by the distant noises of the match above them. They could just make out the crescendos of the crowd and the booming voice of the announcers. Sounded like a good match, thought Aldai, *Damn. It could at least be boring and uneventful, with old-timers barely able to move, so that we aren't missing anything special.*

He checked his communicator and saw a message from Irina, putting it away before Bekka or Halderford started asking questions. Maybe she was up there in the crowd. It didn't sound like her kind of thing; she hadn't exactly taken the conversation bait he'd dropped about the Slamball match, and he hadn't pressed in in case he came across as a violence-loving brute. He needed more information to know for sure.

They'd exchanged a few messages since running into each other in the recreation deck, but they hadn't exactly cracked beneath the surface and found their chemistry yet. He'd need more groundwork to know whether he had to take the framed Powerhouse shirt off his cabin wall and pretend it was just a minor interest for him. But he couldn't shake the idea that maybe she'd avoided discussing Slamball because she was going to the match with someone else. *I mean, she was stunning enough; she could be dating a Slamball player, for all Aldai knew.* He felt a jolt of jealousy from his wandering thoughts, and cursed himself for it. *What have you got yourself into?*

"Quelin's having a good season," posited Halderford. Aldai and Bekka were a bit taken aback. It was true, Quelin was having a good season; he'd run an average of forty-two plays per match and scored two point three on average, but they were surprised to hear Halderford offer up such a statistic.

"He is," said Aldai. "Surprised me a bit. There were rumours he'd been out in a transport that decompressed, and was lucky to make it back alive midway through last season. Seems to have recovered from that, though, at least if you take his scoring record."

"Up to seventy-six passes a match, making first team on every occasion," replied Halderford, again to the other's surprise. "Bet you didn't think I'd come up with that kind of knowledge." Aldai imagined Halderford making a rare smile, hidden in the darkness.

"You are full of surprises, Sergeant," said Bekka.

"I do the fantasy league with my sons," Halderford replied.

Aldai raised his eyebrows. He'd forgotten Halderford even had sons. He gave off the impression of someone who would go back to his cabin, lock the door and read old musty books. *You think you know someone. Perhaps Halderford has a hidden sociable side, back in the warren of habitation quarters buried in the middle layers of the Port.*

"Eyes up," the sergeant whispered. "Two heat signatures far end, possibly kids but take no chances."

They moved through the forest of regularly-spaced struts, making little noise as their soles rolled heel to toe with each step. Aldai took point, moving ahead with pent-up anticipation that had filtered into him from the crowd noises above, ducking under the angled L-bars that branched out from the struts to support the floor above. He could make out excited whispering and the dim light of an artificial light source dancing around. He heard the rustle of people, and rounded a large box to see a young couple hiding in the darkness. He cleared his throat as he flicked on his torch, angling it away from the couple to limit their shock. There was a scream of pure terror as the pair took in the Special Ops team that had suddenly appeared over them.

"Just some kids," said Aldai to the others, partly enjoying the scene of frantic scrambling as they went from half clothed to fully presentable in a fraction of a second. "You two realise this area is strictly off limits and the whole port is Code Red, right?" he said, with a relaxed sternness. It was clear that they would never be doing this again in their lifetimes after that scare.

"We're sorry sir," said the boy, his voice quivering as he pulled himself together. "Please, we we're just fooling around." The girl looked at him aghast, as if his comment had overridden the surprise intervention from three military officers.

"This was a bad idea at the best of times," said Aldai. "Stay near the habitable zones. You don't know what's lurking around in the off-limits areas."

He was slightly unsure of protocol from this point. They were expecting some sort of terrorist, far less so a couple of teenagers. "Do we call them in?" he said to Halderford.

"Please sir, we didn't mean anything, we won't do it again, honest."

"I think they've learnt their lesson," said Halderford, as he motioned for them to leave with an outstretched arm. "Get out of here. Stick to the quiet areas around the back of the Concourse. That seems to be where all the other teenagers hide these days." They immediately gathered their belongings and raced away through the door, clearly in no mood to ever enter an off-limits area ever again.

"Ah, to be young and in love," said Bekka, after they'd resumed their watch from the far end.

"I'm not sure they were necessarily in love," joked Aldai.

"You unromantic fool," Bekka said, punching Aldai in the arm. "I bet you broke lots of girls hearts when you were their age."

"I was always the perfect gentleman," he said in response, hearing Bekka scoff audibly.

The Slamball sounded frantic above. It must have been reaching a tight conclusion, because the crowd was louder than ever. He wanted to be up there now, in the stadium, or even on the pitch. He reckoned he could still move just about like he once did. Special Ops kept you in shape at least, high altitude body-groans aside, so he'd just have to get some game time to sharpen up his play and learn the formations. He could be up there right now, running up the side wall in the dying seconds, somersaulting over a defender like Landarus used to do, and curving the ball into the goal. There would be nothing stopping him, and everything stopping him.

The final hooter sounded through the floor as the crowd cheered. "If anyone tells me the score before I get to watch the highlights then I can't vouch for my actions," said Aldai.

"You'll literally have to walk through the station with a blindfold and ear protectors," said Bekka. "Not even the great Aldai, one-time Slamball player, can make that kind of play."

"Hmm, not unless you guide me like an old, blind beggar."

"You trust me to walk you to your cabin?" she said. "Who's to say I won't walk you into the recreation pool?"

Aldai laughed. It was hopeless. Not only had he missed what sounded like a great game, but he was destined to be unable to even see the highlights reel without knowing the score.

"Looks like it was quiet on the watch front," Aldai said to Halderford.

"Quiet is good," came his response, as they made their way back to the military section.

.

Chapter 8

Caellyn awoke from her sleep shift to find herself still in the first room of the Venusian Facility. They'd set their suits to rigid, so that the limbs locked in place, and tried to sleep through the night cycle, their equipment humming gently as they stood like three stone statues.

Caellyn and Seerman had taken it in turns to watch Kowalski and monitor the storm. If the howling winds abated at any point, they needed to take the slimmest window to get Kowalski back to the lander. What it meant in reality was that you stood alone in a darkened room on an alien planet the temperature of fire and the pressure of a one-kilometre depth of ocean, in a Facility where the First Expedition had disappeared. Then there was the possibility that Kowalski's suit power would trail off, and you'd watch him disintegrate in front of you. After all that, when your sleep-shift came round, you were at least pleased to close your eyes.

When Caellyn awoke her brain tried desperately to believe it was back in her cabin on the StratoPort, surrounded by her fabric hangings and the wallscreen. In her dozy state, she tried to formulate the walls into the right shape, and expected the sounds to be that of her neighbours as they thumped their way down the corridor to work. Instead, as her senses came into focus, they registered the inside of the pressure vessel, and the dark obsidian walls around her. Her arms were stuck down by her sides in the suit and her hands felt the manual interfaces. She checked the Earth-time clock on her heads-up display: 07:15. The StratoPort would be waking up, and heading to work bleary eyed under the shining sun. Whatever they faced it had to be better than the depths of the Facility on Venus. She shuddered.

Kowalski, shit.

He was still there; she could see his head moving slowly as he breathed in his sleep. She checked his readout on his mecha-arm, and saw it registered thirty five percent. It was holding at least. She checked hers: seventy six percent.

Her hearing slowly localised, and she registered the banging and scraping of the storm outside. Even without opening the outer door Caellyn could tell that it hadn't eased. *Shit.* It must have been a distant volcanic eruption that had pulled the clouds into a pressure spiral. She prayed a quiet prayer for it to ease in the next twelve hours.

"Morning," came Seerman's voice through the comms, registering a small amount of static as Caellyn's ears popped a little.

"Storm's still going," she said in response.

"Roger." He unlocked his suit arms so they went from rigid and frozen to loose and mechanical, looking like a sculpture coming to life. "You won't like me saying this, but we're going to have to leave Kowalski," he said.

Caellyn shook her head. She knew it was coming, but hearing Seerman say it so matter-of-factly was a body blow. It was a grim reality, a down and dirty thing to do. She turned to look at Kowalski as he was slowly waking up to a suit still leaking power and having lost the ability to communicate. He met her gaze and gave her what appeared to be a smile. She unlocked her suit from its rigid sleep-form and raised her mecha-arm to wave. "He'll be fine, Caellyn. His best chance is to stay here and wait out the storm. We gain nothing by staying here, too. We've got a mission to do, and a schedule to keep. Seven days is all we've got. That's all the risk assessment can guarantee us against this hell-hole atmosphere. I'm sorry, but we've got to press on," he said, his usual calm tone wavering slightly.

"I know," Caellyn said in reluctance. "But it doesn't seem right."

"We've got to make contact with the Star-Sphere today. The faster we get down and back, the faster we get out of this place. Kowalski's best chance is to stay here. He'll meet up with the others when the storm's subsided, and we'll see him at mess time this evening."

Caellyn turned, not wanting Kowalski to see her lips move

"I don't like it. It doesn't feel right just to leave him behind."

"I know Caellyn, I don't like it either, but we've got a job to do. Kowalski would want us to make progress, that's why we're all here."

"Okay," she said, looking down at one of the mangled drones. "You tell him."

"Of course," Seerman replied. He tapped Kowalski on the shoulder, motioning with sign language that they were to head back into the structure, and that time was running out. Kowalski nodded solemnly, trying to project confidence and understanding against a pained expression that was trying to break through.

He would understand. He would understand why we had to do it. Caellyn looked at him as if it was the last time she would see him and gave him another wave, hoping that the bionics of the suit would convey her reticence. It was excruciating not to be able to talk to him. Kowalski motioned to his power supply and gave her a thumbs up, as if he was sure it would out last the storm, but it did little to reassure her.

"We've got to go," came Seerman's voice. "He'll be fine. We'll see him back in the ship when we return."

"Roger," came Caellyn's response.

They left Kowalski, barely lit as his survey lights were turned as low as possible. Caellyn looked back to see him one last time as they made their way down the passage. Tears welled up in her eyes that she couldn't wipe away through her helmet. Kowalski had helped her as she fumbled through training exercises she was barely capable of doing because her normal habitat was a classroom or an office. When they did low Earth orbit training, she had frozen in fear when she lost contact with the spacecraft's grab rail and started floating away until her safety line snapped tight and spun her around. Kowalski had confidently floated up to her and guided her back. Leaving him behind was like burning every favour and throwing gratitude in the bin. But the worst thing was that she knew Seerman was right. There was little they could do; they had to press on. They'd been told to prepare for this eventuality, and it had been drummed into them many times that the mission was bigger than any of them. But it didn't stop the resentment building. And right now, it was Seerman's command that embodied that emotionless doctrine.

They followed the shallow-angled elevator shaft down to the first room, passing the buttress check-point. Caellyn's interest in its keypad had depleted, and she barely thought of it as they trudged on through the darkness. Whatever answers those keys revealed, whatever happened when they were pressed, was immaterial right now.

Seerman led on down towards the labs. His suit bobbed and rolled as their footpads clanged on the hard floor, ringing methodically like a metronome. It felt like he was leading Caellyn to an execution, and she was only dutifully following because there was a baying crowd around her that left her no choice.

She extended her feed tubes and ate what could just about be referred to as breakfast, consisting of a mixture of water and protein paste. It was warm and lumpy, like a poorly made porridge that lacked flavour. And yet despite the feed cutting out when the breakfast ration was finished, she wanted more, as if its dull texture was at least firing neurons and distracting them from other thoughts.

Walking down the shallow incline, urging one mechanically enhanced step after another, Caellyn was suddenly met by a passageway on the right. It split off at a ninety-degree angle to the main hall, and had the same makeup. It was bare and featureless, like a slot hewn into a rock. It led into darkness beyond, and as Caellyn shone her gun torch down its extent, she made out nothing discernible; it just went on into the distance.

"This wasn't here yesterday," she said to Seerman. He stopped and turned around, as if to consider it for the first time.

"I don't remember," he said. "It all looks the same to me after a while."

"I'm sure of it," Caellyn replied. "I mean, I remember this layout even before yesterday from the drone footage, I've never seen this passageway at all before."

"Caellyn, it can't just have appeared," Seerman after a pause, trying to disguise uncertainty in his voice, or perhaps simply trying to divert the conversation. Maybe he was right; maybe she had just missed it. In the darkness, it had just never been noticed. It bore no evidence that it had recently opened or appeared. There were no features to indicate that a door had been there, and no slots that it could have slid into, just smooth wall butting into smooth wall. The inside wall didn't look as if it had just been fashioned. It had the same texture and appearance as the main wall, black and obsidian.

"Should we investigate it?" she said, drawn into its dark expanse and wanting to leave nothing unknown.

"That's a negative," came Seerman's response. He was already making forward. "Move onwards, we need answers before we run out of power ourselves."

"Copy," Caellyn said quietly. She stared down it a few seconds more. Seerman turned to continue walking, at which she hastily made to follow, looking back to check that it hadn't disappeared as soon as her back was turned.

"You know when I was your age, I was posted to Mars colony," said Seerman. "I wasn't much for one to follow the rules back then. We took out a rock buggy and drove it up a giant hill next to Mars Base. In the low gravity we flew nearly a mile before we hit the ground."

"You broke the rules?" she said.

"We got in trouble, of course. We cracked the front axle of the buggy and had to walk back. We only got halfway before the station commander met us and dragged our sorry butts back to the colony. We got reduced rations and deck cleaning for two weeks."

"Ouch."

"It was worth it, though. You know we calculated we crossed three hundred and twenty dropships before we landed. I reckon that was an all-time record for humanity."

Caellyn gave a reluctant smile.

"Never got a medal for it, mind, but I'd do it again in a second."

He's trying to distract me. He's trying to distract me from Kowalski, from dark and empty corridors that appear out of nothing. How does he remain so calm? It's either supreme confidence or a lack of care. She drank warm water through the feed tube. It tasted of iodine. Twenty-four hours in these suits and it must have been entirely recycled by now.

"You know I was military once upon a time," he carried on. "But only for a few years. My dad was Space Division, wanted me to go there too. He used to say there's no point waiting for someone else to solve things, you've got to get out there and make it happen. I wanted to get off the Earth, and get off the StratoPort, see the galaxy, so it fitted. There was optimism back then. I mean, you know, there's optimism now, but it was different then."

"Venus will save us," Caellyn whispered.

They walked in silence for a while before arriving at the lab system. Shadows spread out and glided over bare walls as their lights surveyed the area. Caellyn almost expected it to have rearranged itself, and felt a little surprise when it was still exactly the same as the day before, the two pillars supporting the ceiling in the middle and the eight rooms waiting patiently at the side.

"Sir, I want to see that the drone is still there."

"Caellyn we need . . ." came Seerman's response.

"Sir, please, I just need to see it."

He motioned with his arm, allowing Caellyn the brief indulgence of her curiosity. She walked into the third

143

room, the alcoves bare and lifeless like before. She rounded the third before finding the remains of the drone, unmoved from yesterday. It looked helpless and pathetic, sprawled out and with three bullet holes through its shell. Whatever energy it had to lunge at her the previous day had been extinguished. It could have lived, or been repaired, and now it was just left here. She felt a pity for it that surprised her, before her thoughts turned to Kowalski, left helpless by the entrance. Maybe he was there now, running out of power, alone and trapped by the storm.

"Would you have left me?" she said to Seerman, anger rising in her voice.

"Caellyn?"

"Would you have left me by the entrance, if it was my power pack leaking energy?"

"Caellyn, this isn't the time. We've got a job to do and we don't have a choice. You know what's at stake."

"You would have left me, wouldn't you? I can't do it. This isn't my fight. You just don't care; it meant nothing to you to leave him, did it?" She came out of the room of alcoves but struggled to look him in the eye.

"I'm not sure what I would have done," he said calmly after a pause. "Kowalski is Space Division and ex-military himself. He knows the score. You don't spend a career separated by thin sheets of metal from the atmosphere of space, or the surface of the moon or Mars, without accepting certain realities. But you're not, so things might have been different."

Might have been different? What's that supposed to mean? And anyway, she knew it wasn't true. He would follow through with his god forsaken schedule whatever the cost. "What about your children? You lied to them, you left them behind."

"I had no choice!" he shouted, then tried to compose himself in his suit. "You think they gave me a choice?" He raised his hand against his visor as if forgetting he couldn't place a hand on his forehead. "We all have made sacrifices. When they brought us in and told us the First Expedition had disappeared, I won't lie; I tried to get out of it. It's fair to say none of us would be here if we had been given the freedom to decide. But I've never failed a mission, and I've never lost someone so far, and I'm damn well not about to start now. I wouldn't have left you. I could only leave Kowalski because I know he had more courage than he lets on. Sometimes you have to bury your feelings about possibilities, and deal with what you can. Let your emotions come later, after the mission is over, and after we've made progress with the Star-Sphere and are on the way home."

Caellyn pushed away tears that she knew she couldn't hide within the confines of the suit and pushed her mind back onto her surroundings. Seerman was right. You didn't have a choice. You were in the belly of the beast, and at this point, you just had to keep going.

"I know what you're thinking, Caellyn," he said with an air of exasperation. "Where are the First Expedition? I think it too. I keep thinking they'll appear around a corner, somehow still alive. But you know their leader

145

was a hot-head. *He* volunteered to come here, something about fame and glory. That tells you everything you need to know. They probably pressed a switch or followed a corridor. If we keep to the mission and avoid distractions, I promise you we'll make it through this. We just need to focus on the mission, find information to help us understand the Star-Sphere, and we'll make it back to Earth."

Damn him. Damn his convincingness. That was what persuaded me to come to this planet, and it was all just a ruse by a man under duress. Well, perhaps that isn't fair. He's genuine enough. And at least he's trying to provide a scrap of reassurance.

"All right," she said, finding some confidence amongst the rubble of her thoughts. It was the confidence that came from the perseverance of human endeavour, and the dullness of emotion when there's no other choice but to continue.

"Good, let's head on" Seerman said in a short tone.

The route led away down another shallow elevator shaft. It was the last stretch before the control room, and it was the stretch that Caellyn's team had studied the most. It had curved edges where the walls met the floor and ceiling, and instead of the floor being one long flat surface, it was a series of long shallow steps. It still had the two grooves running down it, ignoring the steps and taking the most direct route along the passage. They'd theorised that the steps were perhaps to help people escape if there was some sort of power system failure with the Star-

Sphere, but the answer was hidden in manuals that were nowhere to be seen.

But when watching it on the StratoPort you could pause and rewind it and cut to different sections. Now she was here, after an hour or two of walking, it gave an entirely different impression, and it felt like the steps were vertebrae and they were walking through the skeleton of a colossal animal.

She noticed an orange light flashing on her display, indicating one of the internal fans had seized up. It took her by surprise but she quickly calmed her nerves. There were twelve fans in total—she remembered that much from the boring lectures on suit engineering—so losing one wasn't a problem. She decided to keep it to herself, and tried to focus on the display, using it to fill her mind rather than the dark flat walls and floor, and noticed that the breeze they had registered yesterday had increased slightly. Still no more than the faintest movement of air that exposed skin would just about register back on Earth, but nevertheless puzzling her.

Seerman stopped in front of her, freezing in position. Caellyn followed suit, straining her senses for what caused Seerman's hesitation. She could make out the entrance to the control room up ahead just beyond Seerman's bulky environmental suit, but saw no reason for alarm.

"Sir?" she said, as he stood motionless for a moment.

"Nothing," he replied, after a pause. "I... thought I saw something, but it was nothing. How's your suit holding up?"

"Fine sir, nothing malfunctioning," she replied.

They entered through the open bulkhead into a large control room. It had several banks of curved desks arranged around the large panoramic window at the far end. They were made of black rock like the walls, and empty of features.

They made their way to the window, passing another failed drone that was braced up against a corner like a wounded soldier. That was a brave one, thought Caellyn. Poor thing made it all the way down here before malfunctioning. Second place, only beaten by the one that glimpsed the Star-Sphere and made its way out again. They walked up to the window and stared out across the expanse.

It was the giant reactor hall, circular and as big as a stadium. It had a shallow curved disc across its base and walls that rose hemispherically to create a domed ceiling above. In the centre, raised a few metres off the ground, was a plinth, and on it floated the Star-Sphere itself. Sixteen orbs, each the size of a beach ball, each hanging weightlessly in the air and occupying a position on the surface of a larger invisible globe.

"My god," whispered Caellyn. "I half expected it not to even be real."

"I've never seen anything like it," replied Seerman, his normally focussed veneer peeled back.

"They're just hanging there in the air..." said Caellyn, trailing off and lost in wonder.

It was a small reward, but it was a sight that almost made the entire mission worth it. Whatever it was, the mechanism carried beauty and elegance. The orbs looked so serene and calm, balanced on nothing but air. They had climbed Everest, and were rewarded with a view from the top of the Earth, one that few people would ever have the courage, bravery and dogged foolhardiness to see. Now they just had to make it back down with a large chunk of the summit.

"One impossible task done," said Seerman. "On to the next. Hell, they expect us to come back with answers. What good is it if we can't operate it? And we're the ones that need to figure that out. Check the room for information."

Caellyn moved over the right side and spotted some features on the end desk that she hadn't noticed before. It was more keypads, but this time embedded into the desk surface so that the individual keys didn't protrude. There were three banks of eight keys, and a larger key to the right. She placed her hands on the desk to steady herself to lean in for a closer look, before remembering the hit of feedback she'd got from the wall near the entrance. Her muscles tensed in anticipation, but it never came. Whatever that energy was, the desk wasn't transmitting it, and the surface was smooth to the touch through her mecha-hands, making a sonorous noise as it echoed the clanks of metal on obsidian.

The keys were blank like the ones on the buttress. The larger one must have some sort of greater importance, but she looked at it with derision, as if its siren call to be pressed was falling on deaf ears or experience. She moved on and checked the walls and corners of the room for any sign of markings or a scrap of helpful insight into the machine, but none was forthcoming. She hoped for even a portion of another Mural, but it was just empty space. They would have to figure the Star-Sphere out like a linguist with only a fraction of the Rosetta stone.

"Some more keys, no information," she said.

"Roger that. I found nothing either. Heaven above. The Government needs answers... If I come back empty handed they'll... well, let's carry on. There's an open airlock over here to get us into the reactor hall. There has to be something down by the orbs."

They made their way through the hatchway, finding a path that wound down to the edge of the floor. Caellyn cautiously scanned her data feed, but found no radiation spike or extraneous data, nothing that indicated that it was dangerous to be here. Or at least more dangerous than the ambient atmospheric conditions of Venus. They slowly walked down the path, trying not to look at the drop on the right, before arriving at the edge of the reactor hall base.

"It's clear in here," said Caellyn, noticing that the atmosphere didn't produce its usual haze in the middle distance. It was dimly lit from the centre of the ceiling, and you could see right across to the other side, more than a hundred meters away. It was a welcome change to the close corridors they'd walked through. She looked up, taking in the gigantic space and the outlet in the ceiling that the drones had never captured. "Sir, that corresponds with the mural," she said feeling some self-satisfaction. "The orbs create a line on the mural that shoots into space. That's at least consistent with the hole."

"Copy that," came a gruff response. It wasn't exactly the kind of depth of information they needed. But what did Seerman expect from her, or any team member? They had so little information to figure it all out.

The basin floor was covered in knee-high ridges that spread out radially from the centre like a sundial. They were spaced evenly around the circumference, numbering about thirty or so, and they lessened in height the closer you got to the plinth. As the explorers crossed the reactor hall floor, following the shallow curvature down, the central dias rose above them. It's plateaued surface that housed the Star-Sphere was above head height, and reachable by stairs that ran all away around it. They ascended them and found themselves on the edge of its surface, facing the hovering atmosphere-shaping engine only a few metres away.

The orbs were relatively small, each about half a metre in diameter, and together they spread around the surface of a larger invisible globe about three metres across. It was small compared to its surroundings, but its unnatural levitation gave it an unnerving feeling of immeasurable power.

"The scanners aren't picking up on too much," said Caellyn. "They can't determine material composition, and the energy readings go haywire when I scan the centre of an orb. The balls are odd, sir, they appear to be..." She trailed off, trying to make sense of the readings. "They appear to be cool, sir. They appear to be around thirty degrees Celsius."

"Thirty degrees? Heck, like the inside of our suits," said Seerman quietly, lost in amazement. That at least made some sense; if they were going to shape a planet into a habitable paradise then they'd need some way to ensure it got to the right temperature. "How are they doing that?"

"I honestly have no idea, sir. I have very little to go on."

"Right, right," he replied shortly.

"I'm not registering any distortion or energy patterns around the outside. We can go closer, sir, if you think it's appropriate."

"They didn't give us any brief on this bit," he said frustratedly, lost in thought. "They just said recon the orbs. What the bloody hell are we supposed to figure out from this?"

"Sir?"

"We need answers, Caellyn. If we don't come back with goddamn answers they said they'd..." he trailed off again, sounding anguished. "You're the Venusian xeno-archaeologist, what do we do from here?"

It took Caellyn aback. The reassuring Seerman was suddenly pressing her with pointed barbs. She was relying on him for guidance, not the other way around.

He's right. I'm supposed to be the expert on this. She suddenly felt exposed and exasperated, but tried to pull her thoughts together.

"There's no temperature change on the outside of the suits, and the temperature of the orbs is incredibly localised. It's as if they're in a thermodynamic pocket, sir."

She took a step forward.

"Sir, I have a hunch about how it works." Maybe it was a shred of courage. Maybe it was a chance at glory, at being the one to figure it out, to a lifetime of adoration. Maybe it was the fact that Seerman was expecting miracles, or treating her as a spare part who lacked the courage of his usual team members.

"Caellyn whatever you're thinking, just be careful."

"I understand sir, I just... I'm going to tap one of them."

She moved forward cautiously, step by step. As she got closer to the Star-Sphere she got a sense of something in the air: electricity, magnetism, or some form of energy, and it left a dull taste in her mouth. She checked the sensors, but they registered nothing. She detached the multi-purpose stick and slowly raised it towards the nearest orb. It just floated there, unresponsive to their arrival, uninterested and condescending of gravity. It was smooth on the outside and almost featureless. It was as if it allowed no light to escape it, and yet gave a solid appearance as if it was conveying its geometry through other senses that you couldn't quite pinpoint.

"Are you sure this is a good idea?" said Seerman, as he stepped down the top steps of the plinth to provide a small amount of cover.

"I...I think this is our best shot of finding answers," came her response, deep in focus.

The stick slowly crept nearer and nearer the surface of the nearest orb, Caellyn watching it intently as she guided it forward, like she was performing brain surgery or installing fissionable material into an atomic bomb. The stick made contact with the surface of the orb, with the lightest of touches.

There was an almighty bang. The orb went translucent and Caellyn was flung forwards like she'd been hit by a steam train. Her head struck the inside of her helmet as the force of the blast overrode the internal damping, and even the padding of the helmet failed to prevent her blacking out.

"Caellyn!" she briefly heard Seerman call, before everything went dark.

She came to a few moments later, her vision blurred, and she could see nothing but white. Her head rang like a bell and she could feel a small trickle of blood down the side of her temple.

"Caellyn, are you all right?" came Seerman's voice, concerned.

"I'm all right, I think." The systems on her heads-up display flashed orange but appeared to still be functional. "Where are we?"

"We're still in the reactor hall. You took quite a hit. Your visor is full of condensation. Take a moment to breath, let the steam clear."

"My god..." she said, realising she was winded pretty badly. "I wasn't expecting it to be that powerful." It took a while for her senses to recover. The steam slowly dispersed, and her strained breathing returned to normal as her chest muscles untwined themselves. She slowly made out the shape of Seerman through the droplets on her visor as they gradually evaporated. She tried to sit up, only managing it as the suit compensated her efforts.

"I thought you were gone for a minute there," said Seerman, also out of breath.

"What happened?" she wheezed, as her body tried to relieve itself from the hypertension of the impact.

"When you touched the orb there was a flash of light, it pulled you instantly into the centre. I was lurched forward as well. It happened in a fraction of a second, but I saw the light shoot up out of that hole in the ceiling. I managed to pull you out of the orbs. They went translucent for a while. Whatever you did, it better be worth it," he said.

"I think it was," she replied. "The orbs are in an equilibrium, equidistant from each other and equidistant from the centre of the larger invisible globe. Disrupting the equilibrium would initiate the machine. It made sense that if they were closer together it was likely to trigger it. I just didn't think that it would be that violent and powerful to the lightest of touches," Caellyn said, finally feeling the security of knowledge, and a creeping self-pride appeared that turned into an excitement of discovery. *That was a stupid thing to do. Almost as stupid as coming here in the first place.*

They stood for a while as she regained her breathing, her body reminding her of its pains and groans at being pulled into a planet-shaping device. Then she refocused on Seerman, who was eyeing up the orbs in deep contemplation.

"If pushing them together initiates the machine, can we pull them away?" said Seerman.

"It's possible," replied Caellyn.

"How possible?"

"I...sir, I don't know. I was going on a thin hunch to get them to initiate. If you try to push one of them away from the larger globe, rather than towards it, it may be fine. It may just be moving the orbs together that initiates it, or it may be disturbing the equilibrium either way, it's difficult to tell."

Seerman stood a while longer, thinking over the next move.

"Well, I can't let you have all the glory. Stand back, give me your lever."

Caellyn retreated to the edge of the platform, a certain satisfaction taking over that this time Seerman was following her lead, before it fought the dread of losing him and being left alone in the bowels of the Facility. She took a step down the stairs of the plinth for minor protection if the machine went off again.

"I touched it with the lightest of contacts sir," she said, realising it was worse to watch someone prod an alien power system than to do it yourself.

"Copy that," Seerman said, as he picked one of the lower orbs and slowly moved the lever closer to its inner surface. He took an age, as if he was building up the courage to touch it. The lever made contact, but this time there was no bang, no flash of light.

"I touched it," he said through gritted teeth. "I'll try a little more force." He composed himself again, bringing the lever into contact with the ball's inside face to push it away from the others.

"I saw them all move a little," said Caellyn. "I think it's okay; it's moving them towards each other that initiates it."

"I'll push it a few centimetres," came Seerman's response, his voice belying his tense muscles. He pushed the orb lightly again.

"They're all moving!" Caellyn shouted. "Sir, they're rearranging as you push that orb out."

The orbs were redistributing, staying on the surface of the large invisible globe and maintaining their equidistant relationship as one of their siblings was pulled outwards.

"Okay," Seerman said, sounding shaken.

"I think we can take one out." Caellyn said.

"Copy."

"Sir, we can remove one of them!" Caellyn said, feeling a sense of accomplishment. "If we can rig one of the hover barges we can take one out! Sir, are you all right?"

"I'm all right," he said, out of breath. "Just a little lost for words. We should head back up, report this to the StratoPort, they'll be pleased for some progress at least."

That made sense: nothing mattered apart from the schedule. They'd just initiated an alien device and his immediate focus was on what came next. He was right, but it didn't shake Caellyn's optimism as she took in her surroundings. They might be in the reactor hall deep under the surface of Venus, like two ants that have crawled into an abandoned nuclear reactor, but they had achieved the impossible.

Another impossible achieved, another to go, Caellyn thought, the optimism fading at the thought of the next task, and the several hours of walking back up to the surface. And Kowalski. She checked her Earth-clock as it registered 15:14. She realised that Kowalski's energy would be almost empty by now. She shuddered with guilt and revulsion, pushing away thoughts of his body crumpled and embalmed in his suit.

She looked up at the large panoramic window of the control room overlooking the reactor hall, and her heart stopped for a beat. She could have sworn she saw something standing there watching them. She blinked and it was gone. *It's just your imagination. Keep it to yourself.*

Chapter 9

Aldai awoke to find his holo-screen still on, and the familiar tones of the morning news lady in his ears. *My head... I must have fallen asleep watching the re-run.* He rubbed life back into his face and rolled over, knocking an empty synth-alcohol canister off his bedside ledge.

Powerhouse won a close game 5-4. It was hardly competitive; there were so many substitutions that it was just pure entertainment, but you still couldn't help get drawn into replicating every dodge, lunge and goal celebration, even when you knew what was coming. The result was spoiled by the delirious chanting of the Powerhouse fans as soon as the game finished. There were some good plays in it however; Landarus hadn't lost his touch, at one point spinning by two players half his age and curving the ball past the keeper as if he was playing on Martian gravity. *How do the old-timers do it? Landarus must be about fifty and he's still spritely. Even Tiernan completes the Special Ops bullet-run like he's in his twenties.* Aldai soothed a throbbing leg and muscles that felt the dull ache of morning.

There was a tension in the news lady's voice that caught his focus. He turned up the volume to hear a concerned newsreader reporting a surface temperature jump. Point seven in a week; no wonder she looked agitated. It had been holding steady the last year, but maybe it had just been biding its time. Maybe it had reached a natural thermal buffer, in deep earth deposits, that stalled the slowly rising temperature, before becoming saturated and withdrawing from a momentary fight at the front line.

A nervous official was being interviewed, reminding everyone that the StratoPort was well out of the way and wouldn't be affected. But he seemed less convincing when he told people that, by their best estimations, the Rift wouldn't collapse. The Rift had held steady for a hundred and fifty years, trapped in a natural equilibrium, even becoming larger as the speed of the winds increased, but no one knew for sure whether you would wake up one morning and it would be gone. Without the Rift, the SeaPort would be trapped, and the StratoPort would be isolated as it slowly ran out of fuel and human necessities.

A call came in and his wallscreen went from a forest scene to a soft glowing red, with the familiar quart-beat of the military channel. The walls damped so that no noise could get in or out, and Halderford's voice came through, "Report to Ops, thirty minutes," before cutting out without expecting a reply. Aldai acknowledged it through his comm-watch. He had the quickest of showers, the water barely touching his shoulders, and put on his civilian clothes to head to the Ops centre.

Team-6 trickled into the locker room, Rongal only making it with a minute to spare as Halderford watched the clock turn over with the silent pressure of military drill expectations. He seemed neither disturbed that Rongal was last, nor surprised that everyone had assembled on time. He waited patiently for the last seconds to pass before turning to the team, as if to remind them that when he gave them a deadline, it was formal and required careful diligence.

"No uniforms today," he said, as Rongal caught his breath. "We've been called in to Intelligence."

Aldai's heart rose and then sank. This meant either answers or more questions, and certainly not both. A small box opened in his mind, begging for information on the Gaunt-man, before he shut it to prevent its insidious curiosity from spreading and capsizing the ship. He allowed some hope for answers, but braced himself for a half-truth, or a frustratingly slim glimpse of the inner workings. The reality was that they would get none of that, and this was another public relations exercise in response to the temperature spike.

They took a quieter route up to Intelligence, avoiding the main Concourse, where crowds had gathered to babble and vent at the increasingly hopeless surface conditions. They grated on Aldai. People eked out a life in two main ways: some loud and openly, like a child stomping on flowers, and some reserved and quiet, burying the nagging threat of finality and putting their

161

heads down and carrying on. The two types tended not to mix well. *A temperature jump brings out the stompers. They'll tire themselves eventually.*

They strode along empty corridors, occasionally passing bewildered citizens lost in thought, who bowed out of the way as six tall, broad-shouldered men and women marched past. They took an elevator from near the centreline hub, up ten floors and then radially outwards, before it glided to a stop and the doors slid open onto an abandoned office floor. Climbing three more sets of stairs, they found themselves in the Intelligence foyer.

They were met at reception by the same lady as when Aldai and Bekka came up to report the Gaunt-man's den. She was shrewd in posture, with old shoulders hunched forwards and eyes like a hawk. She'd made them feel most unwelcome before, eyeing them with a glare that bored into your skull and warned you to turn around for your own safety. After her, they had been pleased to be shuffled into the dark-walled interrogation rooms. Information auditors asked them over and over to recount the events that led them to discovering the Gaunt-man's den. The impassive staff took down notes without expressing surprise or condemnation of an inhuman presence in the Undercity. When they left, the receptionist shot them a similar glare, etching another unwelcome face into Aldai's mind to sit alongside the Gaunt-man's. *She was probably hired for such a purpose, maintaining a perch over the foyer and only moving to peck at grain scattered by Orcanciz.*

This time she at least gave them a half smile, or perhaps a not unwelcoming smirk, that said she knew why they were there, but wouldn't tell them. She pressed buttons or keys behind her desk and an Intelligence Officer appeared shortly after.

Instead of going to the interrogation rooms, they were taken further into the department, where they were ushered into a conference room with a large rectangular table and six chairs laid out. The officer showed them in, and then closed the door without saying anything.

"Not even any coffee," said Jones, looking as tired as Aldai.

"They're probably hoping you'll fall asleep," said Bekka. Jones glared at her playfully, but didn't quite have the energy to respond. Bekka registered a minor sense of victory.

"No biscuits either," Rongal interjected, not intending to keep Jones and Bekka going, but with a purpose that simply represented an empty stomach.

"Do you know what this is about?" Aldai asked Halderford, but Halderford just shook his head a half-turn.

"I can honestly say I don't."

After a few minutes the door opened and Orcanciz walked in, carefully closing the door behind him before assuming a commanding position at the front of the room. His wide face was blotched with rosiness.

"Team-6, you are to be inducted into Intelligence. From now on all your missions will be classified as Code Gamma, and you will report directly to my team," he said with authority. He paused afterwards, as if there was an element of choice to the statement, and they could leave now if they wanted to, but his body language made it perfectly clear that they would all remain in their seats.

"Team-2 were involved in an altercation a few days ago. Given your recent Code Gamma mission, which I thank all of you for keeping secret, and the discovery by Aldai and Bekka, you will now be reporting through Intelligence."

The team turned to look at Aldai and Bekka, who had kept the discovery of the Gaunt-man's den secret from the others. Perhaps Orcanciz had deliberately dropped that grenade of information so matter-of-factly to test the team's reactions. Perhaps he was trying to see if Aldai and Bekka had leaked, but the genuine surprise of Team-6 would tell him they hadn't. Even Halderford had a look of intrigue, though it carried an air of respect that they had done the right thing in keeping it secret from him. Jones, on the other hand, looked incredulous, as if he'd not been invited to a birthday party.

"I want to make a few things clear," said Orcanciz. "Your lives will now be different. You will have access to information that, if disseminated to the wider Ports, could cause significant difficulty to the remaining survival of our species. There are always hard decisions that have to be made by those in charge. In our current circumstances, where we've been chased by the storms to these last vestiges of humanity, there are difficult decisions aplenty, and in the past, there were even harder ones."

Aldai felt like this was an introduction meant only to prepare them for bad news. It felt like the beginning of an excuse, before a terrible crime or misdemeanour was divulged.

"You ran into a Gaunt-man in the Undercity a week ago. I imagine this raised many questions in your mind, and I appreciate the sacrifice you made, not pursuing those questions. Had the situation not brought us to this point, I know that you would have taken that information to your graves," Orcanciz said, with an odd stress on the last sentence, so that it felt more like a threat than a reminder.

"I imagine it caused you a certain amount of surprise to find out that there was a man, barely human, walking around on the station. Imagine what would happen if this information got out to the general public."

"What was he?" asked Jones, trying to sound confident but unable to stop a squeaky edge to his voice. Orcanciz carried on as if the question hadn't been asked.

"There are certain secrets, certain things that happened, and were lost and forgotten when the StratoPort lifted off the ground. It was a desperate time, and hope was hard to find. There were many lines that were crossed, because many lines *had* to be crossed in order to ensure the species survived. Those lines had been placed in times of relative peace. Some were crossed because they were no longer applicable when the circumstances changed, but, sadly, some were crossed in desperation, when they should have been maintained as our unwavering moral boundary. Unfortunately, the human spirit only bends so far against adversity, and society is a delicately balanced entity," Orcanciz paced to the right slowly, repeating words that it felt like he'd said many times before. They were heavy for him to say, but he delivered them like a well-practiced speech.

"When hope was slim, a geneticist by the name of Albateranin proposed that we modify human gene seed to be able to survive on the surface. If we couldn't fight the storm, then maybe we could survive it. Instead of running from an impossible enemy, we adapt and live with it. He called it artificial evolution, and proposed changes in metabolism, skin, sight and lungs. I have to interject that nobody would approve this in the present era, but these were different times. They created modified embryos and grew them into living half-humans. They sent them out onto the surface to test their survivability. Some lived, many died. What you saw the other day was a descendant of those."

Aldai took the information in, turning it over in his head like nervously shuffling a pack of cards, unable to make sense of it. The team sat in silence, all with similar expressions on their faces.

"The mutations went wrong and became hostile. Albateranin lost contact with those able to survive, as they resented what he had done to them. He thought he could fool nature, but it is not a force that can be bypassed. His creations had an aggressive temperament, like wild animals, and his research was shut down. They thought that would be the end of it, because even if some had survived on the surface, none of the female Gaunts could bear children. They assumed they would die out, and a horrific and abominable chapter of human history would be thankfully closed. We don't know how they survived, but the evidence we have, and the evidence you saw, indicates that they are still a threat. They have become more organised and with a more purposeful intention to take vengeance on the Ports."

"How many of them are there?" asked Aldai, anger rising in him, the kind of untethered indignation that has no clear source nor direction to attach itself to.

Orcanciz stared him down. If he'd clearly given this talk many times before, then he must have faced this reaction an equal number of times. "I want to stress that the actions of the past may arouse abhorrence and guilt, but we must live in the present," he paused to let the words sink in. "We are unsure of how many there are; few manage to get into the SeaPort, and even fewer smuggle into the StratoPort. Current geneticists reveal that based on data we've obtained, they are still managing to breed, but they do not have many generations left."

"What data?" asked Jones, with an odd level of enthusiasm, like a fox that smells a hunt.

"Team-6, I impress upon you your obligation to humanity. I impress upon you the delicate nature of our existence. I impress upon you the large number of surviving humans that are living on this station, and that would like to carry on living on this station," he said, again ignoring Jones' question. He had a message to deliver, and was clearly in no mood to turn it into a discussion.

"The Gaunt-men are single minded in their approach. They wish only to destroy the station. We are always interested in diplomacy, and we have made many attempts to open channels of communication with them, but none have been successful. The Gaunt-men will stop at nothing. We have but one choice when so much is at stake, which is to defend humanity against them, and to keep this station, and our hope, in the air. There will come a time when this information can be more widely disseminated. There will come a time when Albateranin will be judged for his crimes, and children will grow up knowing of the horror he inflicted. But in order for those children to grow up, first we must defend the castle."

Orcanciz let the words hang, as if giving a pause for a question, but knowing that it would only be filled with silence. It was true; the StratoPort needed to stay in the air. It was a fragile sanctuary that had to be defended, you couldn't argue with that, but that didn't stop a level of internal conflict from brewing in Aldai's mind. Jones was nodding like a fresh recruit who wanted to be sent to the front line to fight a noble war.

Orcanciz scanned each of them before hammering the brief home with a reminder of their more formal obligations. "Team-6, you made an oath when you joined the military: to defend humanity, and defend the last Ports at all cost, including with your lives when necessary. I am certain that you will uphold your oaths in these testing times. I do not need to remind you of the penalty should you not find yourself able to carry out your orders," he placed his hands on the table as he said those last words, his suit jacket bracing around his bulging shoulders, his medals hanging loosely from the pins, and his stare meeting every one of them, before falling on Halderford.

"Sergeant Halderford, you will remain in this room for the next hour, then I want you to prepare for the SeaPort, leaving on a transport at 15:00 hours. Your mission orders will be delivered on route," he stood up, straightened his jacket and rounded on them one last time. "The Gaunts will show you no mercy. They will be hostile, and they will fight and kill where necessary. Be prepared to show them no mercy in return, not because they deserve it, but because your lives depend on it, and so do the lives of everyone you know and everyone you hold dear." With that, Orcanciz left the room, not allowing any questions, but not expecting any either. None came, and the door closed roughly, leaving six shell-shocked members of Team-6 with minds buzzing and military doctrine trying to quiet the rowdy thoughts, like a judge banging a cudgel for order.

They sat in silence for what felt like an age, before the door opened and a concierge entered with coffee and an array of pastries, silently leaving them in a corner before walking out, as if the room full of contemplative, quiet special forces was completely normal.

"Well, that's a relief," said Jones, immediately making a line for the coffee.

Aldai joined him, realising that he was hungrier than he realised.

"I would never believe it if I hadn't seen one myself," said Tiernan sombrely. "But his face has haunted me, and his rasping voice. It's been very difficult not to mention it to anyone, like finding a hornet's nest that you're told not to warn people about." He rubbed his face, as if urging some blood back into it.

"Do you think he's right, that there's no hope for them?" said Rongal.

"You heard Orcanciz," said Jones in reply. "He said they'd tried diplomacy, but you can't talk to people that won't listen."

Aldai looked at Halderford. He'd barely moved since Orcanciz had left the room, he simply sat there, his hand resting on the table, fingers poised. Maybe he already knew that information, and he'd just been keeping his team in the dark. He gave nothing away: no compassion, no anger, no surprise or umbrage. What else did he keep from them? Everyone did a job on the StratoPort while facing only the tip of an iceberg, having to trust that the part of the iceberg under the water was being managed dutifully by everyone else, but it was different when you were being told to hunt down half-humans like dogs.

It lit a spark in Aldai's mind that he tried to prevent settling on the combustible tinder. "What's it like on the surface?" he asked Halderford in a provocative tone. "You've been there, right? People say you used to run missions there before it was blacklisted."

Halderford barely moved, as if he hadn't even heard the question.

"This was news to me too Aldai," he said after a pause. "It's true, I've been to the surface, and it's a hostile mess of winds, dust, darkness and heat, I never imagined that anything could survive on there."

"Be prepared for hostility," said Jones, as if his brain was catching up on Orcanciz's words. "At least we'll finally get some action. I didn't join the military to chase shadows." he said with growing excitement.

"Just remember which end of your gun is the dangerous one," said Bekka.

They sat in silence, only occasionally interspersed with conversations as the information sunk into their brains. They all became more aware that they'd been asked to stay here in order to monitor their reactions, and so whatever thoughts they were having slowly settled to the bottom of their mind as their military focus crept back in.

"Meet back at Ops centre at 13:30," said Halderford, before they departed. "Be prepared for a drop to the Seaport."

Irina! Crak!

He'd been due to meet her the following evening. He'd been running it over in his mind, thinking where they'd meet, where they'd go, what they'd talk about, and her big brown eyes that he was going to get to stare into once more. He imagined her perfume, and her lithe figure in a cocktail dress and heels. Now he'd have to postpone the pleasure in order to head down through the Rift and into the damp confines of the SeaPort.

Chapter 10

The drop hangar was about two thirds of the way down the Undercity, nestled between Levitation Engines 3 and 4. It was perched on the edge of the outer wall, and looked over the Rift, from where it could watch dropships descend into the depths and rise out of them like bees following foraging flight paths.

Team-6 took the larger cargo elevator to give them room to sling down their packs and equipment. It was bare on the inside, and scraped and dented from too many years of being crammed full of crates and boxes. It creaked as the bracing cables lowered it down through the StratoPort. Without the benefit of solid foundations, the giant structure couldn't help but flex, and that meant that long elevator shafts often struggled to maintain a dead-straight trajectory through it. The drop hangar express elevator did a better job, as it was fitted with dampers and suspension like the elevators in the upper cone. It could ride the rails as they moved slightly under tolerance, but that was a luxury unafforded to mere cargo. Aldai winced. Being lowered in a clunking box didn't exactly calm your nerves before getting in a drop-ship that was going to fall like a stone.

After a few minutes, the elevator hit the floor buffers and they pulled open the doors to find themselves in the drop hangar. It was full of a din you could barely talk over, and the pressure pulled away from you. The hangar bay doors struggled to prevent leakage of atmospheric pressure that huge air conditioners, braced near the ceiling opposite, were constantly trying to fight.

There were three sets of bay doors lined up against the outer wall. Each was angled near the horizontal, and two of them had drop-ships poking through, each with its nose clamped into a robust looking mechanical vice. Even a partial view of the ship showed how big they were, extending up several decks and reaching down many more, considering the part of them hanging below the bay doors, hidden from view. They were more rockets than drop-ships, tall and proud, only really designed to go straight up and straight down, but they were surprisingly nimble and controllable.

One of the drop-ships was surrounded by a group of maintenance staff in colour-coded overalls, pointing and shouting at each other as they prepared it for flight. To the uninitiated they looked like an unorganised rabble, but they knew exactly what they were doing. The ships arrived and left two times a week to create a constant transfer of goods and fuel between the Ports, as well as occasional passengers on their way to and from a SeaPort secondment. However, it looked like there was an issue with cargo. They were taking smaller crates off the upper section of the ship, presumably to make way for their last-minute charge of Special Ops passengers.

A man in grey overalls signifying authority waved them towards the passenger area, and they were led into the waiting room. The door closed with a hiss as the room pressurised to full atmosphere. Their bodies nonchalantly adapted, all too used to dealing with varied pressure environments. You just ignored the dulling of senses and pain of pressure build-up in ears and tubes until it relented to a satisfying return of function.

"You think they'll let me fly it?" said Jones, immediately throwing down his pack and heading over to the window overlooking the hangar floor.

"I think they're more likely to strap you in with extra restraints," said Rongal, pulling one of the heavy, cast-iron chairs out and sitting down to fiddle with his necklace cross.

The waiting room was empty apart from the Special Ops team. If anyone was due to go on this flight, they would have had their schedule mercifully postponed, to drop to the SeaPort later in the week.

The room was large and had an array of tables and chairs. Around its outside was a ledge attended by high stools, as if to give it the appearance of a sophisticated café, and a paper stand was positioned by the door for reading material, layered in newspapers that looked long past their recycling date. There was a coffee pot that Tiernan was emptying into plastic cups, and around the wall were sparsely positioned artworks that looked like they were produced from one of the high schools when Aldai was young enough to be there. The room couldn't escape its industrial function however, and the floor was covered in dark marks, the walls carrying a certain grime from being used as a lunch room by maintenance staff who'd spent the morning elbow deep in rocket parts.

It brought back bad memories for Aldai. The drop of the ships only matched the drop of his stomach at having his early twenties taken away from him to be spent in the artificially lit corridors of the SeaPort. The lack of sun made your bones feel old and clouded your outlook. He shuddered at the thought, and considered Sam, at the beginning of his stint. At least this trip for Aldai would be short.

He looked over at Bekka, her face pale. They all probably were, even Tiernan, who'd dropped more than once. The drops generally went without incident, but every decade or so a ship would be lost. Aldai lightly kicked Bekka's boot and nodded to her, giving her a look that asked if she was all right. She nodded back with a brief smile.

"Who's this a first time drop for?" said Rongal, putting up his own hand.

Bekka put up hers.

Jones had also clearly never dropped before, but was dealing with his nerves by overcompensating on energy. He was up at the viewing panel, staring intently at the final preparations they were making to the ship. "It's just like the elevator right?" he said, his back to the group. "And once you hit free-fall it'll be calm and relaxing. Apart from a little weightlessness, nothing to worry about."

He's trying to convince himself. Aldai kept quiet, hiding his own reservations and finding some solace in the fact that he'd done it before, and it was someone else's turn to feel it for the first time. Nothing gave you courage like seeing someone else more afraid.

Through the viewing glass they could see the final preparations being made to the drop ship. There were mechanics overseeing the pumping of fuel and charging of batteries, with gently steaming cables attached to the ship like umbilical cords about to be released. Below and out of view, where the main body of the ship was held in the large side clamps, similar activities would be undertaken by maintenance staff in pressure suits to withstand the external environment.

The ship itself was about five metres in diameter. Its nose, currently nestled into the powerful looking vice clamp, was dotted in viewing ports that gave the pilots the good visibility that was needed to manoeuvre it into the StratoPort on the return journey. Down the top of the rocket, beneath the pilot's cabin, were three large stabilisation ailerons that were currently housed against the rocket like a bug storing its wings. When the ship dropped, they would open up and guide the vessel on a straight path all the way down to the SeaPort. Interspersed between the stabilisation wings were the guidance harpoons.

When the ship rose towards the StratoPort after a long ascent, it would slow its trajectory as it aimed to position its nose in the vice clamps, to secure itself to the mother structure. In order to aid its manoeuvre, as it got close it would fire out many magnetic harpoons that would socket themselves into targets on the lower drop hangar. The harpoons would then be tensioned and used to assist the main and manoeuvring rockets to make the locking contact. It was an impressive sight to see, and looked like a sea squid trying to grapple onto the side of a whale for support.

Once the vice clamp gripped the nose, the ship would be secured, and the large side clamps would grip the lower ship to make doubly sure of that fact. Then the hangar bay doors would close around it, and the hangar would pressurise, before the weary and shaken passengers disembarked and the cargo was unloaded.

It was a brute of a machine. Once upon a time, flight was attempted by gentlemanly aristocrats in elegant and delicate flying machines made out of balsa wood and stretched fabric. Their craft were beautiful, with shallow curved aerofoils to turn the air downwards without the air even realising what was passing through it. A dropship, on the other hand, was designed to drop like a stone and rise like a rocket. It cared not for style or grace, just the violent mixing of oxygen and methane to create a burning plume behind it that turned into a cloud of steam, that slowly dispersed until it was sucked into the dark Rift-wall.

It wasn't a wholly clean process either, despite their best efforts. Most power on the StratoPort was generated from the four Fusion Reactors, but that kind of energy doesn't get a heavily laden drop-ship up fifteen kilometres of altitude, and the drop-ships were too small to house a gravity cascade like the giant Levitation Engines. They ran on good old fashioned rocket fuel. You would suck oxygen out of the atmosphere and liquify it to make one half of the fuel, and turn seawater and carbon dioxide into methane to make the other part. The methane fuel was mostly produced in the SeaPort using the power from their fusion and geothermal plants, while the liquid oxygen was produced in both the StratoPort and SeaPort. Overall, once the fuel had been generated and burnt in the drop-ship engines, the net result was taking oxygen out of the atmosphere and replacing it with carbon dioxide, but it was an inconsequential burden on a galloping environment spiral.

The mechanics were shouting at each other and waving arms in signal-code, and they released the last few cords from the machine as a man in red overalls walked around with a check-slate, presumably doing a final inspection. He motioned a thumbs up, and after a few minutes the waiting room door hissed open to minor pressure change that stung eardrums, before a concierge gave them a forced hospitality smile and motioned to them that the craft was ready.

They walked across the hangar floor and up a gangway that had been wheeled over the bay doors, giving access to the side hatch of the ship. Ducking into the passenger section, they found nine seats spread around the internal circumference, with a ladder that ran upwards to a second set of passenger seats a floor above, and the pilot's cabin above that. They secured their equipment under the seats and inside the netting attached to the thin central column. A grey-overalled staff checked each of them as they pulled over the chest restraints. Jones had gone white as a sheet, while Rongal had his eyes closed and even Tiernan was staring upwards as if trying to gain the attention of the gods and asking them for safe passage.

The grey-clad staff left, content that the passengers were secured in their cocoons, and Team-6 nervously shuffled in their seats, trying to get blood flowing under the tight straps and heavy chest restraints that came over their shoulders. A drop pilot poked her head through the door, her bright face looking pleased to be carrying such esteemed cargo, when normally it was just boxes and containers.

"Welcome all," she said in an infuriatingly positive tone of someone who did this twice a week and it barely raised her heartbeat. She climbed up the ladder to strap herself into a gimballed seat in the pilot's cabin, and a moment later the co-pilot appeared and dutifully followed her.

Aldai tried to peer out of the windows from his cramped and restrained harness. There were view ports positioned between each seat at two heights that gave a reasonable view of the outside of the craft, although the top ones were obscured by the stabilisation wings in their stored position, and only a few of the pilot's ports two floors above showed some light coming through, the others blocked by the vice clamp.

"Commencing pre-flight checks," came the pilot's voice, as the ship whirred with the spinning of pumps and gyroscopes, and there came the uncomfortable clunking of actuators extending and ailerons flapping back and forth through the outer skin wall next to them, sounding as if the craft was pulling itself apart. Aldai could see over the hangar deck that was now vacated and presumably open to the pressure of the stratosphere.

"All systems ready," crackled the co-pilot's voice through speakers dotted around Team-6, the scream of the drop-ship's systems now deafening like a race car on the start line. Team-6 steadied themselves against their brace harnesses. The bay doors slowly opened, letting in the mid-afternoon sunshine, and there was a heavy jolt as the large side clamps let go of the craft so that it was only held by the vice clamp at the nose. "Get ready for drop," came the pilot's voice, still unnervingly calm. "Brace against the supports and have a nice flight." Aldai dared himself to imagine the view below, just empty space and the Rift patiently waiting for them. How the pilot remained calm at this was beyond him.

"Ready," said the equally impassive voice of the co-pilot. Then, there was a heavy clunk from the vice grip above them, and everything seemed to go quiet.

"Freefall initiated," the pilot said, as if the lurch of stomach wasn't indication enough. It was probably just the pilot showing off her self-control compared to six Special Ops who were now grimacing as their bodies reeled from the unnatural feeling of unopposed gravity. Rongal looked as if he was about to black out, and even Halderford had his teeth clenched involuntarily as he gripped the bars on the chest restraint over his shoulders.

The stabilisation wings deployed, opening up the view to the sky around them, and rocking the ship as they were buffeted by the air before the control systems quickly got a handle and the wings locked into place. After what felt like an age, but in reality was only about ten or twenty seconds, conditions stabilised.

"Terminal velocity reached, stay in your seats," came the pilot's voice. Jones was mouthing something, but no sound was transmitting over the din of the air rushing past the ship, the whir of cabin pressurisation, and the popping of ears.

Aldai looked upwards to see the StratoPort disappear from view through the pilot's port holes, slowly shrinking before becoming a mere dot in the sky. Five kilometres below the sky station, the Rift-wall appeared in the side ports as they reached the cloud surface level. As they descended further it got darker and darker as the sun was blocked from view, and lights flickered on in the cabin to illuminate the inside and the sky above became a disc of dimming brightness framed by the edges of the Rift.

The ship started shaking, hitting turbulent air, and it rocked and shuddered, the aerofoils groaning under the strain of buffeting cross winds as rocket stabilisers fired around them to keep them going in a straight line. Debris clinked on the outside wall, sounding too close for comfort to the passengers bracing themselves in seats next to it, and they could see droplets of rain streaming over the ports that now showed little but the darkness beyond.

"Preparing for landing," came the pilot's voice, and a few seconds later the rockets fired into action, pinning the passengers to their seats as they felt the intense upwards force. The descent slowed, and Aldai simply gripped the chest support handles until he waited for the familiar soft impact that indicated it was finally over, and they had touched down on the SeaPort landing pad, poking out of the sea.

The drop-ship reached its destination to the dull thuds as the magnetic harpoons stabilised it against the platform. Clamps held the bottom in place, jealously gripping the new arrival to prevent it changing its mind.

Aldai smiled to himself, pleased for it to be over, and remembering the words written across the SeaPort landing pad. Stamped in large standard lettering was the phrase "WELCOME TO EARTH."

Chapter 11

The landing platform started its descent into the SeaPort hangar below. Darkness hid the slowly passing walls from view as the drop-ship travelled through the connecting silo tube. A grinding sound reverberated around the craft from heavy metal chains slowly rolling over pulleys, and the platform occasionally jolted as the shiplift's sea-sprayed mechanisms fought the elements. They heard two giant doors close above them, shutting off the view up through the Rift and silencing the howling wind that whipped around the tube. Lights flickered on, illuminating grime-streaked panels through the view ports, and more silo doors opened beneath them as they passed through into the hangar bay, which was abuzz with activity.

As they entered the hangar the view opened up. Through drips of water from the silo-tube above, they saw another drop-ship being worked on to the flash of welding sparks, and an inspection team walking around with clipboards and clean overalls. Everyone in the hangar was so engrossed in their work that few even looked up as the shiplift mechanism clunked loudly and the drop-ship reached its final resting place.

"Never gets any easier," said Tiernan, as if he'd seen more than his fair share of drops in his fifty or so years, his leg bouncing involuntarily.

The hatch opened from the outside, and a familiar smell swarmed into the cabin. It was musty and damp, with tones of body odour and kerosene, and it permeated the SeaPort, feeding off the humidity and imprinting into every wall and fabric. The only relief you'd get from it was when your nose adjusted and whatever you were smelling just became normal.

Aldai felt a sense of familiarity. *At least the pressure is stable.* The ceiling above was dotted with pressure tubes that kept atmospheric pressure inside the submerged hangar. *And the temperature doesn't fluctuate.* The surrounding sea made sure of that, providing a stable heat sink for habitable conditions, even if the polluted water was hungry to corrode through walls and make its way inside.

Leaving the craft to the splatter of heavy droplets still seeping through the inner silo doors in the ceiling, they were met by the yellow light of artificial lamps and the din of workmen amplified by the metal hull of the hangar. Their boots found the familiar metal grating that covered the seaport walkways, and they stepped over a workbot water-vacuum trying endlessly to fight the ingress of water and hoover it back out into the sea around them.

"Welcome to the ocean," said the concierge, just about managing a hospitality smile. "Follow me to the docking bays. It's just a short submarine ride and then you'll be in the SeaPort proper."

The SeaPort itself wasn't directly under the Rift. In fact, when the StratoPort lifted into the air no one knew about the other station. No one knew they'd need it.

The StratoPort itself was merely contingency. It wasn't supposed to be a last sanctuary. It was contingency while humanity tried one last gasp effort to stop the worsening climate of storms. It was contingency that became sorely needed when that attempt failed. Instead of saving Earth, it caused an Acceleration Event that scoured the surface.

Floating aimlessly in the sky for fifty years, the StratoPort eked out a new life for the lucky few who were on board. But soon the endless recycling and material stores were wearing thin, and travel through the clouds became hazardous beyond compare.

But nature hadn't completely turned its back. Through a sorely-needed stroke of luck, the Rift opened, and the StratoPort had a lifeline once more.

Humanity headed back down to the surface, hastily modifying dropships and setting up the SeaPort hangar. Then luck smiled again, and not far from the Rift they found a huge underwater military facility. It was South America's own contingency, hidden from the world under the South Atlantic off the coast of Brazil. It was abandoned but fortunately still operational and had fusion power and deep-sea mining that could replenish stores of rare resources. It became the SeaPort, and humanity had a base on Earth once more.

Aldai listened to the submarine's propellers whir through the dark sea, now under the storm itself, then felt the echoing impact as it made contact with the SeaPort dock.

Team-6 exited the sub and were led into a waiting room with windows covered by privacy slats that clattered as the door closed. In the corner was another robot with a heat lamp aimed at mould that it was scraping away.

A short, stocky man entered the room after a while. He was bulging out of his uniform as if overweight, but his body proportions indicated that a large amount of his bulk was muscle. He had a grim face, beady eyes, and a sharpness of movement that discouraged idle conversation.

"Sergeant Qualtum, Team-2," he said in a gruff voice, shaking everyone's hand roughly without making eye contact. "Follow me; we should be able to make the cell-reaches by evening."

Team-6 looked at each other with raised eyebrows. So much for pleasantries. But perhaps that was a good thing. The less time you thought about where you were the better. Focus on the job, keep your head down. It worked in the StratoPort and it worked in the SeaPort too. Halderford shouldered his pack dutifully, and the others followed.

The SeaPort was a sprawling mass of disjointed structures spread out across the seabed along the shallow marine shelf near the coast of Brazil, before the ocean floor dropped off a cliff towards the deeper waters beyond. It was a tangled mess of podded districts, modules, warehouses, power systems and habitation centres that extended across its thin disk-like shape.

You couldn't stay down here long. People had tried to stick it out in the early days, but after too long your bones became brittle, and the dry, rattling cough that most people got during their stay would turn into lung-rot. Worse than that was what the lack of sun did to the human mind. After a few years, you craved it more than anything else. You needed to feel its warmth on your skin and its rays on your retinas, and feel it travel down optical nerves to nourish the brain. Soon the SeaPort was abandoned for habitation and the only people down here were those on conscripted service.

Aldai caught up with Halderford and Qualtum as they made their way along the walkway towards the Main Chamber. The two sergeants were walking in silence, as if nothing needed to be said, despite the myriad of questions that needed to be answered. Qualtum had failed to explain where the rest of Team-2 were, and Orcanciz's briefing on the Gaunt-men was a spanner in the works that was causing Aldai's mind to judder and start. Maybe that's where Qualtum's prickliness came from, to deflect people who wanted to ask questions they shouldn't be asking.

The Main Chamber was at the centre of the SeaPort, a large, domed structure, scattered with a disorderly arrangement of chairs and tables where people ate, drank and gambled their evenings away. A circular window at the top may have one day let in glimpses of light, but now just showed black water beyond it, dripping into buckets strewn over the Main Chamber's metal-grated floor.

Six walkways, known as the Spokes, spread out from it like points of a star. Each was wide enough for five people to walk abreast but cluttered with extraction pumps and hoses. Further from the Main Chamber they presented an obstacle course of cordoned-off sections and uneven floor gratings. Beyond the Spokes, modules and districts sprawled out into the Outer Reaches, many of which had been long abandoned; you could walk for miles amongst them and not see another human being.

The Main Chamber was the best bit of the SeaPort, comparatively speaking. Depending on who the Seaport Overseer was, it could be full of raucous card games or drunken gambling and occasionally a bareknuckle fight, organised or otherwise. It was generally kept to a decent level of civilisation, but normally towards the end of a two-year tenure the Overseer let the reins loosen a little. It had provided Aldai brief respite and entertainment, but he had mostly kept to the side when he was down here, playing cards with a grizzled old man who was on his third service. He'd taken far more of Aldai's money than Aldai cared to admit, though most of that had occurred in combination with large amounts of moonshine.

They passed weary looking faces, eyeing up Special Ops with a certain suspicion and inquisitiveness, but not enough to indicate that the military presence was unusual in any way. They'd stare, as if hoping for news that their SeaPort stint might end early, occasionally releasing a bone-rattle cough before averting their gazes and getting back to their daily tasks.

Sam. Aldai hoped more than anything to see him now. For his benefit, or Aldai's or both. As they neared the Main Chamber, Aldai strained to see his friend amongst the people who'd clocked off shift early, gathering for evening meal service in the distance.

But before they got to the communal centre they took a left, passing through a doored bulkhead and into one of the many smaller round walkway tubes of the SeaPort, its ceiling covered in cables, some of which were severed and hanging down so that you had to swing your head around them as you walked through. A robot was climbing the wall to clean away the grime that dripped down in streaks, and the corridor went from relatively clean to dark green as they passed its progress.

"They're everywhere," said Jones. "Like sewer rats."

"Wait 'til you see the actual rats," Rongal replied.

After taking a series of turns like making your way through a maze, Qualtum arrived at a heavy side bulkhead and opened the door with a large set of keys on his waist, the door requiring a shoulder barge to open before he ushered them inside. They found themselves in a side room that opened into the small SeaPort Special Ops base. The main room was square and surrounded with lockers, with an archway that led through to cells, interview rooms and bunks. Closing the door, Qualtum lowered his pack and turned to address the team.

"We're heading out past the deuterium mines to the old cell blocks. Just beyond, there's an off-limit area that is our strike target. Team-2 was performing missions there last week when we encountered a hive of Gauntmen. We engaged them in combat but were ambushed from the rear. There weren't many of them but we were forced to retreat. One killed, two wounded. Our mission is to attack from the West of their last known position and put them to sleep."

"How many did you count?" said Halderford, puffing out his stomach with a rare hint of insecurity at being outranked by Qualtum, and having his team ordered around.

"We think about fifteen," he replied, sucking air through the side of his mouth. "But there's no telling how many they'll be. They've managed to find a way in to the Outer Reaches in the last month or so; we don't know how. We've been running recon and harrying them to try to push them back but it's cat and mouse. Our inventory of sensor cams is low, and they manage to take them down, so it's difficult to say numbers for sure. We've just got to get boots on the ground and take them out where we find them. Keep your guard up at all times. Pack for one night."

"Yes sir," Halderford said, turning to the team. "Camo gear on and full headsets."

"Yes sir," they chimed, trying to get used to the awkward new chain of command. They smeared dark paste on their faces and packed overnight bags, leaving their excess luggage in the few lockers that weren't damp and mouldy.

They left the chamber to wind back into the labyrinth of walkway tubes. They passed bulkhead after bulkhead, through poorly maintained sections with lights half hanging from the ceiling that flashed on when Team-6 came through and blinked until they passed. These were passages that rarely saw use; they tried to avoid public areas now they were in full combat regalia. The only evidence that people had been there recently was a moonshine den in an offshoot room. *So that's where they made it.*

They arrived at the Deuterium mine entrance, a section of large-diameter tube that led to a wide blue bulkhead. It had an imposing round central door for transport containers, and several human-sized doors on each side.

Aldai could hear the familiar gentle hum of huge pumps, their vibrations traveling through the structure, as they sucked in water and split out the heavier elements. The deuterium would be siphoned into bottles and put into storage. Only a small amount would be needed to fuel the reactors for years, but they were taking no chances. Who knew how long they'd need fuel for.

He had visited during his two-year conscription. He'd befriended a technician who gave him a personal tour, taken in by her warm smile at having someone exhibit an interest in her work. She showed him around, reciting tedious technical information, both of them pleased to have distractions from SeaPort life. She'd worn a perfume that made the air smell like flowers rather than its normal musty hues and had let her long blonde hair hang over her lab coat. She'd stood close to Aldai as she showed him the centrifuge systems, until his hand caught her waist and neither moved away. She'd turned to stare at him with searching eyes, the pretence of deuterium mining having fallen away, until she pressed up against him and they found themselves breathless in Aldai's cabin bed shortly after.

They'd circled each other for the next few months, like suns caught in mutual gravity. They lived separate lives until they'd need another's heartbeat against their chests, the taste of soft sweat on their necks and the moan of ecstasy in their ears. Then her assignment ended and she disappeared back to the StratoPort without even a goodbye. When he returned, Aldai had bumped into her once. She had a husband and two children, briefly making eye contact before looking the other way as if they were perfect strangers.

They crossed the Deuterium mine entrance and went through a bulkhead on the other side, Qualtum kicking aside a pumping robot that seemed to be conserving energy in front of it. "Keep your rebreathers to hand; the sections onward from here are less structurally sound," came his voice from up ahead.

Aldai fumbled at one of his shoulder straps until his hands recognised the mouthpiece's t-shape. He studied the walls with suspicion, but they seemed solid enough for now. A few hints of corrosion on some of the bracing ribs, but otherwise they looked as if they could just about hold together.

They switched to torch light as the ceiling strips failed to come on, now that they were far outside maintained sections, and the metal walkways became uneven where some of their ground supports had rusted away. After half an hour of walking, getting into a well-rehearsed routine of opening and closing bulkheads as their Special Ops train passed through them, they reached a door whose turn-wheel was resolutely stuck in the closed position, and even Aldai couldn't shift it with a discarded pipe braced against a door strut. Qualtum checked his augmented map on his wrist device and they retraced their steps to a different offshoot and made their way around it, soon finding themselves in the old cell-block.

In front of them were three long sections, each heading off at a different angle from the entrance. They were lined double height with cells, long abandoned by staff and criminal alike, but covered in wall markings, discarded bedding and rotted magazines as if they had been vacated in a hurry. This block hadn't been used for inmates in well over a century, when a newer facility was tacked onto the SeaPort on the other side. Aldai shuddered at the thought. Prisons through the ages had always been grim places, but to be incarcerated here, or even in the newer facility, for more than a two-year assignment was torture for anyone. It worked well as a deterrent, at least.

Qualtum motioned to stop, "Five-minute break. The den is up ahead ten minutes."

Aldai found a seat in an old cell and ate part of his evening rations, squeezing nutrition paste out of silver packets and drinking water from his canteen.

"So, this is what the SeaPort is like," came Jones' voice from next door

"There's better bits," replied Tiernan, standing in the central area. "Five times I've been down, two assignments, three missions a long time ago. Every time I hope it's the last time I see it."

"You see the moonshine room back there?" said Rongal. "At least it's got that going for it."

"If you want your liver to turn the colour of sea water," replied Aldai, hearing a trickle of laughter. "If you get a decent batch it's a lot better than the synth alcohol on the StratoPort, though. One batch actually tasted quite good, in fact so good that almost the whole facility was out of action for a day while they nursed hangovers. But most of the time its average at best."

"Well, I'm not looking forward to it," Jones muttered, his normal shine having dulled a little.

They shouldered their packs and made through a bulkhead in the far end and into large tubes that were even danker than before. Aldai checked and double checked his rebreather, almost expecting the walls to fall apart at any moment. After the second bulkhead Qualtum gave a signal to enter operations mode and they dimmed their lights and muffled their footsteps. They passed through an old office capsule, that had ancient looking computers long past useable, with mould growing over the keypads and old barnacles on the desks and monitors, as if at one point it had been underwater. Another capsule had a large generator in it that had been stripped bare like a picked skeleton.

Then Qualtum gave the signal to engage.

They passed through two more bulkheads, bracing against the doors and moving through doors with rifle cover before taking point on the other side, Qualtum directing them with the Special Ops command signals like an orchestra conductor, until he motioned for them to take extra care as they came to a larger door. Tensing up, he quickly spun the door wheel, At the familiar click of the lock disengaging, Bekka pulled it open and Qualtum swung his rifle through with full-beam torch on. They stood motionless for a few seconds, listening for any movement inside but hearing none. Qualtum carefully stepped inside, swinging his torch light, bright enough to blind anyone in there, around to check the extent of the room.

"Clear," he said, relieving muscles that were ready to pull the trigger and take the impact of ambush bullets in response.

They entered a cylindrical room, like a giant tin can lying on its side, with a grated platform along the bottom and a raised platform at the other end, giving the impression it was a conference room, or theatre or venue for revellers many decades before. Qualtum gave the signal to secure the place, and they scoured the few entrances and exits. After holding positions for a few minutes in silence, Qualtum relaxed. "They're gone. This is where we engaged them last time. It's like playing cat and mouse through these tunnels. One minute they've settled in an area, the next minute they're moved, only to reappear somewhere else. Check the room," he commanded in his short tone.

They scoured every corner in their torch light, finding a discarded jacket that looked similar to the worn cape of the Gaunt-man they saw in the StratoPort, but finding no other traces. Bekka did a scan, finding the hallmarks of plasma residue on the walls.

"Where are they getting this from?" muttered Qualtum, lost in thought, the edge taken off his confidence as he faced the place he'd been in a week before, deep in a firefight. "Let's head back to the cells. There's a communicator there, and we can contact base, see if they've picked anything up on sensors. But there's miles upon miles of empty tunnels down here; they could be anywhere."

They trudged back, retracing their steps but finding little to recognise in the repetitive sprawl of bulkheads and corridor tubes. Aldai noticed the remains of a rat, looking almost the size of the cats that hunted them in the main section, but otherwise there was little to give you bearings, and they were reliant on Qualtum's lead to guide them.

Arriving back in the cell block, Qualtum pulled out a briefcase hidden behind a tarpaulin under a cell bunk and turned the scroll locks until it clocked open and he set about initiating it. He disappeared down one of the far cell block arms and they could hear the muffled edge of his voice reporting from the distance as they spread out again into the cells.

"Stay put here, we'll spend the night, awaiting further orders," Qualtum said on his return, stringing a hanglamp from the gantries of the floor above, illuminating the room and casting striped shadows onto the nearby cells from their half-open bars.

Aldai spread out in one of the cells, taking off his boots and rolling up his combat trousers, damp from wading through low level water in some of the corridor tubes that had leaked. He cursed the conditions and pulled out a bar of solid protein-carbs and ate it, its bitter and tangy flavour revealing that at least some care had been put into its taste, compared to the standard nutrition paste.

Food was one aspect of the SeaPort that was better than the StratoPort. The food on the StratoPort was grown in cramped hydroponics farms, with the sole intention of growing algae and insect crops as quickly as possible, before grinding them into a paste that was at least more palatable than the ingredients would be separately.

Down in the SeaPort there was no sun, but there was sea food. There were fish that could survive in the depths, often odd and prehistoric in appearance, that were caught by drones flying through the deep water trailing large nets. They had scant meat on them, but the flesh they did have was like injecting gold into the bloodstream. Every now and again a school of fish would pass by, lighting up otherwise empty radar sensors, as they roamed the dark oceans searching for life to support them, but they had become rarer and rarer as the years went by.

The fish was the delicacy, but there was also a small ecosystem near the surface, with floating algae that seemed to survive on the little sunlight that crept through the clouds, that in turn caused intermittent flocks of plankton. And not too far from the SeaPort were hydrothermal vents supported colonies of mussels.

The sea still provided, just. It meant that you got some semblance of nutrition from a natural food chain that the body so dearly craved. But you only got it in the SeaPort. Some fish made it to the StratoPort, but it was mostly intercepted by those on Secondment to the SeaPort, and no one quite had the heart to stop that practice.

Qualtum came around distributing silver packages, barely making eye contact as he handed them to each person. Aldai recognised the fish-bar packaging instantly, salivating at the welcome surprise. *Qualtum might be all right after all.* Nothing reinforced leadership like appealing to people's stomachs. Not quite the scraps of fish meat served in the Main Chamber, but nevertheless a close second. The fisheries department would clean the fish off the bones and combine it with nutrition paste into a bar, occasionally with mussels if there were any about. They were rationed at one a day, and they provided both a welcome reward and a potential punishment, when they were taken away for misdemeanours.

Aldai wolfed it down, savouring the flesh that gently flaked apart and rejoicing at the burst of a mussel that his tastebuds had waited a decade to experience again.

He closed his eyes and tried to imagine he wasn't in the SeaPort. As the light source swung gently in the centre of the room, disturbed by the vibrations of the team moving about, he tried to imagine it was the sun, and he was heading out across an empty sky to throw a magnet rope into the clouds. It was serene, the sun hanging gently above, enveloping the stratosphere in its rays as the clock ticked over lazily.

He imagined the return journey they'd get to make in a day or so's time, sitting back in the dropship waiting for an almighty blast of rocket engines to lift them off the ground. He imagined the StratoPort closing in on the viewscreen, and the relief he'd feel at returning there.

He remembered the return all those years ago when his SeaPort assignment finished. The mood in the ship was high: a group of people finishing their two-year stint and returning to the sky. He remembered one bald man singing all the way up. But there was a tinge of sadness there. The dropship wouldn't get closer in his memory, and the StratoPort just stayed out of reach.

A sudden memory seared emotional pain across his thoughts, and he closed his eyes tightly as unwelcome tears briefly formed in the corner of his eyes. He held his eyes shut as he tried to reform his thoughts, pushing that memory away, closing his mind off, pushing thoughts down, and focussing on others at the surface. He breathed deeply, opening his eyes to check no one had noticed, but the team were all dispersed around the room and minding their own business with earphones and fish-bars. Qualtum and Halderford were sitting on two chairs in the centre, keeping watch and barely talking, which probably suited both of them. No one had noticed, but Aldai's mind ran with frustration and painful memories that he clamoured to control.

Halderford whistled quietly: a call to alertness. He snuffed out the hang-light and they all waited in silence, Aldai fumbling around on the bench beside him in the darkness, finding his rifle and silently pulling over his helmet and visor.

After a few moments they could hear something approaching, as distant bulkhead doors opened and closed. He heard Halderford and Qualtum, quiet as anything, move their chairs into one of the side cells, only audible to someone who knew what to listen for. The bulkhead down the far end opened and closed, and Aldai saw a light source dancing around the hall from a torch light that the person was carrying.

Then, the footsteps stopped, and the light became directed more purposefully now, searching around the cells as if the person had suddenly got the feeling they weren't alone.

The man took a few steps tentatively forward before he heard the cock of a rifle and a sudden flash of light, recoiling as Qualtum directed a full beam at him.

Aldai joined the fray, sliding quietly out of his cell and lifting his rifle towards the intruder. He half expected to find a Gaunt, but it was just a fairly average-looking person, still reeling from having a light and rifle pointed his way. He was covering his eyes and cursing.

"Stand down," said Qualtum's voice. "Team-2 code delta-two-omega."

Halderford was already restringing the hang-light as the bewildered Special Ops took in the scene. The man was crouched down rubbing his eyes, muttering something under his breath that sounded like a string of curse words. As Aldai urged his pupils to refocus to the now dim-light, the face became visible, and he was suddenly struck that he recognised it. It was the man with shoulder-length hair from the trio when he'd first met the Gaunt-man.

"Any news?" Qualtum said, as if knowing exactly what was going on. Aldai exchanged quizzical glances with the others, all looking as dumb-struck as he felt, but all knowing that now wasn't the time to ask questions and have things explained to them.

"You scared the life out of me," came the man's quiet response, his thin face etched in seriousness. "You should have let me walk on through."

"Copy, but if I'm not mistaken, you're armed and may have fired if you'd noticed us first."

"Maybe so," he said, looking around behind him. "I can't stay."

"Copy, do you have anything to go on?"

"They're up past the outer ring, in the old warehouse habitat. That's all."

Qualtum nodded, and the man walked off. But as he did so, he eyed up the curious group of dark-clad military personnel that had appeared out of nowhere, their faces smeared jet black with camo paint so that all he saw were inquisitive eyes staring back. He caught Aldai's stare with a look of revulsion on his stern face, as if he was disgusted at these humans entering his domain in the far reaches of his SeaPort. Aldai gave back as good as he got, his jolted mind still racing. This man was answers. This man was colluding, helping the enemy. Aldai felt an untethered anger that was trying to latch on to something around him.

Once the man was long gone, Aldai moved around to Halderford who was a few cells away, trying to relax.

"What the hell was that about?" Aldai said quietly.

"It's need to know Aldai, I'm sorry, just forget it happened."

"Do you know?" Aldai said, with an air of irritation.

"I'm your Sergeant, Aldai, I will be privy to things that I can't disseminate to the team."

This infuriated Aldai, despite it being standard procedure. Every mission they went on was based on Halderford having more information than them. They followed his orders, earned their surplus rations, and turned up the next day. But this was different. He felt a fire burning within him. Maybe it was the claustrophobic, dark SeaPort, or the fact they'd just been told there were genetically modified Gaunt-men around that they had been tasked to execute quickly, no questions asked. There was only so much you can fumble around in the dark, being kept at arm's reach from truth and answers, especially when your finger hovers over the cold metal of the trigger. Right now, Halderford was the blockade of authority. God, that man infuriated Aldai sometimes. He was so impassive; he gave so little.

Halderford stood up and moved closer to him. "Trust your eyes Aldai," he said. "You know the score. You know that even if I knew who he was, I couldn't tell you. And there are many layers above me, I work on fractals of information; we all do, that's our job. We're the tip of the spear, but the tip of the spear doesn't always get to choose where it points. That's the job we do. That's what keeps out part of the machine turning."

It wasn't an answer, but it was enough to at least stop Aldai in his tracks. Damn, he was irritating, even in his calmness. Sometimes he frustrated Aldai more than anything on the planet, and especially so when he wouldn't even let Aldai be angry at him for it.

"We're spending the night here, move out at 04:00," Halderford said.

Aldai paced the floor, finding a cell down the far end away from the others to collect his thoughts. He stared at the walls, trying to decipher century-old scribbling that looked like a name and a date. He was trying harder than ever to imagine that he wasn't in the SeaPort. *Andalucía.* He imagined the rolling hills he would one day settle in. The green grass, the gentle breeze, the swaying trees. He needed it now more than ever. Goddamit, Venus had to work.

He heard footsteps and Bekka came into his cell and sat on the bunk next to him, as if sensing he needed someone right then.

"You all right?" she whispered.

"Yeah." he said. "It's just this place, it brings back bad memories."

"Down here?" she replied, her voice soft and calming. "I can imagine it's not exactly a holiday."

"It's not that," Aldai responded. He sat quietly for a moment, thoughts racing around in his head. "It's... when I returned, that's when I found out my dad was gone."

"Oh my God, Aldai," she whispered. "I'm so sorry, I didn't know. What happened?"

"I don't even know, that's the worst thing. They said it was aggressive cancer, and he hadn't messaged me because I had enough on my plate with a SeaPort assignment. Then mum said he'd been diagnosed and jumped. I didn't know what to think. Maybe she was just trying to wind me up, but I never found answers. She hated him. He was just a goddam seed. I hated him, but not all the time. I was so angry, angry at him, angry at myself, angry at the world for letting it happen," he said quietly, tears welling up in the corners of his eyes. Bekka reached out and put an arm over his shoulder.

"I don't know what to say," she said. "That must've been awful, you must've been strong to get through that."

"He was just a goddam seed," Aldai said, placing his head in his hands. "He was barely around, growing up, so I convinced myself I didn't need him, but when he was gone..." Bekka shifted over, leaning on him so that he could feel the warmth of her body against his.

"That's why we stick together, that's why we do what we do. Is that why you joined the military?"

Aldai sat quietly for a while, composing himself. He leaned back against the cold metal wall with a more rigid self-control.

"I did it straight away," he said. "I walked straight up to the military quarter and signed up. Pretty soon after I was put in Team-6. It was exactly what I needed, I just let the regimented days consume me, one after the other, one mission to the next. Halderford was moved in shortly after I joined. I'd follow him anywhere, but crak, he irritates me sometimes."

Bekka smiled; that was something they could all agree on. He was an exemplary Sergeant, and it was no small wonder why he hadn't been promoted from that position, but while his calm demeanour was one that carried authority, it certainly got on the nerves of Team-6 every now and again.

"I get that," Bekka said, pushing up against Aldai.

They sat like that for a while, occasionally hearing the others move around down the far end of the cellblock, and Aldai feeling the warmth of Bekka's body, the rising and falling of her breathing, and the beating of her heartbeat. Somehow, despite it being coarse standard issue, her jacket felt soft against his, and her hair gently touched his cheek and hung loosely over his arm.

After a while, their heartbeats slowing to gentle rhythm, she shuffled in her position, Aldai feeling her whole body move against his, and she leant over and whispered in his ear "You know I have a thing for mutts," before getting up and heading back towards the hang-light, returning to her cell.

He lay down on the bunk, with a half-smile of surprise, as his mind swam with the current. He looked up at the ceiling, seeing someone had drawn a wingless dragon across it, its body writhing and curving from head to tail, as it bared its teeth to whoever used to sit in this cell. He set his watch for 03:50 and slowly drifted off to sleep.

Chapter 12

Caellyn stepped down the side of the Star-Sphere plinth, carefully placing one mechanically assisted step after another, as she and Colonel Seerman started their long walk back to the Venusian surface.

On reaching the bottom step she noticed a dark tree branch lying next to one of the raised fins.

"Sir, there's something over here," she said to Seerman, peering down at it. It looked like a blackened tree root, splitting into thinner and smaller branches along its length. It was elongated, looking as if it moulded itself into four fingers near the end, but there were no discernible knuckles or flexion points. Its surface looked like rubbery, porous skin, and there was a sever mark where it appeared to have been chopped off from something larger. Seerman joined Caellyn, staring down with equal curiosity and horror.

"What is that?" Caellyn said.

Seerman took his stick and tentatively tried to roll it over, finding the tissues soft and spongelike.

"It looks as if it's been here for a while," he said, a tinge of weariness to his voice. The effort to move the ball of the Star-Sphere outwards had taken the edge off his usual stern confidence, as if his fifty years of experience was finally catching up with him. Or maybe it was the fact they were stuck in the bowels of a Venusian Facility where people disappeared, and now there was evidence of some kind of twisted lifeform.

"I can't handle this," said Caellyn, her voice full of remorse. "What the hell is that?" she repeated in an agitated way.

"Caellyn, look at me," said Seerman. "We don't know what that is, it could be ancient, it could be hundreds or thousands of years old."

"You're right," she said, taking a moment to compose herself.

"We have a job to do, and the next step of that job is to make it back to the surface. We make it back to the surface, and then we know we can remove an orb, and we report back to Earth for further orders. Whatever else is going on, it's not our concern right now. We just have to shut it out. Another team can come here in the future and worry about that."

Caellyn shut her eyes, breathing heavily. "Yes sir," she said, meeting his gaze and finding some confidence in his grim resolve.

Where he found it was beyond Caellyn. Maybe you just get used to walking a high wire after an entire career in the Space Division, sitting on rockets that could blow you to smithereens and trusting pressure boundaries that kept out environments that would kill you instantly. And all while having your trust entirely in someone else's work. Your whole life was in the hands of engineers and designers, and your life managed in risk charts and contingency meetings. After that you were just a passenger in someone else's endeavour. You would just have to blank out the danger and force your mind away from possibilities. But it wasn't something that Caellyn was used to.

"Let's go," he said, turning to head across the reactor floor. "We'll be up there by evening."

It took half an hour to make it back up to the control room, crossing the shallow curved floor between the fins and winding up the ledge to the control room airlock. They found it empty, to Caellyn's relief. Whatever she had thought she'd seen from the plinth below had either gone or was just a figment of her imagination.

Walking up to the labs, she tried to block out the Facility around her. She focussed on the displays inside her helmet and ran unnecessary diagnostics to distract herself by studying the incomprehensible technical readouts, simply to have something to focus on that wasn't bare obsidian walls. She gripped her bolt pistol through the brain interface, occasionally relieving unconscious tension that had built up as her body clenched inside the pressure vessel.

Her suit was holding, at least. An actuator had seized and one of her coolant tubes had ruptured when she was pulled into the Star-Sphere, providing a second orange light to join the malfunctioning fan from the day before, but it was minor, overall.

They reached the labs, Seerman signalling to stop for a break, and Caellyn drank water through her feed tube that she was sure was warmer than last time. Still, it was nourishing, and she realised how thirsty, tired and hungry she was. They'd spent nearly thirty hours in these suits, sleeping broken shifts the night before, and her body was beaten up and weary. He temple ached from where it had struck the side of the helmet, and so did her left hip and shoulder that must have taken the brunt of the impact as she was flung forwards an hour or two before.

What am I doing here? Exhaustion ran over her. She was no soldier, no space cadet, no hero. Her normal environment was sitting at a desk, working in an office, or hiding away in the hydroponics deck. The scariest thing she'd ever done was to allow an old boyfriend to take her out in a shuttle. He'd tried to impress her by flying close to the top of the cloud, despite her protests, and shortly afterwards she'd given him his marching orders. She hadn't even been to the SeaPort, and bore no desire to go in the slightest, not even for the adventure of it that was a mild draw for some people.

She'd actually wondered if she might get away without going to the SeaPort entirely. Her mother was unusual in having never gone, and Caellyn was always suspicious of that fact. Maybe it was a perk of being high up in Central Government. When Caellyn questioned her about it she always just said it was lucky, and that it probably meant that Caellyn had the lucky gene too. Pulling strings, more like. The dishonesty annoyed her. She felt guilty for having the possibility of avoiding the SeaPort assignment, while everyone else disappeared below the clouds for a few years. She only tolerated it, and didn't press her mum further because she had the conflicting emotion of being pleased and thankful for the protective power. It was the most direct indication her mother really cared about Caellyn, anyway. She wasn't cold, but her attention was always in short supply when she buried herself in her work, and Caellyn lost count of the times she used to turn up late after school because she was working long hours.

The guilt bored away at her, though. The seed of guilt lies dormant, even if it doesn't grow, and when she would go to the odd SeaPort leaving party she'd keep a low profile and avoid conversations about "service". When her friends asked about her parents, she'd ended up lying and saying her mum had been down twice.

Perhaps that was why she'd agreed to go to Venus. She resented the idea of being the odd one out, even in its privilege. Protectiveness is a double-edged sword and can turn into doubt in your abilities, and then it turns to resentment. Deep-rooted confidence only comes from proving things to yourself, and in that respect Caellyn felt lacking. There was something in the back of her mind. The guilt was there, a drive to perform civic duty, to fulfil obligations and feel grounded amongst others, not to have to rely on feeling superior when other people brought it up.

Her brother said he'd go. He was too young to understand what he was saying, and it was just teenage posturing, but it annoyed Caellyn until she shut him up by saying there were rats down there the size of dogs. But what did she know? She'd never faced difficulty. She'd only ever known the StratoPort, the joys of bunking off school and breezing exams, and landing a comfortable job poring through the videos of a potential civilisation on Venus.

So, when Seerman came to her in the hydroponics floor, it all seemed to click together. He'd offered her a chance to change the tracks, to plant her steam train heading in a new direction. She'd reluctantly agreed. When she'd told her family the cover story, that her SeaPort duty had come up, her mother's face had gone pale and her dad looked indignant. But her brother looked a mix of shock and awe, and it almost made the whole trip worth it. She had felt a weight lift off her shoulders, despite the knowledge of where she was going. It was the feeling you get when you finally repay a long-owed debt.

But now the full reality was dawning, and she cursed herself for being so foolish. *This isn't my fight; this isn't my job. This is death in dark corners. Or death in a boiling, roasting oven. There's little fulfilment in these dark obsidian walls and hidden passages that could conceal a whole expedition without a trace.* She fought a lump in her throat as she imagined being back in her cabin watching 22nd century comedies through a lazy Sunday afternoon.

She wanted more than anything to leave. She could do it too. She'd just have to carry the bolt-pistol through to the habitation chamber and point it at Arundel until she agreed to fly the ship out of the atmosphere and back to the *Molniya-V.* It would be easy. Hell, she could just lock them all in the bunk rooms and fly it herself with her basic pilot training. But her conscience yapped in the background, and she remembered the serious faces trying to "persuade" her to go, readying hidden threats. Her career would be ruined if she returned having jeopardised the whole mission, maybe worse. Who knows what they threatened Seerman with. She cursed herself for lacking the bravery to go through with an exit plan.

They trudged on up through the labs, every step a minor victory against a fear of being assailed at any moment. Caellyn's mind turned to the off-shoot corridor that had appeared out of nowhere. She told herself not to even look at it. As the approached its location, she kept her eyes trained on Seerman's heels, watching the ankle joints pivot, and the metal leaves on the rear-facing back legs articulate. The yellow coating was already dulling, and where suit parts moved against each other it was starting to wear through from the repetition of movement after having walked several miles without refurb.

Then it was there on the left. She caught a glimpse of it out of the corner of her eye, as Seerman flashed his torch at it briefly as he went past. She gripped her bolt pistol and leant down to grip the sheath of her combat knife, steeling her emotions. As it passed, she got a feeling of rain on her back, from her nervous system misfiring, as it expected some sort of impact. The feeling urged her forwards, but she pushed it away and tried to cool her nerves. As she put a few metres between herself and the corridor, she turned to look, but only saw the empty elevator shaft and the thin dark void where the corridor broke the wall line.

A spasm of relief hit her. The door *must* have been there all along, she told herself. Or, perhaps, just an automated system kicking in after millennia. Nothing had appeared out of it, so it must just have been harmless. Maybe it was the storm, causing a pressure difference that pulled it open. That must be it. She felt muscles release and took a deep breath, her lungs welcoming the extra oxygen after having been constrained by tight chest muscles.

They were doing it. Impossible task after impossible task. A shred of excitement shouldered its way into her thoughts. They were going to do it. They were going to solve the Star-Sphere for humanity. She imagined her friends' wide-eyed faces as she told them she was once pulled into the centre of the device, because she'd had the audacity to tap it with the lightest of touches and reveal its secrets. And when she could finally tell her scamp of a brother that she'd been to Venus she'd get bragging rights for a lifetime.

They passed through the buttress check-points, too tired and beaten by the internals of environmental suits to care about investigating keypads further, and made their way up the final elevator shaft.

Kowalski.

She'd almost forgotten about him. Her thoughts had been so focussed on the Star-Sphere, shadows and severed organic-looking branches, that he'd passed out of her mind. More guilt. They'd left him there, and her brain hadn't even had the courtesy to remember him. He could have been sitting there, slowly watching his power fall away, until the pressure systems failed, the coolants spluttered their final expansion, and he was crushed and boiled inside out.

She strained her ears to listen for the wind. She begged it to have stopped, so Kowalski could have made it to the Lander. She wanted to run, but Seerman kept pace at walking speed. What was he thinking right now? He was the one that had chosen to follow the precious schedule.

They closed the final tens of metres to the entrance room, seeing the ceiling level off up ahead, from the small incline back to horizontal, and summited the final peak as the view of the first room rose above the obsidian floor horizon. Seerman looked to be straining his torch, his mind clearly on Kowalski too.

"He's gone," he said.

Good. At least his suit wasn't sitting there like a burnt-out husk. "I can't hear the storm," she replied.

"Me neither."

They checked the corners as they entered the room, but his suit was nowhere to be seen. The entrance was empty, save for the scattering of broken drones.

"Let's get out of here, I need a coffee," she said, surprising herself with a level of calmness.

"Copy," Seerman replied, with some amusement and exhaustion in his voice even through the crackled comms.

They passed through the dogleg entrance and Caellyn heaved on the entrance door, hearing the scraping as it slid wide open. The storm had gone, and so had the dust-fog. She was met by a ghostly beautiful scene of the entire U-shaped valley, as she took it in from the top of the incline back to the valley floor. The whole ground, rocks and soil alike, was red with a rusty edge, and tinged green in the dullness of light coming through the clouds above. In the distance to the right, as the valley opened up, was a mountain range, leading to a central peak that looked like a super volcano.

Ahead of her was the ship of the First Expedition, standing unmoved, still waiting patiently for the return of its crew, despite its mortal wound. But the lander of the Second Expedition was nowhere to be seen. Caellyn searched the valley, the horizon and the sky.

"*They've fucking left us!*" she shouted.

Seerman arrived at her side, barely able to hide shock and panic from his face before trying desperately to steady himself.

"Arundel, Yakun, do you copy?" he said, the comm pitch changing as he switched to the long-distance channel. "Venus lander, do you copy?" he repeated, but there was no response.

"They've left us!" Caellyn shouted.

They'd done it, Caellyn thought, they'd only gone and done it. She was angry beyond belief. But part of her wasn't even surprised. She had thought of doing it herself.

Maybe it was karma for leaving Kowalski. Maybe he'd re-joined them and led them to safety after his nerves were shredded by power failures in his suit. But no, he wouldn't do that. That wasn't him. Seerman was right, he gave the impression he'd do the right thing even if it meant painful sacrifice. He wouldn't leave her and Seerman behind, not unless it was absolutely necessary. It was probably Yakun; it must have been. He'd got spooked by a rock, taken the controls and piloted the ship as far away as possible.

Caellyn raged until she ran out of anger, to find it replaced by a dull hopelessness. *We're going to die here.*

"Venus lander, do you copy?" Seerman called out again.

Caellyn fell limp in her suit. She closed her eyes. She didn't want to admit it, but she wanted anyone at that point: her mother, her father, a friend, someone to appear in the distance. It was a ridiculous thought, but that didn't matter. She just wanted to believe it so badly that when she stared into the distance, she almost thought she could see someone through the heat haze.

"Seerman, we copy, closing in on your position," came a response in her ear. Arundel's voice. Caellyn was ready to berate them with every ounce of remaining energy, but the colonel interrupted her.

"Copy, craft. You had us scared there for a minute."

"Sorry, sir. We had to take off with the storm. We got pretty high to avoid it and decided to save thruster power until you returned to make sure we didn't have to take off again."

"Roger," said Seerman.

Bullshit. They should have returned as soon as the storm finished. That was their duty. They'd stayed up in the sky because they were afraid, and it was a damn foolish thing to do. What if they'd rushed out of the Facility needing urgent medical attention?

"Is Kowalski with you?" Seerman said.

"Kowalski? No...he's with you, right?" came the response.

Caellyn and Seerman exchanged worried glances through their visors.

"He stayed behind by the entrance; he was having comms problems," said Seerman. "He was going to meet up with you when the storm subsided."

"Sir, we've been monitoring the entrance. No one's come out; we would have noticed."

Caellyn's heart sank. The radio silence felt like it went on forever.

"Just get down here," snapped Seerman.

"Yes sir."

After a few minutes, the craft appeared as a dot in the sky. It gracefully arced around, leaving behind it a light green vapour trail of sulphur rain that boiled off its wings as it lost altitude. It swung around them, down towards the end of the valley, before making a final descent along the valley floor, landing softly near their original touchdown point.

Caellyn and Seerman waited for what seemed like an age in the decompression and environmental chambers before they could finally take off their suits and enter the

Lander's habitation zones. When the final light shone green, Caellyn burst out of the suit, feeling her limbs light and free as they moved unaided. She wolfed down several glasses of cool water, her body craving the liquid as she felt it spread across her body and rehydrate dry sinews.

Seerman came down hard on Arundel and Yakun for not returning. He gave them a tongue lashing and then checked the sensor history, looking exasperated as it confirmed Kowalski never came out. The colonel disappeared into the communications room as Caellyn went for a shower. The water stung bruised body parts, and gave her a brief shock as the dried blood on her temple came off on her hands. She ran the med-scan over it and put on comfortable clothes before heading back out.

Yakun and Arundel were looking shell-shocked and sheepish around the main circular table. But Caellyn's anger had receded, feeling a little pity for them after Seerman's dressing down. It wasn't something they were likely to do again. But she held on to an air of indignation.

"What's it like in there?" asked Arundel.

"Dark, quiet," Caellyn replied.

Yakun passed Caellyn a coffee, either sensing she desperately needed it or simply trying to make a peace offering, and they sat in silence for a while, Caellyn occasionally drip-feeding the details of the past few days when she could muster the energy, as their brains tried to form themselves around the situation. She told them of the keypad by the buttress check-points and Yakun perked up, fascinated, and looking incredulous that they didn't push one of the buttons. She told them of the Mural, and the half-alive drone. She described the hanging orbs, their thirty-degree surface temperature as they were stuck in their thermodynamic pocket, and described herself being pulled into the machine. Yakun hung on her every word, and looked ready to head in there himself. She mentioned how they had to leave Kowalski. She struggled to say the words, dreading their condescending judgement.

But to her surprise, Yakun even came out and said they'd done the right thing. "Even if you could have shared power, which the klumps who designed them didn't factor for, although a power transfer would be an additional risk I suppose, anyway, you'd just all be wasting time there and all running out of . . ." He trailed off, realising what he was saying.

Caellyn decided not to mention the side passage that appeared out of nowhere. Or the darkened branch on the reactor hall floor. Some things wouldn't be helpful if shared.

Seerman returned, bringing with him an old bottle of scotch, the label crisp and broken. It must have been several hundred years old. He sat down and ran his thumb over the label, before laying out four small drinking cups. He twisted off the seized-on cap with force that required his whole torso, and poured out equal measures. Even without tasting it they could sense its potency in the air.

"I think we've got to accept that Kowalski has died," said Seerman sombrely, clasping the cup and staring at the table. "Wherever he is, his power would have run out by now."

"But there's technology in there right?" Arundel responded. "Maybe he found a way to keep himself powered?"

"Other than the Star-Sphere," said Caellyn, "We saw no other indications of power. And even if he did find some, he wouldn't be able to interface with it to power an Earth-made environmental suit."

"It's possible but unlikely, Arundel," said Seerman. "Caellyn's right I'm afraid. Here's to Kowalski, may his soul find some peace."

"And find a way off this planet," said Yakun, as they all raised their cups and drank. It was the most flavoursome liquid Caellyn had ever drunk. It hit every tastebud with a sledgehammer and left fire down her throat. It tried to break through the dam of emotion she'd been holding back, but she managed to hold herself together just enough to keep those emotions at bay.

"I've been in contact with Earth. Tomorrow we head back into the Facility and bring out a Star-Sphere globe, we're to take it up to the *Molniya-V* so we can study it without having to withstand this atmosphere," said Seerman, with an equal level of solemnity. "We're all going in. Two isn't enough, in case something goes wrong, and we aren't to leave anyone else alone, Earth order. We stay together from this point on."

His order was met with silence, as if they all agreed. No one wanted to be left alone at this point. But perhaps more than that, they all knew that no one could quite be trusted to stay on the ship and not make the decision to leave.

"This is crazy," said Arundel

"It doesn't matter," said Caellyn. "We've been in and out, and can move the Star-Spheres. We can get one out, that's all that matters now."

"Roger," said Seerman, as he got up and capped the scotch, taking it back to his bunk luggage. Maybe they'd drink the rest on the way home. "Yakun, prepare four suits for the next day-cycle."

Chapter 13

Aldai's watch buzzed lightly, waking him from his sleep. He lifted himself up, the SeaPort cell-block dimly illuminated from the hang-light that was restrung for morning preparations. His arm was numb from sleeping on the hard bunk of the cell, and his leg itched from sea water, his trousers still damp from the day before. Nothing dries quickly in the SeaPort, unless you bathe it in the inviting glow of an infra-red heat lamp. Every SeaPort cabin has one, and every person gets mildly addicted to it during their two-year assignment, if only because it keeps away the rashes and infections.

As he put on his boots, his eye caught a square object on the floor under the bunk. He picked it up to find it was a wallet. He checked it through, finding nothing but gnarled leather, and smiled to himself at the thought of its long-lost owner. It looked old, like it belonged in a museum, and he stuffed it in a side pocket, deciding it would be a good present for Wes's son. A five-year-old boy would no doubt relish a keepsake that used to be owned by an ancient hardened criminal, found in the Outer Reaches cell-block.

Qualtum was fully packed and prepared, looking like he'd been up all night without losing an ounce of his zeal.

"We've got intel to back up what we heard yesterday," he said to the small huddle of Special Ops. "One of the sensors went dark around the warehouse. That means either the conditions took it down or the Gaunt-men did. Either way, that's where we headed."

His voice focussed their minds, engaging military preparedness. Nothing wakes you up like being reminded you might end the day pulling the trigger.

"Let's roll out," Qualtum said. Halderford nodded at Aldai, who nodded back and took down the light, so that their world was once more lit only by the beams of torches.

They followed the tube corridors and bulkheads back to the tin can stage area. Qualtum took point again, applying the same precaution and rigid preparedness as the day before. He shot a full torch beam through the hastily opened bulkhead door before giving the all clear, and signalling for the others to follow. It was empty still, and they gave it one more brief survey before they continued towards the warehouse district.

The tunnels took them around a derelict power module that had broken away from the main structure and now lay on the sea bed. Its struts had disintegrated and crumpled many years before, leaving a series of broken tube corridors that once connected to it. The structure around them groaned more than usual as ocean currents washed over the severed arms, and they moved on cautiously until Qualtum stopped and indicated another dead-end bulkhead.

"Washed out," said Qualtum, shaking his head. Aldai walked up and shone his torch through the view slot. Sure enough, when you pressed your eyes against it, you could see the murky depths of water that had filled the passage ahead. "I'll find another route. We'll have to go around."

He checked his Sergeant's wrist-link, lost in concentration as he manipulated modules only visible through his visor. How Qualtum could make sense of direction, even with the augmented maps, was beyond Aldai. All the corridors looked the same. But he'd got them this far, and whatever route he chose, they'd follow closely or risk being lost in miles upon miles of the SeaPort labyrinth, that might take months to traverse before they found civilisation again. If they survived that long in the maze. Some of the tunnels smelled like previous residents hadn't been so lucky.

At one point, they climbed up a small ladder and crawled through a service duct that you could only get through on your elbows, with your legs sliding and grabbing for purchase in the low passageway, pushing your pack ahead of you. It was only then, with his head against the steel grating and the walls close by, that he realised how much life existed down here. Despite it being pitch black, there were hair-thin spiders, white as ghosts, that scuttled away behind pipes and through gaps in cladding, and Aldai's torch once caught the reflection of two tiny eyes peering out at him before their owner scuttled back into the shadows.

A few bulkheads down, they opened a door to find a rush of water pouring through. Instantly bracing themselves and reaching for their rebreathers, they all waited patiently to see if the water level stabilised, finding relief that it did.

"Water, water, everywhere...." sang Bekka quietly. "But not a pumping robot in sight."

They waded through it before finding themselves at the entrance of the warehouse district. They passed through to be met by a surprising sight. Inside was a double-height chamber covered in old, ornate metalwork. As the metal twisted and interleaved, it created the impression of trees and vines curling over themselves, and in the middle of the room the structure reached out to support what must have been a sign. It was embossed at the sides, but its central section was bare, flat sheet, its message worn away long before, and only a few flecks of paint remained.

"What is this place?" he heard Jones say, just behind him, quiet enough to be barely audible but loud enough to echo Aldai's thoughts. It reminded Aldai of an old Victorian library he'd seen in a history book back in school, that he tried to read with the utmost teenage brevity so that he could leave class and head to Slamball practice.

"It's beautiful," Tiernan replied just above a whisper. "It must have all been painted back in its heyday; can you imagine that?"

He stood looking around it, running his torch over the shaped metal of the balcony that ran around the upper section of the room, as complex shadows danced behind. It made a stark difference to the functional design of the StratoPort. There, ornate craftsmanship had been a secondary factor behind the need for cable routes and rapid manufacturing.

The entrance room, with the standard rounded corners for pressure bracing, gave way to another circular tube corridor that split either way in a T-junction. Qualtum motioned to enter quart-stealth, and they dimmed their lights and softened their steps, as much as you could on metal grating that creaked as it felt the unusual weight of people passing overhead.

They split into two teams, Aldai, Qualtum and Tiernan taking the right passage and the other four taking the left. As Qualtum led them around, they passed into a section where the walls changed consistency. Instead of being metal they were plastic, and the air felt cooler and less humid. They followed the corridor and found it had many offshoots to small cupboard-sized rooms. Each was packed to the ceiling with small containers arranged across the wall in a gridded frame. Tiernan looked as if he wanted to stop and investigate every single one, and Aldai couldn't help but feel the same. He couldn't deny his own inquisitiveness at what was stored here in such conditions. But Qualtum showed none of it, and was pushing on ahead. Tiernan turned to Aldai and raised his eyebrows with a slight shake of the head in amazement at what was around them, his wrinkled face showing placid astonishment even through the camo paint.

Qualtum signalled to turn off torch light, and they switched to night vision. Through the grainy haze of green, they passed through an open bulkhead and into the first cavernous warehouse.

It was a huge space several stories tall and about a hundred metres in length. It was full of crates roughly scattered, some taller than head height but most small and box-shaped, stacked to shoulder height, in a loose arrangement that left winding paths across its extent. The water was a few inches deep across the floor, and some of the sides of the crates had rotted or fallen away, their contents strewn out, providing hidden obstacles as Tiernan, Aldai and Qualtum moved their feet carefully to avoid the splashes of disturbed water.

Aldai felt a deep curiosity about the contents of the boxes, but it was difficult to make out what they were through the night vision. One box, it's side nowhere to be seen, looked packed full of figurines, while another, its entire structure almost disintegrated, contained a tangle of ornate sticks.

Aldai kept an eye across the tops of the boxes as they walked, ready to respond to any sign of movement. He occasionally paused and switched to thermal cam, but was just met by a wall of monochrome dark blue as everything hid behind ambient temperatures. Qualtum signalled to stop, and they crouched down behind some crates as he manipulated his wrist-interface.

"I'm not picking up any heat signatures in this hall," he said, and Aldai and Tiernan agreed. "Let's head to the next one."

The map was something Aldai dearly wanted to see at that point. Not for the mission, but in order to get a sense of the size of this place. It was uncharted territory, at least as far as your average person knew, and didn't appear on the public wall maps dotted around the main chamber. It just seemed to go on and on. If it wasn't frequented by Gaunts, then it should have been treated like an excavation.

Towards the back of the first warehouse the crates were thin and tall, and one looked as if it had recently fallen away from its contents to reveal a human figure. Aldai did a double take, switching to thermal but registering no heat. As they moved around it, the night vision picked up on its various surfaces and it appeared to be a sculpture of a woman holding a baby. It looked religious in nature, as if it had once taken prominent place in a cathedral, worshiped by thousands and surrounded by choristers and organ music, and now it stood unprotected in a dark warehouse under the sea.

They climbed a set of stairs to a gantry that overhung the rounded corners where the wall met the floor, and passed through a door into a short passage connecting the two warehouses together. The second warehouse was of similar size to the first, this time full of similar-sized rectangular containers on the right, four feet high and twelve feet long, that created a regular criss-crossed set of walkways and long alleyways down to the far end. To the left, taller containers hid their interspersed walkways from view. The floor was dry in this one, with the preserved artifacts finding fortune compared to their damp neighbours in the warehouse before. Aldai scoured the room in thermal mode, but again it was just monochrome blue.

Qualtum gestured to move through the taller boxes on the left, before stopping, his body rigid and still.

"Scout 2 has registered targets," said Qualtum. "Follow intercept, warehouse through left wall," he said, motioning them towards it, knowing they'd be right behind. They moved quickly, sacrificing a level of stealth in order to weave their way around boxes to join up with Halderford's team. They passed through the connecting tube and found themselves on a gantry overlooking another warehouse with the same layout as the one they'd just exited, with a grid of smaller boxes in front of them, and larger boxes against the far wall.

There was light coming from the far corner, enough to blind the night vision, so Aldai switched to thermal, seeing two groups, one where the lights were, and another that must have been Halderford's team, moving through the boxes towards them. He could hear the faint sound of voices over the distance, as Qualtum led them as quietly as possible, hunched over, through the grid, approaching from the side as Halderford's team closed in on the Gaunts' position.

As they neared the middle, they heard Halderford's voice as he engaged, followed by a series of frightened screams as the Gaunts reeled from their discovery.

Qualtum motioned to keep eyes peeled around them as they stopped in their tracks and searched the warehouse for ambush before heading towards the commotion, checking each long alleyway as they moved from grid section to grid section in case there were Gaunts crouched among them. But there was something about the noise up ahead, it wasn't the voices that Aldai was expecting. Some of the voices didn't sound like the angry, hoarse man that Aldai had seen the week before.

"There are women and children," came Halderford's voice through the comms.

"Roger," said Qualtum. "Kill-order."

Aldai was taken aback. His heart froze as he heard Qualtum say the words so calmly. This wasn't the fight he was expecting. He was trained to kill; it had been drummed into them during training. But he'd never actually had to do it, and he was damned that the first time he'd take a life would be from unarmed families. Even if they were half-human genetic mutants, the result of barbarous experiments, there was enough humanity in their eyes and the screams of the children for it to feel wholly wrong. Halderford must have shared his sentiment because there was no ringing out of shots, just the sound of people shouting and pleading. Qualtum cursed, and went to double down on his hunched speed, but Aldai grabbed one of his broad shoulders and spun him against the side of a container, causing him to lose his footing as they crashed onto the floor to a clatter of metal grating.

"Sir, you can't be serious," he shouted. "Are you sure..." but Qualtum steadied himself and launched back, his weight overpowering Aldai and pushing him against the crate behind him.

"I've got my orders, you follow yours," he said, finally making eye contact with Aldai, his beady eyes carrying zeal and anger. Aldai met his gaze with resignation, as they heard the commotion getting louder up ahead, Halderford shouting over the cries of the Gaunts as he tried to wrest control of the situation. Tiernan stood behind them, a model of military professionalism, as he aimed his rifle in the darkness for cover, while Qualtum pushed into Aldai's chest again and made towards the Gaunts.

Before he could even get fully to his feet a clunk landed not too far from Aldai, and a flash bomb went off. Carbine needles zipped overheard, and he heard a blood-curdling wail as Tiernan collapsed limply to the floor next to them.

"Tiernan!" he heard himself shout as he shut out the pain and focussed on staying alive. There was gunfire all around, echoing off the warehouse walls to create an almighty din. Needles zipped over their position crouched behind boxes, and it sounded like Halderford's team was engaged in a firefight too. His senses swam as he tried to regain composure, his eyes refocussing from the flash bomb. His visor had compensated out the worst of it, but it still shocked his system.

Qualtum slammed a device onto the floor and a red flare shot up into the air. Spinning like a Catherine wheel, it hovered at its vertical extent and illuminated the entire scene in an ungodly red glow. He motioned to Aldai the direction of the ambushing assailants behind them, and fired some covering needles in that direction. Supporting Halderford would have to wait; they had their own problems to deal with. Aldai braced against a crate, spotting a Gaunt duck for cover near the entrance where they came in. He held his position and waited for a body to peek above a box. Seeing a flash of movement, he trained a shot on it, and a puff of fluid spurted in the red light as his carbine needle punctured skull.

They heard a cry from the ambushing Gaunts and saw shadowy figures retreating across the warehouse. Aldai fired more covering needles, fizzing through the air, and Qualtum moved up a few boxes. The Sergeant then took point as they advanced across the warehouse. They moved forward in tandem, one box at a time, catching red-tinged glimpses of the escaping Gaunts, until Aldai braced against the side of a crate and Qualtum joined him.

"They just split," Qualtum said. "One's heading to the back of this warehouse, the others heading to the one we just came from. You take that one. I'll drop the flare. Switch to night and engage." He keyed something into his watch that caused the spinning flare to immediately go dark and all light in the area to cease. Aldai switched to night vision and pounced towards the Gaunt's position, seeing him stagger as he climbed up the stairs to the exit gantry, blinded as the lights went out. Aldai fired a carbine that looked to strike the Gaunt's leg, as he let out of howl of pain before disappearing into the connecting tube.

Like the Gaunt before, he was ungainly in his movement and unnaturally fast considering his skittish gait, but Aldai was in no mood to let another one get away. He followed suit, climbing the gantry and passing through into the neighbouring warehouse.

Now Aldai was the apex hunter. He switched to thermal, seeing the trail of warm blood on the floor. It led to a faint glow around the side of one of the tall crates, down one of the alleyways of the grid. He watched the Gaunt move and shadowed him, taking control of the chase. As the Gaunt cut left, so did Aldai. As the Gaunt retreated a grid space, Aldai closed in. He watched as the Gaunt lunged to the side and fired some needles towards him, but he'd already braced against the side of a crate. He could hear the Gaunt's heavy breathing, its leg wound exacerbating its rattle-breath. He was working the Gaunt towards the corner, and as they closed in, he threw his own flash bomb to the side, on the Gaunt's only escape route, and it worked. Aldai watching it flounder into the corner and a dead-end between containers.

He braced against the crate wall next to the stub of a corridor.

"You're cornered," he said, before remembering the kill-order and cursing. Killing in a firefight is easy. Killing someone trapped down a dead-end was a more unwelcome move, and now he was faced with it. Killing without questions was not how Team-6 worked. But he knew he shouldn't be trying to talk to it, to bargain or reason. He should be pivoting around and firing more needles through its skull. The Gaunt stayed quiet as it breathed heavily and let out a rasped cough.

Then Aldai's pain caught up with him. He remembered Tiernan's lifeless body lying prostrate on the floor of the other warehouse. He thought of Bekka and Halderford in the other group, finding a sudden pang of fear that they may no longer be alive. The Gaunt rang a shot out towards his location, and that was all he needed. Anger descended on him and he rounded the corner, shot the Gaunt in its gun arm, one in its side, and covered the distance to the reeling corpse so that he was standing over it with his gun pointed down at his head.

"Give me one good reason not to pull this trigger." Aldai's trigger finger wavered and resisted pulling the final blow. The Gaunt looked weak and frail, staring up with a strained face, trying to hold some resolution against the barrel of the gun.

"Mercy?" said the Gaunt, wheezing as his side bled and his lungs struggled. "The others would have killed me already. You don't know who we are do you? What did they tell you? Mutants? Aliens?"

"What does it matter?" Aldai replied, letting the man talk. "You're trying to bring down the StratoPort. You're trying to end humanity."

"End humanity?" said the Gaunt, his voice trailing off. "We are humanity. It is *you* that destroyed *us*, you floated up in your castle while everyone else choked under the clouds."

Aldai was left speechless, his mind racing against the thoughts. Could this half-human really be a descendant? Could it have survived all this time, with the sun blocked out and the global storm punishing the surface? He didn't believe it; he didn't want to believe it. The Gaunt tried to reach towards his gun, but his leg wound had made it too painful to move, and he simply winced and coughed blood.

A shot rang out in the distance, briefly startling Aldai, before he refocused on the Gaunt.

"What are you talking about?" he said, losing his authority as his moral footing became less secure.

"You really don't know, do you?" said the Gaunt, sensing Aldai's hesitancy. "We survived. We survived while you just left us behind up in your flying Port. You don't deserve your freedom, your sunlight," he said. "There aren't many of us left. We survive in underground shelters, eating scarce food and dying in our hundreds. The storm takes us, the earth takes us, and every generation we get weaker. And you don't even know."

"It's not possible," Aldai said. "Nothing can live on the surface."

He'd heard it a million times. They'd grown up with tales of how the storms had rendered the surface uninhabitable. Travel to the surface had been blacklisted. You couldn't even land a craft these days. But he'd never seen it for himself. Was the Gaunt lying, or had the StratoPort been living under its own lie? He thought of Orcanciz, hoarding secrets, giving kill-orders to subordinates with rifles, to execute blindly without being given the knowledge to apply moral judgement.

"It's too late anyway," said the Gaunt. "We have people on the StratoPort right now, with enough explosives to bring it to the ground. It's too late for us, and it's too late for you. We're the same, you and I," he said, before putting all remaining energy into leaning over towards his gun. His hand strained as it clasped the gun handle, leaving Aldai no choice. Aldai pulled the trigger, putting a carbine sliver through the Gaunt's skull to a light splatter of blood on the wall behind. The Gaunt's body went limp, sagging down, as the crumpled needle tinkled on the floor behind.

Aldai stared at the body, taking in the sallow cheeks and withdrawn eyes, unsure what to believe. He couldn't help but feel pity, but whatever the truth was, it would have to wait. Jesus! Taking down the StratoPort. If the StratoPort came down.... well, all that was left was a lifetime down here, or no life at all.

Aldai searched the body, finding only a hand-drawn map and a knife, before hearing approaching footsteps. He whistled out and heard the same tune repeated back.

 Qualtum appeared beside him. He looked like he was about to give Aldai an almighty dressing down, but then he saw the dead Gaunt and simply glared at Aldai before motioning to follow.

The other warehouse was quiet, the gunfire having ceased. They returned to it to find the four remaining members of Team-2 over Tiernan's body, Bekka and Rongal holding watch with rifles poised in case of further attacks. A jacket covered Tiernan's face, and Halderford and Jones were fashioning a makeshift stretcher out of the slats of the neighbouring crate, despite Halderford's arm appearing blood-soaked in the torchlight.

"Report," said Qualtum to Halderford.

"We killed two, the rest got away. Went through a hatch, somehow managed to jam it shut."

"There's a team on the StratoPort," Aldai said. "They're about to blow the whole thing up."

Qualtum eyed him with suspicion. Aldai winced; he had just revealed he talked to the Gaunt instead of dispatching him without a word. He had showed some mercy in the warehouse rather than follow heartless kill-orders. *I did the right thing. Qualtum can rail at me all he wants.*

"Roger, we have to get up there asap." The Sergeant let it go, reserving his judgement for another time.

Chapter 14

Team-6 left the warehouses and headed back to the sub-dock, hampered by the grim burden of Tiernan's body. Jones and Rongal carried him on the makeshift stretcher, his unmoving old face hidden from view in a tightly wrapped tarpaulin that secured him to the crate wood. It was an unceremonious funeral march, through damp SeaPort tubes, for a Special Ops lifer. Somehow they all knew it would end like this for Tiernan. When you forego retirement, you are bound to die on your job. But they'd never let themselves fully follow that train of thought; it just felt like he would go on forever. It shouldn't have ended like this. Not in the SeaPort.

They stayed quiet and alert in case of further Gaunt ambush. They passed the tin-can Gaunt den, and their nerves settled as they found themselves closer to civilisation. But they still stayed quiet. No one quite had the words to say. There was no time to honour Tiernan right now, and no time to let the emotions boil into vapour. It wasn't the right place for it, either. They needed to get his body back up to the StratoPort, back under the sun, before they said words of remembrance and put his soul to rest.

They reached the cell-block and Qualtum called in to base using the communicator. "Seems there's some disturbances up there, maybe you were right," he said gruffly to Aldai after stashing the communicator back under the cell bed. "We're flying back up, asap." That was good news at least. Getting out of the SeaPort and back to the StratoPort was a sorely needed blessing.

They pushed on, past the deuterium mine, Qualtum urging all the pace they could muster, while Halderford played his opposite, positioning himself between Qualtum and Team-6 to protect them from the officer's exasperated backwards glares. Tiernan deserved the greatest of respect, not to be rushed and bungled through hatch after hatch. They all knew the score and the imminent threat above in the StratoPort. They moved quickly but carefully, as if Tiernan's spirit was still alongside them, watching them to ensure his body made it back to civilisation.

As they neared the centre of the SeaPort, the tube corridors became larger again and lit by the blinking strip lights. Qualtum stretched further ahead, taking Bekka with him to run interference. It was mid-morning by now, so most civilians would be halfway through their first shift of the day, but there would still be people scurrying about, and it was in no one's interest to see a group of Special Ops carrying a dead body back from the Outer Reaches.

Aldai caught sight of a woman up ahead, wearing the dark grey SeaPort communications uniform. She looked surprised as Bekka skewered her into a side corridor to keep the following train hidden from view. Aldai smiled. When Bekka was in operations mode she was a force to be reckoned with, and you wouldn't want to find yourself on the wrong end of her tightly focussed wrath.

A med team were waiting in the SeaPort Special Ops centre when they arrived, ready to take Tiernan's body. It took some persuading for Team-6 to relinquish it, Jones even saying he'd carry it up himself on his shoulders, but in the end they relented. The med team assured them Tiernan would be up on the next scheduled flight, and so Team-6 were forced to say solemn goodbyes. Aldai nearly choked as they peeled back the tarpaulin for one last time. This was one mission Tiernan would have to sit out. He'd been there from the start, ever since Aldai joined Special Ops. A mission without him would feel incomplete, like losing an arm, and all that were left were memories and phantom sensations.

They repacked their equipment from the lockers and wiped off the camo face paint before departing to the sub dock. The sub whirred its propellers, pushing design limits so that the small craft shook as it zipped through the dark sea to arrive back into the bustle of the SeaPort drop hangar.

Their drop-ship was just finishing its final preparations, hissing and steaming as it stood ready beneath its silo tube. Team-6 made their way to the waiting room, where they were caught by the questioning glare of workmen who wondered why they had been called in for an unscheduled rocket lift. But they looked away just as fast. Sometimes it wasn't worth risking a comfortable life to ask questions you didn't need to know the answers to.

Aldai waited until the door of the waiting area was closed before saying something had been growing in his mind.

"They're us. They're humans," he said, in a low angry tone.

"Careful what you say," said Halderford, watching him intently. Qualtum was fixing him with a stare that suggested he might explode at any moment.

"The government lied to us, the Gaunts aren't modified, they aren't experiments, they're just the people we left behind," Aldai carried on.

"You trust them?" interrupted Qualtum, angry and spitting, standing up as the team sat around in a circle. "What about your dead comrade? I've had to bury three of my team in the last year to these animals," he said, his body unmoving but rigid with tension. "You believe what a desperate man tells you. That's exactly what they want you to believe. That's how they recruit sympathisers." He eyed up the rest of the team as if challenging anyone to defy him.

Aldai's head swirled in mixed messages. Goddamnit. He'd killed two of them. Two lives extinguished. The face of the second was prominent in his thoughts. Whatever they were, it was a life. He'd shot one dead at point blank range. He'd never killed anything before, and now he'd had the displeasure of watching eyes go blank and blood splatter out of skulls. It revolted him. The whole thing revolted him. And what about those women and children screaming? Maybe he'd killed a father, or a grandfather. And he didn't even know what they were. Maybe they were just animals, maybe they were just single-minded Gaunts trying to destroy the last sanctuaries. But nothing deserved to live in the Outer Reaches, treated like vermin and cast aside as outsiders.

He found himself standing up too, squaring off against Qualtum. "You didn't even try and reason with them did you? It was always going to be a slaughter. What if they are humans? What then?" Qualtum moved forwards, head to head. He was a few inches shorter than Aldai but no less fierce. Aldai was broad, but Qualtum carried a bulk of muscle that said he'd give him a run for his money.

"As far as I remember," Qualtum hissed. "They fired on us first, and they tried to slaughter *us* first. And need I remind you, they're currently trying to slaughter the StratoPort." Aldai held his stance against the bristling Sergeant, feeling the prickle of adrenaline across his body as it readied itself for a fight. "You want me to drop you off on the surface?" Qualtum continued, as if hammering home the point. "You want to see if you could survive out there? On what? With what? Don't be fooled, Aldai."

Halderford stood, his voice slow and methodical. "When we recover the sphere from Venus," he said. "And reverse the climate, then we can deal with what we find on the surface. Right now, we have to deal with the present, and right now in the present we have to stop the destruction of the StratoPort. It doesn't matter who's trying to destroy it, or what their motives are, we simply have to defend it."

That was something that Aldai couldn't argue with. Crak, Halderford irritated him sometimes. He wasn't even allowing Aldai to be angry. Aldai had just wanted to rile someone up and get them bogged down in an argument. His twisting, rolling thoughts just needed to grapple with someone else, and Qualtum was a powder keg that would blow out and channel some anger. He sat back down as Qualtum held his rigid pose, watching him back off with the malice of authority.

Rongal twisted in his seat uncomfortably. "They took Tiernan, man," he said, unable to contain his emotion. "Goddamnit.... god damn it."

"They'll take any one of you if you give them half a chance," Qualtum interjected, taking a seat himself and keeping his eyes trained on Aldai.

Jones had been studying his rifle, as if trying to pretend that the conversation wasn't going on around him. He was counting his rounds meticulously, and then counting them again, before checking the remaining clips around his waist. The eager young soldier desperate to see violent action had dulled, like a sword rusted in blood. Maybe he'd killed one too, in Halderford's firefight in the warehouse, but it wasn't something they'd ever talk about. "It always seemed strange to me," he said, cutting through the tension with a philosophical tone, that surprised everyone. "When we read about the raising of the StratoPort and the failed attempt to reshape the atmosphere. You never heard about what happened to the people. I mean, Jesus, they must have all died when the Acceleration Event scoured the surface. But you just never read about it. It's like they've been wiped from history."

"What do you want to read?" said Rongal, trying to hold back tears. "I know one thing; these aren't human. They're genetically-altered aberrations. I mean, the surface is blacklisted to humans. How could they live there unless they had their mutated genes? They're doomed anyway. You heard Orcanciz. They're running out of generations, and now they're just taking ours. God help us. They need to be stopped, for Tiernan's sake."

"It's a bloody shit show," said Jones, leaning back in anguish. "I mean they don't deserve it, right? We need to put them down like..." he said, stopping mid-sentence as if he was rethinking a poor choice of words. "We need to put them down. But you know who I'd like to put down most of all? Albater.. whatever his name was, the scientist who created them. If I saw him I'd put a needle through his head no questions asked. But it's just strange, when I look at the Gaunts, they just, I don't know, make you think about what we left below the clouds all those years ago."

Qualtum was still watching them all, as if waiting to pounce on anyone that was looking to rock the boat.

"Well, you know what, the StratoPort isn't much," Rongal replied. "But its home, and it needs to stay in the air. And there's no reasoning with genetic mutants that just want to destroy. You talked to one, Aldai? What do you think?"

The question took Aldai aback, his thoughts still swirling with scorn and indecision. But he couldn't disagree with Rongal.

"There was no reasoning, just diatribe. Just anger," he replied.

"There you go," said Rongal. "Let's put a stop to their destruction."

Aldai didn't know what to think. There were times in his life he wanted to bring the StratoPort down himself. When the train wobbled on the tracks, you saw it for what it was. There were brief times when he actually saw it as a bloated monstrosity, an undeserved sanctuary. But then he'd get swept along in life, and those feelings would pass. He thought of the good things. Sam, Wes, even his mother. He fumbled in his bag and found the wallet from the cell-block. He thought of Wes's son's excited face as he stared at the keepsake of an ancient criminal. There was new life up there. Maybe he'd get a permit and have kids of his own. Maybe Venus would succeed and he could have a family on the dusty green hills of Andalucía.

The workmen finished their preparations, clearing the hangar floor, and the concierge came into the room and signalled it was time to leave. Team-6 crossed the gantries, stepping over the pumping robot that was still trying to keep the walkways dry, and passed into the drop-ship.

Aldai stowed his bags and sat, locking in the shoulder brace. It took a few attempts to jam into the receiver, its aged clasp worn down from too many missions. This ship was older than the one they came down in, and the inside walls were faded and the floor panels were mis-matched where some had been replaced. It didn't exactly fill you with confidence as you sat on a volatile mixture of rocket fuel, but you didn't exactly have a choice.

The drop pilots came in, looking a similar vintage to the ship itself, as they wore leather flight caps like dogfighting mavericks. "Sirs," the pilot said respectfully. He climbed up to the gimballed flight chairs, closely followed by the co-pilot, and the whirring and clunking of the ship started.

The overhead silo doors open, causing a shower of water to cascade around the viewports, and the platform slowly started to raise them upwards. It lifted them through the hangar until the viewports saw nothing but close metal walls of the silo tube that extended from the hangar roof to the surface of the sea. The silo doors closed, and above them the larger storm doors opened to a groan of weather-splashed metal bearings. They heard the noise of the storm, and the swirling as air currents licked around the hull. Aldai leaned inwards, peering through the pilot's view ports above them, trying to catch a glimpse of the faint disc of the top of the Rift. But it was obscured from view at this depth, and all you could see was darkness.

Still, they were on their way back up into the upper atmosphere. It filled Aldai with a sense of joy. The SeaPort was getting to him. They'd only been down for a day, but he found it oppressive. It played on the mind and clouded the judgement. It changed thought patterns and diverted his conscience. Right then, all he wanted was to be up on the StratoPort again, running standard assignments, patrolling some boring part of the Port and watching Slamball. It didn't even matter who was playing, he just wanted to be in the stands watching forwards twist past defenders and smash goals into the backboard to the ecstasy of the crowd.

The launch platform clunked into its final position, and the drop-ship stood resolutely exposed to the base of the Rift. It rocked slightly as it steadied itself, and there was the light splatter of rain that tapped on the hull. Then the rockets flared, and they were surrounded by white vapour as the ship lurched off the platform and into the air. It juddered with uncomfortable vibrations, occasionally buffeted, pressing them into their seats, so that all they could do was tense every muscle against the G-forces.

They ascended quickly and started to see light come through the windows. It was faint at first, getting brighter until you could lean forwards and see the sky through the upper Rift. Aldai stared out of the pilot's cabin viewports, entranced as the disc grew larger and larger. The first rays shone through the craft as they neared the top of the storms. It nourished the soul like nothing else.

Then Aldai saw a streak across the sky ahead of them. It was a craft, but it was trailing black smoke. It arced around until it was blocked from his view. He heard the pilot's worried exchange above them, and craned his neck to see through side ports. Bekka had seen it too, and gave him a worried glance, as they suddenly heard the rattle of gunfire, saw flashes of tracer bullets fly past the windows and heard a zipping thud from below them.

"Punctured main cargo," said the pilot, his exasperated voice audible over the din. "I think they're coming around for another pass." The shuttle jinked to the side, their ascent slowed, as stomachs lurched and fingers gripped the bars on the shoulder braces.

"Drop into the Rift, use it as cover!" Qualtum roared up towards the pilots, and whether they heard him or not, Aldai felt the uncomfortable sensation as the rockets spluttered out, and gravity started to pull them down.

"Copy," came the pilot's voice through the speakers They saw the Rift walls reappear around them, before they felt the reassuring blast as the rockets refired into life, steadying their descent. Aldai glanced at Qualtum who looked like he wanted to get out of his seat and fight the other craft hand-to-hand. Rongal was throwing up, his head bowed. Bekka was pale as a sheet. Aldai looked up again, seeing the craft finish a high turn, bending downwards, its route marked by the black fumes it left behind as it came around for a second attack.

The punctuated shots of gunfire rang out again as their attacker opened another volley. Aldai closed his eyes and prayed to whatever god was listening. But as it started, it was followed by an almighty bang, and he looked up to see an explosion of black debris and the craft streaming past them. It passed unnervingly close, as the pilots skilfully fired side thrusters to jolt them sideways to avoid it.

Aldai caught a glimpse of the enemy ship through the side port. It was rusty and battered. It looked like one of the shuttles from the StratoPort, but corroded and worn. It had panels that were roughly welded onto it. It looked as if it had been made out of scrap. It swung past them, down into the Rift, and Aldai turned to see it crash into the Rift-wall, instantly whipped to the side and crumpled like a leaf in the strong side winds.

"Bloody suicide mission!" shouted the pilot through the speakers. "Who the hell would do that?"

The Special Ops remained resolutely quiet, neither offering an answer nor being able to speak after having their organs lurched inside out.

"He banked too hard; wing sheared as he pulled too much G. Not a good pilot, I'll say that. Bloody hell. He was about to shred us with that second pass. Whatever you are fighting, just make sure you win, I'm very partial to staying alive," he said, with the dogged humour only a pilot can find.

Aldai slowed his breathing, feeling some relief at still being alive, his legs and arms tingling at the unnatural sensations. *Give these pilots a damn medal. In fact, give Qualtum one too.* Well maybe that was a step too far. Qualtum had his head bowed, eyes closed, his normal bluster subsided.

The ship stabilised, listing on one side, before rising above the cloud wall again and slowly ascending towards the StratoPort. Aldai searched the remaining sky in case there were any further assailants, watching the station grow from a distant dot with eager anticipation.

The Port got larger and larger until you could see the details of the tangled mess of the Undercity, and Aldai finally allowed himself some relief when he spotted the landing lights designating the hangar. Their ascent slowed until they almost stopped. It felt like they were close enough to reach out and touch the neighbouring brackets and panels of the Port, the pilot showing immense skill to guide the ship in such close proximity. They heard the bolt-fire of the harpoon guns socketing into the receptors, and the drop-ship grappled onto the side and danced laterally as it was pulled into position beneath the vice clamp. The rockets still fired below them to maintain their constant altitude, and the pilot cabin viewports went dark as the nose engaged the heavy vice. A jolt rang through the ship as it was grabbed, and then a secondary one sounded below, making the floor feel a reassuring amount of solid. Then the rockets finally went quiet.

They waited patiently for the hangar outside the ship to repressurise before the belt clips of the shoulder restraints released. Aldai was the first to stand, bracing himself against the central pillar on wobbly legs, but he backed away to allow Qualtum to leave first, as a concierge finally opened the side hatch.

Chapter 15

Team-6 were met by a Special Ops staffer. He was a young man with a baby-like face who looked like he should still be in school.

"Sir!" he said to Qualtum, giving an exaggerated salute as Team-6 assembled on the hangar floor. "Teams have engaged around the Heart, stuck in firefights. We think they're targeting one of the Fusion Reactors," he shuffled nervously, moving his arms behind him then back to his sides. "They came out of nowhere. But we've just registered a ship piercing through the outer skin near the Concourse. We need you to head up there and intercept. There's a shuttle a few blocks up to take you to a hangar above it."

"Copy," said Qualtum, slinging off his pack and holstering spare ammo cartridges around his waist. The others did the same, rummaging around in bags and ripping essentials from them, like a pride of lions tending a fresh kill.

Qualtum motioned for them to head to the express elevator, and they left the beleaguered staffer to take care of the pile of heavy equipment. As the elevator doors closed, Aldai watched with amusement as the staffer unsuccessfully tried to lift a pack onto his back. The elevator smoothly engaged, but before it had even picked up speed it slowed and stopped at floor a few decks up, where a transport was waiting for the Special Ops.

"Back out so soon," Bekka muttered. Rongal looked like he would give anything to never leave the solid floor of the StratoPort again. *At least transports are more stable than the brute force rockets of the drop-ships.*

The transport lazily swung out into the midday sun before steadying itself and zipping up around the side of the StratoPort. As they flew past the outside of the Concourse, its large panoramic windows looking smaller from the outside compared to the giant bulk of the station, they saw another makeshift craft that had latched itself onto the side like a tick. Qualtum motioned to it out the transport window. It was gently smoking black fumes. It must have gripped the side and blown its own entrance hole.

They landed in a hanger and quickly took another elevator down two floors. Stopping between decks, they opened a hidden passage onto one of the high walkways near the Concourse ceiling. Aldai's legs, still getting used to solid ground from the trials of the drop-ship, reeled again at being precariously high over the shops, bars and restaurants below them, with only a wire strung along the sides of the gantry walkway to keep them from toppling over the side.

A small flock of birds buzzed around them. They looked angry, as if they were trying to shoo away intruders that shouldn't be walking around their private quarters up in the ceiling. Maybe they had nests nearby that they were defending.

One stopped on the safety wire, looking up at Aldai with an inquisitive expression. He couldn't help but feel the sparrow was trying to communicate with them. Maybe they could sense the danger their home was in, and were urging the Special Ops to defend it, or maybe they were trying to warn them, or guide them to their prey, like the birds that used to guide tribal hunters in Africa.

Aldai waved the bird away and stared down into the scene below. It was eerily quiet. The concourse should normally be bustling with people as they took lunch breaks or met up with friends. Without the stir it looked sterile and bland, like an architect's model before they added the embellishments that brought it to life.

"Need eyes on the targets," said Qualtum.

They all watched the forest of white and grey walls, trying to spot any movement that might indicate the Gaunts below. Aldai flicked to infra-red, seeing various groups of people huddled in shops and rooms.

"I see them," said Jones. "Moving past the fountain."

Aldai picked them out. It looked to be a group of about five, but it was difficult to tell as the tangle of walkways above them obscured their movements from view. They were heading towards the centre of the station, carrying large shields, and one looked to be carrying heavy equipment around its shoulders. Two others were stretchering a device. "Sun's wrath," he said. "I think they've got a bomb."

"Copy that," came Qualtum's response. "We've got confirmation from on the ground too. Split up, Halderford, take Jones and Rongal and shadow them, but keep a distance. Aldai, Bekka, you're with me, we'll try and flank them, cut them off."

Aldai still hadn't got used to taking commands from Qualtum. He followed the lead but it just didn't feel right. It should be Halderford orchestrating them. For so long they'd been a simple, well-oiled machine. Halderford knew them better than they knew themselves, and they moved like a single unit, expecting and anticipating every action. Qualtum cared nothing for that. He was simply pulling rank, presiding over a tenure of subordinates and directing them with cold orders.

Halderford, Jones and Rongal dropped on abseil lines to a platform below and made their way down the height of the Concourse to reach the floor, to follow the Gaunts like stalking wolves. Qualtum motioned Aldai and Bekka back to the elevator, taking it up, across and down to the side of the Concourse. The doors opened next to the entrances of the surplus rations warehouse whose heavy shutters were down like they were expecting a nuclear explosion.

"We'll try and cut them off by the Auckland food court," Qualtum said, leading them across open foyers towards the centre. An occasional set of frightened eyes peeked out from behind the entrance to an office, while along the ceilings red lights flashed all around, and large, red, block text scrolled across screens telling people to stay inside at all costs.

The cat was most definitely out of the bag. There was no way that Orcanciz could cover this one up. The Gaunts were walking through the main parts of the StratoPort in full view of the public. Whatever happened, things would change, thought Aldai. Maybe for the better. With less lies from the Government. Well, as long as the StratoPort didn't drop out of the sky. Aldai's stomach lurched at the thought of the whole station falling away from him.

"We think they're heading to a main vent line near the centre," came Halderford's voice through the comms. "But they've changed course, turned left. They've taken hostages: a man, woman and a boy."

"Shit," muttered Qualtum, before acknowledging. "We'll have to cut through Vaal district."

"Sir, those vent lines," said Bekka. "Grief, they run straight down the centre of the Port. It could rip through the whole station."

"Copy that," replied Qualtum gruffly.

"There's an amphitheatre next to them if I remember, sir," she continued. "We can cut by the pool."

Qualtum checked his wrist-pad, pulling up maps as they walked briskly onwards, then acknowledged Bekka with a nod and doubling down on speed. They shot through an office, workers cowering under their desks, and found themselves at the Auckland food court. The smell of food hit them as they dashed through it. The aromas, normally as bland as the grey and beige food that was served, actually smelled tantalising. Aldai realised he hadn't eaten a proper meal in twenty-four hours, just processed ration bars, and his stomach groaned. But it would have to wait; he'd come back and feast later.

They moved on, past the pool, it's water still, and arrived at the back of the amphitheatre. Its fan shape spread out from near the central column of the StratoPort. It had entrances either side, one next to its intermission foyer, opening onto the circular landing that ran around the central column of the Port, and another back entrance that led into the higher tiers of the auditorium. Qualtum led them past the empty ticket booths to find themselves at the top row of seats. Stairs ran down each side towards two exits either side of the central stage that was covered in props and scenery. It displayed an elaborate forest with a bench in the centre, set out ready for a play that evening.

"They've set up barricades at the central service column," came Halderford's voice through the comms.

"Copy, we're approaching through the theatre," Qualtum replied.

"You'll land right on top of them," Halderford replied. "We're to the side. They've brought cutting torches, and they're trying to burn through to the duct beyond. They've got guns to hostages' heads."

They followed the exits around the stage and made quietly across the wood-panelled foyer beyond, to where it opened out onto the landing area that surrounded the central column. They could hear the fizz and splutter of torches and raised voices coming from the Gaunts as they frantically tried to execute their plan. Bracing up against the side of the opening, Qualtum fixed a mirror to the front of his gun, peering around to get a view of the commotion beyond.

A voice rang out, hoarse and wispy, undeniably from a Gaunt. "If we see you move an inch, we'll execute these hostages."

They heard the woman cry, and the man try to comfort the child, until the dull thud of a gun butt quieted him. Qualtum ignored it, staring at his gun mirror as he counted, mouthing numbers, before turning to Aldai and Bekka and drawing the scene quickly on the floor.

He turned back to shout a response. "Let the family go and we can come to some arrangement." He fiddled with his wrist-interface.

A stone-cold lie, thought Aldai. Qualtum would execute the Gaunts given even the slimmest of chances.

"What could you even offer us, sunwalker?" came a different voice from the Gaunts, this one a little clearer, before its owner spluttered out a cough. The first voice could be heard chastising him for even engaging them in conversation.

"If we see even a glimmer of movement, we'll execute the hostages," the first voice rang out again. "And if we see more movement than that, we'll set off the bomb where it stands."

That sent a jolt through Aldai's stomach. They were desperate beyond compare. But he at least sensed an opening with the second one, who was entertaining dialogue. He exchanged glances with Qualtum, who looked like he was thinking the same thing. They needed to take out the first voice at least, and maybe the second could be reasoned with. Maybe. Qualtum looked away, deep in thought, before reaching for his ear as he listened for a message.

"Two approaching us from behind," he whispered, signalling Aldai and Bekka to head back into the theatre and engage. *Goddamn, how many are there crawling over the Port?*

They moved back across the intermission foyer and Aldai poked his head around into the amphitheatre, spotting movement up by the back rows. Shots whizzed past his head as he swung back behind cover, and carbine needles dug into the wall opposite. Their grouping was sporadic, lacking accuracy. At least they weren't good shots, Aldai thought as his heart ran double time. He signalled Bekka, before lunging out and firing cover shots in their direction and diving down behind the front row, moving across the front of the stage towards the stairs on the far side. Bekka followed, firing her own shots and crouching down at the near-side end seat.

They heard rattled breathing from the top tiers, but it was difficult to focus on compared to the commotion that was building behind them. Back at the central landing, Qualtum's voice rang out against rasping threats from the Gaunts. And then gunfire. A firefight had broken out, and they heard the wailed screams of the mother and son.

Shit, they executed the man. Then the screams stopped, and all that rang out was the firing of rifles.

Incensed, his adrenaline flowing, Aldai caught Bekka's eye as they hunched down at opposite ends of row A, and signalled her to provide cover as he made his way up the stairs. Bekka's carbine spluttered out needles towards the higher seats, and Aldai made his move, bounding up the steps in a crouched position, stopping just before the top. The Gaunts hadn't seen him, and he caught a glimpse of them through the chairs as they both jumped upwards, firing down on Bekka's position, one of them getting caught in Bekka's fire and reeling backwards. It screamed in agony, and that was all the distraction Aldai needed. He rounded the end seats.

One Gaunt was clutching its face and convulsing on the floor. The other was standing and firing down at Bekka. It turned, noticing him too late, and Aldai fired indiscriminate needles through its head and upper torso. It fell limply on the floor, where the other one had gone quiet. Aldai pumped needles into the second one's back just to make sure. Another two notches on his tally. He'd deal with the emotions later.

Bekka. He bounded down the stairs, a dread taking over that she might have got hit in the return fire, and finding relief as she heard him coming, and her head popped up, meeting him with a face framed in the light from the theatre lamps above. His heart pumped back into life.

Then a bang knocked them both staggering. And another, almost flooring Aldai.

The air sucked out away from them, as they were hit by a forceful pressure wave. Depressurisation? No, the pressure had returned, as his hearing rang like a bell. The bomb? No, they were still alive, and they weren't falling as gravity took them. It was a grenade of some sort, not military issue; they were far more directed. This was crude and rough. He regained his senses, Bekka shaking her head as if to rattle her brain back into position, and they ran back into the foyer.

Qualtum's bloodied corpse was lying where they'd left him. He'd taken the full blast of the grenade, and it had split him open. But there was only one blast mark. The other must have been Halderford's team. The rifle fire had gone quiet, punctuated by only the occasional single shot.

He didn't even think, he simply threw the smoke bomb onto the Gaunt's location, hearing it instantly hiss out its dense grey gas. He flicked on infra-red in his visor and moved out of cover. There were two Gaunts left. He dropped one with needle fire, as the other dived down behind a makeshift shield. He advanced purposefully, hearing Bekka moving beside him.

"I'm holding a kill-switch, you kill me and the whole station goes down," came a voice through the gas. "You're standing next to a device that'll rip a hole in the side of the station wherever it goes off." There was a spluttering cough. It was the second voice, the one that had dared to ask what Qualtum could offer. There was a chance, at least.

"You don't have to do this," said Aldai, his finger poised on the trigger as the smoke cleared, so that he caught a glimpse of his prey, crouched up against a buttress jutting out of the curved central column, nestled in behind a plate barricade. He was holding a gun in one hand and a kill-switch in the other. Across his chest was a vest that also looked like a heart monitor. Crak, they were serious.

The Gaunt glared at them through the corner of his eyes as he pressed the side of his head up against the buttress. "It's too late, there's no going back."

"There's always another way," said Bekka. "There's always something that can be done."

The Gaunt shook his head slowly. "Do you know how many lives of suffering you caused, and what it's like to live in those conditions? I'd give a thousand lifetimes to live just one under the sun, and I'd take a thousand lives to make you pay for what you've done." It sounded laboured, like he was reciting someone else's dogma.

There was an opening. "We didn't even know you existed," said Aldai. "The authorities kept you hidden."

The Gaunt spat and scoffed out loud "Sak! Do you think that's supposed to help? Outcasts, and you didn't even know we existed?"

"But not anymore," said Aldai. "Now everyone's seen you. They kept you quiet; they kept you hidden because they knew that if the population found out about you, there was no way that people could live with themselves, knowing you were out there. The collective conscience, it looks after everyone. We'll make room."

"You think these people care about us?" he said motioning to the Port.

Aldai took his eyes off the Gaunt for a moment and looked around. It was a grim pile of bodies on the floor, each contorted into a different death throe. There were four Gaunt corpses, and then there was the family: executed, collateral damage in a war to end the last vestige of humanity. A dead man, woman and child. He clenched his jaw, fighting the urge to turn and add this Gaunt to the death toll, as his moral compass swayed around like a flag in a hurricane.

"They'll offer you sanctuary," he managed to say, desperate for the Gaunt to surrender. "There's space in the SeaPort for more people. They'll increase rotations, and you'll get to live up here on the StratoPort. This could be your home."

This stopped the Gaunt in his tracks. It was as if a dawn slowly rose inside him. Aldai was saying words he never thought he'd hear. The Gaunt's brain was ticking over as he tried to grasp it, his eyes widening as if an uncontrolled joy was spread through his bones for a moment. He could live next to the sun, the sun he so desperately needed. If he destroyed it now, he'd never get to live that life.

Aldai watched the Gaunt intently down his rifle. This was progress. He hadn't dropped the kill-switch. There was something in this creature that didn't want to do it. They must have planned this for years, but now he was faced with it, with the other Gaunts dead, he looked desperate for a reason to stay alive. Inside was some remnants of a human being. Just for a moment, it had

262

seemed like Aldai had managed to take that defence down. But then it passed, and the Gaunt laughed a dark steely laugh to himself.

"You think I could live here as an equal. Look at what we've done, look at who I am. I've seen the look of revulsion in your eyes, I feel it every time we talk to your kind. You think they will let us live here, as if we're one and the same?"

"If you've seen the look on people's faces here," said Bekka, "Then you'll know we've faced desperation too. You must have seen it down in the SeaPort. We haven't felt your struggle, but we've known our own. Everyone here understands the desperation we're all in. We all have to find extra strength to live in these circumstances, and we'd find extra strength still to make it work."

The Gaunt eyed Bekka with caution. He still had one hand holding the gun and the other gripping the kill-switch. They were walking a tightrope and holding onto this man by the thinnest of threads. Everything they ever knew hinged on him not releasing his thumb, detonating the device and ripping a hole out of the centre of the Port.

"They've found success on Venus," Aldai said. "There's a chance we can reverse the climate, we can make the surface habitable. But we need the StratoPort to make it work, the device is no good if there's no humans to make it work on Earth."

"What hope is there on Venus?" the Gaunt said half-heartedly, as if reciting more words that had been forced into him by someone else. His conviction was falling. His hand had lowered a little, his muscles looking like they were relaxing the tiniest of amounts.

"We can offer you sanctuary," said Aldai. "We can guarantee your protection, and that of your family." The Gaunt's head twitched to the side, the smallest glint of a tear beading in the corner of the man's eyes. Aldai pushed home the advantage. "Do you have children? You have a son or daughter?"

The man was quiet, as if the memory of them was too much to bear, and as if they were watching him now, too young to understand what he was doing, and why it was necessary.

"You can have sanctuary up here, you'll get quarters. The sun rises over the concourse every morning, the sky is always clear," Aldai continued.

It was too much for the man. Aldai watched his thoughts coming to a conclusion, like a coin spinning through the air, with equal chance to land heads or tails. The Gaunt reached towards his chest. Aldai remained motionless, his body preparing to be blown to smithereens. All he could do was wait. The Gaunt twisted a central dial, dimming a blinking light on the heart monitor, before unclipping a strap across his chest. Aldai watched, every part of his body pleading for the man to co-operate, his sinews bursting in the frustration of being powerless to do anything but just look on and hope.

The heart monitor slumped off the Gaunt's body, and he deactivated the hand-held kill-switch, placing it gently on the floor, and then letting his arms hang loosely by his side, resigned to whatever fate awaited him.

Aldai's trigger finger wavered, as if it wanted to take one more life. It was following instinct, and the reflex actions of war. All it had to do was squeeze, for instant retribution. But the fight was over, and he couldn't do it. He thought of the one he'd shot against the wall in the warehouse district, its face still haunting his thoughts. And this one was now unarmed and surrendered. Without the other Gaunts, and without the vest and kill-switch, this one looked helpless and weak. Pity swam over Aldai. Whatever the Gaunt cause was, this one was just a desperate being trying to survive, and to that Aldai felt some compassion. He knelt down and put a hand on his shoulder, and the man looked at him with fear and trepidation.

"My family..." he whimpered. "My daughters..." His cheeks were sallow, his face pale, his eyes receded and glossed over. But the eyes were unmistakably human. Whatever else they were, genetic monstrosities or otherwise, inside there was still a humanity glaring through.

"It's going to be all right," said Aldai, as Bekka quickly pulled away the weapon and bomb gear.

He turned around to see a mass of people on either side, Security and Intelligence Officials, who he hadn't even noticed arrive. He'd been so focussed on the Gaunt he'd lost any bearings of people around him. He saw Rongal standing amongst them, his leg soaked in blood, a grim expression plastered over his downcast face. Aldai searched around for the others, but saw no sign of Jones or Halderford. An Intelligence Official moved over and tried to lift up the Gaunt and put cuffs on him, but Aldai pushed him aside.

"I'll stay with him," he said. "No cuffs." He felt Bekka's touch on his arm, turning to see her face, her soft features a mixture of pain and reassurance.

"The team?" Aldai said.

"I'll check," she responded, urging him to go with the Gaunt, as the Intelligence Officers gathered around them with some insistence that they should move. But somehow Aldai already knew the answer. They were dead. Halderford, Jones, gone. The pain was suddenly unbearable. He pushed it aside, trying to focus on the task at hand and deal with those emotions later when alone. He realised he was gripping the bony arm of the Gaunt tightly, the Gaunt barely even noticing.

He pushed the hurt away, and focussed on the words he'd said. As his thoughts ignited like rocket fuel, he focussed on one thing at a time. The next thing was the Gaunt. He'd promised him sanctuary, and that was the next thing to focus on. He'd stand by him. Shit, maybe he didn't deserve it, but Aldai couldn't grapple with the tangle of facts right now, and his hand wouldn't let go of the Gaunt. As the tide of emotions roared, this man was a life ring to hold onto. He would walk right up to Orcanciz and show him the Gaunt's humanity. He would make Orcanciz feel what he felt. That gave Aldai's mind a momentary distraction as the adrenaline fizzing around his systems slowly left his body.

He would make *one* thing right. He would right *one* wrong. It was a purpose that at least sated his running mind, as the Intelligence Officials led them away.

Chapter 16

Aldai felt alone. He was surrounded by people, flanked on either side by a guard of Intelligence Officers, as he and the Gaunt were led up to the Intelligence Department, but he felt alone.

His team had been everything to him; he'd been with them through most of his adult life. They'd spent countless hours on duty in the Undercity, crawling through tubes and patrolling around the giant Levitation Engines and under the Heart. They'd spent many hours sitting in the dark, watching for signs of movement, waiting for a drug-runner or loner to unwittingly fall into their carefully laid traps. He'd had to put up with an endless spiel of youthful overconfidence from Jones, and the only occasional surprise from Halderford when a good mood allowed his private life to spill its secrets. Their laughs, jokes and reciprocated tactical movements were buried into Aldai's conscience, forming foundations in his neurons. And now they were gone, the team ruptured, and neurons fired into dead ends.

His emotions swirled in a pallet of colours. Anger, fear, loss and pain. His arm burned. He hadn't even realised he'd been grazed by a carbine round. He focussed on that, to try and push the other thoughts away. Five Gaunts dead. He'd killed five. He didn't even have a choice. He'd just been thrust into a fight he knew little about, and taken lives without the chance to question. The guilt of killing was only overridden by the pain of what the Gaunts had taken from him.

He wasn't alone. He found some resilience, and a brief floor to stand on, and he focussed his thoughts. There was vengeance and redemption. The Gaunt was his ticket. The Gaunt was the key to opening the Intelligence-shaped box and putting right this misfiring mess.

The Gaunt was still in a resigned state, walking just ahead of Aldai, who still held his arm. The man had chosen his fate, thought Aldai, and now he was alone too. *What on earth was I thinking? Offering him sanctuary? That wasn't mine to guarantee.* He'd manipulated the man; he'd poked and found the chinks in the armour and then exploited them. This man had a family. He had daughters who he wanted to see again, and Aldai had used it. He cursed his foolishness. *What salvation could I offer? How could I promise him a family up here? I've doomed him, this is my fault. His fate is my fault.* The Gaunt wouldn't get to see his family. Aldai chastised himself. He should have let the pale man carry out his mission, or he should have pulled the trigger. It would have been mercy. But no, that wasn't right. That wasn't goddamn right. *I will fight for this Gaunt. I won't abandon him.*

Aldai's feet found firm ground. He was walking on the StratoPort, and it was still in the air. He was alive. He'd done it. It caught up to him how close they'd come to total destruction. He looked around at the walls as they trooped past, seeing hope in every faded ceiling tile and every scuffed panel. This was home. It wasn't much, but it was home. He wanted to push the Gaunt away, feeling revulsion. He wanted to wash his hands of this vile mess and get back to normal. He wanted to see Wes and Sam, to double down on his plans for Andalucía, and scour the library for any books on vineyards. He wanted to take out a transport and go fishing once again over the clouds. He didn't even care if the mag-lines caught nothing, he just wanted some level of normality, some backstop to the maelstrom.

But there was no more normal. The man in front of him was proof of that. He'd seen the frightened stares of people hiding in offices and shops when the Port was in lockdown. What would they think of the Gaunt? They would rip him to pieces. They would look and gawp in horror and anger at his alien features, seeing only a twisted figure that barely looked human. They wouldn't look closely at his eyes and see the flash of humanity and see past the visage. Only Aldai had done that.

They were both alone. They had both lost everything. They were two men facing an uncertain future. Goddamn, Venus had better succeed. They could reshape Earth and live on opposite sides of the world, the humans and the Gaunts, in blissful ignorance of each other. He'd even promised it, he'd told the Gaunt Venus would succeed, and he'd even said it with an air of certainty, as if he had really believed it himself. They had to find the Star-Sphere, make it work and reshape the surface of Earth. It could be a paradise once more. *We have no choice.*

However, something in Aldai's mind said that the Gaunts wouldn't enjoy it as a paradise like he would. And the sound they made when they breathed, the difficulty they had speaking, the ungainliness of their movement. It was as if every step, every word, and every exertion was an effort, a fight to survive. But maybe the sun would heal them. Maybe it would flush warmth back into their skin and their bones. Or maybe they would fall apart in several generations, and Aldai had stripped this man of his only chance at redemption. Maybe the Gaunt's only release was the destruction of the StratoPort, and promises of anything else were a death sentence as their malformed genes pulled them down.

It didn't matter now. They were in the elevator, packed tightly with people. Aldai stood next to the Gaunt, wanting to say something but unable to form the words. The Gaunt was in his charge; Aldai had made sure of that. Whatever the score, he wasn't going to let the Gaunt be taken away straight into the care of Intelligence. Whatever was right or wrong, that would most definitely have been a false end. Orcanciz's moral compass had broken many years before, that was clear. There was no way Aldai was going to let the Intelligence Officers swoop in and immediately remove the Gaunt. He'd fended them off by the central column, and convinced them to back away with pure conviction. The Intelligence Officers hadn't known what to do. They weren't outranked, but something in their minds told them not to push it, that the rules could be bent this one time.

The elevator reached the height above the Concourse and started to move horizontally, through the veins of elevator routes that criss-crossed the StratoPort. They were like a molecule of blood, being pumped around by a central heart. They were helpless, stuck in the endless flow, unable to gain control of their direction and velocity, just being swept along by the current.

The cat was out of the bag. This was big, thought Aldai. The Government had been lying to them. Now everyone would know about the Gaunts. Now, everything would change. The children's stories of ghouls and vampires would be thrown away, and a new civilisation would have to be built. The Intelligence Department would be decommissioned and its secrets spilled like flowing blood. People needed to know the truth. Their lives needed to be guided by the truth.

But then Aldai thought of Orcanciz and General Gumpert and the President. *Christ.* These were large, proud men. These were men who prided themselves on leadership and revelled in power. They wouldn't appreciate being cornered with their backs up against the wall. Aldai felt a prickle run up his spine. He realised he was now the tip of the arrow for the Gaunts. Whatever the Gaunt faced in the Intelligence, it would be Aldai alone that had to defend them.

This was a mistake. *What on earth am I doing?* He had no idea where to go from here, he'd promised this man a life on the StratoPort for his family. He'd promised him that Venus would succeed, and he'd promised him the surface of the Earth. And now they were heading to the Intelligence Department for Aldai to deliver it. The Intelligence Department. A place where they barely acknowledged questions, let alone answers. They just took notes and disappeared down corridors.

He remembered how they had split Team-6 up for cross examination of their facts, as if they didn't even trust their own Special Ops. He was reminded of the kill order. Jesus. Qualtum hadn't even blinked. He'd seen a collection of Gaunts with women and children, and he'd ordered an execution without question. That bore all the hallmarks of Intelligence and Orcanciz. And Team-2 had probably been doing that for months. How many had they killed? How many had Qualtum shot down in cold blood? That was on Orcanciz's hands. Aldai felt the strap of his gun over his shoulder. He hadn't even realised he still had it. He was walking fully armed. His hand curled around the pistol grip as his mind raced.

Aldai didn't know what to believe. He was alone. He looked around the elevator. There was the Gaunt, his breathing sharp and hoarse and getting faster as the elevator ride went on. Around him were impassive Intelligence Officials, wearing dark trousers and jumpers, with flak vests that barely seemed to fit, as if they rarely put them on. Someone must have hastily pulled them out a store cupboard to protect officers confused about heading onto the front line. They probably never expected to leave the Intelligence District. They probably hoped their job would simply be to hide in a distant office and preside over secret information, lording over the rest of the StratoPort.

The doors opened and they faced the foyer of the Intelligence quarters. There was the hawk-like lady on reception, her eyes searching the group with pin-sharp detail. She looked at the Gaunt, but her face didn't contort. Instead, her eyes moved onto his with a death-stare of malice. Aldai looked away.

The Intelligence Officers moved forwards out of the elevator and Aldai felt a pressure on his back to follow them. He tried to usher the Gaunt, but found some level of resistance. It was as if he had frozen. Perhaps it had dawned on him what a hornet's nest he was walking into.

"I've got your back," said Aldai quietly, cursing himself for more fragile promises, and motioned him forwards, finding the hesitation give as the Gaunt followed his guidance. They were ushered through the slate-grey corridors, past offices and meeting rooms full of people craning to see what was going on, and past libraries of files upon files. Aldai felt he was going deeper and deeper into the brain of the StratoPort, and he longed to know what was on those papers and recordings. His faith in everything was being shaken. Without the facts, he didn't know if he could trust anyone. Not his school teachers, the Government, and least of all Intelligence.

Halderford. He knew he could trust Halderford. He didn't always give them the full picture, but he trusted him beyond all else. He'd known Halderford for what felt like a lifetime, and he'd never once not let him down. Every order, every mission they'd been on, he'd been a rock, a source of guidance and surety in the chaos around them. He played his cards close to his chest, and crak, he irritated Aldai from time to time, but you never got the sense you were being lied to. You never got the sense you might be doing the wrong thing. And now he was gone.

Anger and remorse swelled up in Aldai, to the point where he almost couldn't bear it. Halderford had been a reference point, a stake in the sand. It didn't matter what was going on around them when Halderford was in charge. He made the right decisions, and Team-6 followed through on his command. That was all there was. That was all there needed to be, and now it was gone.

They were guided into a nondescript room with no chairs, no windows, just slate-grey walls and a door. Aldai and the Gaunt were left standing in the centre of it, and two of the Intelligence Officers, now armed with assault rifles, followed them in. The Gaunt was trembling. He shouldn't be here, as a prisoner on the StratoPort. And the Gaunts shouldn't be outcasts, treated like dogs and living lives under the clouds. This was a slim and fleeting chance to change that.

After a few minutes Orcanciz came into the room.

"Aldai, I'd like to congratulate you on your efforts today, the entire StratoPort owes you the greatest of debts. You'll be rewarded as a hero, and I'll make sure personally that you are put forward for a medal of honour."

It took Aldai aback. It blindsided and disarmed him. A hero? It hadn't even occurred to him. It actually felt good for the briefest of moments as his mind formed around it. His mind tried to swell, but then it found the weight of present circumstances and reformed on the solid purpose. But before he had a chance to respond, Orcanciz was addressing the Gaunt.

"Sir," said Orcanciz.

Sir? Aldai was equally dumbstruck. He certainly hadn't expected Orcanciz to address the Gaunt with such reverence, or even respect.

"What is your name?" he said.

Holy sun. His name? Aldai hadn't even thought about it. He hadn't even asked. Orcanciz was stripping away his footing. Aldai had been ready for an argument, a fight, and instead he'd been left dumbstruck.

"Ryl" said the man hoarsely, staring at the floor

"Well, Ryl, we are forgiving here. What you did today cannot be overlooked, but we are always looking to open dialogue, and there are always opportunities and ways forward," he said, with a level of kindness that left Aldai reeling. He suddenly realised he was still holding Ryl's arm.

"They need sanctuary," Aldai said, staring down Orcanciz. "They cannot be left outside of the Ports, we will find space and make it work," he said, as he held himself together through gritted teeth as his body felt like it wanted to crumble.

"Now Aldai, or course, that is what we want too."

"Promise me!" Aldai said. The two Intelligence Officers were standing motionless by the door, unmoved by the conflict in front of them. "Promise me that you'll give them sanctuary. Promise me that you'll give this man sanctuary, quarters, let his family come here too." He said the words with as much conviction as he could muster, but he felt like he was light rain on Orcanciz's polished metal.

"Aldai, why don't we go into the next room and discuss this. We'll make sure Ryl, here, is well looked after. We have no ill-will towards him."

"Promise me!" shouted Aldai, tears forming in his eyes. His team had been killed. He'd lost everything. This was the only thing he had right now. This was the only redemption laid out in front of him. Maybe not for Aldai, but at least for someone else. The fragile existence in the StratoPort clawed at his mind. The anger was swelling. One of the Intelligence Officers was now staring at him, watching the gun and his hand in case Aldai made any sudden, foolish moves. Aldai swallowed hard and managed to diffuse the fire spreading in his mind.

Orcanciz held up his hands in a defensive pose, somehow maintaining his relaxed demeanour.

"Aldai, we can't stay like this forever. We'll take good care of Ryl. Unless you're planning on staying beside him forever, then why not come into the next room and we can talk about this."

Aldai was stunned, he didn't know what to do. He suddenly realised he was gambling with no chips, with a

277

weak hand of cards. He had nothing to go on. He felt like railing against them, but they would simply absorb it.

He realised he still had his gun. He could take out the guards before they'd even noticed what was happening. They looked rookie and ill-trained. But Orcanciz had a holster strapped around his waist. He looked like the type that could pull the trigger fast, even if his years of desk pushing hadn't been all that kind to his physique. But what would that achieve? He was stuck in the bowels of the Intelligence Department. Goddamnit. Worse still, he'd walked in there willingly.

"Ryl, I'm going to have to go with Orcanciz," Aldai said, resigning to defeat.

"I understand," the Gaunt said hoarsely, unwilling to turn and look at his captor. Aldai wanted to reassure him, but he couldn't lie again. He wanted to say that if nothing would happen to him, and if it did, the Aldai would make sure people found their accountability. But it was no good. He knew Ryl wasn't safe. And he knew he had walked Ryl right into the middle of this.

"I'm sorry," was all he could say, and he let go of Ryl's arm. Orcanciz gestured towards the door with a poorly-hidden look of relief, and Aldai left the room, Orcanciz blocking off his chance to change his mind as he followed closely behind. Back out in the corridor, an officer took Aldai's gun, and two more passed by carrying restraints. Aldai desperately turned to catch their intentions, but they entered the room and the door closed behind them.

"He'll be all right," said Orcanciz, ushering Aldai down a corroder and into his office.

It was well decorated with wallpaper and elaborate plaster coving on the ceiling. It looked as if Orcanciz was trying to make it feel as if it was a stately room back on the old surface. On the wall hung a painting of a steely industrialist who stared out over the room with the command of superiority. Maybe it was one of Orcanciz's ancestors. But then again, maybe it was just a random painting Orcanciz had hoarded. It was certainly a rarity. Aldai had never seen an original like it before.

Orcanciz's desk was wooden, with chip and repair marks, and a rug spread out across the floor. It was like a treasure trove of long-lost artifacts. It would have created a regal presence if each item hadn't been mismatched. As it was, it looked like the room of a man who hoarded treasures that other people couldn't have, to remind them of his authority. It was to impress upon people that Orcanciz bore the keys and remnants of the surface, to the old world, while everyone else had identical bare cabins.

Orcanciz motioned for Aldai to sit on a decoratively embossed chair, with a comfortable padded seat that was rare on the StratoPort. Orcanciz went to sit in his own chair, slightly larger and with a broad back, behind the desk.

"Aldai I want to thank you again for your actions today. You are a hero. You saved many lives. The attack on the Heart was a diversion, and the group that you accosted was the real threat."

"What are you going to do with Ryl?" Aldai said, trying to be ambivalent to Orcanciz's praise, but finding that the idea of being a hero seeped into his consciousness and started to spread out through his mind. He pushed it away and doubled down. "They deserve sanctuary. You can't keep them secret anymore; everyone saw them."

"Of course, of course. Ryl will be well looked after. First what we need is calm. You saw the faces of the population; they've just gone through a traumatic event. We need calm, and we need things to return to normal."

"What normal can we return to?" interjected Aldai.

"I understand," Orcanciz said. "Of course, things will change. But first we need to question Ryl. We need to secure the station, to make sure we are defended against further attacks and to make sure we understand the lie of the land."

"If you hurt him..."

"We won't, Aldai, I give you my word. And I completely understand your concerns and desire to give them sanctuary. It is something we want, too. But it needs to be done in the right way. We need to understand how many of them there are, and where we can house them. We need to draw up plans and strategies, we need to perform reviews in order to investigate how we can make it work. All of this takes time, but right now we need to return to a certain level of calm."

Aldai was being painted into a corner. He felt it, the anger. Orcanciz's words were empty, intended to pass Aldai off. But his weapons had been dulled and taken away. Orcanciz was telling him what he wanted to hear and giving him nothing. It was bluster intended to divert and suppress.

"But you know, Aldai." The leader shifted forward in his seat, and changing his tone to a more direct one. "Running the StratoPort requires difficult decisions. Let me tell you something. Something that few people know. When they floated the StratoPort into the air, just before the Acceleration Event, do you know how they selected who went inside?"

Aldai shook his head; he honestly had no idea. He wracked his memories of history lessons and conversations, but it had never occurred to him. It just wasn't something that was ever discussed or talked about, as if to avoid unearthing inconvenient truths. You just didn't consider horrors that you couldn't change. It wasn't taught in history books, and parents hushed inquisitive children or scared them quiet with ghoulish fables.

"They selected people based on factors. They needed a certain amount of each profession. They needed a certain number of men, women and children. They needed the correct distribution of ages, so that the population was sustainable and steady. Numbers, Aldai, that is how they selected people. They assessed a large number of people based on statistics. They took the right people from all over the world. It was chance. We are the lucky few. Our numbers came up, or those of our ancestors."

"What happened to the rest?"

"They came from all around the world, people of all nations, and tried to live near the StratoPort on the ground. Even before the Acceleration Event, they would try and get into it in large numbers. The surface was already difficult to live on. After the Acceleration Event the clouds thickened and darkened with anger and volcanic debris, and they still tried to get in. They used makeshift craft that could barely fly through the gathering storms and high winds. We were like a life-raft, but there were thousands of people around us, enough to sink us and drown everyone. In fact, after the effort to change the climate failed, and if it wasn't for the Acceleration Event that scoured the population, it's quite possible that the StratoPort could have been swamped. What would you have done in that situation? If you had been in charge of the life-boat, too small to save everyone, what decision would you have made, Aldai?"

Aldai went quiet, trying to think quickly. It was a trap. It was intended to silence him. "But they survived, didn't they? They survived on the surface!"

"No," said Orcanciz, shaking his head. "No one can survive on the surface. Difficult decisions have to be made all the time. Leaders like ourselves, we have to keep the population in order, keeping their hope alive, and most of all, keep people busy in their lives, so that there is some level of normality, some feeling of humanity. It is a difficult task, but it is a task that needs to happen to steer humanity through this difficult phase. Soon they will return from Venus, and then we shall begin the next phase."

"You believe there is hope in Venus?" said Aldai.

"Yes, yes, of course," said Orcanciz, almost dismissively. "Aldai, you are a hero. You should enjoy it. We will take care of Ryl, we will look after him. We will start to draw up plans for cohabitation, and we will run studies to see if we can host the Gaunts here, but first of all, we need the population to go on, we need to return things to normal. You are a hero. The whole StratoPort will see you that way. They will cheer and adore you. Can you play that role? Can you help humanity to survive in difficult times, despite difficult decisions? Can you be a leader?" Orcanciz said to him, with kinder but piercing eyes. It wasn't a question. And despite the imposing care, there was a hint of malice behind it that made Aldai fully aware that he wouldn't have any other option.

He sat, thinking over an endless number of conflicting thoughts. They rolled over each other, fighting, growing and diminishing. Nothing made sense, so he pushed them away and focussed on what was in front of him. But what was left? He was powerless. He had let Ryl be taken away. All that was left were memories of dead and bloodied corpses. The family that the Gaunts had slaughtered as hostages. Five Gaunts on Aldai's tally. Halderford, Jones, and Tiernan. The sea around him was choppy, and he closed his eyes, knowing that all he could do would be to float along with it until he gained some clarity.

He nodded to Orcanciz and managed a faint smile, trying to give him an air of certainty and confidence. Orcanciz smiled back, relieved and reassured. But it was the expression of a man who just needed to leave so that he could firefight the next challenge, and his eyes were already glancing towards a report on his desk. Aldai was one simple task amongst a workday of similar difficulties.

He was just doing a job. He cares little about the individuals he presides over. But even amongst everything else, it gave Aldai a fraction of what he needed right then. He could be washed along for a while; he could be their hero for the time being. He had no choice but to do it. He was being carried along by the currents. When he washed up on a bank, that's when he would find some order in his thoughts. *When a box is opened, the act can never be undone.*

Chapter 17

The next few days passed in a blur for Aldai. He and Bekka had turned into reluctant heroes of the StratoPort, their faces all over the news and the local paper. There was even some footage of the final moments as he talked down to the bomber. Some brave or foolish kid had filmed it on a wrist watch from a distance, catching blurred and shaky images of the Special Ops staring down at the Gaunt.

They were swept up in the public relations machine of the Intelligence Department. They had a constant schedule of events, interviews, dinners and ceremonies. They were mostly kept apart, barely seeing each other, and only having the briefest of moments to catch up and discuss what painful tasks they had laid out for the day. It was the Intelligence way: divide and conquer. People were easier to herd when they were by themselves. They were each assigned an Intelligence Officer who shadowed them, ferrying them from one assignment to another and feeding them fixed lines to say.

Neither had the energy to resist at that moment. It was a tidal wave of pressure and control, and it rolled with a momentum that prevented any urge to try and stand still. There wasn't even time to think to begin with, and just as you were trying to make sense of the situation, another camera or microphone was thrust in front of you and you recited more words that slowly became easier and easier to say. And in some ways, it was a blessing. There were thoughts you didn't want to process, that kindled and burned in the back of your mind. The grief of loss and the uncertainty of the future. Being busy was all that was keeping those thoughts away, and at times the next event was a welcome distraction.

But the questions were relentless.

"How did you find the coolness to talk to the terrorist?" a reporter asked, sitting opposite Aldai in the television studio, half cosy lounge, half a mess of old cameras and cables.

"What did you say to him?"

"Are there more of them?"

The reporter didn't even care. The questions were meaningless to her, as she barely acknowledged answers and moved on to probe a different angle of attack in order to extract ratings and further her career. Aldai tried to pass his actions off as something that anyone would do in the circumstances. Maybe if he was humble they'd leave him alone after a while.

Afterwards a junior assistant came up and asked him to sign her lucky baseball cap. She bit her lower lip and fumbled with her jumper. Aldai noticed a tattoo peeking out of her neckline. Later that night he found it went down her back and over her left arse-cheek. Well, being a hero had some perks. Maybe it wasn't all bad. She kept away the loneliness of night, when your brain tried to consolidate your situation, something he was desperate to avoid doing.

As for the questions on the nature of the Gaunts, he wasn't sure what to say in the slightest. The Intelligence Officer that shadowed him to every public event just gave short instructions.

"So, I say that the Gaunts are aliens from Jupiter?" Aldai tried, the Officer walking slightly ahead of him in silence, as he chaperoned Aldai to the opening of a new hastily-assembled theatre.

"Negative. They are the distant descendants of the experiments of a crazed scientist, spawned during a desperate time, and barely surviving, their gene-seed warped, giving them an unnatural anger and hatred."

Every time the Officer gave the same answer, dutifully recited like the slow reading of an ancient text. He probably worked through his instructions every evening before he went to sleep, to burn their teachings onto his retinas. No humour, no small-talk, just doing a job and trying not to engage with Aldai. Crak, he was frustrating.

"Right, and how do you spell the name of the scientist?" Aldai would ask. That would get him. That would at least show a chink in the armour.

"A-l-b-a-t-e-r-a-n-i-n."

Aldai shook his head; this man was impossible. Maybe he was a robot. Maybe Aldai could open his brain and reprogram him with some humour.

"What's happened to Ryl? Can I see him?" Aldai asked.

"Negative."

"But is he all right?"

"Sir, I am not authorised to know that information."

"Can you find out? It's important, you know, for if I get asked a question on what happened to the Gaunt that was taken into custody."

"Negative sir. Just say he has been securely detained. You are to reassure the public that there is no further danger."

Goddamnit.

One day, when the Officer left him, he wandered up to the Intelligence Department. He would get answers himself. He was a bloody hero; they'd better let him right through. He arrived there expecting to have his skull bored into by the hawk-like lady, who would probably flap her wings and chase him away, but to his surprise he was met by a different person on reception, a young man with a black buzz haircut. The old hawk-lady must be away stretching her tattered wings.

Aldai walked straight up to him and demanded to see Ryl. The receptionist coolly denied him, and two other Officers with holstered pistols appeared at the side of the entrance foyer, looking nonchalant but clearly delivering a message.

Aldai asked to speak to Orcanciz, but he was told he was very busy at this time with other business. He was told, in a pleasantly passive-aggressive voice, that the leaders were being run off their feet trying to help the Ports recover from the attack, and that they wouldn't have time to answer questions from the public. He left empty handed in frustration.

He toed the line. He didn't know what else to do. You could see fear in the eyes of the population. There was an edge in people's demeanours that said they were waiting for another bomb to go off at any moment, or waiting for the floor to fall away. Every clang that ran out through the structure of a steel girder flexing itself as it thermally expanded in its daily cycle and every thump of a pump misfiring caused hushed conversations across café forecourts to stop, as people held their breath for a few seconds before resuming idle gossip.

And against people's fears, the spiel from the Intelligence Department was working. The Gaunts were malformed crazed terrorists, and no one thought otherwise. They had executed a family of hostages and tried to blow the station out of the air. They were public enemy number one. Absolutely no one cared who or what they were. They were outsiders, the opposing army, baying at the city gates. It galvanised and united people and distracted them from the trauma of an untimely death that everyone on the StratoPort had nearly experienced a few days before.

Now wasn't the time to speak of caution. It wasn't the time to talk of the humanity in their eyes, or to speak of the dark corners of the SeaPort Outer Reaches that no intelligent being should have to spend a lifetime in. It wasn't the time to mention that the Gaunt had a name. And it certainly wasn't the time to talk of cohabitation. *Damnit, Orcanciz won.* Aldai scolded himself for being foolish enough to even ask. *What was I thinking, demanding that the authorities should make room for them? The public would rip them apart, shun them back where they came from.*

Anti-Gaunt fever swarmed over the Port. There was a morbid excitement to it that made it impossible to fight the addiction. People were desperate for any change to their mundane lives, stuck in a steel cage in the stratosphere.

As the days went by, the events came less and less often, and he felt more himself. But as he tried to get back to normal, he found that there was no real normal to return to. Everything had changed. He was given leave from Special Ops to deal with the remaining requests of the Intelligence Department, but it left too much time to think. He needed a mission, to be back in action. But what action was there left? What he needed was Team-6, but they were gone. The anger within him swirled around, trying to mask the loss of Halderford, Jones and Tiernan. It tried to find an outlet, and Gaunt-fever was all too easy for it to settle on. He tried to push away the images of their desperate faces, and instead join in with the chorus of resentment rushing around the Port. It worked at times. It kept the wind in the sails.

Rongal had survived. Aldai and Bekka went to see him in the hospital. He was being treated in a first-class room that had panoramic views over the clouds, and was slowly recovering, his leg in a cast angled up in the air and bandages wrapped his waist and face. He was angry too.

"I don't know how you did it," he said.

"Did what?" Aldai responded, lost in thought, barely acknowledging what Rongal was talking about

"Managed not to kill that Gaunt straight off. I would have done, given half a chance, as soon as he dropped the switches, bang, right through the temple," he'd said.

"I guess I just wasn't thinking straight," said Aldai in response.

"I'm just looking forward to getting out of here," said Rongal, "And getting back into the action. Did you hear they're sending teams down to the surface? Can you imagine it? Sign me up; we need to find their nests and take them out before they try something like this again." He twisted as if eager to get out of the hospital bed, despite his body in medical slings.

It was true; it came up on the news over the next few days. Teams were being sent down to the surface to hunt out the Gaunts. Aldai expected to be asked, but the request never came. He asked around, but no one else in Special Ops seemed to know anything about it. Either they weren't happening, or Aldai was being kept well away from the fighting for the time being. He was torn between wanting to be part of the action, back on missions and amongst a team, and knowing that if they were being sent to the surface, they were executing desperate Gaunt families.

Aldai had too much time to kill. He found himself walking the decks, occasionally bumping into random people who thanked him for his heroics. They asked about who the Gaunts were, and whether there were more of them. Their faces were painted with worried expressions, and they muttered things like "I hope they get them all," and "They deserve to live under the clouds," to which Aldai just nodded and moved on.

At one point he found himself on the hydroponics deck, wading through the tangled trees until he stumbled across the far window. Feeling a sense of solitude, he stared out through the plastiglass and wept, letting the loss climb into his mind, before pushing it back down when the tears ran dry.

He thought of Ryl. There had been no news. The Intelligence Officer just showed his vacant discipline whenever Aldai asked. What on earth were they doing with him, or to him if he was even still alive? Intelligence had swallowed him whole, and now he was just the ghost that he resembled.

When Aldai's life got caught in an eddy, that pulled him out of the sweeping current of his new StratoPort life, Ryl's sallow face would creep into his mind. It would haunt his dreams and wake him to a cold sweat.

There was a ceremony to honour Bekka and Aldai. It took place in the main Concourse, and half the population tried to attend, so many in fact that they had to turn people away, and there were rumours that they had to apply extra levitation to that side of the Port because of the mass of people. Poppycock of course. More PR. The people were fairly inconsequential in weight compared to the Port itself.

The crowd had cheered, and Aldai and Bekka had managed smiles and waves, soaking up the adulation. It was an out-of-body experience. Whatever the crowd felt, it was disconnected from Aldai and Bekka's feelings about it. But strange as it was, they couldn't deny it felt good. To the people they were heroes.

Aldai had gone up to the Crescent to have a drink alone, to collect his thoughts. He'd hoped to find some peace and quiet, a momentary sanctuary from the madness going on around, but even the barman had bought into it. As he passed Aldai his drink, he asked if he could put Aldai's photo up on the wall. Aldai managed to deflect it in a kind but forceful way that said no, and never to ask again. It was a technique he'd honed after a few days of similar requests. Walking away, he found a stool with a view over the concourse, but just as his eyes glazed over in daydream, Wes arrived. It interrupted the brooding that Aldai had planned, but he was pleased to get caught up in mindless chatter for a while.

"You realise you're now my son's hero right?" Wes joked. "He wants to go into the military. I forbade him, of course. I said he needed a proper career like an accountant or an engineer." Aldai laughed. "I'm serious though, he just runs around with this toy gun saying he's shooting the Gaunts and that he'll defend the StratoPort himself. I think he'd sign up today if they allowed 8-year-olds in the military."

Aldai enjoyed this. Wes got on his nerves sometimes, but right now he just wanted to hear an endless babble of someone else's news, some level of normality.

"Wait, they don't let 8-year-olds in the military do they?"

"They don't," said Aldai with a wry smile.

"Then how come they let you in, right?" his friend responded. "He loves the wallet, by the way. Thanks for that. Beats any present I can give him for the next decade." He carried on, changing the subject to talk about how his wife was worried about the Gaunts. She wanted Wes to go up to Intelligence and demand that they tell him the truth. She almost went up herself, but he had managed to stop her.

"You hear they're letting Sam out early? I mean up early?" Wes had said, barely noticing that Aldai wasn't really responding to his chatter. "Apparently the whole schedule's up in the air, Sam's back up here in a few weeks."

That was good news. At least because they worked better as a three rather than Aldai having to deal with Wes by himself.

"We're heading straight up to the nightclub when he's back. I've already squared it with Melissa. I mean, when I say I've squared it, I told her, and she said no, and then I'm going to do it anyway. You can bring, what's her name...Irina?"

Aldai had completely forgotten about her. With everything that had gone on, she'd completely passed out of his thoughts. They hadn't messaged since before the SeaPort, which felt like an age ago. He briefly thought about the delicate curve of her neck and her gentle laugh and confident posture that accentuated her natural body, but it was fleeting. Everything had changed since before. And anyway, she was probably already hooked up with some other Lank. His thoughts of her fizzled.

He shook his head at Wes. "No, that was just two trains in the night. Count me in, though," he said, to which Wes slapped him on the back.

"There's the robo-cop I know, I'll go and warn the bar keeper to make sure they have enough drinks."

Then there was the funeral. It was a military affair, with the coffins of Halderford, Tiernan and Jones lined up at the front, the StratoPort flag draped over them. Rongal made it out of hospital and attended in a wheelchair with his leg jutting out like a cannon, his tears revealing an equal amount of sorrow and threat of retribution.

The bugler rang out the military anthem and it was overwhelming. He found Bekka's hand clasp his, and her eyes were full of tears too.

They found themselves in a small coffee kiosk in the office district afterwards. It was a quiet area with hardly any passers-by. It was good to finally be alone with Bekka after a hectic schedule of appointments dragging them apart.

"I miss them," Aldai said. "Even Halderford. God, he got on my nerves, but I wish he would do that one more time."

"I know what you mean. Whenever I see a clock almost strike the hour, it makes me think of him anally waiting for the exact time to begin an exercise. A stickler for punctuality! I can't imagine the mindset that would make someone do that, but it worked. He was a great sergeant. And I still have Jones' voice nagging in my ear. It's just not quite the same without them. But you've got to move on, right, keep moving forwards."

"You're right," he replied.

They shared stories of the good times with the team. It was cathartic and warming to the soul. That moment, hidden away in the coffee shop with no one else around, was a better send-off than any of the ceremonies. The honour guards and the funeral paled in comparison to the memories.

He was pleased to be with Bekka for this moment, making him laugh and forget the world for the briefest of afternoons. She wore a black beret with a netting that hung over her eyes, framing her deep brown pupils. They'd known each other for so long but he couldn't help himself get lost in her perfume and melodic voice. They'd just been friends, but now every time she moved her body it sent a jolt of electricity through him. She'd clasped his hand over the table, and they had stared into each other's eyes for a moment, unsure of what to do or say, before Aldai had changed the subject onto Slamball, and how he had resolved to get back into the sport.

He actually got a game in, for the Powerhouse no less. He was rusty as hell, but he was allowed on as a later substitute, to the cheers of the crowd. Hero status had all sorts of perks, but he knew it was probably fleeting. He was just riding a wave of good fortune that would stop as soon as people realised he wasn't quite Slamball team material. But he surprised himself, and the crowd, by saving a goal and then spinning a ball down the field, catching the side wall and finding a striker who scored. The release of endorphins was incredible.

There were engagements left, right and centre for Aldai and Bekka. There was even talk of going down to the SeaPort for a morale-boosting mission. They'd reluctantly agreed. They weren't exactly given much choice. Life went on, which meant the Ports resumed their normal hustle and bustle. Drop-ships rose and sank, and the sun turned over in the sky. The world slowly felt like it did before. But there was a niggling feeling that Aldai couldn't shake. *Once the box was opened, the contents were forever revealed.*

When Ryl's face woke him from a nightmare, his thoughts would wander to Ryl's family. His wife and daughters, who were grieving a husband and a father. They were still there, alive, under the clouds. They were trapped down there in a shallow grave.

Orcanciz's words rang through his mind. He'd been taunting Aldai, playing with him. They were all just numbers, selected because of statistics, with the good fortune to be on the StratoPort when the Acceleration Event snuffed out the lives of an entire planet. As he thought it over and thought of the Gaunts fifty thousand feet below, it dawned on him the horror that those early residents of the Port must have lived through. They had made it onto the life raft, but they had to sit in it, clasping onto its fragile buoyancy, as the cries of those suffering around them clamoured in their ears. It made Aldai's skin crawl. They were up there in the sun, while everyone else was below, dying in their billions.

And heaven above, what of the friends and family you left behind? For every person whose number came up, there would have been tens of acquaintances and relatives who weren't so lucky. As a population was stuck in the metal cage in the stratosphere, those other people were choking under black skies and dying in darkness. Aldai almost hoped they were lied to. He actually hoped that there was an Intelligence Department at the time that lied to everyone and told them that the death on the surface was instantaneous.

No wonder there were secrets that were tightly controlled. No wonder the history books covered little of those events. Orcanciz had told him that to make him have to wrangle with the thoughts. It was punishment for daring to storm into his department and make demands. Ryl was experiencing that right now. He was up on the StratoPort, while his family were below the clouds. And Aldai was experiencing it though him. The memories of humans left behind were being kept alive by the Gaunts that still skulked on the inhospitable surface world.

On days when things were quiet, he found himself wandering more and more. Trying not to be noticed, he even went down in the Undercity, walking through endless industrial sectors, occasionally running into workmen and women who thanked him for what he did. He walked back to where he and Bekka had found the Gaunt's den. He pulled back the panel but found the inside cleared out and empty. He'd hoped to see something. He'd hoped to run into a Gaunt so that he could explain what was happening, and perhaps get a message to Ryl's family.

One day news broke that the Gaunt that was captured had died of natural causes in the detention blocks. Ryl was dead. The news channels said it was proof of how weak and frail their bodies were, cursed by the unnatural experiments, and a contributing factor to their anger. The report said how it meant that their bodies were adapted only to the surface, where they belonged, and poorly at that. Aldai knew it was a lie.

The world was messed up. They were caged by the StratoPort and caged by the lies of the Government.

He walked into Special Ops stores and found a grenade. He concealed it in his pocket and walked down to the Heart, straight into reception, and asked for a tour. A scientist with large round glasses greeted him, smiling at meeting a hero, and showed him around. He thought about it. He'd just have to pull the pin and watch the whole thing go up in smoke. It was a bloated monstrosity, and it deserved to go down. But he couldn't. He sheepishly returned the grenade. No one had even noticed.

You just had to keep going, staring at your feet, one day at a time.

"Tell me again about Andalucía," Bekka whispered, lying against him on his bed, her soft breath on his neck.

"There'll be a vineyard, olive-green rolling hills, dusty brown soil that will grow the ripest of tomatoes, bursting with flavour."

"That sounds good."

"And wine like you've never tasted."

"I've never tasted wine," she replied dryly.

"Oh, right. Yeah. Well, then at least no one will realise when the first few batches are terrible." They laughed. Her chest moving on his side was all the life he needed.

"And some little Aldai's running around," Bekka said after a pause.

"Whoa! Easy there!" he replied in shock. "One step at a time. Anyway, they've got to actually bring back the Star-Sphere first. That's gone remarkably quiet, right? The news has been nothing but Gaunts."

"And the strapping hero, Aldai."

"And the heroine, Bekka. You're not getting out of more lifeless ceremonies and dinners that easily. You know, I think you were the contributing factor in convincing Ryl to stand down. Maybe you should take all the engagements solo for a time."

She poked him in his ribs as he squirmed. They lay in silence for a while, the mention of Ryl's name bringing up thoughts that went nowhere good.

"You're right, though," Bekka said, "Venus has gone quiet. But they would say if the mission had failed, right?

It's been a few weeks since the Venus Celebration, assuming that actually coincided with the day they landed. Maybe they're on their way back and the Government just doesn't want to get people's hopes up."

"They better hurry up. There was another surface temperature jump this morning. Two in one month; it's getting worse. There haven't been such rises in years. It makes you wonder how much time we have left. If the Rift collapses...well. It all just needs to be reversed. I mean I've got brackets to make and grape seeds to sow in Spain." It was a quick distraction to a pleasant dream. "Oh, they've given me my own team. How about that, Team-7. All new recruits, apart from one guy, you remember that staffer? The one with the baby face. He's in there too."

"No way, that's amazing. So, what type of Sergeant will you be, huh?"

Aldai smiled a melancholy smile. "I'll be like...well, I don't know. That's for the recruits to decide. We start training a week on Tuesday. I'm going to run them hard the first few weeks, mould them into warriors."

"I'm still in Team-6, returning to duty next week. Some old lady's come out of retirement to lead it. Just me and Rongal left of the originals! Urgh, but he's on a revenge drive. Keeps talking about doing god's work to clean up the Gaunts. I doubt we'll be involved, though, whatever's happening on that front. Still, you've got your work cut out, getting your lot in shape."

"Yeah, but I'm looking forward to it, getting back to a routine at least. No more hero worshiping from annoying crowds. I hear the Sayen cartel has seen a resurgence; all the good-will is causing people to want to lose control of reality for a short time. I'll take the recruits down there as soon as possible and get their teeth cut on some drug-runner hunting."

Bekka kissed him on the cheek as the wall-screen faded from a river delta scene to the jutting mountains of the Old Americas. Dusty red rock formations broke up into the old sky, where a sun, obscured by wisping clouds, was creating long shadows across the red-rock floor. A long track of road ran east-west across the scene, for ancient travellers to lazily head along, while a flock of birds danced around one of the mountain tops.

Outside, the real sun, an angry ball of flame, lashed the StratoPort with high altitude rays. It descended towards the horizon, getting lower in its daily cycle as it swirled around the Earth. As it disappeared from view, it turned the sky red, diffusing the world in a rich sunset before its light dwindled. Then it passed to the far side of Earth, to fight the underworld, restore order to the chaos, and be reborn the next day.

Life in the stratosphere would go on, one day at a time, and one sunrise after another, and Aldai would rise and set with the sun. Bekka, Halderford, Sam, Wes, his mother; they were all stitches in a tapestry, interwoven amongst countless others on the StratoPort. Each thread bore resemblance to those before, re-used and repeating. Life, love, purpose; the same patterns played out in every strand. Even when the fabric was becoming dry and brittle, as the temperature around them rose.

One day Aldai entered the Concourse near the ceiling to see Irina in a small bar. It was themed like a candlelit grotto, and she was sitting close to a Sayen cartel member. He recognised the man immediately; he'd arrested him a decade before. He must've spent years in a cell, and yet here he was, acting like a good citizen. He felt like walking up to them, slamming the man to the floor and taking him away in cuffs.

He shook his head. *That kind of thinking won't do me any good. Maybe the Sayen cartel runner is reformed. Either way, his life is his own.*

Aldai checked the time. *Bekka will be at the Crescent right now.* She filled his mind and painted out his future. His thoughts dissolved until all that was left were Bekka's eyes staring back at him. The planet storms and temperature spikes were irrelevant when she smiled, and the metal structure in the stratosphere felt like home. The bell tolled above, and he made his way to the express elevator. He keyed in level four, and felt it descend.

Gravity always pulled. The StratoPort always struggled to stay in the air, endlessly on the verge of giving up its fight and being consumed by the Rift. The Levitation Engines maintained altitude, keeping humanity afloat, but the planet was always waiting below. The fabric of their lives stretched out, twisting in the stratosphere. The weave always tried to look upwards, to the sky and stars, to beyond the confines of Earth. But the past was below, a past that couldn't be left behind. They were drawn backwards, and inescapably tied to the possessive world beneath.

Chapter 18

"I need to run diagnostics on the expansion valves," Arundel said. She'd been white as a sheet all morning. Perhaps something to do with going into an alien Venusian Facility that had consumed Kowalski and made him disappear without a trace.

"Make it quick," Colonel Seerman replied in frustration. "It's only been two day-cycles since we landed. Just...check them over, we need to be out of here by oh nine hundred."

"Yes sir, just following procedure," she replied. "The manuals say that if the lander is to be left alone for more than a few hours then..."

"I understand, Arundel," Seerman responded. "Just get it done."

The colonel wasn't exactly full of colour himself. He was pacing around, trying to herd Yakun into finishing the environmental suits and hover barges, occasionally disappearing to check on his progress in the decontamination room, before coming back with a look of minor exasperation. He was muttering to himself when he couldn't find his fabric skull cap that seemed to be lost in the pile of dry-clean, and reminded everyone every five minutes of the morning schedule.

Caellyn tried to stay out the way. She surreptitiously sipped her coffee and ate nutrition sludge that was rehydrated from a packet stamped with "porridge." It was a dry and clammy bowl; the water hadn't evenly mixed through the paste, but at least it filled a grumbling stomach.

She actually hoped Arundel would discover a catastrophic failure that meant they would have to abandon the surface and head back to the *Molniya-V* in orbit. If they couldn't guarantee the integrity of the ship, it would be foolish to continue with the mission. She even thought Arundel might "find" one. Despite the coolers working efficiently since landing two days ago, she wouldn't have been surprised if Arundel's head appeared from the panel declaring that one of the valves had just ruptured into its casing, and that was it, that was their pass home.

But after slowly checking the filters, auxiliary power systems, pumps and flow paths, Arundel certified them as working to ninety-four percent capacity, well within tolerance. They ran out of excuses.

"Time to go. Let's suit up," said Seerman impassively. No one replied, but everyone headed to the gear room and began the arduous process of sliding into the fabric overalls covered in sensors, and then into the metal suits themselves. Caellyn was immediately reminded of sore body parts, as they found the same resistance that had buffeted them on the previous two-day excursion. The outer casing closed around her while the internals expanded to support her inside it, and her hands grasped the controls. Her view became framed once again by the visor through the pressure vessel.

As they all finished preparations, they headed into the pressurisation chamber, waiting patiently as the atmosphere leaked in around them before stepping out onto the surface once more.

Despite everything, the view was beautiful. The fog was long gone, and although the sun hadn't moved in the sky, the clouds above looked like they were letting a little more light through. Instead of looking like a rock canopy, they were now more like a thick veil of many layers of billowing silk, frozen in time. The U-shaped valley was glowing in the flat light, and the cliff wall next to them looked imposing in its full view, like the outer defence wall of a medieval castle running off into the distance. It made Caellyn feel small and insignificant, a fleeting traveller moving in an ancient landscape, unchanging in millions of years.

"Everyone's suit holding up?" Seerman said through the comms, as they walked up the incline to the Facility door, each pushing a hover barge. Caellyn's suit creaked as it got used to withstanding the pressure again, but the groans of flexing metal had become second-nature background noise.

"I should hope so," came Yakun's response. He'd had an unnatural level of quiet optimism as they had left, probably from burying dread and anticipation and focussing entirely on discovery. Caellyn struggled not to break it by telling him about the corridor that appeared out of nowhere or the alien-looking tree limb that was severed in the reactor hall. The less Yakun and Arundel knew the better.

"Yes sir, suits are fine," Arundel responded shortly.

They reached the entrance door and briefly paused, contemplating the point of no return. They took one last look across the valley floor, flat and empty apart from the two Landers below them, the ships looking like two faithful chargers that would wait patiently until the planet consumed them. Then the team turned and disappeared through the dog-leg entrance passageway.

"These walls are incredible," said Yakun, mesmerised by the technology in front of him in the entrance room. "It looks organic, or intelligent, some sort of coating flowing over them. I know, I know, don't touch them. I won't."

It was like he'd forgotten about Kowalski, or maybe he just didn't care about anyone.

They moved on, slowly down the first elevator shaft. The fear of walking back into the unknown was at least somewhat offset by heading there with greater numbers, as the four suits clanged and thumped step after step that reverberated off obsidian walls.

On reaching the buttress checkpoint, Yakun climbed the stairs and was equally in awe of the key pads. Caellyn briefly remembered her own feelings of excitement and wonder, but those emotions were nowhere to be seen this time around. Any desire to investigate the buttons or to press them, had long since evaporated.

"I think we should press them," said Yakun.

"That's a negative," called Seerman, moving towards the base of the stairs as if he was ready to pull him away in person.

"Yakin stop being an arse," said Arundel. "I just want to get out of this place. Nothing good is going to happen if you touch those keys."

"You don't know that," he said. "Maybe it'll activate the whole Facility, maybe it'll make the air breathable, we could live down here."

"Yakun that's enough," interrupted Seerman. "We have a job to do, and we're not here to take unnecessary risks."

"I just think, what if Kowalski did that, what if that's where he disappeared to?"

"You want to disappear too?!" shouted Caellyn, stunning herself and everyone around her. "Get down from there, Yakun, Arundel's right, let's get an orb and get out of here. We've got a long walk ahead of us. Come back here later on a separate mission and play around with buttons, all right?"

It seemed to work. He sheepishly retreated and they moved on in silence, deeper into the structure. Caellyn shook her head. He was like a child trying to test boundaries he didn't understand. At least he was a damn good technician. You could just about forgive his eccentricities when he worked mechanical miracles.

He had spent the evening adapting the hover barges based on Caellyn and Seerman's description of the orbs. They'd been exhausted, physically and emotionally, but he had kept going, keeping them up until he'd finished extracting all the information he needed. If the hover barges were to support an alien power orb, then they conceded that it was a necessary sacrifice.

"How heavy are the orbs?" he had asked. That was a question which had stumped them. They had looked dumbfounded at each other for a few seconds, hoping the other had somehow logged an answer.

"Not too heavy, maybe like they had the same density as water?" Seerman tried.

Yakun tutted in an irritating way, "Okay, I'll just factor in a wide tolerance. We'll take several barges so we can double up to bring one orb out. And you say they were room temperature, like thirty degrees, and you touched them with your grabber, but it didn't shatter at the temperature gradient?" For some reason Yakun infuriated her with his tactless, blunt approach.

"No, the sticks didn't snap, we'd have told you if they did," Seerman replied dryly.

"Very strange," Yakun replied, as if not believing them. "Well, I suppose that at least means we should be able to mount one on the barges. Extraordinary, you know, if we can get them back to Earth. We'll have more than just a planet-shaping device; this technology could be very useful across a wide range of fields."

"One step at a time, Yakun," Seerman had replied, as they tried to walk away and get some sleep before Yakun noticed they were gone.

Still, his optimism, or perhaps his lack of awareness of danger, was a welcome distraction. Caellyn wished she had his naivety right now, or at least his ability to become consumed in a task, so that the surrounding circumstances didn't matter.

"Where does this off-shoot go?" came Arundel's voice, as she walked ahead of Caellyn, who was bringing up the rear of the four astronauts.

The side corridor. It was excruciating not to tell her about the way it had appeared from nowhere. Sharing would have eased the burden, but Caellyn knew it wasn't the right thing to do. It was bravery to keep it to herself and Seerman. Keeping Arundel and Yakun in the dark was necessary for making things go as smoothly as possible.

Then it dawned on her that they weren't far enough down the second elevator shaft. The corridor she'd seen was about a hundred metres ahead. They had only left the buttress room about ten minutes ago, so there's no way this could have been the side corridor from yesterday. A chill ran over her skin despite the heat. Arundel had stopped, staring down it, while Yakun and Seerman slowed and turned ahead.

"What is it?" said Arundel, staring at Caellyn's face. "You look like you've seen a ghost. You're scaring me, Caellyn. What's down there?"

"I don't know," she managed. She composed herself. This time she was sure, this corridor hadn't been there before. She knew it had appeared from nowhere. She shouldn't have doubted herself. But then it left the grim reality that there really were corridors appearing in the walls. It was like the first one, joined smoothly to the main side wall, heading into a darkened extent that the torches couldn't reach. "We don't have time to investigate," she said. "Whatever's down there we'll have to leave. We've got to make it to the Star-Sphere."

"Everything all right back there?" came Seerman's voice, his tone slow and purposeful. He'd seen it too. He must have walked past it, knowing that there was now another unresolved danger between them and the entrance. He knew as well as Caellyn did that these tunnels were appearing out of solid wall, looking like they'd been there for centuries, jutting against the main wall as if their structure had been born in the same process.

Caellyn wanted to scream. She wanted to tell Seerman that no, everything wasn't all right. That this was madness. But she found a scrap of solid matter in her nerves. It was as if she was outside her body, and someone else was controlling it.

"Everything's fine," she said, surprising herself. "Just these cross corridors," she replied.

"Keep alert," was his only response.

They moved on slowly down to the labs, passing the second side corridor, it's insides as dark and black as the day before. Reaching the labs, Yakun at least provided a distraction in his urgency to see the Mural of the star-spheres. They managed to tempt him to leave only by reminding him that the real thing was an hour's walk away.

Time passed slowly inside the pressure vessel environmental suits, their bodies gently swaying from side to side as they carried on. When they finally reached the control room they stopped to catch their breath and slow their heartbeats.

"It's beautiful," said Arundel, as they stared at the Star-Sphere through the view glass that overlooked the reactor hall. It was, in its own way. Sixteen orbs that ignored time, gravity and the oppressive heat of the furnace of Venus. They hung in a globe like a jewel cluster, their material worth more than all the diamonds on Earth. Small in comparison to the size of the vast reactor hall, they looked as if they were patiently waiting to prove their immense power.

Yakun had gone quiet, and it didn't even take too much effort to lure him away from the control panel on the far desk. His suit had registered a major actuation failure on the way down, but he had managed to reboot part of the system while the essentials carried on in the background. It was lucky it had happened to his suit or they didn't know what they would have done. It had frightened some reality into him, and his enthusiasm had all but waned into a desire to get in and out as quickly as possible.

They passed through the open airlock and slowly made their way around the curved platform to the edge of the reactor room floor, then crossing the fifty metres or so of its base until they arrived at the plinth that the Star-Spheres hovered above. They climbed the steps until they found themselves face to face with it once more.

"We can push them out from one side, but we need to first establish if we can touch them at two points. Any volunteers?" said Seerman

"I'll do it," said Yakun.

That surprised Caellyn. Maybe there was some real bravery or conscience to be a team player behind his scatter-gun exterior.

"Okay, but slowly," Seerman instructed. "Make sure to first push it outwards from the inside. Once you've moved it a few centimetres, touch it on the other side with your other arm, but only lightly at first."

"I understand," Yakun replied solemnly.

He walked towards the device, as Caellyn and the others backed away. Yakun positioned himself slowly next to the orbs so that he could reach the inside of the one hovering at waist height in front of him. He moved his arm inside the invisible larger globe, and slowly brought the end of his suit-arm into contact with one of the balls. Caellyn braced herself, her body ready to be flung forwards again, or to see Yakun combust in a ball of flame, or the device to fully initiate and tear them all into shreds of metal and flesh. But nothing happened. The orb moved slightly, and Yakun was standing there in one piece. The remaining orbs repositioned as he moved one globe out a few centimetres, before giving it the lightest of taps on the outside. It worked. There was no catastrophic reaction. He carefully removed his arms and looked at them, his eyes bright through the suit visor.

"That was incredible," he said, some of his vigour returning. "I think we can touch them on both sides, based on that tap. I don't understand how, but we can definitely manoeuvre them."

"Copy that. Well done, Yakun," Seerman replied. "Let's position a barge and see if we can remove it fully. Here goes nothing."

Caellyn stood on one side, Yakun on the other, and Seerman stood directly outside of it, positioning the hover barge next to the globe and extending its bracing legs to take the initial weight of its future cargo.

"Ready?" said Yakun, and they nodded. He reached inside the orb again to push the globe outwards. He moved it slowly, as the remaining globes rearranged, remorseful as one of their siblings was being removed, forming a new shape so that they all maintained their equidistant relationship.

"Careful," said Caellyn, as Yakun pushed it beyond the few centimetres they'd managed before. Yakun brought his second arm into contact with the outside of the globe so that he was holding it between his hands.

"I'm holding it," he said, his voice wavering and strained. Caellyn stared at his face, looking for any sign of the unexpected, but it was just a picture of intense concentration.

"It feels heavy, but I think I can just about support it if I need to," said Yakun. It was still maintaining some of its own levitation, but it was succumbing to gravity as it was pulled further from the device.

He placed it fully in the dish of the hover barge.

"There's still some elastic force trying to pull it back," he said. "But it falls off quickly away from the larger globe. The barge looks like it can take its weight. We can remove the leg supports and float it to the edge."

They move slowly in unison, taking each step methodically and carefully, until the hover barge sat motionless unsupported near the outer edge of the plinth. They all held their poses, watching it intently for a while, before slowly calming taut muscles as they realised it wasn't going anywhere.

"How about that!" he exclaimed in excitement. "We did it!"

"Well done, all," said Seerman.

They stood dumbfounded for a while, marvelling in their success.

"Where's Arundel?" said Caellyn with sudden panic. "She was standing just there."

They looked around. She was gone. There wasn't even a trace. There was nothing to hide her. They were in a giant shallow dish with few features apart from the plinth in the middle. They walked around it, but it was clear she was nowhere to be seen.

"Did she leave?" said Yakun, a rising exasperation in his voice

"It takes ten minutes at best to get back up to the control room," said Caellyn, feeling unnerved and exposed. "There's no way she could have made it, we were only turned around for a few minutes."

"Check the floor," said Seerman.

They walked down the steps and around the base of the plinth, but there were no marks, no gaps, no line that could possibly be a hinge line or a panel that could be removed.

"Sir, it could have been one of those side-tunnels," Caellyn said, her vocal cords tightened. "Just appearing in the floor, be careful where you stand."

"What tunnels?" said Yakun. "You're saying those side tunnels just appeared? They opened since we got here?"

"They appeared, Yakun," Seerman replied sombrely.

"Sun's wrath!" Yakun cried. "Why didn't you tell us that? That seems like quite an important thing to tell people walking past them!"

"For what?!" shouted Seerman. "Keep yourself calm, keep looking for anything that might indicate where Arundel could have gone." But Yakun was climbing back onto the plinth. "Yakun, I'm ordering you to stand fast. You knew there were many unknowns in here, get back down here," said Seerman.

"You walked us into a bloody death trap," he said, reaching the top of the plinth. "I'm getting the hell..." but he was cut off, as if in shock. "What the hell is that!" he screamed.

He stood motionless, as if he was pinned in place. Then he took a few steps back, unsteady on his feet, losing balance and picking up speed off the top of the plinth.

"Yakun!" shouted Caellyn, as he started to fall backward onto the floor. She moved forwards instinctively to try to catch him, but he crashed to the ground, landing hard on the floor, and there was a crack like a lightning bolt.

Caellyn nearly threw up in her suit. That bolt meant only one thing. It was a severe pressurisation, as a chink in the metal armour opened up and let the Venusian atmosphere in. It would have filled the suit in a fraction of a second, turning him into a boiled, evaporated skeletal mess. She could barely hold herself to look, but the inside of his visor was splattered with blood that had dried before it even touched the glass and nothing was visible through it.

She stared at Seerman aghast, the crumpled body of Yakun at her feet. Seerman's face was pale and motionless, as they both tried to steady themselves. Caellyn gagged again, holding back her stomach as the acid burned on the throat.

"Sir, we need to..." started Caellyn, but as she said it her mind went blank, as if she had an idea that just vanished. "We need to..." she said, trying a second time but to no avail. Seerman stayed silent, until he simply turned and started climbing the plinth. Caellyn instinctively followed, as if whatever Yakun saw was preferable to being left down on the floor of the chamber alone.

But she reached the top and there was nothing. The orbs sat motionless, like before, now in their new configuration of fifteen, with the sixteenth sitting harmless on the hover barge to the side.

"What did he see?" said Caellyn.

"It doesn't matter," replied Seerman quietly. "None of it matters."

"Sir?" Caellyn replied.

"It's over Caellyn," he said, staring blankly at the wall in the distance. "We've lost three people. I've never lost anyone on a mission before. Do you know what they threatened me with if the mission failed?" he said, lost in his thoughts.

"Sir, look at me. We have to carry on," She tried to force eye contact with him.

"There's something here, something around us. We're helpless, we're just being picked off. We never should have come." He carried on, his voice wavering.

"We have to fight; we can make it back to the surface," Caellyn said as she shook his suit as if to jolt his mind into its normal focussed configuration. "We have an orb. We just have to make it out of here. We can do it, sir."

He looked at her, his eyes wide. His pupils were dilated and skin tight. But as he met her gaze, his features relaxed and reformed. They slowly reshaped themselves into his normal confident demeanour.

Whatever she had done, it seemed to have work. He blinked hard and knocked himself back into the present. He was a fighter and he wasn't done yet. Caellyn surprised herself with her persuasiveness. Or maybe Seerman had realised that he simply couldn't handle not being the one with the brave face. Either way, Caellyn pulled him out of his trance for a brief moment.

"You're right," he said quietly. "You're right."

Caellyn looked around. The scene was eerily quiet. The air felt still, as if every molecule was standing rigid to attention. There was no sound apart from the hissing and spluttering of the coolant systems inside their suits. The whole reactor hall was a bare, empty tomb. The only feature was Yakun's metal husk lying on the floor. Where the hell had Arundel gone? Where was she now? She'd been subsumed into the wall or the floor. She was either dead or alone in the hidden recesses of this god-forsaken place.

Caellyn should have been afraid. They were being picked off, one by one, deep under the surface of Venus. She should have screamed and run. But there was something inside her that didn't give in. There were reserves of courage, of something. Maybe it wasn't courage; maybe it was foolhardiness. Maybe it was simply an ability to detach her emotions when her back was well and truly against the wall. Whatever it was, it was giving her some clarity, where Seerman seemed lost.

In the far corner, opposite the control room, she spotted another corridor. It was like it had appeared just then while her back was turned. It couldn't possibly have been there before; she would have noticed it.

"Sir, over there, there's another corridor."

"I know," came Seerman's solemn response. Just as she moved to grab his arm and pull him slowly out of the Facility, a clattering rang out far above them, up by the control room, and Caellyn tuned to see the airlock door swing closed in the distance. She stared at the control room window above them, with a morbid beat in her heart, trying to make out shapes, trying to see something in the darkness of the windows.

It was hopeless. They were trapped. They were trapped like rats in a maze, or a fly in a flesh-eating plant, having been lured in to meet a slow and painful death. There was clear intention from *something* to pick them off: an alien entity or the Facility itself. An intelligence was manipulating and feeding off them. The severed root-limb. She had to see if it was still there. She turned to look for it, leaving Seerman transfixed on the corridor. He hadn't even flinched at the closing of the air hatch, as if his thoughts had stuttered and dropped off a cliff. Caellyn searched for the hand, looking among the shallow fins, but it wasn't there. *Shit* she thought.

She was losing her mind. It felt like a dream. It felt as if the atmosphere was inside her suit, and she was sweating through intense heat and pressure. *Focus.* She focussed on her breathing. *Slow it down.* One breath after another, she lowered her heart-rate. Her emotions were numb and distant. But then something grew in her mind.

"Sir, I think they want us to take the corridors."

Seerman was lost, just staring.

"Sir!" Caellyn shouted. It seemed to work; he turned, briefly recognising her, as if taking her in for the first time. Terror broke over his face before he shook himself to his senses.

"Sir, I think we have to take the corridor. We don't have a choice. We'll die if we stay here. We have to find out what's down there."

Seerman nodded slowly, fighting rigid muscles to agree with her. She watched him, hoping he would snap back into the old Seerman, hoping he would find that reassurance that he'd given her the past few days.

She thought about the tree in the hydroponics deck. She thought about Seerman sitting against it in casual clothes, convincing her to come to Venus with him, reassuring her that he would lead the mission full of confidence. But that Seerman seemed as far away as the StratoPort. *He is lost; the mission was the only thing keeping him going. The mission gave him focus, it gave him reassurance, and without it he is adrift. Now it's down to me; there's no one else.*

"Sir, let's go," said Caellyn quietly. She looked around, her body tingling as it feared hidden doors and entities appearing and disappearing with every turn. Nothing around her felt solid or trustworthy. But the reactor room was the same. There was just the corridor, calling to them. Holding Seerman's arm, she moved them slowly towards it. They crossed the floor until they were at its entrance. No marks, no hinges, no join marks, just a void. She took a deep breath and walked into it. It was dark and close, Caellyn walking forward first, shining a light down its extent, seeing only endless blackness. As they walked down its length, a mist started to appear, a slow fog hanging in the air. The heads-up display skewed momentarily with distortion before snapping back into its programmed layout.

What do they want me to find? Where are they leading us? She walked on forwards through the mist. *What does it even matter? They've left us no choice. There is only one way forward.*

After a while the corridor opened up into a wider, more circular passageway. It looked organic, as if it had been cultivated. It looked like trees had grown up around the sides, melding together as they grew, to create a single surface.

"Caellyn," said Seerman behind her. "I need you to know something."

"Sir, what is it?"

"I told my son I was heading to the SeaPort but I'd be back for his college graduation. He was studying aeronautics like I did. I told my daughter not to get married before I returned. I lied to them; they bloody forced me to lie to them. I need to know that if I don't make it..." he trailed off. "I need to know that if I don't make it, that you'll tell them where I went, that you'll tell them I'm sorry."

"Of course, sir," said Caellyn, her eyes welling up.

"I need to know you'll tell them I love them, and my wife, tell her I love her, that she was everything to me. Tell her I never would have gone if they hadn't threatened..."

"Sir..." It was as if he'd already given up. As if he'd already resigned himself to his fate. "Sir, we're going to get through this, you can tell them yourself."

She moved on, anger filling her thoughts. She wasn't going to die down here. That was what she was angry about. Or maybe it was Seerman's resignation. Maybe it was this goddam Facility. Maybe it was the life she might not get to return to herself.

This can't all be for nothing. We will find something in these tunnels. There has to be something down here. Then she found a glimmer of hope.

"Sir, they could have killed us already. They want us to live. If they didn't want us to live then they would have already taken us," she said, finding hope in her own words. It was scarce hope to go on, but it was hope nonetheless. "Sir, they want us to find something down here."

But there was no response. She turned around, knowing what she would see, and sure enough, he was gone.

Then the anger boiled inside her. It was fuelled by fear, by hopelessness, by loneliness. She was angry at everything. She was angry at Seerman for convincing her to come. She was angry at the planet, she was angry at Kowalski for his suit failing, she was angry at Yakun for dying. She was angry at herself.

But she was all alone. And her courage left her. With Seerman gone, her reserves depleted. They'd been keeping each other buoyant, and now there was nothing to balance against. He'd evaporated into thin air, and so had the last ounces of security.

She turned to see a giant entity slowly ambling towards her down the larger passageway. It was twelve feet tall and looked like the roots of a tree. It had many black legs, or arms, or tendrils, that spread out from a small upper body section, each splitting into further branches that touched the floor as if they were gripping onto its smooth surface. The roots were moving one after the other. There were eight, ten, maybe twelve main arms, each taking it in turns to move over the others, propelling the beast towards Caellyn. Above its upper body, was a face, or at least it could have been a face. It was triangular, with two large eyes draped over the edges, like a cross between a mutt and a praying mantis.

It moved silently towards Caellyn, and she turned to run. She begged her suit to move fast, but it was no use. The joints hissed and creaked as they tried to push it as hard as possible towards the smaller tunnel. If she could just make it back there then the giant entity might not be able to follow. But the suits weren't designed for speed. The coffin pressure vessel rolled from side to side and warning lights flashed on her display as she hit design limits. She screamed at it in anguish. She slowly turned to see the progress of the beast behind her, and found it was standing right there, looming over her, one of its roots reaching out so that it was almost touching her visor.

She felt her world darken, as it just faded away to blackness. She felt an energy coming from the alien, like it was charging her body with electrostatic force. It felt like the damping in the walls, but now all around and through her, running over her teeth and through her hair. And then everything went dark, and she lost consciousness.

Chapter 19

Caellyn awoke, her eyes struggling to adjust to the brightly lit surroundings. She pushed away the bleariness and the world slowly came into focus.

She tried to make sense of where she was. She looked up at the ceiling that was slowly passing: she was moving. She tried to move an arm, but it was pinned down. She tried a leg, and found it equally restrained.

She was on her back and could feel herself being supported by something that didn't feel solid, as if she was gently floating on a bed of air. Its surface felt cold and hard, unsuited to making a human being comfortable. She could make out that she was in a large corridor, large enough to fly a dropship through, and she was being slowly transported along it.

I'm dead. This is the afterlife. But then she noticed the ceiling; it was made of the same material as the corridor they'd found themselves in at the base of the Facility. This time it was off white, but it had the structure as before: an irregularity that suggested it had been grown. *The alien.* She remembered the sensation of being blacked out, and it stung her brain again, so that she had to pull it together and restart her mind with simple thoughts.

Above her a series of lights gave off a warm glow. They passed one by one as the corridor moved by around her. They gave off a strange heat that bathed the skin in light like the sun, and it made the skin rejoice as it fed photoreceptors like flood water over broken ground.

Then she gasped for air. And her lungs filled. She was open to the atmosphere around her. Her suit was nowhere to be seen, but the air around her was breathable. It was nourishing. After days breathing recycled air from her environmental suit, she'd forgotten what fresh air tasted like. In fact, this air was fresher than even on the StratoPort. Even that air had been through pressurisers and filters, but this was clean. It was almost painfully clean. Her lungs were so used to having to fight, to pull the oxygen out of the gas mixture and reel at its unnatural components, that she had to prevent herself taking full breaths as it felt like her chest might explode. She breathed heavy, short breaths until her blood vessels became sated and her lungs stopped clamouring.

Seerman. Yakun. Arundel. Maybe they were alive too. *Shit, not Yakun.* A dread filled her as the memories of his unconscious suit came back to her, acting as his final resting place and tomb. He had seen danger, and it had cost him his life.

She needed to move. She tried to struggle, but nothing worked. She could feel her body, but whatever was holding her in place was so tight that she couldn't budge an inch. She could move her eyes left and right, and that was it; everything else was paralyzed.

The corridor narrowed, and the walls became straighter and flatter. Their surface was still unorganised and irregular in the way that only nature can achieve, but whatever had grown to form the walls had been pressed and coerced into a smoother finish.

Then sculptures appeared on both sides. They were made of the same organic-looking material but grown into shapes that looked almost human.

She swallowed hard and almost choked as her unmoving body refused to adjust in normal ways. She strained her eyes to their lateral extent to try and get a better view of the statues passing by. They looked like mummified humans, forever fixed in a final pose like they'd been hit by the ash-cloud of a pyroclastic flow and instantly petrified. But there was something odd about them. They passed on either side like a museum or trophy cabinet, but each one was slightly different. In each one the proportions and outline were wrong. In one the arms were long and large, with stocky legs and an elongated skull. Then another went past, this time smaller. It was human, but squat and rounded. The arms looked as if they jutted out from shoulders too high, making it look unnatural and in a permanent state of discomfort.

As she travelled on, more and more passed her. They were all different, all with some semblance of humanity but all with different mutations and variances. Then, out of the corner of her eye, she spotted one that looked familiar. It was human, and human as she knew it. She gasped as for a moment she thought it resembled Seerman, but it was too difficult to see through the strain in her eyes as it slid by. No, it couldn't have been him, she thought. He was alive, somewhere else, he had to be. She was seeing things. She'd just wanted to see something familiar.

But then the statues stopped, and the wall opened out again, and she felt a revulsion. They were a display of conquests or experiments, lined up in a corridor, and she was the next test subject. Fear gripped her still body.

She heard a stuttered, almost electronic, groan come from behind her, and her hearing caught onto a constant pattering of heavy feet, like an army marching out of step. It had been there all along, but her senses had only just caught up with her. She knew what it was. She felt a cold sweat pore out of paralysed limbs as she realised there was an entity behind her, pushing the slate bed along. *What on earth are these beasts?* She remembered its gangling root-like limbs, its imposing height, its mesmeric movement as it slowly glided towards her.

Against every sense of resistance, she tried to strain her eyes upwards, to see what was there, and she caught sight of it. Standing over her was another alien. But it looked different. It was of similar size to the first, but this time it was thicker and broader. It was covered in a dark bark-like skin that was gnarled and twisted, but with an even temperament that suggested the bark was crafted by the hand of a designer. She could just about make out a head before it leaned forwards. Two large eyes fixed on her, and her world went dark again as she blacked out.

* * *

She awoke again to the sound of a human voice.

"Caellyn! She's coming around."

She recognised that voice, but her mind was full of fog, and she couldn't place it. She couldn't place anything at that point. Her eyes slowly let in light, and she saw a face she wasn't expecting. It was Kowalski. Her heart leaped with joy. He was alive.

"Kowalski," she managed to murmur.

"It's all right, Caellyn, you're safe for the moment, take your time."

Relief flooded through her; it was the first time she'd felt safe in about a week. It caused strands of muscle to uncurl after having been stuck in rigid positions over the last few days. The constant threat of the Venusian atmosphere and the dark corridors of the Facility had kept her subconscious on high alert. Despite everything, she absorbed his voice and felt a level of reassurance. The sound of Kowalski's words, the breathable atmosphere, the solid floor; her muscles relaxed so they felt like goo.

But she had no idea where they were. Kowalski was sitting next to her, perched up against the side of a room, as the walls slowly curved out of the floor.

"Where are we?" she said, as blood returned to her extremities and her nervous system tingled back into life.

"We don't know," he said. "Just take some time to acclimatise."

She took in her surroundings. It was a large cube of a room, made of the white organic material. The four walls, ceiling and floor were all square, and each joined another through a radius to smooth out any sharp lines. She was braced up against one of the curves. She felt the texture of the organic surface. It was hard, like plastic or glass.

There was Kowalski sitting next to her, and then, sitting in the middle of the room, were two people she didn't recognise. She racked her brain as to who they were, but she'd never seen them before.

"The First Expedition," she said quietly to Kowalski.

"Yes, this is Boldun and Parker."

They waved at her half-heartedly, barely acknowledging the newcomer as they crouched over something in the centre of the floor.

"Where's everyone else?"

"It's just us," Kowalski responded. "It was just them, the First Expedition, for a long time. I told them we'd arrived on Venus a year after they did, but they said they'd counted a year and a half in here. Once a day the aliens turn out the lights in the ceiling. Perhaps they're showing us a minor mercy by at least giving us night to sleep in, but it's very easy to lose track of time in here."

"Crak," Caellyn said, her mind returning. She stared at the two astronauts from the First Expedition. They were completely bald. Even their eyebrows were gone. In fact, so were Kowalski's, though she'd recognise him anywhere from his sheer size and broad features. Then she touched her own head, and found she was bald too.

"They take our hair," Kowalski said. "Sorry about that."

"What do they want with us?" Caellyn said, sitting up and noticing the light source in the ceiling. It felt natural and warming as it illuminated the room. She looked over at the two astronauts from the First Expedition who were all but ignoring her. They threw pebbles into a pile on the floor, looking like they were playing some kind of game.

"We're not sure," Kowalski replied. "Once a day one of the walls disappears and one of the Reapers—that's what we call them—one of the Reapers comes in and blacks us all out, like a coma. Like the one you were in when you arrived. Then we come to and the wall is back, as solid as ever, and they've left three bowls of food. Occasionally they take one of us, but we don't remember anything until we wind up here again."

"I heard one make a noise, like it was communicating," Caellyn said. "It sounded like a stuttered wail."

"We've heard them do that, but I'm afraid to say we aren't fluent Reaper yet," Kowalski replied. "Parker thinks they're just toying with us, that all this was just a test, an experiment," he lowered his voice to a whisper, "They've been in here a long time, you can imagine what that does to the mind."

Caellyn looked around the room. It was bare. She couldn't imagine spending a year in here, maybe more, being constantly made unconscious and counting days by the dimming of room lights. It was just big enough to run around in, but you'd be running in circles, just seeing wall after identical wall pass you by.

Frustrated at being ignored by the First Expedition, she got up, steadying herself on legs that didn't feel like they'd walked in a while. A head-rush split her forehead, and she took a moment to wait for the blood in her brain to settle. She moved towards the two astronauts, finally getting their attention.

One had rounded features and a large flat nose that seemed to be accentuated by the lack of hair on his bald head, while the other was thin and had a pointed, split chin. The one with the large nose reeled slightly as he saw her approach, as the other one eyed her suspiciously.

"Caellyn," she said, throwing out a hand for pleasantries.

"Parker," he replied, standing up. His suspicion broke for a moment as he remembered how to greet another human being. "This is Boldun. Welcome to the afterlife," he said.

"He's joking," Kowalski interjected from back by the wall. "We think."

"Another from the second expedition," Parker continued in a posh ringing accent. "We thought we'd be here forever, just the two of us, before Kowalski over there turned up a week ago."

"A week ago?" Caellyn replied. "But he only disappeared just over a day ago."

"Ah well that's the coma, you see," Parker replied, as Boldun stayed on the floor fumbling with pebbles. "You never know how long you've been out for. Let me give you the tour. Boldun stand up!" he snapped, and the other man jumped to attention. "Sorry about him," Parker continued, "Hasn't taken well to being in here. Difficult to keep the mind together, you know." Caellyn shook his hand, as Boldun smiled without eye contact. "Now let's see, which wall is which? I always forget; you have to look for the little imperfections in the graining. Ah yes, that's the main wall, the one the Reapers come through in their armour."

"Their armour?"

"That's what we think it is. We all saw one on Venus before we were taken and brought here, without that bark stuff on. We think they put it on to protect themselves in this Earth-like atmosphere, and their natural environmental habitat is Venus." He scratched his shoulder and cursed quietly to himself. "Now, where was I? Ah yes, over there is the toilet. You just walk up to the wall and the door appears, or rather disappears, and there's a hole in the floor. We think it's a toilet. Well, we've been using it as a toilet, and the Reapers haven't stopped us. That's about it, I'm afraid. Now if you don't mind we are just in the middle of a game of Gotch," to which he went back down on his knees and resumed the throwing of pebbles as if Caellyn wasn't even there anymore. She went back over to the wall and sat next to Kowalski.

"We need to get out of here and back to the Lander," Caellyn said, loud enough for the First Expeditioners to hear. They ignored her and carried on with the game.

"Of course," Kowalski replied. "But we're not even sure we're on Venus anymore. We get the briefest glimpse of a large corridor outside before we black out, but that's all we've seen."

"We can't stay in this box," she replied, staring around at the walls. "What... what happened to you? After..."

"Me? My power was running low, I feared the worst as the storm wasn't abating. It got down to two percent and I heard a noise down the elevator shaft. I thought it was you and Seerman returning, but then a Reaper appeared and blacked me out."

"Jesus, we were down in the reactor room at the time."

"I know," Kowalski replied. "They were watching us; they were there all along. Maybe Parker is right, maybe this was all just a trap. They could even have been watching humanity on Earth, from here, the whole time."

"I.... the Star-Sphere," she whispered.

As she said it Boldun and Parker stopped their game and turned to look at her, as if she'd said words that brought up a long-lost memory within them. They looked as if they were grappling with old thoughts stored in the back of their minds.

"We don't know if it was even real, or if it even worked," said Kowalski.

"We have to try to get out," said Caellyn. "We have to get out of here and find where we are. What about Seerman and Arundel?"

"We haven't seen them," Kowalski replied. "What about Yakun, you didn't push him out the airlock did you?"

"Dead," she replied. "He fell off the plinth. Suit cracked open." She closed her eyes as she said the words, fighting back tears.

"Oh my god, I'm sorry," he said in a strained voice. "Goddamn. He deserved better. We all do," he murmured.

Caellyn fought a tidal surge of emotion. She thought of Yakun turning up for mess on the *Molniya-V* covered in machine soot. She thought of Arundel and Seerman, maybe alone in their own cubes. She thought of the picture of Seerman's children that he had tacked onto his bunk head in the Lander. As the feeling rose, she fought back tears.

Noticing from the centre of the room, Parker motioned her over, as if a whisp of empathy had found its way back into his brain after over a year with just Boldun for company. She walked over, wiping her cheeks and kneeled next to them.

"Caellyn, we have a plan," Parker said in a hushed voice. "But keep your voice down, we have no idea whether they listen in on us or not. We don't think so, because we don't seem terribly significant to them. Anyway...oh, yes. When they come in, once a day, they black us out into a brief coma. We lose consciousness, but we've been trying to fight it. We can resist it, more and more each day. We don't think they notice us doing it. Boldun has managed to stay awake long enough to almost touch one of them."

Finally, some fighting spirit. She nodded back. Boldun just stared down at the pile of pebbles on the floor, trying to pretend they weren't next to him talking.

"Boldun, show...sorry what's your name again?" he said

"Caellyn."

"Boldun, show Caellyn, here, the splinter."

Boldun straightened his right leg and pulled a shard of something out of his combat trousers. It was a long black splinter of thin material that converged to a sharp point at one end.

"I've got this," he said, half grunting as if he'd almost forgotten how to speak. "I think I am getting better at staying awake, I think I can jab one soon."

"What he's trying to say," interjected Parker with frustration, "Is that we can take out the guard, and try and escape."

Caellyn smiled; hope at least. That's all they needed. Something to make it feel like they weren't completely trapped in this cube. She went back to Kowalski and closed her eyes, trying to collect her thoughts. After a while the light in the ceiling dimmed, and natural exhaustion took over.

The days passed, as the ceiling light went on and off periodically. They slept when it was dark and tried to keep themselves busy during the light. Parker and Boldun would play the game religiously in the centre of the room. Parker would normally win, but occasionally Boldun would sneak a victory and howl with delight, as Parker sulked in the corner.

They taught Caellyn how to play. They had a number of smooth round pebbles, looking like they had been hewn naturally on a beach, and you would line them up in piles and try to take the opponent's by redistributing one of your piles around clockwise.

Parker and Boldun took great pride in beating her at first. But then she beat Boldun, and he looked as if he was going to stab her with the shard, before Parker held him back, and so she decided to leave them to it for a few days. They couldn't help but step on each other's toes and ruffle each other's feathers in the cube, and it was all they could do to try and maintain some order.

The Reapers came in once a day and blacked them out. Caellyn tried to resist, but it felt impossible. It was like an elephant was sitting on your brain, and you were trying to resist it with thoughts alone. One day she felt she managed to make some progress, but it was like fighting a heavy anaesthetic. The next day, the progress was gone, and she was out like a light.

Every day they'd come out of the Reaper's coma to find four nondescript bowls of grey liquid. It actually tasted not too bad. It was better than the StratoPort nutrition paste. It was salty and sweet, and there was the slightest floral hint that almost suggested real fruit had been put in it. The bowls were delivered on a tray, and some days there were more pebbles on it.

"We think they give them to us to keep us entertained," said Boldun one day, breaking the silence of the game they were playing. He and Caellyn had resumed the occasional face-off, once the ground rules had been made clear to Boldun about acceptable behaviour. He'd seemed genuinely remorseful about his earlier outburst and had tried to play Caellyn more often once he relaxed, and once he realised she treated him with more humanity than Parker did. Caellyn obliged, out of affection and pity, but mostly to pass the long hours in the cube. If the Reapers really had given them the pebbles for entertainment, then it was a small patronising mercy.

"You got the shard from the tray?" said Caellyn one day, realising that the tray was the same material as the shard that Boldun showed her.

Boldun nodded. "They didn't even notice. Whatever they are, we don't seem too important to them."

That made sense; they were like caged animals. They'd been trapped for study, with only the smallest fleeting care for their well-being.

"We're trophies," Parker said, sulking in the corner that day, for some reason or another. "You said you saw statues in the corridor. Maybe we're next."

"We'd already be there if that was so," Kowalski interjected, keeping a tight lid on Parker when he was wound up.

Occasionally one of them would be taken. A Reaper would come through the door unexpectedly and they'd awake to find someone gone. The person would be away for a few hours before being returned, none the wiser as to what had happened.

One day Caellyn was taken. When she came to, she was stuck rigid to the board again, this time in an upright position. Her heart froze as it forgot how to beat. In front of her was a large window of the same composition as the view screen in the control room of the Venus Facility, and beyond it was one of the Reapers. It looked similar to how she'd seen them on Venus, without the bark-like exo-skin.

The Reaper was moving around what looked like a laboratory of growth-like structures. Some seemed to glow when the Reaper approached, and as it would reach out one of its root-like limbs a light would shoot into the wider structure like an electrical current. Occasionally she saw the light zip towards her through the floor, and she would feel jolts of electricity, and the strange damping that went through your bones and left you tasting dull metal. The Reaper looked to be varying the power, and occasionally walked up to the glass and stared at her from close range as she tried not to pass out from fear. But the jolts of damping were never too painful. Whatever it was doing it was at least not hurting her. It felt like it was experimenting, to see her response to the currents, testing if her body could withstand them.

When she returned to the cube the others were astounded she had been awake during it.

"So that's where they take us," Parker said. "Gives me the creeps, you almost don't want to know that kind of thing. Did it make any noises, like it was trying to communicate at all?"

"No, no noises. It came up close and stared at me a few times. Heck, its eyes bugged me out. I almost passed out when I tried to look at them. After that I tried to look anywhere else."

Parker treated her with a level of reverence after that, but it bordered on jealousy, as if he had wanted to be the first to see something other than the cube. But in the days that followed the cycle went back to normal, just lights on, food left, and lights off. Parker lost it one day and just started screaming and wailing, and Kowalski had to pin him to the floor while he calmed down.

A few days later Parker was taken, but he never returned. After a few hours, Boldun started worrying, until the following day only three bowls were left by the Reaper. Boldun cried to himself in the corner and was inconsolable.

"We have to get out of here," Caellyn said to Kowalski, as Boldun went quiet, only letting out an occasional whimper.

"I agree," Kowalski replied. "Boldun said he was managing to resist the blackout comas long enough to swing his arm. I think you should check on him. He doesn't seem to acknowledge me as much as he does you."

Caellyn gave it a few hours, and the next morning Boldun was at least more responsive.

"Can you resist them long enough?" She said to him, as they sat in the corner and ate the thick grey liquid in the bowls. "We'll only get one shot at this."

"I think so," he said. "I don't know. We better do it soon before they take anyone else."

"I agree. Boldun, I'm not sure what we'd do without you. But we only get one chance at it, are you sure you can strike the Reaper?"

"I'm sure," he said after a pause, with a quiet fiery conviction.

Chapter 20

Boldun crouched by the wall, just to the side of where the door would appear and the Reaper would walk through. He held the shard down by his side and his lips moved as he ran through his thoughts in nervous anticipation. Caellyn and Kowalski waited patiently in the centre of the room, playing a game of Gotch, but barely concentrating on it as they waited for the Reaper to arrive.

Caellyn braced her mind. She had made a little progress in trying to resist the blackouts, enough to feel like she was at least pushing against a dam wall before the water came rushing over the top. Over the past days and weeks, Boldun had tried to teach her how he was managing to resist it, and she had felt it work a small amount. But it felt difficult beyond compare, and every time the Reaper arrived, she was out like a light just as her thoughts marshalled themselves into some sort of defence.

Boldun explained that you needed to focus all your mind, lighting up every neurological pathway, because if even one was dormant then the Reaper would find its way in and spread out across your brain, putting you to sleep. He'd muttered like a madman, but you couldn't argue against his results. Whatever he was doing it seemed to be working for him. Boldun explained how you focus your mind on an image or a memory, simultaneously taking in your surroundings. The deeper you went into your thoughts, and the more you were able to absorb from the world around you through your senses, the more you'd be able to hold onto them against the mental barrage from the Reaper.

Caellyn first tried the hydroponics deck. She thought of the trees, the musty smell, and of being caught in the sprinklers when water gushed through their dry pipes once a month and drench everything across the deck. She thought of returning a sodden book that she'd desperately tried to dry out over her cabin heater, and the look on the librarian's face at the warped pages.

But it didn't work. It didn't seem to be a strong enough memory. Next she tried her school days. She'd been class captain for the intra-year touch-Slamball tournament, and scored a goal deep in injury time to win the semi-final, to the adulation of the small crowd of parents, families and teachers. Her dad was jumping up and down in the stands and her class lifted her up onto their shoulders. They lost the final, but it didn't matter; they hadn't expected to get so far anyway. It was about the comradery and the carefree days afterwards where the entire class was floating on a cloud and boys chased her like squabbling sparrows.

But neither seemed to be working, and it was a mental strain to be able to remember such events, so far away, and what felt like so long ago. She fought back tears at the memories, when now she was trapped in a white cube, separated from everyone she cared about on the StratoPort by uncrossable space and time. *We have to escape. I have to push through the pain and fear and make it work. I need even the smallest defence against the Reapers.*

She remembered the day that the Venus find was first communicated to the public. She was fifteen. It broke on the morning news. The mural was in a picture behind the news-reader's head, and they were excitedly telling the viewers about a new hope that had been found on our neighbouring planet, hope that could blossom into the redemption of Earth. They talked of facilities and Star-Spheres. Caellyn didn't quite understand what everyone was so excited about, but her mum came into their living quarters with the broadest of smiles and a light in her eyes. It wasn't something Caellyn had seen in her before. Normally she was impassive, said little in the mornings, and turned up late after work. She would nonchalantly asked them about their day, but hardly listened to answers as she read data sheets and huffed about delays and inefficiencies.

But just that once, all the distance disappeared. It was like a curtain was raised, and her real mum came out for the first time. She took her daughter down to a hideout she used to use when she was fifteen herself, down in the Undercity, and they excitedly chatted about everything life could offer. Caellyn saw her mother in a different light, as a person, and it was the first time that she had cherished some level of similarity to her. There was warmth and security to her that had been buried beneath the humdrum of their daily lives.

It brought tears to her eyes as she thought about it now, the memory waiting in the back of her mind like a loaded bullet against the Reaper's mental onslaught.

They had no idea what time it was; there was no way to tell in the cube. They simply waited with anticipation for the Reaper. The noise of the Gotch discs sounded like bellowing drums as they lightly skittered over the organic-hard floor. The walls felt even more oppressive, like a prison, and it felt like they were closing in, and the cube was shrinking. They waited for the entrance door to dissolve, to see glimpses of the passageway beyond, their only hope of escape, behind the Reaper clad in its protective suit.

Focus on the walls, thought Caellyn. Focus on the patterns, the imperfections. There was a bulge over on the right side that almost looked like an elephant head. There was a shallow recess in the ceiling that Caellyn imagined was a lake on Earth, surrounded by stump-dead trees, withered by acid rain. No, she pushed that thought away. She changed her mind. It was a shallow lake surrounded by *live* trees, blowing in the wind, like one of the images on the wall-screens in the cabins.

Time seemed to pass intangibly in their white cube prison. Boldun stayed crouched by the door in a state of readiness. He was mouthing thoughts to himself, preparing his own memories, filling his mind with imagery that would ground him and hold his consciousness awake against the overwhelming power of the Reaper's telepathy.

And then it happened. The door in the wall dissolved, and there was the Reaper, slowly moving into the room.

Caellyn felt the darkness coming, and she tried to push it away with her mind. She tried to focus on the details of the hideaway in the Undercity, the smile of her mother and the excitement in her voice. She focussed on the present, the cube around her, the surface of the Gotch pebbles, and of Kowalski, his body already going limp as the darkness took him. She felt the drowsiness of sleep as the Reaper advanced, and her vision became separated and blurred.

She caught sight of Boldun moving in the corner of her eye. He was there, swinging. The Reaper hadn't seen him. He swung the shard through the air towards the shell of the giant beast in front of them. Caellyn wanted to shout out, but drowsiness consumed her, and she felt herself slipping away, the blackout taking hold.

But it didn't take her. There was a loud bang, and an awful sucking sound like a decompression event. Caellyn was coming to, but she suddenly felt heat, intense heat on her skin, like she'd been splattered with molten lava. It burned and sizzled on specks up her right arm and across her chest. She was dotted in pain that seared as it cooked layers of flesh. She cried out in anguish. She heard Kowalski's voice, also screaming, and then her consciousness returned.

Boldun was a gruesome mess. The Reaper was too. It had fallen over and was a tangle of armoured limbs on the floor. Boldun's shard must have struck through the Reaper's armour. Inside the Reaper's outer shell was the immense temperature and pressure of the Venusian surface, and with its containment breached, its insides were forced out in a fraction of a second. It had liquified and sublimed its entire body through a small crack, and it was now splattered across the floor and up the wall, red-black globs and chunks looking like the worst murder scene you could imagine. Boldun was among that somewhere. He'd taken the brunt of it, and it had seared the flesh off his bones like a molten pressure gun.

"Caellyn, the door," came Kowalski's voice. It was open.

Gagging at the smell and still reeling from the pain of molten spray across her body, she stood up and steadied her legs.

"Let's go," she said. There was no turning back. Whatever was out there was their last hope. Better to die fighting than live caged. They moved fast. The door could disappear at any moment, and they wouldn't get another chance. They ran around the lifeless husk of the Reaper, saying a silent prayer of thanks to Boldun that would never be repaid, and found themselves in the large corridor.

It was the same one that Caellyn had awoken in the first time. It was large enough for a drop ship, its curved roof far above them. You could walk an entire army of Reapers through here, standing four abreast, with ample room above their twelve-foot height. To the right it headed into the distance before curving upwards and out of sight. To the left, about a hundred metres away, was an end-wall with a series of round holes near its base. They stood for a moment dumbstruck, trying to assess their options with all the haste they could muster, a last roll of the dice that they would strike lucky with an escape route. But the rest of the corridor was featureless. If there were other options, they were hidden behind more invisible doorways.

The wall behind them stayed open, as if inviting them to go back into the cube-cell.

"There's a breeze coming from those holes," said Caellyn, feeling it on the bare follicles on her arm, from the ones that weren't singed and burnt, with their nerve endings deadened.

They both started running in that direction. There were four holes, each at chest height, that looked just about big enough to climb through. It was only a hundred metres away, but it felt like however fast they ran they weren't running fast enough. A horn rang out down the corridor, deafeningly loud. Caellyn turned to see two armoured Reapers come out of doors that hadn't existed a moment ago.

"We can make it," shouted Kowalski. "Don't look back."

They pounded the floor, putting every energy possible into howling leg muscles, squeezing out any power from sinews that wanted to stop. They heaved air, trying to run when their bodies wanted to freeze solid in fear. They were closing in on the holes but could hear the soft padding of the Reapers behind them. She turned; she couldn't resist. But the Reapers weren't closing. This time it was Caellyn that was free to run unimpeded and the Reapers who were wearing protective suits.

They were almost at the wall. Caellyn thought she could see light coming from the holes. The current of air coming from them was stronger, and then she saw a flash of green on the other side. Her view was blurred and jarred from the exertion, but it looked like something green and natural. Too late now to turn back. Whatever it was, it was their only choice.

The last tens of metres seemed like an impossible hurdle. With every step it felt as if the holes got further away. But then they were upon them, diving into them, scrabbling through on knees and elbows like fish convulsing in the open air. They skittered down the small tubes, lashing their feet in case something grabbed onto them, and steeling their minds in case the blackout appeared at the fringes.

The end of the tubes came into view. Ahead, there was a scene that didn't look right. It looked like a meadow. There was green grass stretching out over a wide expanse, and a forest of trees on the left-hand side, curving around into the distance behind a tall hill. It looked exactly like one of the videos of Earth from the telescreens in the cabins on the StratoPort. Caellyn almost stopped, fearing she was about to bump into it, that it couldn't be real. But then she found herself falling and landing on soft muddy ground, and then she was inside it, feeling grass beneath her toes and soft earth under her hands. Kowalski arrived next to her.

No time for orientation. "The trees," he said. Without hesitation they ran across the meadow, feeling a light wind whip over them and the uneven soil crumbling as their feet padded down. The sky was bright and summery, and warmth beat down on them until they made it under the tree canopy above and hid behind a large oak, surrounded in light brush and covered in thin vines.

"What now?" said Caellyn, breathless. "Where are we?"

"I don't know," Kowalski said, also heaving air. "I think we're inside some sort of dome. Look, the wall by the inlets goes upwards."

Caellyn dared to look back, expecting to see the Reapers coming through the ducts, but the meadow was empty. The ducts must have been too small for them to fit through, and they were nowhere to be seen, but she still expected them to walk through invisible walls or appear out of thin air.

Kowalski was right, though. The walls stretched up from the four holes until they were lost in the sky. They looked gently curved in all directions, as if they were in a colossal Bio-dome. It felt like the hydroponics deck, but more full of life. The hydroponics deck was a tangle of plants, but they were bare and dry, desperate for moisture and sustenance, and cowering under light tubes in the ceiling. Here the flora was free to grow as nature intended. She leaned on the tree, feeling its bark, rough and solid.

Unexpected joy spread through her. It felt like her brain had been a caged animal, and now it had been let out to pasture on green fields, and it revelled in its freedom, bucking and cavorting in pleasure. It was being fed with natural sights, sounds and smells that it so desperately needed, that filled receptors that had been denied their natural counterparts for so long. A primal urge within her was met and sated, and a warmth settled on her thoughts.

The wind rustled through the leaves overhead and buffeted through the trees into eddies that her skin reached up to meet. Small bugs flew lazily around them, and the call of a songbird echoed in the distance. The air was fresh and clean, and the dappled light settled on fallen leaves and roots across the forest floor.

"We've got to get further in," she said. "They'll be in here looking for us any minute."

"Agreed," Kowalski replied, and they moved on through the wood. They passed gnarled tree after tree, winding through the forest maze. They climbed an embankment, slipping and scrambling with legs that weren't used to such inclines, and especially not ones covered in loose soil, but making it to the top to hear the sound of running water.

There was a stream below them, trickling down a steep valley, and they ran to it, Kowalski falling over and rolling the last few metres. They thrust their heads into it and drank long and hard. The water was icy and fresh and quenched thirst like nothing else. After they couldn't drink any more, they collapsed on the ground next to it.

"Is it Earth?" Caellyn said.

"I don't know," Kowalski replied. "But whatever it is, it's better than the cube."

"Jesus, they kept us in there when this was just a hundred metres away? And the First Expedition was in the cube for a whole year."

"What do they want with us?" muttered Kowalski.

"Boldun was a brave man," she said, feeling a jolt of pain at his memory. "I think he knew he wasn't going to escape with us, but he did it anyway."

"That he was," Kowalski replied solemnly.

A crack of a branch sounded down the valley.

"We should get up to higher ground," Caellyn said.

They followed the stream upwards until they were met with a large rock face, the stream cascading down from above in a waterfall that splashed and pattered into a small pool below. Climbing over the rocks, they ascended above it, carrying on with weary legs. The trees thinned until they reached more open grassland that led up to a peak.

"I think we should stay under the trees. Who knows what else is in here? If we're being watched or chased, then we stand a best chance of surviving by keeping under cover," Kowalski said, and Caellyn agreed. But even without the view from the peak they could see out over rolling hills beyond, as well as back to the Bio-dome wall behind them, just visible as it blended into a sky that looked open and expansive.

"This place is huge," Caellyn said quietly, taking in the sweeping tract with wonder, as Kowalski sat down next to a tree. Caellyn suddenly noticed his leg had been seared badly by the molten Reaper. "Oh my god," she said.

"It's all right," he replied with a strained expression, as the adrenaline left his system, and the damped pain that it was suppressing started to return.

"Can you carry on?"

"Sure, but I just need to rest for a bit and catch my breath." They sat in silence for a while, taking in the sounds of buzzing flies and fluttering leaves.

"Kowalski, I'm sorry," Caellyn said. "I'm sorry we left you in the Facility."

"It's ok, I know it was Seerman's decision. But you know it was the right one, you had to go on."

"I'm not sure it was," she replied. "This whole mission was a failure. Maybe if we'd stuck together, we'd have stood a better chance."

"You know," Kowalski said quietly, "I think as soon as we landed it was too late."

They heard another crack of a broken branch and stopped, dead quiet. They stared into the forest ahead of them, looking for movement. Hardly breathing, they listened for any sign that they were being watched.

Then, something appeared from a bush. It was a giant cat, three feet high and stalking them with grace and menace. It was odd and ungainly, with what appeared to be two sets of eyes: the top two larger and surrounded with dark purple patches of fur, the two smaller ones nearer its snout. It had six legs, the middle two splayed outwards to brace its sideways movement, the large paws at the front bristling with claws that looked like they could slice through metal.

It snarled a deep growl that reverberated off the trees around them. They both stood up carefully and adopted coiled poses to face off against the beast. Searching around for any kind of defence, Caellyn caught a glimpse of a sharpened stick lying on the ground near her. It was a broken branch, forged into a point. She tried to inch towards it but the cat flexed and changed its tone.

Suddenly the big cat pounced, launching its weight at Caellyn so that all she saw was claws and teeth. She dived to the side, just quick enough to miss it, as it clattered into the tree, sending shards of bark flying as it desperately tried to right itself, its limbs flailing before finding steady ground.

Caellyn heard Kowalski roar, and turned to see him land a large log on the beast's head, driving it down onto its skull. But the wood merely crumbled, and the cat shook its head as if it barely noticed. It steadied itself before lunging at Kowalski and sinking its teeth into his throat, its huge weight knocking him to the floor with ease. Without thinking twice, Caellyn grabbed the sharped branch and launched herself at the cat's back, driving the spear into its neck with all the force of her anger. She drove it from the memories of Seerman, Yakun, Arundel and Boldun. She drove it with every ounce of fear, and with every difficulty that she'd felt on that goddam hell-hole of Venus. She felt the branch run deep as it parted flesh and scraped off bone, and the beast spasmed momentarily before slumping to the floor.

"Kowalski!" shouted Caellyn. She heaved the bulk of the cat off him and took one look at his neck, contorted at an unnatural angle, with blood pouring out of it from gruesome wounds, and knew that he was gone. She cried out with the pain of having lost so much, and the pain of being alone once more.

Then a noise rang out behind her, stuttered and dislocated, and unmistakably a Reaper. She felt her world go dark, and the blackout washed over her as her body went limp.

Chapter 21

Caellyn awoke in another test chamber. She was inside a transparent column, in a large tube of breathable air. But this time she wasn't strapped to a board. She had freedom to move in the tubular space, and she tested her arms and legs tenderly. She pushed against the organic-hard floor and tried to lift herself up onto her knees.

Outside of her tube, she could see a Reaper, its head bowed as it worked away on consoles and interfaces. It briefly glanced up as she came to, but it appeared to be unconcerned with its test subject's consciousness. It looked down just as quickly, ignoring Caellyn's startled response, and resumed whatever ungodly tasks it was completing.

But this one was different. It was larger than the others, with a broader head and more limbs. Its face had sharper lines, like a well-defined jawbone. Its eyes were brighter, more incandescent, giving it a royal quality. As it moved, it seemed to float, its proud head keeping still above its body, as the many root-like limbs shuffled below.

It must be a Queen, the leader of this hive of aliens. Even the room looked more regal, with the consoles that grew out of the floor being smoother and more refined. They still looked as if they had been grown, covered in minor imperfections, but grown under greater obedience, and the organic material had better followed the commands of its artisan creator.

Caellyn collapsed on the floor, pressing her forehead against its uneven surface. Her mind hurt with loss and hopelessness. She'd lost Kowalski twice. She'd watched Boldun be turned to molten liquid. She'd watched Yakun boil and be crushed inside his suit. Seerman and Arundel were gone.

But, perhaps, Seerman and Arundel were still alive.

There was still hope.

There was still hope, and Caellyn wasn't done yet. She pushed herself up on her arms before standing to her full height, pushing back her shoulders in defiance. The test chamber was four or five metres in diameter, and she strode forward to the glass-like transparent column, facing off against the queen. "What do you want with us?!" she shouted at the top of her voice, releasing spittle of emotion, as desperation and resolve roared inside her. But the Queen just ignored her. Its face looked consumed in its work, lit by the faint glow from the panels, and the alien barely noticed her screams. She banged on the glass, its surface warm to the touch. But again, the Queen just carried on with its tasks.

Caellyn wanted to smash through the glass, run at it with all her might, but the Queen wasn't wearing any protective armour. The atmosphere on the outside was Venusian, and if she broke free, she would be crushed and cooked in an instant. She sank down on her knees, focussing her mind, preparing herself for another unknown fight.

She looked to the side and caught a glimpse of a second test chamber, identical to the one she was in. Her heart leapt for the briefest of moments as she hoped to see Seerman or Arundel in it. To see them like this, despite being trapped like a fly in a glass, would have brought some comfort. But it was empty. She cursed herself for wanting someone else to share her fate.

A series of lights came on, illuminating a channel that ran from one side of the room to the other across the front of the test tubes. At either end it disappeared into a hole in the wall, and to the left she could see a glowing blue light, slowly increasing in intensity.

The Queen hard at work, sending electrical signals that flashed across between the interfaces, until in the far wall a door suddenly opened. Caellyn jumped in her skin as in strode another large Reaper. It was of similar size to the Queen, and moved with confidence, with its head held proudly atop its twelve-foot height. The Queen turned to acknowledge it, and they both raised their heads sharply, and transmitted splintered, broken sounds, that caused uncomfortable vibrations in Caellyn's eardrums.

Then something unexpected happened. The new Reaper walked towards the other tube. It stepped over the channel, and as it got close to the tube-wall, the glass-like column disappeared, and it walked in. It stood on the tube floor looking poised and resilient, as if it was about to be hit by a tidal wave, but it would meet its end with honour and bravery.

The tube closed in around the other Reaper, and it turned to look at her. They were the same, both trapped, both contained in an unnatural restraint.

It looked at her steadily, its pupil-less eyes appearing to focus on her, holding her attention. As it watched her, she suddenly felt some level of damping. It felt like a blackout, but much less powerful, like the damping on the walls of the Facility, and it coursed through her nervous system. But this time there was something different behind it. It felt uncomfortable, and she found it contained emotions that weren't hers. They were scattergun and unorganised, but unmistakably from a different consciousness that was seeping into her mind. They were garbled and malformed, like a jumbled pile of electrical cables.

It was emotion, and she was sure that the Reaper in the other tube was trying to communicate with her. Her mind wrenched at the unnatural intrusion, and she got waves of remorse, courage, pity and reverence. She clasped her temples, trying to get the unwelcome voice out of her head.

Then the Reaper turned away, having completed its message, and resumed its steadfast vigil against whatever was to come.

The Queen started making chanting noises again that echoed off the walls of the chamber. Its arms became more rigid and outstretched, and it looked like a flower trying to spread its petals for the first time. But then it seized control of itself and lifted a limb towards one of the control panels. The panel morphed, reaching out to meet the outstretched root, welcoming the inputs from the Reaper Queen in a strange symbiosis.

Caellyn heard mechanical noises, like the moving of a conveyor belt, or the scraping of a log through a forest floor. Along the channel, out of the far end, came capsules. They looked like giant seed pods, pointed at one end and more rounded at the other, where a strange blue electricity crackled across the surface. The first capsule moved forward slowly, to be followed by another, and another, until four of them lined up in front of the two tubes.

The other Reaper still stood resolute, its body stiff, and Caellyn felt herself tense in anticipation. She felt the damping start to build around her, in the floor, through her bones and around her teeth. It was like an electrostatic charge through her hair and through her brain.

The Queen moved to a separate, larger panel, closer to the chambers, which looked like an ornate shrine, and raised four limbs, placing them on it with delicate care.

Suddenly Caellyn was hit with a surging pain. The inside of the test chamber was filled with a blinding light, as her optical receptors were bombarded with strange inputs of energy, cascading through the tube. The damping coursed through her body, feeling like it was searching for something, looking for individual strands of DNA. She felt split, as if every atom of her body had been pulled apart one by one, spread out through the air around her.

Her conscience became unconstrained. Her brain could no longer contain it. It wandered, trying to free itself from her mortal body, trying to separate itself from the biological feedback of her flesh. It left her soft tissue and surged into mere energy, before hitting something malleable, that felt like the meeting of a new conscience. It was another mind, an equal, a rival. It met her in ethereal space, to dance and intertwine. The minds twisted around each other, until they became so intermeshed that they were almost indistinguishable.

She felt a connection to the hive-mind of the Reapers.

She felt emotions coming from sources that weren't hers. She heard voices that she didn't recognise and sounds that were unnatural.

Her mind felt the presence of other bodies, and of other brains in the hive-mind. As she was pulled along a searing racetrack of consciousness, Caellyn felt individual Reaper nodes that pulled at her like gravity around planets. Her mind dipped into one for a second, before carving out and back across the thought-space. In that briefest of moments, she felt she was inside the mind of a Reaper. She understood the language, the emotions and the perspective. She felt their infinity, a huge number of voices and minds spread out across the galaxy. She felt memories, thoughts, words and phrases, all in a language she didn't recognise, and yet she understood everything, as she was catapulted simultaneously through a chorus of bodies.

Her mind snapped backwards, lurching into an abyss, before finding itself in the thoughts of the Reaper in the tube next to her. She was in its body, also being seared with pain. But it wasn't resisting. It was in a state of catatonic adulation. It revelled in the pain, and it felt distinction at having been selected.

Her mind flayed out, like a broken and lashing machine belt, flapping in the air, as it searched for new constraint. She found her mind settle in another body, in a huge hall, surrounded by other Reapers. She felt every one of their collective thoughts. They were chanting, shouting. They were making wailing, intermittent sounds, and she was too. She was howling with joy, shouting at the top of her voice. In the centre of the hall was what looked like a tree, only it was moulding, changing shape. It was growing unnaturally fast, shaping itself as its shoots and branches followed patterns of control. It morphed itself into the shape of a human fifty feet tall, standing over the thousands of Reapers watching. The Reapers all raised their root-arms in adulation, in celebration and in worship. They praised this tree-form statue like it was a god. They felt deliverance and emergence, and their emotions reached a height that they hadn't felt in a long time.

Then her mind detached, like a flag in a hurricane freeing itself from a flagpole, before being caught in another mind, snagging and settling on another viewpoint.

She found herself swimming in a memory, in a different time and place. She was with a group of Reapers, at ease in gentle socialisation. As the Reapers passed the time, they suddenly felt a calling of new life. It reached out to them from across the cosmos. In a distant planet they heard the growing of seeds into new Reapers, to join the collective, the young voices reaching over inconceivable distances across the universe. The collective had expanded, and a cycle of life had been completed once again. Reapers had been born on a far-flung planet, and she heard the cries of new-borns as they saw the world for the first time. They were welcomed into the Reaper hive-mind, and she felt joy, the kind of reward that is only released when you have created new life.

Then the world dissolved, and her body was being pieced back together, atom by atom. Her mind was pulled back into her skull, and her senses reformed, as if they'd been defragmented and reorganised. She spat blood onto the floor and tried to steady herself against a body that wanted to flip itself inside out.

She was back in the tube, back in the chamber. The four seeds positioned in front of her were now moving along the conveyor belt and glowing a faint green. She felt disgust, and a distinct awareness that some part of her had been implanted into them. She looked across at the other Reaper, who appeared to be in an equal level of discomfort. The Queen was carrying on with its task, unconcerned.

Caellyn banged on the glass, but it was no use; there was no response. She braced herself in exasperation, and watched the four glowing seeds moving slowly along the conveyor belt until they disappeared through the side wall. But the sounds continued, and four new ones started arriving in the room, fresh and without the green glow. Like before, they stopped in front of the tubes. The feeling of damping rose up around her again, like her individual molecules were being separated once more, each pulled in a different direction, and she felt atomised, turned to mist.

Her mind searched out once more, loose and free. It felt the touch and companionship of the entire Reaper civilisation, millions of minds, each with millions of years of memories. Time was irrelevant, and the present and past moulded together in sights, sounds and recollections. Her mind moved in position and time, across inverted and intersecting planes of neural activity. Her mind was dragged along thought-space highways, erratic and lashing, and then rough and steady.

It settled in the mind of a Reaper standing near a sphere that was translucent and full of swirling patterns. The sphere looked as if it contained the entire universe, mounted in a room that looked like a cathedral. She walked towards it, her root-limbs tingling in unison, as Caellyn's mind coalesced inside the Reaper's. Peering into the sphere, she felt her thoughts spread out across galaxies and constellations, transported to distant planets on the other side of the universe.

She saw civilisations, human civilisations. They bore resemblance to Earth. There were people building mud huts, skyscrapers, flying machines and spacecraft. Her consciousness moved from one to the other, civilisation after civilisation, each striving, pushing, growing, expanding. There were similar people in each, but all different shapes and sizes, like the statues she'd seen in the Reaper corridors. They all looked human, but as if they'd each evolved into different bodily configurations.

She felt the emotions of the Reaper as it watched with satisfaction as each civilisation and each planet lost control, pushed further and further by uncontrollable momentum, producing energy and heat, slowly turning planets hotter and hotter. She watched the screams of entire societies, the rusting of buildings, and she watched entire planets become consumed by clouds. She watched civilisations grow out of control, unchecked and out of balance, as nature's protests were dismissed, and fuels were burned with unabridged desire and desperation. Every human planet was consumed in competition until there was nothing left, and the skies turned dark and thick. The atmospheres worsened until they were no longer habitable. There was anticipation and enjoyment in the Reaper's ecstasy as it watched the destruction unfold.

Then, through the Reaper's consciousness, Caellyn watched the planets, their human inhabitants long gone, slowly grow into Reaper worlds. On every planet, the atmospheres slowly became like that of Venus, and Reapers grew from the ashes.

Then she settled on Earth. It was unmistakable, with the continents arranged in their unchanging shapes. She watched civilisations grow and fall. She watched humans, their body-shapes now familiar, war against each other, fight and pray. She watched cities come and go, growing out of the earth and being consumed by it. She watched the soot rise into the air, with noxious gases pumping, as human consumption escalated. She watched the clouds grow, becoming fiercer and angrier, and the sky become erratic and uncontrollable.

Then a StratoPort rose out of the mist. It hung there for what seemed like an age, and Caellyn saw its population desperately trying to hang on. They were holding out, trying to keep the human spirit alive, and trying to cheat and manipulate nature with every ounce of human energy. But then she saw it slowly dropping, falling, faster and faster, as gravity pulled it. It was released from its perch, burnt-out and riddled with explosions, until it was consumed by the clouds below. Thousands of lives were extinguished, their thoughts and memories consigned to undocumented history. Their struggles were irrelevant against the higher function of human purpose. Their pain, love and friendships were all immaterial, mere distractions, while the human collective fulfilled its natural bargain.

Then she was back in the mind of the Reaper, feeling adulation, letting out a spear of joy across the hive-mind. It was met with rejoicing across the thought-space. There was eagerness in response, in anticipation of new Reaper life.

Another world was ready, and another cycle of nature had been completed. The humans, the creators of worlds, had done their job once more.

She felt the Reaper's reverence of the human terraformers. They had done their job again, changing the climate to one habitable for Reapers. But she also felt an insignificance from the Reaper's thoughts, as if every human was merely a blunt tool in a slow and steady process.

She was back in the tube, feeling like her arms and legs had just been stuck back together. She felt as if nothing in her nervous system worked, because every dendrite, synapse and tendril was re-finding its connections.

The seeds moved along the channel, glowing green, until more appeared from the left, and a new set stopped near her tube.

The process surged again, splitting her apart with incredible pain. Her mind lashed out, this time travelling across the complex they were in. She watched the Facility being grown, carefully prepared to entice humans to travel to Venus, the Star-Sphere being positioned within the freshly grown reactor hall. She watched the Bio-dome grow within the Venusian rock, built from the DNA and memories of the First Expedition. She felt the Reaper's wonder at being able to meddle and play with living humans, in the flesh, when normally they would be long gone from a planet or solar system before Reapers appeared.

Then she was inside the mind of a Reaper tending to the prison-cubes. She was carrying a tray of four bowls of the grey liquid. She walked up to a wall and it disappeared, and inside were four humans. Caellyn half expected to see herself, but it was a different cube. It was Seerman and Arundel!

For the briefest of moments her mind disconnected from the thought-space, becoming human again, amongst a sea of Reaper minds. Her mind stretched like elastic as it tried to pull itself away from the Reaper collective. Her mind, a swirling entity, swelled to unfathomable rage and sorrow, almost bursting and shattering itself into fragments that would be forever lost across the hive-mind. But it held, and the elastic pulled her back. She was back amongst the millions of brains, insignificant, as if she was being swept along in a current from a mile-wide river.

She was back in the Reaper's thoughts, looking over Seerman and Arundel with intrigue and irreverence. She reached out a root-branch and they collapsed in the blackout. They were such weak and feeble creatures, so easy to restrain, so incapable of self-control and living in balance. She laid down the bowls and left, feeling pleased with herself: the satisfaction of feeding hungry mice trapped in a cage.

Time skipped forwards, and she repeated the process. Day after day she would bring the bowls, for what must have been a year, or two years. Then one day, instead of four bowls, she brought three. One of the humans had gone, one that Caellyn didn't recognise. But Arundel and Seerman were still alive, looking older and wearier.

Then she arrived one day with only two bowls, and then only one, and then the pattern stopped.

Caellyn's mind fought to be free once more, washed over by remorse, fighting the surrounding Reaper thoughts. She was like a thorn in a haystack, irrelevant and out of place, pushing against the hive-mind with the intensity of human grief, but finding an immense pressure of resistance.

Then her mind was back in the chamber, but not in her body. She was in the mind of the Queen. She felt power over the thought-space, like a conductor marshalling an orchestra.

But Caellyn felt different sensations in the Queen. She was presiding over the seed preparation in the test-chamber room, and she felt the connections with the control panels as her root-limbs interfaced with them. She felt the drawing of gene-seed and mind-code from both Caellyn's estranged body and the Reaper subjects.

The Queen turned them into a consolidated kernel with satisfaction, before placing it in the germinating nuts along the channel. They glowed green as they accepted the biological information, and the Queen felt self-pleasure as it sent them on for interstellar travel, to flower on new worlds. It felt a personal connection to each seed, as if they were its children. On those distant planets where the seeds eventually landed, the humans would evolve over millions of years, taking different forms based on the environment, but characteristically human in each case. They would slowly spread across the planet, consuming the surface, and terraforming it into a new world for the Reapers, who would spawn from the seed pods when the conditions were right. The new Reapers would grow their own civilisation before the process repeated, and they would send their own seeds off.

But there was no haste in the Queen's process. There was no excess desire, no frustration at the slow pace of the cycle, no wonder or need to push it faster than nature allowed. They lived as part of the symbiosis, and never beyond it. They lived as part of nature, not fighting against it.

In the Queen's mind, Caellyn felt like she had done this before, thousands of times. She felt old, millions and millions of years. She felt a connection to other queens, separated on other planets, only connected to each other through the hive-mind thought-space.

Each one revered the humans like they were perfect beings, who never failed to terraform a planet, consuming it like a virulent plague. And each new Queen that would later grow on each new planet, would save those humans, from the remnants of their bones and fragments of DNA still left, to be sent out and resurrected on a different world, to live once more in a new cycle.

But in all the memories of the queens, they had never had a live subject. The seeds were always germinated by ashes and archaeology. This was a first, the first time they had the opportunity to capture fresh gene-seed and mind-code from a *living* human entity. And this one was strong: the strongest. It had survived when all the others had failed. It was the last, the human leader, and it would germinate pods with new intensity and vigour.

Caellyn's mind reeled, fighting the immense power of the queen. *She was the last one.* The Queen had just thought it. *She was the last human from Earth.* It was a final blow through her heart, skewering her with a dull pain. She felt the sorrow and weight of all humans on Earth, as if every single one of them was crying out to her.

But then she felt power. If she was the last, then she had every human behind her. Every lost voice, throughout history and every voice she knew from her life on the StratoPort was now on her side, shouting at her to go on.

She pushed against the Queen's mind. Her consciousness flicked back and forth as it tried to tear itself away from the collective. For a moment she was back in her own body feeling the searing agony of the germination process, before being dragged back towards the Queen's thoughts. She was grappling with the Queen's mind, and she felt the Queen reel in discomfort at being attacked from the inside out. She fought the alien consciousness, until she found, within the Queen, a nucleus of imagination.

Then she was in the Queen's thoughts, but with everything quiet. The Queen had wrestled control, but paused its processes, its roots still. It was thinking in slow contemplation, searching around Caellyn's mind, considering it with some importance for the first time. The Queen suddenly felt *Caellyn's* emotions. It felt *Caellyn's* pain from being split apart in the process.

The Queen withstood it, but felt sorrow and remorse. The Queen searched around inside Caellyn's conscience, seeing her memories and connections, her feelings and thought processes. The Queen felt her pain at losing friends and family, and of watching the StratoPort fall out of the air. They were emotions the Queen had never felt or even considered. It stopped the Queen in her tracks. The leader watched Caellyn's body convulse and spasm as it was probed and defragmented by the damping, and it felt guilt and regret. It lifted up a heavy limb and paused the process, and Caellyn was catapulted back into her own body, her mind settling in her natural brain, and she tried to breathe deeply through lungs that felt they had just been replaced. She coughed and spluttered, as her thoughts got used to a human body once more.

And then she felt the Reaper Queen in her mind, the world went dark and the blackout took her.

* * *

Caellyn awoke in a small corridor. It was human sized, with the white organic walls of the Reaper technology, the same as in the cube cell. Her mind slowly returned, and she searched her body with her hands, to check it was still in one piece. She felt okay, in fact rejuvenated, despite a lingering sensation of the damping that was still coursing gently through her body. *I am alive.*

Ahead of her was a glass wall. Beyond it was a dusty fog similar to the one they'd seen when they arrived on the surface of Venus. She put her hand up against it, feeling the heat. She was in an airlock, separated from the Venusian atmosphere.

What kind of sick test was this? What kind of final retribution was this from the Reapers?

But there was light in the airlock, and it felt natural and glowing, like sunlight. She turned around to find another glass wall. This one looked out on a scene that made her heart skip: the Bio-dome. Ahead of her was the meadow, with grass gently blowing in the wind. Along the side was the forest, and in the distance were the rolling hills and mountains. Clouds gently hung in the sky overhead, some small and wispy and others like cotton wool. Insects swayed in the air and a flock of birds flew by the window.

It was everything she wanted.

But then it dawned on her. *She was the last one.* She remembered the Queen's thoughts, and her body revulsed as it braced itself at the memory of the germination process. *She was the last human from Earth.* They had taken everything. These goddamn Reapers, they had taken everything from her. But then she remembered what she had seen in their thought-space. They had taken nothing. The Reapers had simply followed a natural cycle. It was humans that had taken it all from themselves. And now she was left to feel the entire burden.

She stared out through the glass wall towards the Bio-dome. She wanted it so badly. Even the brief time she had spent there with Kowalski had been like a drug, and she felt an addiction to the forest, the wind, the lazy sky and the trickling stream.

But it was a melancholy thought. She would be there alone. What was the point if no one else existed? What was freedom worth, if there was no one to share it with? She turned to find her foot land on something that clinked. It was the shard. The same weapon that Boldun had used to puncture the Reaper suit. He'd kept it hidden for months, waiting for the right time to strike, holding onto it as the only hope of escaping the cube. And it had worked. It had sliced through the armour of the Reaper and given them another chance to go on.

The Reapers had given it to her as one final, sick joke. She felt angry, angry at them. They'd done this, they'd doomed her. They'd doomed all of them. Turning all of Earth, and every fleeting human planet, into bones and ashes. Their pain, love and purposes ended as dust in the maelstrom.

The Reapers simply waited for planets to turn to Venus and then grew out of someone else's ruins.

She picked up the shard and walked towards the Venusian sand-fog, raising it up to strike through the glass and feel instantaneous death consume her. But she couldn't do it. The shard stopped in the air, her muscles limp, her will gone.

She turned and looked at the meadow. The landscape called to her, pulled her forward. It wanted her among its hills and mountains in order to feel complete, and she wanted the same thing more than ever. She raised the shard one more time, bracing her muscles and driving it through the air. It struck the glass and sliced through, shattering it into a billion tiny fragments. And as the tiny shards fell around her, she felt the onrush of a different atmosphere flowing across her body. A gentle breeze lapped over her, cool and refreshing.

Gripping the shard, she stepped out on the grass, feeling it between her toes and under her feet, and she ran.

About the book

This novel has been self-published. If you enjoyed this book, I'd be very grateful for any support. A good review or a share on social media would be brilliant. Any and all feedback welcome to one of my social media profiles.

Other books

A preview of my other novel: Augur, is provided on the following pages.

Augur

- Preview -

Prologue

Captain Sarnak watched the monastery gates for any sign of movement. He kept his focus steady despite the deafening noise around him. Nearly half the city come out to see the monks enter the machine, anticipation etched onto everyone's faces, filling the air with energy that crackled through the cityscape.

"What's taking them so long?" Sergeant Antrly muttered to him, standing at the front of the Ropa Greyjacks.

But Sarnak didn't respond. He merely curled the corner of his lip.

So much for a shod perfect schedule.

A seasonal gust tumbled over the parapets of the imposing walls. Sarnak's eyes traced over the ornate structures and hand-carved spires. He strained his ears, trying to listen for any noise from the four hundred augurites. *What's holding them?* They would be lined up behind the thick oak doors right then. One long column spilling out of the cathedral that the monastery enclosed.

He wouldn't blame those men and women for delaying. He shuddered at the thought of the sacrifice these monks were about to make. This cold autumnal day was the last time they would see the outside world. At the end of the procession, they would enter the Augur, be sealed inside, and their long vigil would begin. From that point, it was their responsibility to guide humanity from isolation, forever separated from the consequences of their decisions.

He clenched his jaw, the air condensing as he breathed out.

Sylvia.

He wished she was here, not a thousand miles away in Terceira watching him on the live vid-screen. He imagined her hands tensely holding her handkerchief. *One last time.* Then he'd join her in the house they'd built on the Atlantic archipelago.

The sea.

That was a pleasant thought. It took him away momentarily. Crashing waves, one after the other. Gulls calling as they rode updrafts over sun-baked cliffs.

"Captain, should we do something?" came a voice through the comms.

"Negative, we wait." Sarnak replied.

What could they do? It was out of his hands, with orders keeping him in the dark.

Don't talk to the monks.

It's a damn stupid rule.

Sarnak remembered the anger he'd felt in the towering offices of Aires Meridian Aves Corporation. He was supposed to be in charge, like he had been for countless other escort missions, whether dignitaries, presidents or gravsen pilots. He'd overseen victory parades, military convoys and the movement of secretive technology. But in every case, he could talk to the subjects, discuss contingency plans and get a feel for their mindset. You had to know the thoughts of those you were helping. Only then could you be sure you would be able to get them to their destination safely.

But escorting four hundred monks you'd never even met? And you couldn't even talk to them? Sarnak had slammed his fist on the desk of Commissioner Halsen when he'd told him that AMA had insisted on it.

"It's essential that the augurites are not influenced before they enter the dome," Halsen said.

"You need this to go perfectly?" Sarnak replied. "But we're transporting an unknown entity!"

"The monks have been in isolation for the last few years. They know precisely their responsibilities; you won't have any trouble from them." He sat forwards, placing his wrists on the table. "Assume they will behave perfectly and worry about everything else. I have complete faith in you."

Maybe that was the problem. Complete faith.

People threw it around too much these days. The government placed complete faith in AMA Corporation. The public had fallen in line and given complete faith to the Augur. Everyone was relying on the monks, with complete faith, to guide the future safely.

"I'm just a human being, Commissioner. Complete faith is an illusion. I'm still fallible, just like anyone else, just like those monks."

"Sarnak, you know what I meant. Have faith. Sealing Day will go smoothly and the Augur will be a success."

"You sound like a damn politician!" Sarnak spat, his fist hovering above the table again. But he relented, flexing his fingers and sighing deeply. "Do you really believe your words? Do you really believe this is the right thing to do?"

Commissioner Halsen turned in his seat to look out the window. They were in a makeshift office in an AMA high-rise, bare apart from a standard issue filing cabinet, but the views over Ropa were spectacular. The city sprawled in the distance. Buildings covered every square inch of the ground, the suburbs dotted with clusters of skyscrapers. And in the centre was the Augur itself, the colossal domed structure that dominated the skyline of Metro Europa.

"This is our chance to deliver a brighter future," Halsen said. "Perhaps our last chance. Once the machine is operational, we can see the dangers before they happen. The world will be a safer place."

"I hope you really believe that. Taking the future out of the hands of those who live it is a dangerous gamble. It would be hard, if not impossible to undo."

"The public voted for it. The people want it. AMA Corp have been planning the machine for decades, and the monks have spent most of their lives learning their responsibilities. This city, the world even, cannot take another disaster. One more and there won't be anything left."

"The city will get by just fine, like it always has."

Halsen moved over the filing cabinet and rifled through dividers, finding the paper he was looking for. "The world isn't like it once was. Nano-infestations, gravity bombs, neural nets and rogue AI's. Not even you can stop everything. We need something more to tackle this. We all have to pass the torch."

Sarnak sat back and rolled his shoulders, looking up at the drab ceiling tiles. He sighed and sat for a while contemplating. "I just never thought it'd be like this. To a bunch of sanctimonious martyrs."

"Well, perhaps me neither." The Commissioner adjusted the embroidered cuffs of his tunic. "But their sacrifice is desperately needed. The augurites will work together to guide us away from disaster."

Sarnak shook his head.

Maybe Halsen is right.

The greyjacks could only do so much. Ropa struggles to get by, sometimes swamped by a tide of its own people. And it only looked to be getting worse. If humanity was going to survive, it needed greater guidance.

Maybe the Augur is necessary.

But crak, it was a risk. Putting the future in the hands of monks shut off from society? Monks he'd never seen in person. How could he trust that they'd do the right thing, using a machine designed by a corporation that he knew little about?

"What about Ran Fawn? Have you met him?"

"No, but I imagine you would like to," Halsen smiled. "I would have suggested that AMA Corp allowed you an hour with him before selection, if they'd have let me. I've heard about your officer interviews. They say no-one comes out of that final exam quite the same, but those that pass are the best damn officers going. And not one has a bad thing to say about you."

Sarnak snorted gruffly. "If only all my colleagues agreed."

"I'm sure they do. You didn't get your fifth stripe for nothing. You have a way of seeing through people and understanding them. I pride myself on similar skills. I want to know who this Ran Fawn is behind the media personality, just as much as you do. If we can't test him, how can we trust he is the right person to lead the monks inside the machine? Unfortunately, there are some decisions we have to give to others."

Sarnak shook his head again and leaned forward in the chair. What did he expect, that he'd convince them to cancel the project? Whatever his misgivings, the Augur was happening, and no one could stop it. "I'm too old for this," he sighed.

"The world keeps going, doesn't it? In all my life it feels like it's driving past me like a steam train." Halsen pulled open a drawer and took out a fountain pen, turning the silver relic over in his hands. "Everything was different when I was a young man."

"Even the hamburgers."

Halsen laughed.

Sarnak breathed deeply. He sat back up in his chair, meeting Halsen's gaze. "I take it the military is on standby?"

The Commissioner's movements stopped. He carefully put down the pen, neatly perpendicular to the edge of the desk. It wasn't public knowledge that opposition in the other mega cities had been growing as Sealing Day appeared on the horizon. It was a long time ago that the world population centres had voted unanimously for the Augur. Portland and Beijing were starting to have doubts.

"Most of that is highly classified, but you won't get any trouble, I assure you that. Focus on the march. And if I'm not mistaken, the retirement celebrations afterwards."

"One thing at a time," Sarnak smiled.

"I hope you have at least some way to mark it planned; I'll keep my eye out for an invite. But you will be missed considerably. Whoever succeeds you will have tough boots to fill."

Sarnak raised his eyebrows. He remembered what it was like when he took over, fresh faced and daunted by the responsibility. Somehow, he knew it would be different for his successor. "If the Augur works, they won't have anything to do at all."

The monks would defend the dome themselves. One of their first tasks would be to eliminate the possible futures where the Augur would be destroyed. When Sarnak was told that it sent a jolt of uneasiness up his spine. A machine that prevents its own destruction sounded like a whole mess of an idea. But if you believed the Augur was the right thing to do, then it was something that was tied up in the parcel. *What if it fails? What damage could it do if things go wrong?*

The thoughts unnerved Sarnak. *Put it out of your mind.* It wasn't his job; he'd done his stint. His path was with his wife Sylvia, and the villa they'd built on the Atlantic coast of Terceira. One last assignment, and then a hard-earned retirement was theirs, and the future was someone else's.

Now Sealing Day was upon him.

The great gates of the monastery slowly opened outwards. The group of greyjacks held firm to witness a rare glimpse inside the hallowed ground. As the heavy doors patiently swung, they revealed the first ranks of the four hundred monks, staring back out at the police force. They were wearing their distinctive ochre robes, with calm and resolute expressions on their faces. Lined up in neat rows, the men and women were standing alert with the confidence of instilled doctrine.

At the front was Ran Fawn. He stared directly at Sarnak, composed and self-assured.

Sarnak met his gaze firmly. *So, this is the leader, the one with utmost responsibility for ensuring the success of the Augur project.* Sarnak scanned him from head to toe, looking for any wavering or insecurity.

He'd better be ready. Ran was too far away for Sarnak to get a good sense of the man. You had to be close see that: to watch the way his irises dilated, how he held a stare and how still the muscles around his eyes stayed, how his eyeballs flickered. *Give me two months, I'll put you through the academy training and then we'll know.* That would reveal the mettle of the man, how he responded to each of Sarnak's carefully planned tests.

But all he had to go on were the memories of his media interviews a few years ago. Sarnak would never get the chance to know what kind of person Ran Fawn truly was; no one would. He had to trust in the rigorous psychological analysis of AMA Corporation. But it wasn't a position he wanted to be in.

Don't talk to the monks.

Sarnak turned towards the road ahead. "Roll out, greyjacks," he said into the comms. "I need everyone on high alert. Keep your eyes on the crowds, keep your eyes everywhere. If you see anything out of the ordinary, report it, deal with it. This is a moment in human history that I want to go smoothly. I want no mention of the greyjacks when people talk about this in the future. If they do, we haven't done our jobs properly. Signal out."

He started walking forwards, followed by the police team around him and the monks behind them. He kept the slow and steady pace that they had rehearsed many times, moving along the road flanked by crowds behind barriers. There were people hanging out of windows, sitting in trees and climbing lampposts. Most of the city had come to see the last procession of the monks. Greyjacks lined the route every few metres, hands behind their backs, eyes on the people in front of them. A few turned to take in the sight and to nod to Sarnak. For

many, this was their Chief's retirement parade as much as
it was the start of a new endeavour.

Sarnak fought a lump in his throat and pushed those
thoughts away. *This is about responsibility, and nothing
else.* But he would miss it. At least he was surrounded by
the entire police force for the last mission. They were
positioned in the surrounding city, marshalling the crowd,
flying the air transports and watching intently from central
command.

Ticker tape blew around Sarnak as the cold licked the
hairs on his neck. His wife had told him to bring a scarf
but he'd gruffly refused. He claimed it wasn't winter yet,
and he'd be damned if he wore one in autumn. But the
chill was unseasonably cold, and it permeated to the band
of skin between his police issue gloves and the grey jacket.
They were supposed to fit seamlessly together, but
Sarnak's had long since been worn into incompatibility.
Even the Mayor of the City, when placing a medal around
Sarnak's shoulders back in the 2229 Honours List,
mentioned that it was time for the captain to get a new
coat. The station quartermaster had given up asking
Sarnak whether he wanted new kit in the yearly order.

*The scuffs and tears are the real achievements. That's
when you know you're doing policework.* The cuffs
didn't fit the gloves because fifteen years ago he'd tackled
a synth-addled dealer with an incendium grenade. Sarnak
had barely got his arms up in time for the tough fabric to
protect him from a misfired blast wave.

He was moving forwards; he could hear the march of
four hundred monks behind him over the cheers of the

crowd. Confetti whipped around his face as it was released to cover the monks as they progressed along the route. They walked in unison, like a parade day march. *Why the synchronisation? They are men, women, farmers, engineers. They're not fighters; they're not police. It's damn conditioning.*

Turning to check the monks for security, Sarnak saw them casually waving to the crowds, their faces smiling as if it was a normal walk through the city. At the front, Ran Fawn was taking in the adulation with ease. He was who everyone was cheering for. Without Ran, the popularity of the Augur may not have carried through. He had everyone's support. Even Sarnak couldn't find anything that he didn't like about him, at least on the outside. His address to the Earth last week was flawless. If you were going to be sealed into a machine like a tomb, you would want him there with you.

He looked relaxed, as if you could place the entire weight of the world on his shoulders and he'd support it. He had great posture and a chiselled jawline. *How did he do it?* Sarnak wouldn't have that courage if he was about to cocoon himself in a megastructure. But maybe it was all show, and there were human fears inside his head.

"Sir, we've got a Personal Air Transport taking off on the east side." came the crackle through the radio.

"Shut it down." came Sarnak's response. "I want that PAT on the floor now."

"Yes, sir."

This wasn't good for Sarnak's blood pressure. They were approaching Camen Corner, nearly halfway there.

If one PAT was the worst thing to happen, they could consider that a success. *Scan the crowd. Keep your eyes peeled. Keep everyone safe.*

"Craft was just some darn businessman thinking he's above the law. Even tried to bribe us. We've taken him in."

"Well done, sergeant, keep vigilant."

Sarnak felt old. Autumn echoed his thoughts. The leaves in the trees turned and fell to the ground, losing their shine and turning crisp. In autumn the world around Sarnak got temporarily old itself. Even the birds would leave in search for warmer climates where nature flourished. High above, a flock of geese headed south for the winter, unaware of the human struggle below. They flew in V formation, with nothing but buffeting winds to worry about. The world went on around them in its endless cycles.

"Minor disturbance over by Port Quays," came another voice through the comms. It sounded like a recruit that Sarnak had seen ace the Reality trials the year before. *He must be rising fast.* "Some punk kids trying to spray graffiti in view of the procession. We stopped them, and all they got was, 'COME OUT OF THE DARK,' and 'LET US BE FREE.'

"How about your section, Sarn?" came a familiar voice. It was Captain Pason. As the same rank, he didn't have to refer to Sarnak as Captain on the radio, and he knew this would get under his skin.

"That's Captain Sarnak, Captain Pason. It's fine here at the moment, about to turn Camen Corner. Do you have a fix on the crowd numbers?"

"You don't know them?" Pason replied. He was an irritating one. Sarnak had scuffled with him all the way up the ranks, and he was sure Pason bore a grudge that he hadn't been given the final promotion that put Sarnak in the chief's chair. Sarnak didn't reply.

"Two million along the procession route, another two million around the base of the Augur," Pason said after a short pause.

"Thank you, Captain." Pason didn't deserve it, but Sarnak showed him due respect regardless. He sighed at the constant infighting. He just wanted to do a job. The struggle was enjoyable when you're a new recruit, testing yourself and those around you, but at the end of your career you just want life to be simple and to walk your own path, without others trying to blunder you one way or another.

"You're welcome, Captain. It's been an honour; good luck." *At least he's able to show some decency.*

Turning Camen Corner revealed a full view of the Augur. Its dome shape was a breath-taking sight, worthy of any of the structures that humanity had endeavoured to build. It matched the pyramids in grandeur and the tallest towers in achievement. Five hundred metres in diameter, it imposed itself on the city with an unmistakeable presence, a promise of power and security.

It still impressed Sarnak every time. He remembered when it was just a giant skeletal spider of a building decades ago, it's great dome only fleshed out in superstructure. When he took over as Captain, with responsibility for its defence and safe passage, he'd watched as it slowly took form, became solid and imperious.

"Captain, the crowd's getting pretty excited where the monks are passing. One of the barriers is getting loose."

"Get the police to push up against it. Order the people back."

"Already have done, Cap'n, but the crowd keeps coming. There's a constant inflow from the metro line exit by Ulsa Street. Shall we fire off the flare?"

"Crak, no, not yet, I don't want to cause a scene unnecessarily."

"Cap'n if the barrier doesn't hold it'll be pandemonium."

"I know that. Get the police to the barrier. How long 'til the procession passes that point?"

"I'd say five minutes sir."

"She'll hold. We bought the best; just hang on. Get some police around the back and start pulling people away."

Come on barrier. Hold, damn it.

The crowd noise became louder as they got closer to the Augur. It dawned on him that when they reached the Augur and the monks entered, that was the end of his career. It was frightening; what lay beyond was unstructured and timeless. But freedom and release. He was suddenly conflicted. He wanted the monks to slow down, to take their time reaching the giant computer, to give himself just a bit longer as Captain. He fondly fumbled for the badge affixed to the right breast of his jacket.

But the column moved on, reaching the edge of the forum, a two-hundred-metre ring-shaped expanse around the base of the Augur. There were no structures on it, just an empty space of neatly laid cobblestones. The forum was a natural solid moat around the base of the giant dome, creating an impressive circular no man's land that made it easier to stifle malicious forces at a distance.

The barriers fanned out around the circle, keeping the people away from the dome itself. Greyjacks were manning the circumference in greater numbers, and AMA Corp and military craft were flying high above.

Sarnak marvelled at the Augur one more time, now getting closer and starting to block out the sky above him. Maybe it was even the last time he'd see it. He hadn't really thought much past retiring and moving to the Atlantic archipelago. The gentle lap of the sea, the warm evening sun and relaxing with a cold beer looking out from the villa with Sylvia. Maybe he wouldn't even come back.

For the monks, this would be the last image they saw of the outside world. For them, there was no choice. There was no PAT that could bring them home for a holiday, no turning back. A person cannot see an accurate future of a world they live in.

Fifty would take the first shift, and the rest would be put into stasis. For two hundred years the augurites would keep their numbers steady until the Augur's hard wired end date arrived; its job done. Some might never be awoken. There were no children; that freedom had been taken away from them. Their only legacy was the changes they would make to the world that they would only ever see through simulations. He felt sad for them. *Who are these self-righteous, humble martyrs?*

"Sir...one of the monks..." came a strained voice through the comms, pitched in worry and breathless from exertion.

"What is it?" Sarnak turned to catch a view of the procession and see what the officer was referring to. They were so close; they didn't need a disaster at the last hurdle.

"One of the monks just split: jumped the barrier and ran into the crowd. I'm making pursuit."

Sarnak's heart sank. This was why you needed to talk to the people you were transporting. Complete faith? That was always a misnomer. This wasn't something they'd accounted for in contingency planning. His brain tried to compute the consequences for the machine.

"Captain Pason," Sarnak barked. "Get onto AMA Corp. Ask them what we do. Do we still seal them in?"

"Understood, captain."

Sarnak needed an answer fast. But the procession wasn't stopping. It was like a steam train running on its own momentum, heading towards the two heavy concrete doors that were waiting to be sealed together.

He moved to the side of the entrance to allow the monks to start filing through, willing a response to come from Pason. He chastised himself for failing to prepare for this eventuality. Ran Fawn looked unaware, taking a position near Sarnak as the monks started to enter. As the four hundred passed by, a few looked at him wide eyed, as if they knew what had happened. He doubted even they knew what to do in this situation. One of their own had just abandoned them and thrown away the dogma of a lifetime.

"Seal them in," came the response from Captain Pason.

"Captain, please confirm that this order came from AMA Corp," Sarnak said, urgency racing in his tone, "and was approved by Commissioner Halsen." The last of the monks were now entering the Augur.

There was another pause from Pason. "Confirmation from Halsen, AMA Corp in agreement. Seal them in."

Sarnak shook his head. What on earth was that monk thinking? *You spend your life adopting tenets only to flee at the last minute.* He looked at the dark corridor that led into the Augur and felt another chill. He wouldn't blame anyone for not wanting to walk between those concrete doors. But the monk must have taken on the burden of responsibility long ago, and had just forsaken his brothers, sisters, and the population around them.

Ran Fawn waved to the crowd for one last time. The roar from the people was deafening in response. As the last of the ticker tape fell, Ran Fawn took one final look at the world he was leaving. He took a position inside the entrance as the two bulky concrete doors started to close. Just before he was lost to view, he made eye contact with Sarnak. He looked impassive and bold, as if even when face to face with his sacrifice, he was undeterred. He gave the smallest of nods. Then the doors shut together. AMA construction crews moved in to perform the final sealing.

It was done. The monks were inside the Augur, climbing up to their new home and settling in for the first night.

He stood dumbfounded for a while, listening to the sounds of heavy machinery. A few officers came up and shook his hand, but he couldn't help thinking of the monks inside. He had done it. He had played a part in their purpose.

His comms crackled into life. "Sarnak, this is Halsen. Congratulations on the escort."

"Thank you, Commissioner. What about the monk that didn't go in?"

There was a pause before Halsen replied. "AMA Corp will deal with that. It wasn't to be expected. They send their thanks over to you as well. As far as I'm concerned, that went as smoothly as we could have hoped."

"We should have foreseen that."

"I'm not sure how we could have. And would you have forced the runaway in, even if we'd caught them in time?"

Sarnak didn't respond.

"Captain, it is with pleasure that I wish you the greatest of happiness in retirement. You have been a stalwart of this city, and you can be proud of a long and illustrious career."

"Thank you again, Halsen. Until we meet again."

The population idly dispersed while Sarnak waited. As the crowds and greyjacks slowly left, only a few officers remained in the low, dusky, autumn sun. They made sure the remaining tasks were completed and left the clean-up crews to pick up the litter and ticker tape. The next morning there would be little trace of the events of that day. There would only be the Augur, now operational, having started its watch over the city and the world.

Two weeks later, Sarnak was free. His greyjack uniform was replaced with a light cotton shirt and trousers. On a warm Atlantic evening, he sat with Sylvia, sipping gin and tonic and listening to the ocean crash onto the rocks beneath their villa on the west coast of Terceira.

John C. Sable was born in London, England. He studied at Cambridge University before becoming a Chartered Engineer. He later qualified as a Patent Attorney. He lives in Derby.

Printed in Great Britain
by Amazon

43932419R00225